Football Crazy

Greg Williams writes for *Arena,* the *Face* and
Arena Homme Plus. He is the author of
Diamond Geezers (Fourth Estate, 1997) and
lives in north London with his wife and baby
daughter.

Football Crazy

*

Greg Williams

FOURTH ESTATE • *London*

First published in Great Britain in 1999 by
Fourth Estate Limited
6 Salem Road
London W2 4BU

1 3 5 7 9 10 8 6 4 2

A catalogue record for this book is available from
the British Library.

ISBN 1-85702-978-x

Typeset by MATS, Southend-on-Sea, Essex
Printed in Great Britain by Cox & Wyman Ltd, Reading

For Lisa and Rhianna

Acknowledgements

Thanks to Martin Delamere and Ashley Heath for the support and Ekow Eshun for the space. To the friends and family who've been there time after time, I owe a huge debt and, probably, a drink. Special thanks to Jonny Geller who does deals, and to Caroline Upcher who does words.

Football Crazy

Full name: Lee Joseph Martin Sweeney.

Born: Walthamstow, November 1969.

Married: To Michelle.

Children: None.

Previous clubs: Enfield, Chelsea and Napoli.

League debut: December 1986, against Everton.

Favourite goal scored: The next one.

Best goal seen: Maradona's second goal against England in the 1986 World Cup Finals. Not bad for a cheating bastard.

Most memorable match: The first time I played for England.

Favourite away ground: Anfield.

Best stadium in which you've played: Nou Camp, Barcelona.

Pre-match meal: Spaghetti Bolognese.

Favourite drink: Hooch.

Favourite country visited: America.

Miscellaneous likes: Music, Nintendo '64, PlayStation and sleeping.

Miscellaneous dislikes: Traffic jams, queueing and rude people.

Favourite TV programme: *Blackadder*.

Favourite music: Oasis, The Prodigy and anything by Paul Weller (the guv'nor).

Ambitions: To win the Premiership and World Cup.

What would you do if you weren't a footballer: Don't know, but I couldn't have worked in an office.

Chapter One

Bish, bash, bosh.

The waiter cracked the bottle cap, Lee downed the beer, slammed the empty back on the table.

It was official, he was shaping up for a blinding night out. Lee was feeling it; he'd only been in the joint an hour, felt the rub of fresh glass against his fingertips five times already, each consecutive sherbet trying to recapture the sweet, jackhammer moment when the booze slid along his tongue, coated his throat, rushed his chest and then came home to poppa upstairs in the old grey matter. His Spidey senses were tingling.

Had he deserved this, or what? He'd been working hard of late, nose to the grindstone, sunk bollock-deep in slog. And although getting slaughtered only two nights before a big game wasn't strictly professional, he had developed his own system for getting round the guilt – the more beer he caned the easier it got. No worries on the football front; he'd be there, he'd be keen, and he'd like to see them try and drop him. Anyway, having a couple of drinks wouldn't matter, quite the reverse, it would help to relax him. His missus, Michelle, had been grafting like a bastard too, so when she announced that she was taking her shop girls out on the lash Lee had the perfect excuse to get fucked up at a club where he wouldn't get harassed by punters or tabloid rotters.

So that's how Lee Sweeney found himself in a place like this, with people like this, on a night like this. Half eleven and the music was beginning to swell as the joint filled with the hot and cool of after-hours London who clustered in booths and banquettes sipping cocktails, leaning in to converse conspiratorially and, effusive and assured, capered among the decor of the day, Las Vegas meets Scandinavian modernism – baroque, acid-coloured sofas set on blonde wooden floors, outlandish fruit-clad glasses resting upon Eames-influenced coffee tables.

Look at the form on that! Lee inspected a brace of sun-kissed thoroughbreds who cruised nearby; both had straight black hair scraped back tightly to bring attention to fine, privileged faces. Could have been from Chelsea, could have been from Billericay. Lee couldn't tell the difference any more, sorts all looked the same with their minimal make-up, vertiginous heels, gym bodies and off-the-peg attitudes that let you know they merited a life of unbroken golden moments. Whether they were from Hornchurch or Hampstead they gratified and adorned themselves with labels from the same Sloane Street ponce-parlours, which appealed to Lee for he'd never know quite what he was getting when he made his approach, other than a shufti at an obligatory set of tightly sprung abs and mischievous acknowledgement that he had earned a right to a taste of honey. Sometimes he even got a knock back.

He banged down another drained bottle and gestured to the waitress for a freshie. Sensing laughter, he cast his eyes over a group of seated girls with tan legs aligned in the same direction as if choreographed, cigarettes flourished like conductors' batons in between snatched gasps of smoke, depilated bodies hunched closely together swapping uptown intimacies. A small smile spread across his face. He was where he wanted to be, which was exactly where he'd always wanted to be: monied, spoilt, privileged, famous and – blissfully – with a drink in his hand. One of the girls shot him a glance. He looked away for a moment before considering the group again, by which time there was much giggling and craning of necks as Lee's celebrity aura materialised on the group radar.

He shivered. He could almost feel their hair on his neck, the daughters of stockbrokers and doctors and estate agents and engineers and gangsters and bankers and builders, girls who had no idea they had it so good, girls he would never have even set eyes upon had he not had a gift that had delivered him from all the commonplace, indifferent lives he might have had.

Celebrity. It was the gift that just kept on giving.

He checked his watch: eleven thirty-five. His agent Lou would arrive soon. Lou never liked coming out to places like this, especially on a week night, but Lee had given him the old arm-twister, asked him special like, and Lou had promised that he'd put his son to bed and come over for a swift couple of reserve cognacs just to keep Lee happy. Lou was like that. Lou had class. Lou was staunch.

'Get that down ya.' Another bottle of beer fizzed in front of him. Lee looked up to see Noel Simmons; tall, dapper, mixed race and the owner of Simmons, the eponymously named club in which Lee was in session. The form on Noel was that he'd made a bundle of dough in the mobile phone trade before fulfilling his dream of owning a club that had become a focal point for the capital's schemers and dreamers. Through a presence in the country club scene on the ragged fringes of A-road London, and a mammoth talent for self-publicity, Noel had turned the place into a celebrity haven that mixed the beautiful with the bold who just refused to be left on the pavement with the mugs and wannabes.

Lee had never liked Noel, was scared of him in a non-specific way, but he chose to keep him sweet for the sole reason that it meant Noel kept Lee sweet, which meant that Lee was sitting in a reserved booth in the VIP area, which overlooked the rest of the club. He surveyed the area below, reserved for Joe Punter, and noticed a group of frog-mouthed girls staring upwards with desperate fuck faces, shaking off a week's worth of deep-pile misery with the soothing discovery that a big catch was not beyond their grasp. He turned away. This was his domain. Lee loved booths – intimate but public, like all the best places.

'All right mate!' said Lee extending a hand. 'Fancy seeing you here.'

Noel laughed, he laughed at anything, it was one of the reasons people liked him. Mid-grin, his attention faded. 'Lee, I've just remembered something,' he apologised. 'I'll be back in one minute.'

The man had a sixth sense for a celebrity entrance. Lee watched Noel cruise through the lounge dispensing bogus greetings and ministering faux flatteries to the assembled crowd, holding the attention of each guest just long enough for them to feel as if something significant had occurred between them. Sure enough, two members of Six Pack, the current boy band revelling in a mayfly's existence, made a consciously discreet entrance into the lounge and into Noel's avuncular arms. There was much shifting from the medley of well-formed, machine-cooled thoroughbreds along the way. Lee chuckled to himself; he had lost count of the beers, and the place was beginning to shimmer with life, rendered exhilarating by the peerless promise of booze that offered him likelihood and prospects when he was aware that he had gorged well past his quota.

Noel returned, keeping an eye on the room. He sipped from a glass of Diet Coke.

'Lovely guys,' he said nodding towards the members of Six Pack. 'Good friends.'

'Who are they?' asked Lee.

'You're getting old, mate,' said Noel.

'It ain't me drinking the Diet Coke, mate.'

'Maybe it should be.'

Lee screwed his face into a fierce stare, fixed himself upon an alarmed Noel, before relaxing into a loony grin. Noel laughed.

'I've got to relax, you know,' exclaimed Lee. 'Which is why I come to your fine establishment. Anyway, I don't see you moaning when I have a few in here. Matter of fact, most of my fucking wages end up getting pissed away in your bog.'

4

'We're very pleased to have your custom,' said Noel in a purposefully bogus voice. It was a voice he often used, one of his many tricks implying that, because he knew what bogus was, then he couldn't possibly fall into the same trap himself. Lee, of course, knew better.

'Tell you, it's *dripping* in here tonight,' said Lee scanning another couple of golden navels coasting by the table. Both nodded sweetly to Noel who smiled back.

'Steady, Lee,' said Noel. 'You're a married man.'

'No harm in looking though, eh? Man's allowed to enjoy the scenery, isn't he?'

'Those two that just went by,' said Noel waving a lazy finger. 'They were caught in the bogs shoving Es up each other's arses a couple of weeks ago. I had to give them a warning: drop your pills elsewhere, girls. We don't like that shit in here. I ain't having it.'

'How the fuck did someone catch them shoving things up each other's arses?'

'We got cameras in the bogs.'

Lee sat up. 'You *what?*'

'Joke, Lee. Joke. Female member of staff walked in on them, if you want to know. Jesus, that would be some horrible viewing, some of the casualties we get in here, I tell you.'

Noel beckoned over another couple of drinks.

'You're not driving, are you, Lee?'

'Got the motor in the NCP.'

'Well, leave it there. You're too far gone already. I'll get a driver to take you back. Where is it?'

'Near Redbourn. Hertfordshire.'

'No problem. We'll get that sorted.'

Lee jumped from his seat.

'Oi, oi, saveloy!' shouted Lee embracing Lou.

'Bloody hell,' said Lou putting his hands to his ears. 'It's a bit bloody loud in here tonight, innit?'

'Turn it down, dear,' joked Lee, as if Lou possessed a hearing aid that was turned up too loud. Lou reached over and shook hands with Noel.

'How's business?' asked Noel.

'Not bad, not bad,' said Lou. 'Except for this one pain in the arse client . . .' All three fell about. Lou ordered a cognac and surveyed the bar.

'Where's the perfume then?' he joked. Noel opened his palms, as if exasperated. 'Tell you,' continued Lou, 'it's wall-to-wall talent in here.'

'Family all right, Lou?' asked Lee.

Lou scratched his balding head. 'Thanks for reminding me,' he laughed. 'No, really, blinding. Fantastic. Nathan's a lovely kid, you know. Does something different every day. He's a miracle. Really.'

The music was getting to Lee. The rhythm had crept inside him and he began to move his upper body from side to side.

'How many you had?' Lou asked Lee.

'Just a couple,' replied Lee. Noel stared into space.

'Good,' said Lou, missing the lie. 'Take it easy all right? You've got a game Saturday.'

Lee gurned, but Lou wasn't amused.

'Top sounds tonight,' Lee said to Noel.

'The sound system's a bollock blower,' said Noel proudly. 'State of the art. It'll knock your fucking nutbags off.'

'How much it set you back then?' asked Lou.

'Don't know, mate,' said Noel nonchalantly. He took a sip of Coke. 'Lotta dough. Brazilian quid.'

'Who you got playing tonight?' asked Lee.

'DJ Paulo.'

'Never heard of her.'

'Him.'

'Never heard of him.'

'Top DJ, mate. No Bobby bedroom,' said Noel emphatically.

'Talking of playing,' interrupted Lou. 'Wayne playing Saturday?'

'Should be fit,' said Lee.

'Good. Think you two have been developing a bit of an understanding recently.'

'Yes, we do have an understanding,' said Lee. 'He always knows where my balls are.'

'Thank you Jim Davidson,' said Noel receding into the lights and babble. 'I'll catch you boys later. Nice to see you, Lou.'

'So, you been all right?' asked Lou patting Lee's arm.

'Been fine. Bit tired, but fine.'

'Michelle well?'

'She's fine,' said Lee. 'She's out tonight, staying in town with a mate, so I'm on me Jack Jones all night.'

'Shit, I almost forgot,' said Lou raising his index finger. 'I got one of these sent over today. Hot off the press.'

On the table he flattened a copy of the latest issue of *Hiya!* magazine that had paid a hefty five-figure sum for an exclusive interview and photo shoot with Lee and Michelle at their holiday home near Orlando, or 'Florida hideaway' as *Hiya!* described it. Lee examined his image on the cover. He thought about Michelle, wondered whether the marriage had gone bad or was just stale. Wondered why she was either at work or in Florida, never at home.

'Fuck, I don't know if I want to look at this,' he exclaimed. 'Look at the cheesy grin on my face. Jesus. What a mug.'

'Don't be stupid,' said Lou. 'They've done a blinding job. Quality that is.'

'It's your fault I did that,' said Lee.

'Well, have a moan when you've seen the state of your bank balance,' countered Lou. 'Take a butcher's inside, you'll love it.'

Lee opened the magazine.

'Look there,' exclaimed Lou pointing to a headline with a stubby finger. A Monte Cristo poked from his fist. '"Is Lee Sweeney The Luckiest Man Alive?" Go on, read it. Goes on about Michelle and how beautiful and clever she is and all that and then it goes on about her having her own shmatte shop and you being a successful player and minted and all that. You'll love it.'

Lee examined the words cursorily and began to wish he were anywhere else but Simmons. Something about the words and images recast his mood to one of vulnerability. He was wide open. The noise and the smoke and the people were all crowding him. He thought for a moment about the voice that came to him every month, how he silenced it by running round with Tesco bags stuffed with mullah, how it would only be hushed for short weeks before returning for more, demanding another drop without even knowing that it had never been out of his mind, making him fret, making times seem thinner than they were. He looked at his wife's alert, graceful face and he knew that he was selling her short, was tiptoeing towards catastrophe. During the occasional moments that his head cleared he knew that he was the luckiest man in the world, but somehow he could never bring himself to feel it.

'You all right, Lee?' asked Lou.

'Yeah,' said Lee, distracted, trying to snag a waitress. He ordered another round. He needed another drink, wanted to tune back into the good-times soundtrack, needed to lose himself again.

'You checked out on me for a while there,' said Lou sipping his cognac. 'Everything all right? You happy with it?'

'It's all fine,' said Lee. ''Chelle will really like it.'

All Lee wanted to do was swill some drinks, get lost in darkness. He didn't want to talk any more.

'I'll have to get going in a bit,' said Lou. 'I'll neck this next one and get back to Liz. Promised her I wouldn't be too late.'

'No worries,' said Lee.

'You off yourself then?' enquired Lou matter-of-factly.

Lee stuck out his bottom lip and narrowed his eyes as if in intense thought. 'Yeah, I'll give it the off in a bit, might stick around for one more.'

'You all right to drive?'

'Noel's sorted it, hasn't he? Got a driver to take me back.'

Lou necked his cognac in one and blew his cheeks out. 'Bloody hell that's good.' He contemplated his glass momentarily before standing. 'Right, Mr Sweeney, I'm going to take my leave of you so that I may return to my beautiful family, and I expect you to do the same forthwith.' He pulled his jacket back so that he could adjust his trousers to a comfortable height.

'Right,' he said by way of a farewell. 'Don't do anything stupid, all right? Game Saturday, remember. United. I'll probably call you tomorrow about that Swish! lunch. Be good, Lee.'

With that he was gone and Lee sat alone nursing a beer, letting the music take him away and checking out some blonde piece – he wondered why all the white girls had straight hair, no one had curly or wavy hair any longer – and he knew that he was happier now, alone and with a drink, than he had been since, well, the last time he was alone with a drink. This was his kind of drinking. Proper drinking. No witnesses. No limits. *Look at the top bollocks on that!*

'Sweeney!'

'Wasim, what's happening mate?' Lee stood up and hugged a thick-set Indian in a Stone Island sweater. His thinning cropped hair topped a round, puckish face with wide almond eyes and a jaw that never ceased chewing gum, a result of Wasim's pressured existence running a successful chain of high-street menswear stores.

'Where you been hiding?' asked Wasim. 'Ain't seen you since God know's when.'

'You know how it is mate, been grafting,' replied Lee. 'Sit and have a drink.'

Wasim ordered a round.

'So you seen Warren then?' said Lee enquiring about a mutual friend.

'Yeah, saw him about a month ago. Doing very nicely thank you. Few of us went up that new lap-dancing place he's doing in Edgware,' said Wasim. 'Tell you, there was a bird in there, you folded a fiver and put it on the table, you'll never guess what? She'd pick it up with her arse! That killed me that did!'

'If she's up to Warren's usual standards she'd have an arse so big she could have picked up the fucking table,' said Lee laughing at his own joke.

'Went up Warren's warehouse in fucking Manchester few weeks ago 'cos he's still doing the wholesale side of things, you know. I tell you, it's an amazing place – they've got around two million pieces of clothing in there.'

'Sounds like Michelle's bedroom cupboards,' laughed Lee. His tone changed as he saw Billy Lyle – fifties, corpulent, beige roll neck, snow-white hair – walking towards them. 'E 'are, e 'are,' whispered Lee. 'Look who it is. You two still out of sorts after that lease business? He's a nasty old cunt he is.'

'I ain't scared of that old bastard,' said Wasim curling his lip and searching out Lyle. 'I know where the bodies are buried.' He waved his hand as Billy passed. 'All right, mate?'

'What was that about?' asked a mystified Lee.

'Can't let anything get in the way of business, Lee,' said Wasim with a chuckle. 'You shouldn't believe everything you hear.'

Look at the . . . Both men watched a statuesque blonde in her early thirties shimmy past wearing little more than a see-through sheath.

'Check that out,' said Wasim. 'More plastic than in your wallet.'

'She'd be all right with your beer goggles on,' said Lee.

'Not my type, mate. Looked like a geezer bird to me. Here, you remember my secretary, Mandy? She's on her own now, desperate for a bloke. You know anyone who'd be a good match for her?'

'How about Godzilla?'

'You're a heartless bastard, Lee,' laughed Wasim. 'She's a lovely girl, brilliant at her job.'

'So where's Natasha tonight?' asked Lee.

'Left her at home, mate, don't need the grief,' said Wasim with a chuckle. 'Wanted to come out on me own. Relax. Just wanted to come out and smell the perfume, knowotimsayin? Tell you what though, there's a lot of people fucking caning it in here tonight. Just went for a waz, right, and – you know they got glass doors on the bogs next to the dance floor downstairs? – there's all this condensation on the outside of the door and there's this geezer, off his tits, just licking it off of the glass.'

'Minging,' said Lee closing his eyes in mock horror.

'I'm serious,' said Wasim. 'I ain't joking. I'm like "All right mate, easy." I don't need the grief, mate.'

'It's going Radio Rental,' said Lee.

'Soft & Gentle,' laughed Wasim.

'Latest one I heard,' topped Lee. ' "It's all going Felicity Kendal." '

'Felicity Kendal? Doesn't even rhyme.'

The two sat sipping their drinks watching the dance floor below as the horny, horny, horny laydeez and pee wee playaz threw their bodies into strange contorted shapes.

'You know what I smelt in the bogs, Lee?' asked Wasim.

'I don't think I want to know,' said Lee.

'Archie,' continued Wasim.

'What the fuck is Archie?'

'You know: Archie Gemmill, Amyl.'

'Amyl? Thought that was a queer thing.'

'So did I.'

'Bloody hell,' said Lee. 'I was at this place the other night, right, and this dealer only offered me some of that – wotchyacallit? – Viagra. He was calling it poke. "Want some poke, mate?" he was going.' He yawned. 'Fucking hell. Don't know where that came from. This beer's taking the edge, making me sleepy, I could do with a spot of Luca to sort me out.'

'Love that one,' said Wasim reaching into his trouser pocket, 'Gianluca Vialli, charlie. Fucking love it. Shake my hand.'

Lee knew the score. 'Thanks, mate,' he said as Wasim slipped him a wrap of coke, no more than a gram. 'Don't want no ketamine, though. Don't want to get into no K-hole.' Wasim shook his head. Lee slipped out of the booth and down to the toilets oblivious to the occasional stare he might attract. As ever he had to wait his turn to secure a cubicle. Some nights there was a queue for the cubicles that reached out of the toilet door. Lee wondered at the probability of those blokes all needing to take a dump at exactly the same time. He hoovered up the wrap and, blinking, stumbled re-energised from the bathroom where he bumped straight into Wasim who was brandishing their drinks.

'Let's have a dance,' shouted Wasim. 'I fucking love this tune.'

At that moment a girl floating on her own who wore little more than a slip closed her eyes, threw her arms in the air and gyrated her body so wildly that it was like she was trying to make the music herself. It took Lee back to when he had had a thing for the starry-eyed podium girls. But that was back in the days before he was tabloid fodder, before his life went box-office. Noel had been right – the sound system was blowing his nutbags off. Lee fought his way into the middle of the sweaty, practised physiques and gave it up to the bass that was firing right through him.

Going, going, gone . . .

'LET'S FUCKING 'AVE IT!' screamed Lee. 'LET'S FUCKING 'AVE IT!!'

Wasim threw himself around, dancing with a couple of girls before shooting off in another direction in a wild, private celebration. He pulled closer to Lee.

'Love it, mate, love it!' he shouted. 'You know, all we ever done all our lives is rude it up!'

It was going off everywhere. Lee was on form, king of the

wall-to-wall night people retailing a rarefied brand of exuberant narcissism. How much had he had now? He couldn't remember. *Fuck it!* He felt level for the first time in several days; as the music thumped him this way and that he reached a place where he felt comfortable, away from the intrusion of conscience, the assault of responsibility. He had training tomorrow, but they could all fuck themselves, he was going all the way, he was larging it.

Wasim stepped towards him. 'Come over to Blue's,' he said. 'I'm meeting some people, we've got a table, drinks are all taken care of. Come on, mate, let's go mental, mental, Felicity Kendal!'

Lee stared at him.

'I know you've got training,' said Wasim apologetically, 'I understand, you know, if . . .'

But Lee was already heading for the door.

They passed fleeting eyes and tangled bodies, through blue smoke and lights out of the door into the cool night. Lee giggled to himself. Here we go. It had run away from him again, he couldn't get a lock on anything that might offer restraint, it was like being on a motorway with no exit. That Luca must have been stepped all over. There was a hole inside him that he just couldn't fill.

He'd done what he had to, gone through the motions of a blinding night out but, despite the music and the narcotics and the girls as sleek as otters, the irrevocable truth was that booze was the only thing that conveyed him to a place where he was utterly, and always, himself.

Wasim passed him another bottle of beer, and, as they lurched up the street, Lee felt no pain.

He didn't know what had hit him. Hadn't seen it coming. One second he had felt the steering wheel beneath his hands, sensed the road rushing beneath him. The next . . . SLAP! Right in the mush. BANG! It was like an elbow, or the flat of a hand. He never thought it would hurt so bad.

Not an airbag. They were supposed to be there to protect you, to prevent harm from occurring.

But the thing popped out of the steering wheel like a fucking firework, whopped him right on the hooter. BOOF! Try that for size, son. His foot had gone down automatically on the brake pedal and he'd felt the motor skid to a halt. Silence. That was what he had noticed the most. Total silence. He paused for a moment running an inventory of his vitals. He flexed his ankles. There was no pain in his legs. Thank fuck. He took a deep breath and arched his back, trying to force the airbag away. Fumbling for the door handle he spilt on to the road.

He leant against the car trying to control his breathing. His heart was thrashing and his legs were weak. He slumped on the ground and looked back up the road where a Saab 900 was facing the wrong way, its offside wing mangled, the corner lights smashed, glass littering the road like jewels. He could make out a woman in the car, she was crying. No, she was talking – quickly, hysterically – into a mobile phone. He stood up and looked at his Range Rover. There was similar damage to the Saab, but not so bad. The bull bars had swallowed the worst of it.

Then he noticed the airbag. There was something on it; a sticky, browny-red substance . . . He reached up and touched his face before examining his hand. It was slick with scarlet blood. He felt dizzy. Reached up and rubbed his face, felt the blood thick upon him. His face. Shit. His face.

'You all right pal?' A man's voice. Scottish. Middle-aged.

Lee considered him. 'Blood,' he said. 'Fucking blood!'

'It'll be all right,' said the man. 'Sit down. You're in shock.'

Lee watched the man's eyes as he approached him.

'Who am I?' he demanded. The man looked at him quizzically. 'Who the fuck am I?' shouted Lee at him, as if accusing him of a terrible crime. 'Who the fuck am I?'

The man furrowed his brow and stepped backwards. 'I,

I, don't . . .' he started. After a beat his mouth fell open. 'Jesus Christ. It is you, isn't it?'

'Who? Who the fuck am I?' persisted Lee.

'You're Lee Sweeney,' said the man. 'You're Lee Sweeney. Would you fucking believe it?'

'Thank God,' said Lee softly. 'Thank God.'

Chapter Two

There was a bird singing, warbling its little bird bollocks off right outside the bedroom window. Lee half opened his right eye to test the light. Too bright. It was late in the morning and he could feel the residue of the night's toxic excesses worming its way through his circuitry, evaporating from his muddy, chock-a-block pores. His blood was black, his heart a wrecked hulk and his curdled and waspish stomach had died on the vine. It wasn't going to be easy.

But then it never was.

The first thing he needed to ascertain was the precise extent to which he had betrayed his body the night before and the reciprocal level to which it had gone about the clean-up job – the filtering, the neutralising, the remedying. It was always a big job – like swabbing Wembley after a Cup Final – but his kidneys still balanced and excreted, his liver scoured, his heart – his poor, scorched heart – fired away like some ancient generator in a building gone bad.

A doctor had once told him, 'The regenerative powers of your body are precocious.' He loved hearing that; for Lee it was like finding out that he had some force field protecting him, like he was untouchable. The Ready Brek kid.

So whenever he was lying there in the early morning and he couldn't shift because the pain would have been too unforgiving, when the sweat was so thick beneath him that the sheet had fused to his back, when the smell of his own breath made him gag, then he could think of just one word: regeneration. He said it over to himself, like a chant –

regeneration, regeneration – his body making itself new again, making itself good.

To Lee's mind, given the advances of science, a new body wasn't too much to ask – any old butcher with a scalpel and a few spare body parts could do the honours – but, seeing as Lee was a professional athlete, he really shouldn't have been in need of one. Nevertheless most mornings he didn't feel too clever.

The bird was still chirping away outside the window. Maybe it's personal, thought Lee. Maybe the bastard just hates me, wants me out of bed. He felt mildly guilty – he should really have gone and taken a look, just to make sure the bastards hadn't built another nest. Six months ago a handful of them had decided to build homes in his roof. Lee had the geezer from Rentokil round to sweep the eaves, sealed the thing up with chicken wire, made sure the bastards couldn't get inside again. That'll play havoc with your resale that will. He remembered the geezer stank of aftershave, some cheap crap. Probably overcompensating, though the smell of the sanitary and pest-control business stuck to him like cling film.

Lee tried to lift his left leg. After a while he gave up. He thought of that *Gulliver's Travels* film, when the feller gets tied down by the little people. That's what it felt like.

With a bit of effort he managed to turn on to his side, see if he could slide his legs out, rather than try and lift the weight of the duvet. Trouble was the thing was wrapped round him so tightly he just succeeded in twisting it round himself, becoming even more trapped. He felt like he'd been wrapped in a shroud, like one of those hotel beds where they've tucked the thing so tightly that you need a hammer and chisel to get between the sheets.

True story: other than checking the minibar, that's the first thing Lee did as soon as he rolled into a hotel room. Didn't matter where he was, he went to the bed and ripped the sheets and blankets apart, made sure none of them were stuffed underneath the mattress. He hated feeling trapped, made him wonder what would happen if there was a fire, would he be able to escape.

After a bit of thrashing around, which knackered him out, he managed to pull himself from under the duvet. He sat on the edge of the bed and waited to see if anything important was going to happen. Nothing. If the truth be told he was beginning to feel all there, might even have been able to eat, if there was anything in the fridge. He couldn't remember really. He didn't get along to Tesco's as often as he should.

Next stage – standing up. Mission accomplished with a surprising lack of aggravation. He timidly opened his left eye. No wonder it was so fucking bright: he'd forgotten to draw the curtains the night before. One of the rails was still partly hanging off the wall where he'd clung on to the drapes the other night after a brief dizzy spell. (Brief because it ended in blackout.) He'd promised himself he'd get round to fixing that. He was sure he'd got a screwdriver somewhere downstairs in that utility room or whatever they called it. He didn't like DIY much, preferred to get someone in who knew what they were doing. Someone who wasn't pissed.

Looking out the window he saw the little feller working away, his chest puffed out and his yellow bird's eyes roving around. He wondered what it would be like, having eyes in the side of your head rather than the front. Sometimes he'd have been happy just to be able to see straight. Sometimes that would be a fucking novelty.

Behind the house a couple of old duffers were out on the fairway, wrapped up in their golfing casuals. Gusts of steam billowed from their mouths. He felt a pang of guilt. After all, wasn't that one of the reasons he had bought the place, because of the golf course? The idea was to get out there, get some fresh air in his lungs, make some mates, stay out of the boozer. Seemed like a blinding idea at the time. When he and Michelle had moved in, the chairman of the golf club came round to welcome the new arrivals. He said he didn't care what he'd read in the papers, Lee was always welcome at the club and so was Michelle, although certain regulations decreed that she couldn't actually play, which suited her down to the ground.

But that was before Lee had gone to the club bar for a drink with Jug Ears and King Tut. (Jug Ears because of his mammoth lugs; King Tut, well, because he looked like King Tut.) Things hadn't been the same after that. He'd driven past the chairman the other day in the Range Rover and been on the end of a funny look. Pissed Lee off that did. Made him play funny that night. He'd have to go over and have a word with the old duffer. See if he could patch things up.

Anyway, he was standing there looking at this bird and realised that the men rocking the Pringle and Gabicci were staring up at his bedroom window, getting an eyeful of him stark bollock naked. Cheeky bastards. So he opened the window and gave them a 'What the fuck do you think you're looking at?' and they put their irons in their carts pretty sharpish and gave it the off with a lot of tut-tutting and a 'Did you see who that was?' Lee slammed the window: the cold air was making his balls shrivel. The bird had shot off. Flew off into the bushes by the shed. He was sure he'd got some poison in there. He thought he might put some down on the windowsill. That would shut the little fucker up.

The fresh air made him feel a bit more clever though, the ozone was whizzing round his head. He decided to don a dressing-gown and check the post. He loved the post. They just couldn't stop sending him money in the post. They sent most of it to Lou, so that he could shave his ten per cent off the top, but time after time cheques got through, ending up in neat little piles in the kitchen, jammed in a toast rack that had never been used for toast. He loved that about the post, he loved that people used it to send him money, loved it that they sent him letters telling him *how much* money he had.

The paper would be there as well. He had a column, you see, in the old currant bun – first Tuesday every month. The Lee Sweeney column. He always looked forward to casting his eyes over it, see what was on his mind.

Originally Lee had fancied writing it himself, but had found it impossible to hit the deadlines. The paper had threatened to pull the contract unless one of their football writers ghosted it first. So Lee would have a chat with some gutter rat down in Wapping who would knock something up and Lou would scan a proof. Load of old bollocks, but no one complained.

Then, one morning, with a mouthful of cherry Pop Tart, he turned the page and discovered treachery. One of the paper's 'outspoken' columnists – 'Stan, "the Man" who doesn't mess around' – had described him as 'a drunken, overweight oaf with a questionable attitude towards his profession'. Bang out of order. Lee refused to speak to the currant bun forthwith. After much wheezing and pleading from Lou it was decided that Lee could be removed from the process altogether. Lou would have an amicable chat with the ghost, reveal the innermost intimacies of Lee's life and then exercise his right to full copy approval. Lee called Lou to congratulate him. Said that it wasn't a bad read.

Lee was halfway down the stairs when the doorbell rang. It was a bad moment. Lee didn't want to answer it for two reasons. Firstly, it was the morning; naturally, he was hungover. Secondly, he was wearing Michelle's pink satin dressing-gown. He hovered for a moment, undecided about what he should do.

Greed got the better of him: there was a strong possibility that postie had rung the bell because he had a parcel in his hot hands with the name Sweeney on it. Lee's initial suspicion was that his sponsors, Swish!, had sent down the usual tanker-sized package stuffed with their latest, newest, hottest swag. Lee still found it hard to believe that his appearance in public in Swish! clobber made the nation's teenagers rush to their nearest trainer emporium any faster than they already did. But, apparently so. The back-slapping execs who Lee met every few months for a gargantuan alcohol-soaked lunch were all convinced that they were shifting as much gear as they were on account of Lee. To reciprocate Lee never appeared on television without forgetting to wear a Swish! baseball cap. Make that if he was on TV and he was sober.

Postie rang the bell again. This time harder and for longer. There was anger in it. Lee decided that he would be able to position his body behind the door while sticking his head and hand round to receive the parcel without raising postie's eyebrow. After all, Swish! wouldn't want to sponsor a cross-dresser. A terrible image flashed into his head: he imagined walking into the dressing-room for training the morning a 'Sweeney Answers Door In Woman's Clothes' story was splashed across the front page. He shut it down immediately. It didn't bear thinking about. It was like waking up and realising you'd had a wet dream about Mrs Thatcher. The bell went for a third time.

'Keep your hair on,' he said as he unlocked the door. He stuck his head round the side at such an acute angle that it looked like it had become disembodied, as if it were sliding up and down the edge of the door as part of some horror film. He was just about to go through his 'Glad you enjoyed the game, yes I think we should have had a penalty' shtick with postie when his brain fizzled and popped to another frequency. It was the first time he'd focused properly that day, like looking down a microscope at a messy blurred image and, before his eyes, the whole thing had taken shape and form.

'Lee?' The geezer looked cold. His nose was red and his eyes were watering slightly.

'Colin?' said Lee like he was asking a question, but he knew all the time it was him. The men stood looking at each other, steam rising from their noses in the cold winter air.

'What are you doing out?' asked Lee.

'What happened to you?' said Colin.

'I thought you still had two years to go?'

'Your face, Lee.'

'You can't stay,' Lee said firmly. The air was so cold it caught in his throat. 'No offence. It's just that it's a bad time at the moment, what with one thing and the other. Me and Michelle.' He looked in Colin's face. Last time he'd seen him he had a boy's face, full of menace and mischief. Now he had a man's face, a harder face, a saloon bar face, a face a bit like Lee's. His nose was still large and beaklike, his skin slightly red and his chin had a deep cleft in it. His eyes were milky green, a colour as muddy as the camouflage he'd worn in combat the world over. You could tell he was a squaddie by his hair and moustache. That was sad. No one wore moustaches any more, at least no self-respecting footballer. Maybe some sad case Bulgarian manager still rocked the Lech Walesa look, but no players had moustaches. Not unless they were wankers. Or Dave Seaman.

'Look, Colin, come in,' said Lee. 'I was just about to put the kettle on.' It was too cold to stand on the doorstep.

'Ain't you glad to see me?' he asked. Lee couldn't answer. Didn't know whether it was all right to lie.

'I don't want any funny comments about what I'm wearing. It's Michelle's, all right?' Lee needed to be sure that he was understood. 'First fucking comment and you're back out the door, understand?' Sometimes he could sound like the gaffer, if he tried.

'All right.'

Lee opened the door and Colin stepped into the hallway.

'And wipe your feet.' This was Lee's fucking house and no squaddie was going to mess it up for him. Colin stepped back and exaggeratedly slid his feet across the mat. He was wearing Swish! trainers. Cheap ones. Lee felt like saying that he could have sorted him out. But he didn't want to get into that right then. It was, after all, his brother. Give him an inch . . .

'Nice place, bro,' Colin said, brightening now that he

was through the door. 'Nice place. You got a brew on then?'

'Yeah. Come through.' Lee began to feel like a right knob wearing Michelle's dressing-gown. He could feel Colin's eyes on his back. He turned round to see that, from his skewed mouth, Colin was trying to stifle a laugh, like he was one up on Lee. He'd always hated the way Colin used to do that.

Lee sat him down at the kitchen table and went and filled the kettle up. He could feel Colin taking it all in. It was like being robbed.

'Will you stop looking at me like that?' Lee eventually barked. Colin was getting on his wick already.

'Have you seen yourself this morning?'

'Oh, fucking hilarious. Lee's wearing his wife's dressing-gown. Next thing you know he'll be a shirt-lifter.'

'I don't mean the dressing-gown,' said Colin. He still had his hands in his jacket pockets, was hugging himself like he couldn't get warm. 'I don't mean that. You looked in a mirror this morning?'

'No.'

'Well, you should.'

'Kettle's boiling,' Lee said. 'Back in a minute.' He shot off to the downstairs toilet and peered at his face. A face very similar to Colin's but slightly more handsome: stronger features, good enough for adverts if they put enough slap on and the lighting was sorted. The Austrian blinds Michelle had put up over the frosted glass had robbed the room of most of its light and, at first, he couldn't quite see what Colin was on about. Then something became visible, like rivers appearing on an arid landscape after rain – brown streaks across both cheeks, thick at one end, tapering at the other; in other places, it was thicker, congealed. The effect had been exaggerated by being smeared. Lee thought it was amazing how many times you touch your face without knowing it, especially when you're strung out on a few grams of charlie.

Jesus.

He cast his mind back to see if he could remember how many people might have seen him like that. He remembered ending up in the bogs of Blue's. He was with Wasim. Then Wasim had gone. He remembered some po-faced cow telling him that his behaviour was verging on the offensive when he pinched her arse. He remembered telling her that there was only one virgin on the offensive in that place. Seemed funny at the time. Then he bumped into this geezer off *EastSiders* – runs the butcher's, whatsisname? – they'd met a couple of times at charity dos and that, and he had some gear and they'd ended up in one of the cubicles in the gents shovelling it up their hooters. Lee made a move for home soon after that: he was beginning to feel gimped out, the music was fraying his nerves and the gloat squad was crowding him. He remembered that the car valet gave him a funny look. He supposed that by that time he might have appeared a bit dishevelled. He remembered wondering where his tie had got to and then reaching on to his head and finding that he was wearing a Burger King crown.

As the evening began to re-form in his mind he felt sick and dizzy again. He went back into the kitchen.

'You all right, Lee?' Colin was sitting at the breakfast bar tucking into a bowl of Corn Flakes. Milk hung on his moustache. He looked like a beast disturbed while feeding at a kill.

'Yeah, yeah.' Lee needed a drink of water. He turned on the faucet, tested to see how cold the water was. He gulped some down, its freshness hitting the back of his peaty throat. He stopped to catch his breath. 'Yeah, just cut myself shaving. Came in last night, decided to shave. Must have been pissed.'

Suddenly there was a ringing. Lee looked at Colin, who shrugged his shoulders. 'Don't have a mobile,' he said, his metal spoon scraping against the bowl.

Lee paced up and down the room, his feet slapping the tiles, searching for the noise. It just didn't seem right. The ringing was coming from inside the fridge. He went over and opened the door. The shrill signal suddenly became much louder. He rummaged round behind the cans of Fosters to find his Nokia. Jesus. He must have left it in there the previous night. This was getting worse. He checked the caller ID.

'Lou?'

'Lee. What the fuck is going on?'

'What are you talking about?' He started to feel worse. Lou was wheezing on the other end of the line. He only wheezed when he was stressed. The wheezing was not helped by his ten-a-day cigar habit.

'Where are you?'

'Indoors.'

'What the fuck are you doing there?'

'It's where I live.'

'Areyoushaw? You, you . . .' he paused to take an asthmatic gasp. 'You've got to be kidding me. Why aren't you at training?'

Jesus. Not good. Not good at all. He started heading back upstairs. Colin shouted after him. He wanted to know where they kept the jam. Did they have raspberry?

'I don't feel too good, Lou. Think I might have picked something up.'

'You're not wrong. You're not fucking wrong there,' shouted Lou. 'Have you seen the papers this morning? Have you?'

'No, Lou.' Lee sat back on the bed. There were brown smears streaking the pillows and sheets. More dried blood.

'Looks like you shat yourself last night,' said Colin standing in the doorway. 'Where's the Marmite? Changed me mind.' Lee waved him away.

'Congratulations, Lee. This morning the *Mirror, Star, Sun, Mail, Express* are all carrying pictures of you at Blue's last night with your arm round some bimbo,' gasped Lou. 'But that isn't the bad bit.'

Lee lay back on the bed, resigned to the inevitable.

'Where's the Range Rover?' Lou asked.

'Outside.'

'Areyoushaw?'

'What are you talking about?'

'Go round the front of the house and take a look.' Lee never put the car in the garage when he came in late at night. Didn't trust himself with the bodywork. He peered out the window on the front landing. Lots of gravel. No Range Rover.

'It ain't there, Lou.'

'No, Lee, it's not there and I'll tell you why. It's out on some deserted road near the village of, let me check in the *Mirror* here, Walstead.'

'That's just round the corner, Lou.'

'Apparently you were involved in a road accident last night. Nothing too serious mind, no one was hurt. Minor damage to the motor. No need to wreck the no-claims. What is bad news, though, is that when the woman approached you to swap details you jumped out of the car, shouted "Banzai" and took off across a field, leaving the engine running. Woman said you stank of booze. She only recognised you because her son's bedroom is plastered with pictures of you. I've had the rotters on the phone all morning.'

'I'm sorry, Lou. I went out for a couple of drinks. You know it . . .'

'It would be nice if you had some idea of your where-abouts and actions, but maybe that's asking too much of you . . .' said Lou. 'Fucking hell, Lee, didn't I say to you last night, keep out of trouble? Didn't I say that to you? Why the fuck did you go on from Simmons to Blue's? You make me feel like I'm talking to myself sometimes. Look, nothing bad is going to happen. Worst they can threaten is to do you for leaving the scene of an accident. But this doesn't help us at all, does it? This is no fucking good Lee, no fucking good at all.'

'Look, Lou, I've got to go . . .'

'What were you thinking of, Lee? What was going through your mind?'

'I don't know . . . My brother's downstairs . . . I think he's left the army.'

The doorbell rang.

'Lou, there's someone at the door, I better . . .'

'Don't give me that "there's someone at the door" bollocks or that "I'm running a bath" shit. We've got to talk Lee, we've got to talk.'

'Who do you think you are, Bob Hoskins?'

'There! There!' shouted Lou. The wheezing had stopped. 'That's exactly what I'm talking about. That kind of nonsense. Don't you know when to keep your gob shut, Lee? Don't you know? Well, you should start learning because at this rate you're going to end up out on your arse with your career up the spout. And I ain't being funny now. This ain't no fucking joke. Do you hear me?'

'Loud and clear, Lou. Loud and clear.'

'Good. Now, I'll call Brandwood and tell him you've got an upset stomach, won't be training today. Remember, we've got lunch tomorrow with Swish! at the Ivy.'

'Why?'

'Something about an ad they want to do for the new boots. Determinator, or some crap.'

'I won't have to wear the things, will I?'

'In the ad you will. But don't worry, sounds like a nice job. They want to shoot the thing in Thailand.'

'Course. Stands to reason.'

'Now, you keep your nose clean. Keep your head down. Stay out of trouble. I'll call the gaffer and I'll see you tomorrow, two o'clock. Late lunch. All right?'

'All right, Lou. See you then.'

Lee put down the cordless feeling better. He liked that about Lou. Lou would call up and rage, call Lee all the names under the sun. But once he'd delivered the goods he'd change his approach. He'd give Lee a verbal clump, but once the medicine was swallowed Lou would turn the conversation around. Lee would get off the phone feeling good about himself, good about Lou.

Not like his rows with Michelle. They never seemed to have a point. Their crises had begun to annex the rest of their lives. The boundaries between rows and routine had become indistinct. His hangover seemed to have dried up. He felt like a drink. He trotted back downstairs.

'Colin, are you still stuffing your face, you ugly bastard?' he shouted on his way down. Lee stopped immediately he entered the kitchen. There were two uniformed coppers sitting at the breakfast bar.

'Do you both take sugar?' Colin asked them.

'Two in each, please,' said one of the cops, though he sounded a little distracted. The sight of Lee in Michelle's dressing-gown with dried blood smeared all over his face might have had something to do with it.

'Mr Sweeney?' said the other. It was a question, but he knew who Lee was. He was about forty with short, wiry grey hair and a full, almost bloated face. The other was younger and thinner with blond, parted hair. The older one seemed a little taken aback, so the younger one took over.

'PC Tanner, this is PC Fox. We're from St Albans station. Wondered if we could have a few words with you regarding an incident last night.'

'Course you can,' said Colin putting the mugs down on the counter. 'Ginger nuts?'

'In private,' said the copper without taking his eyes from Lee. Colin sloped out.

'Go and wait in the lounge,' Lee shouted after him. 'PlayStation's got *Cool Boarders 2* in it.'

'Do you want to sit down, Mr Sweeney?' asked the copper. Lee sat down opposite, the breakfast bar between them. The older one sat there with a dreamy look on his face. Couldn't keep his eyes off Lee, like some love-sick teenager.

'Wife's dressing-gown. Mine's in the wash,' Lee said,

28

trying to lighten the mood. Silence. 'And, er, cut myself shaving,' he lied pointing to his boat. 'Clumsy sod, me.'

'Quite, Mr Sweeney,' said the younger one. 'We've come to discuss the incident last night. At present it looks like there will be no charges made and consequently no proceedings. Nevertheless, I must tell you that we're treating this with the utmost seriousness. And there is a strong possibility that a formal caution will be issued.'

'Right,' Lee said.

'Would you like to tell us, in your own words, exactly what happened last night?'

'Well,' Lee said. 'I was coming home quite late . . .'

'It was four thirty, Mr Sweeney, according to the third party, Dr Shaw, who was out on an emergency call.'

'Blimey, it was later than I thought,' he said, trying for a laugh. Nothing. 'And I was tired. Training was hard yesterday and these charity things tend to go on late. I don't mind of course – I'll do anything for the kiddies – but I was still knackered. And I was going up this narrow, windy lane . . .'

'It was a two-lane well-lit road, Mr Sweeney.'

'Well, it *seemed* like quite a narrow lane. Anyway, this other car was pulling out and just as I got towards him I sort of hit it. By accident. Anyway I'd been reading about all this carjacking that's been going on and I sort of lost it and jumped out my car and ran off. I thought I was going to get robbed. Man in my position. Public figure 'n' all.'

'If you'd bothered to check, Mr Sweeney, the driver of the other car was a woman in her mid-fifties. Hardly the regular profile for a carjacker.'

'Ah, but you never know,' said Lee. 'Better safe than sorry. Can't be too careful.'

'So, you, Mr Sweeney, a six-foot professional footballer at the peak of physical condition thought that a middle-aged, grey-haired woman was attempting to steal your vehicle?'

'Well, I didn't really get a good look at her. She all right?'

'She's fine, sir. Just a little baffled.'

'No, I meant, is she all right with the insurance?'

'Yes, she is.'

'Comprehensive?'

'Yes, sir,' said the cop with an irritated sigh. 'And you?'

'Comprehensive, naturally.'

'Mr Sweeney, I have to warn you that although Dr Shaw does not wish to press charges I feel confident in saying that we could have you for dangerous driving. You were positively identified by a Mr Grant, who was a witness to the accident, and who also saw you leave the scene which, I don't need to add, is an offence.'

'Must have been in shock,' explained Lee. 'Sorry. Didn't know what I was doing.'

'We're going to leave this one here, Mr Sweeney, but, if there are any more incidents, be assured that we'll take a strong interest. Take this as an unofficial warning.'

'OK, OK, get the message,' said Lee. Better to roll over and take the beating than face it out. He was beginning to feel nauseous again. He just wanted plod out of his house.

'That it then?' he asked.

'For the moment,' said the younger one. Both of them rose and headed towards the front door. Lee held it open for them.

'Thanks very much,' he said. 'Sorry to be a nuisance.' The younger one nodded and strode towards the patrol car. The other one lingered a while before spluttering: 'Mr Sweeney, my daughter's a big fan of yours and I just wondered if you wouldn't mind . . .' He pulled out his notebook.

' 'Course, no problem, a pleasure,' said Lee. 'What's her name.'

'John,' he replied.

'John?'

'It's, er, a family nickname. Short for Joanna.'

Lee scrawled on the paper, his handwriting shaky. (He wondered why two of his signatures were never the same.)

'Take care of yourself,' he said. The cop burst out laughing and walked off shaking his head as if he'd just met the biggest card in the country. Lee shut the door and breathed a sigh of relief.

Then he remembered Colin.

'Colin? Colin?' he shouted.

'In here,' he replied from the living-room. As it was the place Lee had asked him to sit it was not where he would have thought to look.

'Look, Colin, you've got to go now,' he said. 'We'll talk tomorrow. Properly. You're all right though? You're out for good?'

'No worries, bro, no probs,' said Colin uncharacteristically. He left his cuppa on the glass table in front of the sofa. 'I can see you're a busy man. It would have been nice to talk. I wanted to explain what's going on . . .'

'Come round tomorrow, we'll have a proper chat,' Lee said opening the door and ushering his brother out. 'It's a bad time right now.' The phone started ringing.

'The phone,' said Colin.

'Don't worry, the machine will pick it up.'

'So tomorrow then?'

'Yeah. Call me. You got the number?'

'Yeah. Just now. Got it off the phone while you were talking to plod. What they want?' he asked.

'Oh, just a mix-up. Thought my car had been nicked.'

'By the way, I'll only come round tomorrow if you'll wear that dressing-gown again.'

'Fuck off.'

'Oh, and one other thing. I changed your answer-machine message. For a joke like.'

Lee slammed the door and ran into the living-room. He knew all about Colin's jokes. He'd been suffering them his entire life. The red light was blinking. Someone had left a message. Someone had heard Colin's joke. He punched the playback button and held it down to hear the outgoing message.

'My name's Lee Sweeney,' came Colin's voice, 'and I like a drink. I would come to the phone, but I'm sleeping it off.'

Jesus Christ. Lee's heart sank as he listened to what followed.

'What the fuck was that all about, Lee? Lee?!' It was the gaffer, Kirk Brandwood, doing his nut. 'I've just spoken to Lou Green, but I ain't impressed. It's last-chance saloon, Lee. You never, repeat, never, *ever* think about missing training again. Even if you're dead. I want to see you in my office before training tomorrow. And if I don't like what you're saying I'm going to tear you a new arsehole. Oh, one other thing. You're dropped Saturday.' The message ended.

Lee started thinking. Hard. He had some major decisions to make. After all, what was he going to wear to the Ivy tomorrow?

Chapter Three

It was typical of Colin to pull a stunt like that, turn up unannounced after an on-off absence of nearly twelve years – over a decade in which Lee had only seen his brother for the occasional, snatched Christmas dinner. It was always the same story, he'd turn up with a bag of laundry and flowers for mum, a bottle of Bell's and a few tall stories for dad and a slap on the back and a saucy joke for Lee.

As little kids Colin and Lee hadn't got on. Chalk and cheese, they reckoned. Went right back to childhood. Lee's theory was that before he was born Colin was the family's blue-eyed boy, the one whom all the aunts cooed over, the one who spent most of Christmas Day working his way through a mountain of booty, the child who revelled in his parents' undivided attention.

It lasted two years before Lee came along. By all accounts, he was a bit of a taxing baby. Never slept, just bleated the whole time. Drove his mum and dad overboard by way of small-hour nappy changes and hysterical feeds. Only way they could get him to shut up was to shove a tit in his mouth. Some things never change.

They lived in a three-bedroom house in Walthamstow, opposite a rolling couple of acres of crisp-packet and crow-infested greenery called Knott End. Lee had the smallest bedroom. Mum and dad had the biggest. The living-room and dining-room had been knocked through and ran the length of the house. When mum and dad were out, Colin and Lee would play football in there, but gently in case they broke anything. When they did there was hell to pay. They had crazy paving in the garden and pebble-dashing on the house. It hurt when Lee ran his hand over it, although that never stopped him. Mum put a four-foot statue of the Virgin Mary at the top of the stairs. In the dark, she looked to be alive. Lee and Colin called her Scary Mary.

The Sweeneys didn't have a car because they never went anywhere. It wasn't that they couldn't afford to – both parents worked – it was just that they never got round to it, except sometimes at Easter when they got the coach to Rustington in Sussex to stay with nan for a week. Most kids went with their folks to holiday camp, or Devon, or Spain. Some even Skytrained it to Florida. America. It was really something then, going there.

Lee's father, Frank Sweeney, used to work the roofs: slating and tiling, flashing and pointing, guttering, coping, asphalt and hot bitumen, you name it. Work was always good in summer, so the family never got the chance to go away, to slip out of the suburbs. Mum never seemed to mind that they never went away, she was always too busy at the hospital – she was a nurse at the Royal Northern in Holloway – the church (she did the vases on the pedestals) and with her old ladies. She was a voluntary worker with people suffering from senile dementia. Drool cases. It always reminded Lee of a joke Colin told him: what's forty foot long and stinks of piss? A conga at an old people's home. His mum would have hated that.

Mary Sweeney had what they call strawberry-blonde hair, pale-blue eyes and chalky skin with little brown freckles that came up when she went in the sun. She was quite tall and slight, but Lee could never believe how strong she was. Up until he was about seven she could get both him and Colin under her arms and carry them up to bed, no matter how hard they struggled. Her grandparents, the McCarthys – by all accounts a couple of miseries – had come over from Ireland, but she seemed to have inherited little from them other than her religion. She was always jolly, always talking, had more energy than her kids. They'd be asleep on the sofa in front of the TV and she'd

34

be asking what was wrong with them. She called her sons her 'little rascals'. Dad told Lee that Grandpa McCarthy had died because 'he had a taste for the sauce', but Mary never mentioned her dad, even when Lee and Colin used to make her go through the family photo album. She never drank and used to wear pink slippers with fluffy bits where her toes went. Lee used to put them on and do impressions of her to make Colin laugh. Sometimes when she watched the news with Frank she used to cross herself. Lee loved his mum. Loved her to death.

Lee sort of loved his dad as well, but he was harder to know. Frank Sweeney was a bear of a man – Lee was sure that was where he got his lower body strength from. He had jet-black curly hair and eyebrows as thick and shiny as a slug. His hands were hard and big. He used to let Lee touch them when he was watching TV. In the summer, when the work was good, Frank always had a deep tan. His skin looked like stained oak. It used to make his green eyes stand out and he'd come in after work smelling of bitumen and tell Mary 'your Latin lover's back, your Romeo', and she used to laugh and say, 'Gerroff me, Frank, I'm trying to make the dinner. The *boys*, Frank.'

Sometimes Frank came with the rest of the family to Mass, but usually on Sunday the boys would have to get dressed quietly, so as not to wake him. Mary didn't mind that Frank didn't come to church too often. 'He's a good man,' she'd tell her friends. Lee knew his mum and dad were going to heaven. His mum and dad were good people. When he got rich he offered to buy them a house, but they said that they were fine as they were, thanks all the same. Then his mum died, and Lee couldn't help wondering if it had something to do with him, that the fame and success and money needed paying for somewhere along the line.

As a kid Lee used to think about going to heaven a lot. His mum told him that you had to be really bad to go to hell and that he wasn't to worry about it, all he had to do was be nice to people and say his prayers. He remembered once, when the police had come to the house after Colin and some other boys had burnt down a shed on the allotments, she'd sent him upstairs to his room without any tea and called him 'wicked boy'. That worried Lee. Wicked was bad. Wicked meant you weren't going to heaven and Colin wanted to go with the rest of the family.

Frank Sweeney liked a drink. Because he was so big it never seemed to have much of an effect on him, although every summer, when he used to wear shorts and a T-shirt to work, the family noted that he was getting a little bigger around his waist. In the evenings he'd usually just fall asleep, can of Harp in hand, and Colin and Lee would hold his big, hairy nose until he woke up. If he caught them he'd chase them up the stairs, pretending to be a monster. They loved that.

When Colin started playing up, when the schools were always on the phone and the police knocking on the door, Lee would sometimes hear them talking in low voices when they thought he was asleep. They blamed themselves for what had happened, didn't understand where they'd gone wrong. Mary did most of the talking while Frank kept saying 'You're right' and 'Spot on, love'.

Lee could never pinpoint the moment, couldn't remember exactly when it happened, but at some point, when he was about ten, he felt himself drifting on to the family horizon. Even though he was always home for dinner, coped all right at school, even did his chores, his parents were so preoccupied with their other son, the troublesome offspring, that they seemed not to worry about Lee. It was as if they thought he was the finished item, their task completed.

Colin broke their hearts. Dinners went quiet except for the clatter of cutlery on ceramic. Lee still knew they cared – both of them would say to him 'You're a good lad, Lee' – but it was like Colin had drained them of all their energy as parents. He'd come home from a county game after scoring a couple of goals and his mum would be sitting there in her glasses, reading, and dad would be soaking up a few lagers in front of the box and they'd ask how he'd got on. Lee would tell them and they'd say 'Good lad'. Then Mary would disappear upstairs to run Lee a bath with plenty of Radox. It didn't matter what he said, there was no variation, no shading to their answers. To Lee it felt as if they thought that it was good enough that he had come home. There was a new stiffness in the way they behaved towards him and it slowly crushed him. It was as if they were thinking: 'Thank goodness we haven't fucked *this* one up.'

Little did they know.

Despite his parents' pleas and punishments Colin became increasingly feral. Mary and Frank were in and out of school placating headmasters and soothing teachers, apologising for smashed windows, flooded laboratories, shattered school pantos. His *pièce de résistance* came on a summer's day. Every year new parents would be shown round the school by members of staff and told how their sons and daughters would academically and socially prosper in such a place. Colin, at that time fourteen, along with a couple of mates, decided to offer them a different perspective on life at St Patrick's.

Just as the headmaster was about to address those gathered in the school hall Colin and his mates appeared on the lawn outside, which was visible to all seated in the hall, and the three of them stuck their heads in plastic bags filled with a sticky substance and pumping the base of the bag up and down, mimicking glue-sniffing. After a minute or so they all collapsed, feigning unconsciousness, quite an achievement given that the bags were filled with treacle.

That was Colin's last day at St Patrick's. He was given a free transfer to a school with a reputation for stricter discipline, St Michael's, where Christian Brothers kept young men in line with biblical exhortation and relentless beatings, which was why St Michael's was feared as the hardest school in the local area.

Colin really found his feet at St Michael's, developing his talents for trade (he ministered every teenager's ambitions – from trainers to stroke mags to computers to grass) and the free market (all competitors were ruthlessly hunted down and drummed out of business). He was never tall, Lee soared above him by the time he reached his early teens, but he had a broadness to him that was unusual for an adolescent, a chunkiness that made him difficult to put down, made it easy for him to block doorways.

While the Colin saga continued, Lee's development was just as remarkable, but for different reasons. At primary school he had been selected to play football for the local area. His progress as a midfielder seemed to capture the imagination of every male adult that he encountered to such an extent that he yearned for the day when teachers, his dad's mates and his mates' dads would stop approaching him saying things like, 'Don't forget us when you're famous,' and 'You'll be playing for England soon.' After all, he was little more than twelve years old when this was happening, but somehow they seemed to *know*, like his life plan had been mapped out on some wall chart that everyone was allowed to peruse except him. Their comments would always be accompanied by a friendly mussing of his hair, which eventually led him to having it cut really short so that he didn't have to spend half his life rearranging and flattening it.

As he got older Colin would sometimes come and watch him play. Colin's joke was that he would always offer raucous vocal support to the team against which Lee was playing. He remembered being about thirteen and in the final of a local cup competition. There was all kinds of talk about several First Division, as it was then, scouts being sent down to take a look at him. Colin turned up in fine voice. Lee was playing against some skinny fucker who didn't seem to feel any pain. He had these really hard knees and legs and, early on, every time he tackled him Lee would limp away. But Lee soon got the measure of him, started to find some space and feed the boys up front.

But every time Lee got the ball Colin started up. 'Hit him! Hit him!' he would urge the other team. Distracted, Lee started getting rid of the ball early, knocking it square, hoofing it hopefully into space rather than taking his time and looking for the killer ball. At half-time he got a bollocking from the coach. Got told he was doing himself no favours as Arsenal, Tottenham and Chelsea had all sent someone down to take a look at him. Got told to keep possession a little bit longer, look up and try and do something useful.

The second half started and he got the ball. He turned the defender who was up his arse and looked for the runners. Colin was screaming at the other team 'Hit him! Hit him!' and Lee delayed his pass momentarily as one of the boys had strayed offside. 'Hit him! You're weak as piss!' shouted Colin. Lee was just lifting his leg to pass when he felt a shooting pain in his left leg and he went down. The referee blasted on his whistle and came running over. Lee could hear Colin on the touchline singing 'Let him die, let him die, let him die'. Coach came running over, took a look at the ankle and told him he was coming off. As he helped Lee hobble to the touchline Lee saw Colin's beaming face. He was punching the air.

Coach pressed ice on his ankle and told him not to worry. He'd be as right as rain in a couple of weeks. He could feel the cold of the ground on his back. A pair of trainers appeared next to his head.

'You all right, son?' came a voice.

'Yeah, I think,' Lee groaned. He felt dejected. There was nothing he hated more than coming off while a game was in progress. The man squatted down next to him.

'Frank Tydings,' he said.

'Lee Sweeney.'

'I know,' he said.

'Frank scouts for Chelsea,' said coach over-enthusiastically.

'Wondered if you'd like to come down so that we could take a proper look at you,' said Frank. 'Won't be for a month or so. Should give you time to get over that. Get match fit. Coach has given me your home number, so I'll call your parents for a chat. See what they think, eh?'

'OK,' Lee said. He was smiling now, despite the pain.

'Thanks, Frank,' said coach, as chuffed as if it were him who'd been selected. 'Appreciate it.'

'I'll be seeing you,' said Frank. His gaze returned to the pitch. 'Switch it!' he shouted. 'Switch it!' The ball arrived at his feet. He kicked it back. Lee sat up and looked along the touchline. Colin was still doing his own private jig.

'Who the bloody hell is that?' asked Frank, his voice loaded with incredulity.

'That's my brother,' Lee said as Colin punched the air. The other side had just scored.

Two months later they put him in Borstal.

They came for him at twilight.

It was a Sunday and Lee liked Sundays because he rarely had to play football. Colin had absented himself from lunch without finishing his jam roly-poly, so Lee had been only too happy to wolf down another portion before helping his mum with the pots while his dad dozed on the sofa with the *Sunday Mirror*. He'd cycled over to his mate Kevin's for a pool session on Kevin's quarter-size table before returning in the dark, cold but glowing, in order to catch the Top 40 on the radio.

He was lying on his bed reading *2000 AD*, keeping half an ear on Radio 1, when Colin walked in. Lee rolled over on his bed and rested his head on his hand. This was an honour; Colin's visits were a rare occurrence over the previous year when he always seemed to have somewhere more exciting and dangerous to go than hanging around with his kid brother. Colin stood silently still wearing a Patrick cagoule. Lee thought: Colin had come straight to Lee's room, hadn't even bothered to take his coat or shoes off. Mum was going to have a fit.

'All right, Col?' said Lee.

'Yeah, yeah,' said his brother unconvincingly. He was breathing heavily.

'Number seven,' said Lee, acknowledging the music playing in the background. His brother seemed not to hear him, pulled his cagoule off and laid on the floor, his head resting on Lee's slippers.

'You're going to have to take that Liam Brady poster down some time,' he said.

'S'pose,' said Lee.

'Reckon you might be as good as him one day,' said Colin. Lee waited for the punchline. When none came he sat up. This was unheard of – Colin offering him a genuine compliment.

'Maybe,' said Lee.

'I'm serious,' said Colin. 'You've got to remember that you're good. Don't let anyone talk you out of it. There's a lot of bastards out there, a lot of jealous bastards.'

Lee listened intently. This was unlike his brother. It was the first time Colin had spoken to him this directly, this openly, for a long time, like he was trying to pass on something of import, really trying to reach Lee.

'You know if I've been hard on you or anything it's only because I wanted you to do well,' he said. 'And I suppose I was a bit jealous, you know? But I want you to remember that I was always behind you. You know that, don't you?'

Lee nodded. There was a slight desperation in Colin's voice, like he was upset. Lee felt himself getting distressed, didn't understand what was happening.

'You've just got to keep working at it,' continued Colin. 'Don't let the bastards get you.'

Colin was trying to reach him, trying to convey something significant, but Lee didn't know what. The doorbell chimed. Lee watched his brother's body tense, his eyes clouded over. Lee felt his own eyes reddening without knowing why. He heard his father's heavy footsteps on the stairs.

'I've got to go now,' said Colin. 'But remember what I said. Do it for all of us, yeah?'

Lee nodded as his father opened the door.

'Lee, have you seen your bro . . . oh . . .' he said sombrely. Colin stood up and, without a word, followed his father down the stairs.

Lee rushed into his parents' room and pressed himself against the window. Accompanied by his father, Colin was being escorted to a patrol car by two policemen. Lee watched as the four got inside, and the exhaust belching fumes. He waved to his brother, tried to make some kind of contact, but Colin just stared cold-eyed into the darkness. Lee screamed, banged on the glass, trying to reach Colin for one last time. The car disappeared into the November gloom. Lee screamed again. It was how his mother found him, tearfully rocking against the glass.

'Please don't go, Colin,' he cried. 'Please don't go.'

His mother held him tight. She wasn't to know it but she would hear him make the same plea in ten years' time as she herself slipped from life.

Chapter Four

By way of a reunion Colin and Lee had decided to have a 'Jock night': only Scotch with lager chasers would tumble down their throats. Hunched in an obscure, dingy pub, toying with a beer mat and sucking his way through a pack of B&H, Colin filled Lee in on the last twelve years of his life. 'After a while it's like anything,' he said tapping the ashtray with a cigarette. 'You get bored, sick of the same old routine, fed up with the same fucking faces.' He traced a thick thumbnail over a beer mat leaving an indentation. 'That's why every time I got a bit of leave I didn't come back. Couldn't stand the thought of just sitting at home with dad watching *Blankety Blank*.'

'So what did you do?'

'Hamburg, Amsterdam . . . you know,' said Colin with a smirk. 'Plenty of distractions there, you know. You should see some of the East European birds they got there now. Jesus. Unbelievable. You got to be careful though. This one bloke I knew he got all tied up by this bird and then before he knew it this massive geezer jumped out of a cupboard and gave him a right seeing to.' Colin released a loud, fruity laugh. 'And then there was this one time when . . .'

Lee loved to hear his brother blather, rushing headlong from anecdote to anecdote; it helped him slip from the clutches of his own tension, freed him for a few minutes from the humdrum, everyday fear that he carried with him like others wore a watch. That was what Colin did for him, he took him out of himself.

'So I bought me way out,' said Colin by way of nothing

43

a few minutes later. Lee necked another Scotch. 'Came back. Stayed with a mate in Croydon. Horrible place, but then I could barely remember London. It was like I'd never lived here.'

'You should have called dad,' said Lee. 'He would have liked that.'

'Didn't want to put him to any trouble,' replied Colin.

'He's your dad,' persisted Lee. 'He's only seen you . . . what? Seven? Eight times in the past ten years.'

Colin hung his head, embarrassed. 'Yeah,' he said. 'Sorry.'

'Don't apologise to me,' said Lee. 'It's beyond that now. You've done what you had to do.'

'Don't start that again,' said Colin. It was a reference to their mother's funeral. Despite numerous messages, phone calls and telegrams, Colin had been absent from the service at the Sacred Heart.

'I ain't starting anything,' said Lee rising to visit the bar.

'It ain't easy getting out,' said Colin. 'First couple of weeks I just walked around. Traipsed the streets looking for work, but I wasn't even sure how to go about it, didn't know what I could do.' The brothers looked up as the pub door swung open. The light was fading outside.

'I miss her, you know,' said Colin out of the blue.

Lee nodded.

'I'm sorry about the funeral,' continued Colin. 'Getting back from Germany, you know, it ain't easy.'

Lee shrugged. 'She was a religious woman,' he said. 'She would have liked for you to be there.'

'I'm sorry I didn't come,' repeated Colin. 'The hospital. I know it can't have been easy.'

'She talked about you,' said Lee toying with a glass. 'Asked when you were coming.' Colin bowed his head. 'Me and dad. We told her you were on your way,' continued Lee. 'We knew she didn't have long, but we told her you were coming. She was looking forward to seeing you . . .'

The brothers sat silently.

'Dad's never been the same,' said Lee. 'He's sort of given up. He doesn't want to die or anything. He just doesn't care much about living.'

They fetched another round and Colin's monologue continued. As Lee guessed, it was only a matter of time before Colin's luck had changed. Turned out that some old army mate of his had recently inherited a large house with a bit of land up in Hertfordshire, near St Albans. Near Lee, funnily enough. As Colin described it, his pal had been so lonely, rattling around on his own, that he'd let Colin move in. Rent free. As Lee listened, his body still humming from the morning's training session, he wondered at what a strange bunch ex-army people are; big kids driving huge, expensive cars bought in Germany for a pittance. Never putting a penny in the bank for a rainy day, they tooled around the country crashing on sofas, shagging each other's girlfriends and eating cereal three meals a day. Eventually, Lee guessed, the majority end up stuck on the security guard swine shift, descending into depression, and seeking consolation in well-thumbed books about serial killers.

Lee continued to drift as Colin went on about the Chinese fire drill of driving in London now. He used a strange shorthand of words like 'fubar' which, apparently, meant 'fucked up beyond all recognition' and 'sapfu': surpassing all other fuck-ups. It reminded Lee of his own horrors and a condition he might have described as 'traffic panic'. It dawned upon him that there were too many cars out there, too many tooled-up terrors with car stereos worth more than their vehicles. He wasn't joking. Every time he drove into town and was crawling through the acres of chicken 'n' fish 'n' burger 'n' kebab joints and late-nite off-licences and sooty pubs and grotty veg stalls, he'd have his hands gripping the steering wheel so hard that his knuckles shone against the skin before some baseball-capped bozzo hammered out in front of him just itching for a beep of the horn or a flick of the wrist. Just dying for someone to tell him how to drive on his fucking road in his fucking car. Just hoping that some rich fuck in a Range Rover pulled an ill-advised stunt; any excuse to give some chump a good kicking. Lee's advice was never get out of the car. If they can't get you on the pavement they haven't got a chance. Don't get on the deck.

Lee and Colin finished their drinks and headed into town – Colin was thinking about buying a computer. 'They're the future,' he told Lee. He'd even talked about trying an evening class to learn how to use the thing. They were stuck in traffic on the Edgware Road and Colin was rattling on about how his mate with the house had just snagged himself this new TV set that's five-foot wide and how he has over sixty channels, and wouldn't it be great if you could make the whole of one wall in your living-room a TV set, then it could be bigger than real life, and Lee was fiddling with the air-conditioning because he was getting too hot but he wasn't warm enough, when he saw this geezer coming down the street.

He noticed him at first because he was walking quickly, almost skipping along. In his forties, he was unshaven with thick glasses and long, unkempt hair. And he was carrying a package with both hands in front of him, like a cartoon character might hold a bomb with the wick gradually fizzing down. Lee couldn't take his eyes from him. Suddenly the man tripped and dropped the parcel on the ground. A fish supper spilt on to the pavement. The man didn't pause for a second; he dived on to the floor and, using his entire arm, swept the food back into the grey, greasy paper.

He looked around as if others might descend upon him to profit from his misfortune, before he continued on his way. After a couple of steps he pulled open the base of his sweatshirt and stuffed the package underneath, swelling his already not inconsiderable belly. A few stray chips littered the pavement. Pigeons descended and started pecking powdery lumps from them. Colin laughed.

'Did you see that?' he said. 'Filthy fucker just scooped up

his fish and chips and carried on like nothing had happened.' He swivelled in his seat to watch the man disappear. 'Must have something wrong with him. Day release. Nutter.'

It might not seem like a big deal, a man spilling his tea on the street, but it got to Lee. That man was telling him something. He could feel himself falling into a hole, and every acid word Colin uttered lowered him even further. Life is necessarily made of such calamities, its meaning rarely revealing itself except in faint shades and indistinct suggestions, but somehow Lee knew that he was meant to see the man with his funny walk and lost fish supper for it told him this: that even when you're at the bottom of the pile, even when life could not get much worse, there are still things that can happen to you that are just plain miserable, uncompromisingly cruel; that for as long as we manage to stagger on there are always calamities and injustices waiting.

And if there are disasters waiting for those at the bottom then you can be sure that there are disasters waiting for those at the top, and if there is no mercy – that those who have already been dealt a bum hand can get a kick in the groin to add to their woes – how much easier must it be to unleash cruelty upon those who have managed to scrabble their way above the watermark, who are fat from supping the soup of life? He thought about his mother, how she had never committed a bad act in her life, how she had brought only kindness into the world. She'd deserved better than to wither in a cancer ward.

The Cod Man was a turning point of sorts. Lee realised that, sooner or later, the walls were going to cave in around him, that there was little that he could do to hide from the vengeful, destructive forces that, ultimately, would seek him out. He felt like a man stumbling home alone on a moonless night. His card was marked, fate was sealed. Sooner or later everything would go wrong. The Cod Man reminded Lee that he was going under. It was just a question of how long he could hang on, how long he could keep his head above water.

It was pissing down. They were nearing Hendon when it dawned on Lee that he was sick of the sound of his own voice. Colin had turned sullen, so Lee had started talking just to drown out his brainwork, fill the car with words as the traffic stuttered through London. He was droning on about Michelle, and her mother Brenda (or the Crow, as he liked to call her), and how neither of them seemed to comprehend him and how he just needed a chance to work it all out, and how he was worried that his recent dip in form was turning into a slump . . . It happens, doesn't it? You hear yourself and you just want to say, why don't you just give it a fucking rest? Shut your cake hole.

So he switched on the radio and Five Live pops up on the LCD and Lee could hear voices from very far away; so distant that it sounded like a different planet. And he could hear the sounds of summer coming through the speakers, the murmur of sunshine beaming down the ISDN line. Two old duffers were wondering whether this was the best England spin attack that had ever fielded in Georgetown. And all Lee could see, as the windscreen wipers swiped at the sleet, was a vision of livid green. Of pink-faced colonials in straw fedoras, and partisan locals sipping Red Stripe while the laziest of games unfolded its subtle plot. And Lee let out a sigh, something that came from a place deep inside his body, and said dreamily, almost to himself: 'I chose the wrong sport.'

'You what?' said Colin. He'd developed an annoying habit of scrunching up his nose, like a rabbit, when questioning things. Some army power game.

'I said, I chose the wrong sport.'

'It chose you,' said Colin. They came to a stop at a set of traffic lights.

'What d'you mean?' asked Lee.

'It's obvious, innit,' said Colin confidently. 'You're

gifted. You're a phenomenon. People like you come along once in a generation. I mean, if it was a genetic thing, if it was because of who our parents were, or even because of where we were brought up then why isn't it me? Why wasn't I born with what you've got? Think about it. We've got the same mum and dad. We had the same upbringing, went to the same schools . . .'

'Till you got kicked out . . .'

'All right, all right,' said Colin cutting the air with his hand, 'but it was too late then. How old was I? Fifteen? Sixteen? I don't remember now, but the bottom line is that it was too late by then. Even if I'd wanted to there was no way I could have reached your level. You were the youngest person to play for the full school team. You were fucking twelve years old, Lee. You were playing against sixteen, seventeen, eighteen year olds . . .'

'Yeah, and I was a freak,' Lee cut in. 'Everyone thought so. Even the teachers.'

'You weren't a freak.'

''Course I was. I was the only kid in the changing-rooms who hadn't started shaving yet. I was a little kid mixing with adults. Think about it. I was too embarrassed to shower with the rest of the team. Thought they'd laugh at me.'

'Don't be silly, Lee.'

'It's true, Colin. I fucking hated all that, but I had no choice. It was taken for granted that I was happy to be playing for the senior team. No one ever asked me if I wanted to play. I'd just see my name up on the team-sheet every week. Be expected to turn up for the coach, miss the lessons that everyone else was doing.'

Colin chuckled. 'Strange, innit,' he said. 'We were so close as kids. "Thick As Thieves", you remember that song? I'd have done anything for you . . .'

'That's what we get from mum,' cut in Lee. 'That's what she left us. Family sticks together no matter what.'

'No matter what,' agreed Colin. 'No matter what. But

what I was trying to say was I didn't know you hated all that stuff.'

'I didn't *hate* it,' said Lee. 'I just wished I could have been a normal kid sometimes.'

'You were never a normal kid,' said Colin.

'Yeah, I couldn't have been,' said Lee. 'I had you as a brother.' He grinned.

'You were gifted. Still are. So stop moaning, Lee,' said Colin doing the nose thing again. 'Most people would give their right arm to be in your position. I know I would.' He started fiddling with the CD. Lauryn Hill came crashing from the speakers. Colin stabbed at the panel, trying to control the volume.

If he had been listening he would have heard Lee, ever so gently, say: 'You don't want to be where I'm living at the moment, Colin. I promise you that.'

But he didn't.

'I'd give it all up tomorrow just to have mum back with us,' said Lee. He meant it.

'To have the family back together again.'

''Course you would,' said Colin fiddling with the stereo. 'Anyone would.'

Lee went back to his thinking, tried to get inside the scorched circuitry of his mind. Then he remembered why he was feeling so anxious: he was thinking about Saturday. Upton Park. It was the faces in the crowds that really used to do it for him. He'd be getting on with his game, minding his own business, but then there would be a pause and he'd snatch a glimpse of the pink and brown balloons, all of them with huge gaping, red openings. That's how he used to think of them, balloons filled with air, pumped up to bursting, skin pulled as far as it could stretch.

Rows and rows of them, only feet away, their breath hot and toxic in his face. Last week, one of them shouted at him: 'Oi, Sweeney. I fucked your wife.' Lee tried not to, but he looked up expecting to see the culprit having a bit of a hoot, sharing a laugh at his expense. But all he could see was this face, trying to get at him, trying to get inside him. He stared at the bloke, not aggressively, just like he was trying to work out what was going on. The geezer stood up and started gesturing, his face twisted like he was so steamed up that he was going to burst. The crowd started to bubble: one of them had made contact, one of them had got a rise; there was sport to be had. He was an ugly fuck, the one who first shouted – face like a full English breakfast – but that afternoon he was doing all right, that afternoon he'd made the life of someone who had managed to scramble out of the crowd and on to the pitch just a little bit more awkward, a little bit more careworn. It was a victory of a kind.

Sometimes, at night, that's all Lee could see. Faces and voices. That's all he could hear. That's all he could feel.

At that stage of the season the Premiership looked like it was all over really. The team was fourteen points off the pace and the papers and telly (Hansen, again) had been giving them a hard time. Said they weren't up to it. The usual stuff; no bottle, no heart. Lee was off the pace himself, he just couldn't seem to settle. Every time he sat down he just wanted to bounce straight back up again, like his seat was hot. He was like Gordon Strachan, couldn't sit on his arse for more than a minute.

Everyone at the club had sensed that to salvage anything it was going to have to be a cup season. It was clear that Kirk Brandwood, its miserable put-upon chief coach, was under severe pressure from the McKay brothers, the aloof Scots who had bought the club two years before and invested millions (including the purchase of Lee), yet had seen no sustained drive for honours and consequently revenue was disappointing. In turn, Brandwood was making it clear to the team that nobody's place was safe. The players would have to fight each week to see their name on the team-sheet. Woolnough had got stuck into them in the *Sun*. Lee wished he hadn't seen the piece, made him wince. But Woolnough was right, not like that prick Harris.

Some weeks they would play out of their skins, most famously the previous March when they dismantled Man Utd who, until then, had been cutting an imperious swathe through the Premiership yet had had the rug pulled from beneath them by a team of underachievers. It had all clicked; the punters had their day and United were demolished. Lee had wanted to go up to Ferguson, grab his stopwatch and shove it up his arse.

There was a moment after that game that Lee would always remember. He was sitting alone in the dressing-room. The other players, trainers, physio, everyone had left. The place, as usual, was a tip. Empty water bottles had been slung everywhere, gobstoppers of mud were dotted across the floor, bandages and strappings had been strewn where they fell. And Lee remembered one thing. He remembered how much he loved all this. How much he'd wanted this to be his life and, once he had achieved it, how much he had taken for granted, the extent to which he had blithely assumed that it was just the way that things were. And he realised that, sooner or later, it would be gone from his life. It was similar the way he'd always assumed his mum would be there, that the family would be strong, and why he still clung hopefully to Colin.

There were new Lee Sweeneys popping up everywhere – breaking goal-scoring records in their early twenties, earning stellar money, peacocking it down catwalks, shtupping supermodels – and it was becoming more and more obvious to Lee that time was running out, that the patience of the club, his wife and his doctor was disappearing like sand from an hourglass. He pressed his hands down on the wooden benches, listened to a couple of mounted police passing outside and wondered where they kept police horses in the middle of London. He stood up in his stiff club suit. He knew that it was up to him; all the excuses, all the apologies amounted to nothing. They were all to do with other people, what was going on on the outside.

He knew that the salvage job was down to him.

He went into the players' lounge and worked his way through a few lagers before Colin got too leery and strayed towards the Twomacs; the dour Presbyterian Glaswegians were unlikely to react well to his brother's beer-enhanced suggestions on how to run the club better.

The two of them ended up in a country club not far from Lee's place. Lee was lost in music, lost in booze, shaking loose from recent worries when this girl approached him. Lee was aware that, in the past, he had, on occasion, fallen foul of the midnight princess syndrome – a combination of alcohol, desperation and time, which can mutate any old boiler into a vision of something that stacks up nice – but this girl was a top sort. Lee was returning from the bar, lagers in hand, when she tugged his arm.

'You a footballer?'

Lee smiled. He liked her style.

'Your name Lee Sweeney?'

'Last time I checked.'

'Good. Can I have your autograph please?' She produced a couple of sheets of bog paper and an eyebrow pencil. 'I wasn't sure it was you,' she said.

Lee tried to speak, but couldn't get his mouth to work fast enough. The booze was slowing him down. Would have been a different story if he'd copped a gram of Gianluca, but it didn't look like there was a friendly connection around that evening.

'My boyfriend said it was you. He pointed, but I wasn't sure which one he meant,' said the girl watching Lee write.

He handed the toilet paper back to her and picked up the drinks that he'd rested on a black, acrylic table.

'Thanks,' she said and smiled. 'He'll be really pleased.'

'Come over,' Lee said. 'There's someone I want you to meet.' He gave her his extra-monied-celebrity-endorser wink.

'No thanks,' she replied. 'I've got to get back to my boyfriend.'

'You sure?' he asked.

'Yeah,' she said.

'So that's it? An autograph?' He couldn't help sounding surprised.

'That's it,' she said. 'Good luck.'

'Cheers,' Lee said sarcastically, but she'd already turned her back and was fighting her way across the dance floor back to Dave or Mark or Stuart, or whatever his name was.

S'pose you lose some, thought Lee. It was probably just as well. Colin wasn't a lot of fun when he was pissed. Firstly, you could tell he was bladdered, which is never a good thing. Lee hated drunk drunks. Lee's advice to anyone who wanted to take up drinking seriously would be to make sure that people only know you're wankered when you *do* things: when you crash your car, puke up, grope them, hit them, et cetera. If you're going to sit there leaning all over the place, slumped slightly forward, slurring your words, knocking things over and telling people how much you love them well, frankly, you get what you deserve.

One thing that really annoyed Lee about Colin when he was pissed was that he pointed a lot. And the more he pointed the more he jabbed, and the more he jabbed, the more likely he was to poke you in the face and, after he'd poked you in the face, he'd grab you with his clammy, nicotine-stained fingers and tell you how sorry he was, which, of course, was no good to anyone.

'Who was that?' slurred Colin pointing at the girl.

'I dunno,' Lee said. 'Tried to chat me up.' He sipped his beer. It was too fizzy; like those vitamin drinks they'd got him drinking in Italy. 'I couldn't be bothered though. I'm knackered. Stop pointing, Colin.'

Colin put his hand down and watched the girl while he groped on the table for his beer.

'She's all right,' Colin said nudging Lee in the ribs too

hard. 'She's – what they say? – anatomically correct. KnowotImean?'

Lee didn't bother answering him. Since they'd started hanging out together Colin had increasingly been getting on Lee's tits. Lee liked a drink – boy, did he like a drink – but Colin was beginning to attract attention to them, which is exactly what Lee didn't need. Not that night. Not at that moment. Colin, you see, had realised that his tooling around with Lee could be a good thing for his credibility, as much as his bank balance. (When Colin bought a round it was invariably with Lee's money. He had no shame.) Lee listened to Colin jabbering on about the girl and what he'd like to do with her and he realised that while he had a relatively foul mouth, his own swearing was dramatic, done for emphasis, like a chorus in a song. For Colin, it was more of a drum beat – it set the mood for his words, a constant, percussive rhythm.

Lee thought about Michelle, how things were not right between them, how his heart ached for them to be blessed with fresh intimacy. In the public domain it was assumed that Lee loved her for her beauty, or because she was strong, or because they often laughed together. And although these things were all meaningful to Lee none of them cut to the core of why he hung so much of his essence upon her. It was her sanity, her balance that magnetised him. And even though they had been teenage sweethearts, marrying Lee didn't come easy to Michelle, she was too complicated, too complete, for avarice to sustain her. For years they had been a couple, almost before Lee turned pro, and the span of their time together had served to intensify the sparkle of Lee's need. Since the disappearance of Colin, his mother's death and the sombre withdrawal of his bereaved father, Lee had come to realise that the years with Michelle constituted the most sustained relationship he would ever know. Like a talisman, she kept him intact, the auditor of his soul, as vital a part of his make-up as any internal organ. He loved her because she had wanted to be with him for who he was, not what she wanted him to be. She accepted his idiosyncrasies and limitations and, in Lee's experience, this was a rare and valuable thing.

Michelle hated playing the footballer's wife, loathed the counterfeit diversion of the players' lounge, the wives and girlfriends competing with their carnival outfits and high-maintenance hairdos. Once, when Marvin Whitney signed from Leeds, his wife brought their four-year-old twin daughters into the players' lounge. The kids were dressed identically, like they were going to a fancy-dress party; immaculate velvet dresses with floppy hats, blonde hair curled in ringlets. Mum announced to anyone who would listen that the whole rig-out had taken most of the day to complete.

Lee remembered Michelle's eyes sliding over his shoulder as the kids waddled, stiff in their outfits, after their mother, who was virtually wetting herself with excitement, as if she were showing the champions' champion at Crufts. A few of the other wives, who had kids of their own, smiled indulgently or passed comment. Dawn beamed handsomely saying, 'Thank you. *Oh, thank you.*'

He had watched as Michelle put her drink down and disappeared into the ladies' in a flurry of hair and gold jewellery. She returned after half an hour, her eyes red, asking to leave. Lee had had a couple too many, but wasn't in a position to argue. She was silent for the entire journey home; normally when he drove she nagged him to slow down, to be more courteous. The following day she announced that she had a migraine, was moving to the spare bedroom until it cleared. Lee hardly saw her for a week. She hid, blotted herself out, eating nothing but Cup-a-Soup and cereal. He'd take her a cuppa every now and then, but she didn't acknowledge him, lay wordless, wearing eye-shades supplied by Virgin Atlantic.

There was something Lee hadn't told anyone about him and Michelle. Something significant, something people close to them might have liked to have known; it might have explained things a bit. They couldn't have kids. Or, not to put too fine a point on it, doctors thought that Michelle would find conception problematic. Although it hadn't completely put their lives into a state of collapse, put them into a funky paralysis as they worked their way through their daily to-do list, it was an underlying element in their relationship, something that always came between them as they tried to drag themselves onwards.

It had dawned upon them soon after they'd married and stopped using protection. Months went by and still nothing happened. Lee would become aware, from Michelle's mood, that the blood had come. It continued for three years. They had sex for all this time, mostly with each other, and still nothing happened. They negotiated the sperm-count, hormone-level chicane pretty early on; nothing was amiss, Lee was in the clear. But the longer it went on, the closer they got to identifying the cause, the more boffins and counsellors and experts they saw, the more difficult it became. Even money – lots of it – couldn't solve this one. Michelle had IUI and IVF and every combination of trick-timing, hormone-ambushing, egg-boosting alchemy. They were having deadline sex, their love life determined by high-performance watches and decreasing optimism.

It was like a sticky label that wouldn't stay. They were having sex, lots of sex, hourly sex, far too much sex, but somehow it wasn't like having sex at all and the more they had, the less they enjoyed it and the less they were having sex with each other but with a thing, an eventuality that had trampled their lives.

Then, one day, and Lee was never quite sure when, they decided that enough was enough. There were no harsh words, no teary accusations, just a sense of fatigue that swept over them both and hit them only as the truly exhausted can be defeated. They were all played out on the baby-making front, but never admitted it to each other, they just stopped trying so hard. Their sex life continued erratically, although truthfully both of them were drinking so much that it was rarely memorable. Sometimes they'd stop having sex for months, just because the drinking made them feel so much better. People say that drinking numbs you, and they're right. But right then all Lee and Michelle wanted was to feel numb.

Chapter Five

'Jesus Christ,' said Colin. 'The eyes are following me round the room. Spooky.'

Lee ignored him, hunched over the blue baize. Two more balls to pot and then the black . . . Thunk! One of them dropped into the top right.

'Nice one bro,' said Colin with the authority of an expert. They were in Lee's games room at the back of the house which had a view across the golf course. The fading light cast a grey November haze on to the pool table. The far wall was dominated by a framed colour portrait of Lee in full England strip that Michelle had proudly presented him one Christmas. Lee circled the table looking for the best angle for the final colour.

'It's impossible,' Lee said finally. 'Can't be done.'

'Don't be silly,' said Colin. 'Saw Homer do a shot just like that on *The Simpsons* last week.'

Hunkered down on the table, his hand splayed uncomfortably, Lee shook his head. He couldn't be bothered to argue. 'Tell you,' he said. 'Only reason you're any good is you spent all your time in the army playing pool at the tax-payers' expense.'

'Not true,' said Colin as Lee missed the shot. 'We were incredibly busy – drinking, smoking, playing Nintendo, pissing about . . .'

'Thank fuck the Russians didn't invade,' said Lee.

'We wouldn't have noticed,' said Colin.

The front door slammed.

'Looks like the missus is back,' said Colin.

'Last orders, gentlemen please,' said Michelle walking

into the room. She was wearing a long black coat, her cheeks red from the cold. Lee preferred the way she looked in winter. Michelle loved clothes and the winter gave her opportunity to wear plenty. He'd never gone for the girls who showed cleavage in December. No class. She placed a four-pack of Stella on the middle of the table.

'There's the beer you wanted,' she said. 'Go easy on it, cos that's your lot until the weekend, OK?'

She was serious, yet Lee ignored her tone, sweeping her into his arms as if she had not spoken, amused by her admonishment. 'Show some respect,' said Lee, kissing her on the lips.

'I'm serious,' said Michelle. 'You've got to take it easy.'

'Shh,' hushed Lee. 'Game in progress and I'm just about to kick Colin's arse.'

'Kiss my arse more like it,' said Colin embracing Michelle who held back slightly.

'No thanks,' she said pulling a face like she'd just tasted something sour. 'Who's winning?'

'I am,' said both brothers.

'Right,' said Michelle sarcastically. She disappeared from the room. Colin removed the cans from the table and started to size up his next shot. Michelle rushed back into the room clutching a grocery bag and a huge bunch of white roses.

'Have a whiff of these,' she said enthusiastically. Both men eyed her warily. 'Go on,' she insisted. Lee approached her. He had little desire to smell the roses, but he loved her enthusiasm, was thrilled by her excitement.

'Mmm!' he said. 'But not as good as you, my love.' He looked at her with pride, despite the corny line.

'Come on, Colin,' said Michelle acknowledging her husband's look with one of her own. 'Get your schnozzle round these.'

Colin approached her with mock weariness and sunk his face into the petals. 'Happy now?' he asked.

Michelle ignored him. 'And look what else I got!' she

announced to Lee. 'Ta-da!' A large, elaborately designed box of Pandoro swung from her long fingers. 'Your favourite.'

'That is on the money,' said Lee. 'Where'd you get it?'

'One of them little Italian delis in Soho,' replied Michelle proudly.

'You're a genius,' said Lee giving her a peck on the cheek. He loved that she thought of him in banal, everyday ways. 'Back in a sec, just going for a waz.'

Michelle watched him leave the room, pleased to see him happy. Colin played a shot. Missed. Michelle removed her coat, holding it over the crook in her arm and surveyed the garden.

'What did you get me?' asked Colin suddenly.

'A kick up the backside,' said Michelle, joking.

'There's other things you could do for me,' he said with a wink. Shaken, Michelle examined him, assumed that he was joking, hoping that he was.

Lee re-entered the room and examined Colin and Michelle. Something was amiss, the atmosphere gone sour. Colin turned away to chalk his cue and Michelle smiled thinly at her husband.

'Fancy some cake then, love?' she asked.

Lee had picked up his taste for Pandoro while he was playing in Italy. Loved the food out there, couldn't believe the stories of old Rushie having crates of baked beans flown over. Before then he'd never really been abroad much. He'd been to Florida, of course. He and Michelle had a place out there on a compound near Orlando. The residents called it a gated community, but Lee didn't see much of a community; he couldn't even see his neighbour's house, let alone chat to them over the fence. Nigel Mansell was in the same compound. He had a few quid, snagged himself one of the really plush gaffs next to the water. The place had been Michelle's idea, a sanctuary away from the grind of football, the plod of celebrity, a place where Lee might be free to be a very unimportant person.

Lee loved it out there though. Loved it. Visiting was like being born again – nobody knew who the hell he was. And even if he told them they really couldn't give a damn. They thought that football – or 'saawker' – was some kind of nonces' sport, a game for girls and kids. Lee loved being there for the unexceptional pleasures denied him in England, like being able to go to the pictures, restaurants or shops without some stop-at-nothing maniac barrelling up to him brandishing a Bic wanting Lee to autograph his belly. They all came out with the same old crap, how they only wanted a minute of his time, all that shit. Some of them didn't even ask. Some of them just presented him with a pen and paper, stood there, and said 'You know what to do'. When he gave them what they wanted they'd just mutter 'Good lad'.

It was bad in England, but Italy was worse. Even Lee was amazed by the level of football mania over there, especially down south in Naples. Mental. To Lee's disappointment Michelle hated it. All along he'd thought it would be right up her street – all that sophistication, et cetera. He'd been excited by that, thought it might give them the freshness they needed to feel good about each other again. He'd even said that Brenda could move into the villa, but Michelle never took to it, spent more time back in England than in Italy. She was setting up a womenswear shop in the West End. Fair play though, she was stocking it with lovely gear.

Lee endured the Neapolitan attention with good grace; there was something pure about it, something less threatening than the Stone Island mob back home. In Italy it was just part of the deal, part of the craic. He'd be driving along and a couple of lads on a motor scooter would pull alongside, tap on the window and wish him luck for the game at the weekend. Sometimes they'd make elaborate presentation – candles, bits of ribbon, scarves. It was enough to make him rediscover his faith. Almost.

Once Michelle decided she needed a new belt. Lee and

Michelle were just browsing the racks in Versace when the manager ran over, his eyes wide and his brow glistening. Lee looked out the front of the shop to see a hundred Napoli fans laying siege to the shop. Two security guards hastily locked up. The police arrived and Lee and Michelle were shepherded out of the back exit and given an escort home; but not before Lee had signed half a dozen autographs and posed for a couple of pictures with the *carabinieri*. What was it with him and policemen?

Two days later half the fucking shop arrived by courier with a couple of bottles of champagne and a hamper of Italian food (which Lee gave to the gardener) with a note from Donatella offering Lee and Michelle her humble apologies for the distress caused. Michelle liked that, was warmed by the professionalism of the gesture.

It was bad enough when Napoli won, but when the team lost it was unbearable. Lee didn't want to leave the house. And when there was a big game coming up – one of the big Milan teams or the detested Juve – the pressure was so intense that the team would be sent out of the city to a training camp. It was like he was being taken into custody for his own protection and, although she pretended that she didn't mind, Michelle was quietly resentful at his absence. He would return to find a nest of empty wine bottles scattered in the yard.

Most of the players liked it though. Gave them a chance to get away from the wives and all the outside pressures. When he first arrived, Lee found it all a bit strange, very different to England where players are used to picking up fifteen grand a week for training three hours every morning and then going home and playing Nintendo, or catching up on a bit of action with some Page Three princess.

The boys still knew how to have a good time though. By then Lee had developed a taste for charlie. If you're out and about at night in London and you're a face then you always bump into someone who knows someone. There's always gear around. In London it was nearly always covert, but in

Naples the stuff was everywhere. Some Italian chopping up in the bogs at this nightclub once told Lee they were about to partake in 'dried tears of the Virgin Mary'. And that's what it felt like sometimes, as if Mary herself were standing over the city weeping torrents of cocaine into the city's secret places.

When Michelle returned to London to oversee the opening of her shmatte shop in Bond Street, Lee would lie in bed in the afternoon and wonder what on earth he was doing there. On Sunday evenings after the game, some of the players would end up in a club or at someone's house and there were always new people around who wanted to lavish them with drink and drugs and girls. Lee remembered, in his last season, how there was a self-styled gangster, whom everyone was a little scared of, on the scene. They'd pass reverentially into the back room of a seafood restaurant and watch as their names were spelt out in coke. It was done so beautifully that it seemed a shame to hoover the stuff up. At that moment Lee always silently thanked his parents for giving him a name that offered him a manageable amount to snort. Other players weren't so lucky – he was playing in a team with people called Giovanni and Archangelo. That's a lot of gear. Those nights everything seemed to have a bleached look to it. Lee would sit listening to the music – getting right inside it – and talk and sip his drink and he'd suddenly feel sick with fright as if he'd just discovered that he was sitting astride some glowering fault line.

That was when the habit really started, when the need began to bite. That was when, after three seasons – the first winning the UEFA Cup, the second and third winning the Scudetto in consecutive seasons – he might have been able to stand for Mayor of Naples, but, waking mostly with whisky breath, he could barely remember what day of the fucking week it was. On the phone Michelle protested that she was missing him, wished that they could be together, but he could tell from the animated lilt of her voice, the playful tone, that it was the business, the responsibility of commerce, that she found exhilarating. Part of him warmed to hearing her enthuse about the sand-blasted glass she had found for the changing-room doors, but another part of him felt excluded, wished that he'd found a partner who was more easily satisfied, who was biologically different. For both of them to be able to emphatically follow their chosen paths they must live apart. Lee felt it to be punishment of a kind: the shop was her baby.

And although Napoli couldn't stop winning and the throb of the stadium, the drama and the glory, could be felt in every large and small part of the city, Lee began to lose heart. And when he lost heart he lost form. He wasn't able to perform the role he was born to. All he could see were the front players throwing their hands in the air in the way that Italians do, shouting 'Madonna!' and 'Super cazzo!' as he pulled himself from the clinging turf after another dastardly challenge. (This wasn't as bad as the first game he had played when the only word he knew was 'ciao'. He had spent ninety minutes running round the pitch shouting 'ciao!' 'ciao!' trying to get hold of the ball.)

And as Lee's form suffered, so did the team's. After one particularly bad game against Fiorentina, Lee was booed off the pitch at half-time, the Napoli fans gesturing at him as if he'd spat on their mothers' graves. At that time Jug Ears and King Tut came out for a weekend, and stood around after the game with Peronis lost in their fists shuffling their feet and telling him not to worry, that he was bound to suffer a dip in form sooner or later.

Eventually he was called to a meeting with the coach who asked if everything was all right at home. How was Lee to know? He was never there. He couldn't stand being in the place. The villa was too big, too lonely since Michelle had returned to London. The place was silent, there was too much time and space for thinking. The only noises were the cleaner sweeping the marble floors and the gardener with his hose outside. The coach asked about

Michelle. Lee told him that she had promised to come for a weekend, but had yet to finalise any plans. Privately he was convinced that the next Neapolitan she encountered would be an ice-cream. Then the coach told Lee the news. He was worried about him, the club president was worried, and some of the other players had voiced their concern. As there was a break in the regular season, because of an Italian international fixture, it had been decided that Lee would be sent to a fat farm to get him back in shape. Signor Berardi assured Lee that he wanted him to become 'a free spirit' again. Lee sat there fishing for something to say. All he was thinking was, imagine that, imagine a British manager saying, 'I want you to become a free spirit.' Italy was a strange country.

The message was typed and slid under his door. Lee pulled the note from the creamy embossed envelope. 'Signor Lou telephoned,' it read. 'He will arrive tomorrow at 7 p.m.' Lee smiled to himself, understanding what was going on. As much as Lou adored his wife and son he would escape to Italy every few weeks to detox from familial stress. Lee was glad of the company. He'd been on his own at the fat farm for a couple of days and was ready to see a familiar face, even if it was Lou's hangdog mug.

It was an oft broached subject between Lou and Lee that no matter how much money the former made, he never spent any cash on looking good. Lou had never, *ever* looked the part of the high-rolling pimp daddy of England's number one football player. Lee watched him shuffle into the lobby. He'd just stepped off British Airways first class and been limo'd to Lee's marshmallow prison – a sixteenth-century former Jesuit monastery which had been five-starred into a luxury spa and health centre where portly Italians torched calories and whittled away at their waistlines. Lee watched him shuffle towards the reception desk in his crumpled Burton suit and noticed airline eye-shades poking from his jacket pocket alongside a pair of complimentary travel socks.

'Looking good, Lou,' said Lee.

'Lee!' said Lou. 'Good to see you. Looking great yourself. What is this? You've been here only three days and already you're looking better than me?'

'I came in here looking better than you, Lou,' Lee said. 'There's people been stretchered out of here looking better than you.'

'They probably died of carrot juice poisoning,' said Lou being handed a key by the receptionist who had swiped his card and got his signature with the practised efficiency of a nurse administering an injection so quickly that it's not noticed. 'It's hot here. Let's get a drink.'

Lee was under strict instructions to stay off the sauce. The club dietician was nagging him that it was the booze that was causing him to blimp out. Lee decided he'd just have the one.

'Follow me,' Lee said to Lou. They walked into a cavernous room hung with classical paintings. The room was a pale-blue colour with gilt cornicing. A waiter smiled from behind a large, dark wooden bar. Glass bottles were stacked high behind him, a mirror on the wall doubling their numbers.

'Ah, Signor Sweeney,' he smiled. 'Back again. Youa enjoya yourself last night, yes?'

Lee nodded at him and smiled.

Lou got his wallet out. 'What you having, Lee?' he asked.

'Peroni please, Pluto,' Lee said to the barman. It was their joke. His real name was Paulo, but Lee knew he was only too happy to have the piss taken out of him by a Napoli player.

Lou ordered an Irish whiskey and splashed some water in it. Lee ignored the cold glass Paulo had left on a coaster on the wooden counter and pulled deep on the bottle. He placed the empty back on the bar and gestured for another while Lou started on one of the stories that used to make Lee ache with homesickness. It never really went away, but hearing Lou's stories about dullard chairmen, dumb managers and unscrupulous agents all weaving themselves into a scenario of bungs, backhanders and bonuses it made him feel like an exile receiving a dispatch from a distant homeland to which he could never return.

The way Lou talked about what was going on at home you'd think that he had led a blameless life of lily-white trade. Truth was Lou was sunk to the bollocks in it. He was as likely, as anyone else in the business, to meet a manager at a service station carrying a holdall full of used tenners. He was just more likely to pretend that he was above it. The two men sat drinking and watching the sun sink into the Mediterranean. Later in the evening – when it felt like the pink glow had transferred from the horizon to their slack bodies – Lou put his wine glass down.

'Look,' he said. 'We've got to talk some business. I'm going to do this the most direct way I can think of: Giancarlo doesn't want you back.'

Lee put down the shrimp he was working on. He was still smiling from something Lou had said a moment before. 'Say that again, Lou,' he said, his face straightening.

'I had a conversation with him about a week ago and he wants to sell you,' said Lou. He was looking away and holding his palms up.

'Since when?' said Lee, his voice quiet.

'Since a week ago.'

Lee looked at Lou wondering if this was a wind-up. No. Lou never joked about two things. One, his family and two, business. Neither was of any amusement to him. Lee picked up his half-full bottle of Peroni and necked it.

'Can he do that?'

'Yes.'

'Jesus.'

'I know it must be difficult to take this in, Lee.'

'So what are we going to do?'

'We're going to make hay while the sun shines,' said Lou flatly. 'We're going to orchestrate the biggest fucking bidding war the Premiership has ever known for a player.'

'But won't they know the Eyeties are letting me go?'

'Not unless you tell them,' smiled Lou working on his spaghetti. 'It was part of the agreement I got with Giancarlo. They'll go through the motions of wanting to keep you. They've already got someone lined up, some Croatian, ready to take your place.'

'Jesus,' Lee said. 'This is all a bit fucking sudden. They don't hang about.'

'Just as well,' said Lou. 'Faster the better, that way everybody's happy. You play until the end of the season, keep your gob shut and act like you don't know what's going on, then you slip away after the last home game. I'll go and whisper in a few ears, say you're ready to come home, and see who bites. No one's the wiser. Oh, and another thing. We'll be retaining the rights to your name. Whoever buys you, every fucking replica shirt they sell, we get a cut.'

He winked and raised his glass as if to acknowledge his own talent. Lee shook his head, grinning at the bare-faced cheek.

'There is some bad news, and it's part of the reason Giancarlo wants to get rid of you.'

Lee sat straight, waiting rigidly.

'Apparently,' said Lou dramatically, 'the *News of the World* have signed up some bird who says she's been having an affair with you. They've got pictures, the lot. They're splashing with it Sunday. I gave the editor, that fat cunt whatisname, a bell to see if there's anything we can work out but he won't play ball. Boys at the currant bun can't do anything for me either. So I figure we've just got to ride it. What do you reckon Michelle's going to do?'

'Her nut,' Lee said. His appetite had gone.

'Deny everything, Lee,' said Lou firmly. 'Tell her it's all bollocks, a total fabrication. Tell her I've slapped a writ on them and that we're going to take it all the way. Then we'll string her along, say we've settled out of court and you buy her a present, a car or something – maybe she'd like one of them new Mercedes SLKs? I'll back you up and the whole thing should disappear soon enough.'

'Between you and me, it's true, Lou,' said Lee massaging his temples. 'I've known her for a few months.' He motioned the waiter for another beer. 'Couldn't help myself. She's a top sort, speaks really good English, met her when that new Swish! store opened in Milan. She was hired by them to give out baseball caps.' He paused, let out a sigh. 'I get lonely out here you know. I miss my wife.'

'Lee, that's your business,' said Lou waving his hands. 'I'm disappointed that you were indiscreet enough to get caught, that was very stupid, but what you get up to is up to you. What am I going to do? In a way it's good timing. Your name will be everywhere and I've already spoken to the *Sun.* They're running a "Man United swoop for Sweeney" story on Monday. Should jolly the fucking London clubs up a bit. Get them on their toes. They'll be shitting themselves that Ferguson's been out here making himself busy, that it's a done deal.'

Lee didn't say anything. He was thinking about Michelle, about how she was going to feel on Sunday.

'I think I should call Michelle,' he said. 'Prepare her.'

'I'm not going to tell you how to live your life,' said Lou. 'But if I were you I'd do the same thing. Why don't you fly her out here? Get her away from it.'

'Because she wouldn't come. The shop, you know.'

'How can a girl who was brought up in fucking Walthamstow not want to live like this?' said Lou gesturing at the bay. 'She must be fucking mad.'

'Well, she gets bored,' said Lee with the overemphasis of the guilty. 'You know Michelle. She loves her life at home. She likes the shop. She likes to keep herself busy. If she needs a break she goes to Florida.'

'All right,' said Lou. 'Napoli might not want you back, but you've got to play the rest of the season as well as you can. The spotlight will be on you. It would be good to stick it up the Eyeties. Last game's against Inter in a month or so, right? We'll have you out of here that same afternoon. Soon as I get back I'll give the London clubs a jolly-up and see what I can do to help the Michelle situation. By the end of the season you'll be home and dry with a nice signing-on bonus busting your back pocket.'

Lee looked at Lou and wondered what the real story was. Lou had presented him with a *fait accompli*: an opportunity to take the piss, a carnival of cash, a chance to get away with it again. Lee doubted that it was that simple. It rarely was. Napoli had begun to tire of his behaviour. The antics of 'il monstro', as Lee had been nicknamed by *Gazzetta dello Sport* after defecating in the back of a Milanese taxi following what one newspaper described as a 'marathon drinking session with pals' had begun to embarrass them. There had been reports for some time that Napoli would consider reasonable offers and Lou, mindful that Lee probably only had one more major move left in his career, one more chance to mop up the gravy, would not have had to struggle hard with his conscience to put wheels in motion without his client's consent. Lee would never know. Still, what did he care? He was going home.

'The homecoming,' Lee said raising his bottle.

'The homecoming,' said Lou tapping the green glass.

As Lee walked back to his room he looked out across the bay. The moon was full. The sea shimmered like it was daytime. Life wasn't so bad he told himself. Especially as he had a baggie of grass up in his room.

Lou would do the deal and Lee would play a handful of games before the end of the season, before he said goodbye to *la dolce vita*. He sat down in a wicker chair on the balcony and closed his eyes. The blackness in front of him started to swim. He reopened his eyes. Jesus. Out of his head again. He was glad he hadn't ordered anything too expensive to drink, looked like he was only going to yodel it down the bog later.

Lee was worn down and torn up by everything seeming to roll into one. There didn't appear to be any breaks in his life any longer, no punctuation to give structure and meaning to a constant stream of happenings. He thought about calling Michelle, but he didn't pick up the phone. If he was heading for the cliff edge there didn't seem to be any point in giving himself extra velocity.

A few days later the *News of the World* hit the streets. Lee remembered it to this day. He just couldn't believe it: Liz Hurley falls out of her swimsuit and a jumbo jet falls out of the sky, both on the same Saturday. No Sweeney story. They never ran it. Thank you, God.

Thank you, Lou.

Chapter Six

After the business with the car and missing training Lee kept his head down for a bit, made sure the gaffer didn't have the opportunity to find fault. He'd stayed in, ordered pizza, had a few beers, watched TV, even *Match of the Day*. That prick Lawrenson wanking on about Liverpool this and Man United that. Couldn't see past the end of his huge, bulbous hooter. Great player though. Lying in the dark with the blue light washing over him Lee had a better idea, an idea that would land them bumper viewing figures: bird presenters. Tasty ones. Then it wouldn't matter if they were showing some Winkmans Orthopaedic Shoes Challenge Trophy game from Scarborough on a wet Tuesday night, they'd still pull in the punters. That's what they did in Italy. Some of the birds they got there were blinding.

Anyway, for a week or so Lee had really put the effort in. One reputation you can't get as a footballer is as a no-show merchant and Lee's relationship with Brandwood didn't need any more tension than there already was.

One of the lads had once said to Lee that the gaffer looked like a hot-dog stand manager who'd had his pitches queered. There was a hangdog look to him, as if gravity were a stronger force when it encountered his body, that signalled a man who thought that the world was out to get him. In the winter he always wore an anorak, strode around with his hands in his pockets looking as glum as a pack of basset-hounds. It was strange for Lee after being in Italy – the coaches there preferred a spot of Cerruti, made an effort with the old whistle, were partial to a camel coat. Lee returned to London and saw the coaching staff doggedly sporting their sponsored shell suits and anoraks – the flashes and splashes of colour looking like they're the results of a kindergarten finger-painting competition – and he wondered what on earth they were doing with their money. Talk about no standards.

After a week Lee's effort to turn over a new leaf culminated in arriving at training not just on the right day, but early. He pulled up in the car park and could see from the embarrassing collection of wheels – two Mondeos, a Nova and, tragically, a Cinquecento – that only the ground staff had arrived. He looked at his watch, no one would be there for at least a quarter-hour. Maybe, he thought to himself, he should go for a gentle run. Shake off the cobwebs. He opened the car door and planted his right Wannabe on the tarmac. He looked up at the sky (leaden, grim, definitely not pleased to see him) and decided to get back in the motor.

One of the features that had attracted Lee to the Range Rover Vogue was its plush leather interior and the fact that the seats reclined to almost vertical. Allied to the state-of-the-art CD system it was a shagger's paradise. Lee still felt a little tired on account of his getting up so early and having a little bit too much puff to smoke the night before (it was difficult not to be hypnotised by the colours on Super Mario 64 after a half-ounce of skunk) so he slunk back in the car, turned the heater on and let go with *Urban Hymns*. He liked the music but thought that Richard Ashcroft looked a bit skinny, bit of a druggie, maybe. Either that or he liked a glass of Slim-Fast.

Lee crossed his arms over his chest and started to relax, began to drift a little. He started thinking about this thing that he'd heard on the Chris Tarrant show that morning: you only need £5.53 to be a millionaire in Turkey. That was the state of their economy. All you need is a Lady Godiva and a bit of shrapnel and you're wedged up. Imagine that. It was going round and round in his head along with this chorus on the CD and Lee was thinking to himself, I wonder what that makes me? He pondered, if he went there, whether he might be the richest man in Turkey.

He didn't fancy it though. He'd seen that *Midnight Express*. Put him off for life. He remembered once being taken to this Turkish restaurant and this geezer banging on about how these two clubs in Istanbul hated each other so much that it made Glasgow Rangers and Celtic look like a fucking love affair . . . His mind was drifting, his brain started making associations . . . Everything began to shut down. Lee fell deep into himself, listening only to his own slow, restful breathing . . .

BOSH!

He leapt up like he'd been scalded, hitting the horn on the steering wheel, which gave him another shock. He'd had a vision of a grotesque face, hair tumbling from every orifice, thick eyebrows running wild like a neglected hedgerow. Heavy, quivering jowls, cruel piggy eyes and unloved hair, so coarse and steely that you could scrub your kitchen sink with it.

'Lee! Lee!' the voice shouted. 'What the fuck are you playing at?' Lee scrabbled for a hold on reality, realising after a beat that it was the gaffer; the setting of Brandwood's jaw communicated to Lee that he was livid. You could always tell when the gaffer was angry because he thrust his jaw forward, making his lips shrink to nothing and his face elongate to moose-like proportions. He was an ugly fucker. Lee stumbled out of the car into a puddle, splashing Brandwood's nasty nylon tracksuit bottoms.

'Where the fuck have you been?' he shouted, waving his hands around like a TV chef. He leant towards Lee who looked over to the training pitches and saw that the other lads were warming up.

'You're fucking late,' shouted the gaffer. 'Again, Lee. Again.'

'I wasn't late, boss,' he pleaded. 'I've been here for a

while.' Lee checked his watch. He'd been asleep for half an hour. Fuck. Shit. Piss.

'You've got to get a fucking grip,' said the gaffer. 'Time seems to be a concept you're finding hard to grasp. Can you read that fucking watch of yours or did you just buy it because it looked flash?'

Lee looked down at his Rolex Daytona. 'I didn't buy it boss. It was given me by . . .'

'You're missing the fucking point here Lee. Let's try again. What time does training start?'

'Nine thirty.'

'What time is it now?'

'Twenty to ten.'

'So how late are you?'

'Ten minutes.'

'Right, Lee. So what's going to happen is that when everyone else goes home you're going to stay for an extra ten minutes and I'm going to work with you on your own to make up for the bit you've sliced off the beginning. Understand?'

Brandwood fancied himself as a bit of a George Graham figure, but he was too ugly for that. There wasn't a smooth bone in his hill-billy body. He encouraged players to call him 'boss', but people rarely did.

'Sort of private tuition.'

'You're a fucking accident waiting to happen, aren't you, son? Eh? I mean how much do you earn a year? Million? Two? I bet you don't even know. And look at you. A fucking shambles. Can't even take the responsibility to turn up on time. You finished your potty training yet? Or do we need to run through that again?'

'Boss' – nice touch, thought Lee – 'I was here early and I fell asleep . . .'

'The sad thing, Lee, is that I know you're telling me the truth. At least if you said that you had been stuck in traffic or overslept then I could have given you a quick bollocking and that would be the end of it. But what really vexes me is that I know you were here early. I saw your car. Stupidly I assumed that you had gone for a run. But no. The cruel and, I'm beginning to think, inevitable truth is that you managed to park and then fall asleep in your car like some shagged out sales rep.

'What's that supposed to make me feel, Lee? Anger? *Anger*? I'd like to be able to feel angry with you. I would with any of the other lads cos I know they can do better. But you, Lee. No, I don't feel angry with you because I don't really know if you can do any better. I think that this might be it with you; the summit of your capabilities. No, Lee, I don't feel anything for you other than pity and, to be honest, I don't know if you deserve even that.'

Brandwood was beginning to look pretty downcast. Like he'd just realised he'd been sold a pup. Lee thought he'd try and make him look on the bright side. 'Well, at least I'm here now.'

Brandwood turned his back on him. Lee hated it when people did that. No fucker did that to him. Brandwood started walking off before turning and pointing at Lee. Bang out of order.

'We will have a chat after training. Now go and get fucking changed and hurry up.'

On the way to the dressing-room Lee tried to call Lou on his mobile, but all he got was the voice-mail. He wished he'd been able to get through. He was sure Lou would have a thing or two to say to the gaffer. Lou was his friend, his protector. He wouldn't let anyone get away with talking to one of his clients like that. Let alone me, he thought. I mean, doesn't Brandwood know who I fucking am?

Lee had a problem with training – he didn't mind the stretching, sweating or five-a-sides but as soon as the cones came out, he was ordered to find a partner, or one of the coaches started telling him about some exercise he'd seen in a Hungarian training manual from the fifties, he began to lose interest. It brought back memories of a coach from years back who had had the strange theory that the best way to train was not to allow the players to have the ball, thus making them 'hungry' for it when they actually played a proper game. Lee always thought that the problem with that theory was that half the team wouldn't fucking recognise it when they got on the pitch.

The squad went through the usual repertoire of stretching, warming up, scurrying around, shooting practice, dead ball situations and five-a-side. At the end everyone began to trudge back to the dressing-room, Lee included. He was having a chat with Keith Cook who had just come back after a thigh strain kept him out for a few weeks, when the gaffer started yelling, ordering him to come back. Throughout the session – during which Lee had conspicuously worked his knackers off – Lee had come to think that Brandwood wasn't serious about making him stay behind. Thought the whole thing might just have been a wind-up, something said in the heat of the moment.

He was wrong. To the derision of his team-mates he turned and retraced his footsteps towards the waiting Brandwood. The gaffer stood there, hands on hips, his face slightly flushed, a consequence of his still not being quite able to accept that he was not a player any more, but still wanted to take part. Lee had seen the footage of him, back in the day, huffing around the pitch, kicking anyone in sight and roaring at his team-mates to get stuck in. He even captained England. Lee remembered watching the games at home when he was a kid, the gaffer with pork-chop sideburns and long curly hair futilely trying to inspire his lion hearts to the 1978 World Cup. No dice.

'Where do you think you're going?' he barked. He didn't allow Lee to answer. Instead he traced his finger around the four sides of the pitch. 'Jog, sprint, jog, sprint,' he said. 'I think you need to lose some weight, you looked half a yard slow today. Now get to it. I want ten minutes' hard work from you.'

After a beat, Lee set off jogging and sprinting. All the

way round he couldn't work out whether Brandwood was making him do it just because he wanted to piss him off, or whether Brandwood actually thought he was overweight. (Lee's shape was as variable as the weather. At times his body was like some kind of advanced animation special effect. In moments he could morph from lithe to plump.) Anyway, no sense in losing sleep over it. Lee was probably making more money a month than the gaffer did in a season. Maybe in his career.

What was strange for Lee was that Brandwood stood in the middle of the pitch watching him. Arms folded, he planted himself in the centre circle, his beadies trained on Lee like some twitchy prison guard making sure his Category As don't pull a runner on him. Eventually Brandwood blew a whistle. Lee thought he'd show willing and jogged back to the gaffer.

'All right, boss?' he asked.

'In my office. Fifteen minutes,' and he marched off into the distance.

Showered and changed Lee knocked on the door. The first few minutes after training, once he was buffed and deodorised and freshly glowing, was often his favourite part of the day. It was after the pain (getting up, training) and before the pleasure of later in the day. If he was honest it was the only part of the day when he didn't feel like some kind of chemical dustbin.

Brandwood gruffly told Lee to come in. On opening the door Lee offered his boss a conciliatory grin, which he thought might speed along the 'you've got to get your act sorted out' pep talk. He offered Lee a chair with a nod.

'Lee, you are making a habit of serious breaches of discipline,' he started. 'I wanted to get you in here to give you a bollocking about being late but I don't know if there's any point. I can scream at you 'til I'm blue in the face, but it's you that's got to change. I need you to take responsibility. I need to be able to trust you.' The gaffer lifted a cup of tea to his lips. Throughout the movement he never took his eyes from Lee. 'So where shall we start, Lee? Why don't you get the ball rolling.'

Lee was pissed off and didn't mind showing it. For fuck's sake: hadn't he been trying of late? But his better instincts took over. He thought he should try and show willing.

'Well, to be honest, boss, I've not been feeling too great recently. Maybe I'm overtired, or I've got a virus. Like I said, last week I woke up and must have fallen back asleep, cos I just remember waking up at lunchtime and looking at the clock.'

'What can I say, Lee?' said the gaffer. 'A piss-poor attempt at explaining yourself. You know you're so complacent at the moment you can't even be bothered making up a creative fucking excuse. I wouldn't be surprised if you'd told me then that the dog had been sick on your homework. Turning up on time for a week hardly merits a fucking testimonial.'

His tone changed as his anger built. 'For fuck's sake, Lee, give me some credit. I do read the papers, you know. I ain't a total fucking idiot. I mean, there's hardly a lot of consistency in you not feeling very well after spending the night at Blue's club – where I'm sure not a drop of alcohol touched your lips – and getting involved in some motoring run-in at four in the morning. Is there?'

Lee swallowed and nodded as Brandwood stared him down. He had a point.

'Now I know you've got a lot on your mind at the moment. I'm well aware of your personal situation. I'm going to do something I've never done before – I'm banning you from the club for a week. No training, no matches, should give you a chance to get yourself sorted out, clear your head. I want you to keep a fitness programme going on your own. You are still contracted to this club and I expect to see you here next Monday, fit and well and raring to go. And if you put an ounce on I'll turn your scrotum into a tobacco pouch.'

Lee nodded solemnly.

'Got anything to say, Lee?' he asked.

'I won't let you down, boss.'

And, at that moment, he meant it.

Chapter Seven

For Lee, the knowledge that the gaffer was none too pleased with his current performances and attitude was tempered by the excitement of a week away from the grind. On the surface Brandwood was as hard as nails, gave no quarter, but underneath he was smart enough to know that he would only get the best from Lee when his star signing had unravelled some of the more knotty issues that clouded his horizon. Brandwood realised that the papers would see it differently, frothing about bust-ups, ultimatums and transfer lists. He thought beyond that. The only game Lee would miss was a crappy Worthington Cup game against some pikey Third Division no-hoper former hod carriers. They would survive without Lee.

Lee knew that Brandwood was extending himself, making himself vulnerable, so he considered reciprocation. In truth, the idea of detoxing, holing up in some fat farm, didn't appeal. It was too stringent, too unforgiving, and inevitably doomed to failure. It dealt with his body. There was nothing in it for his shredded mind. Lee knew himself well enough to realise that the most likely path to success would be pursuing a kinder, more gentle regime during which he could gently wean himself from those things responsible for his slide.

That night he accompanied Jug Ears to his local for a few swift ones. Just a few, mind. It was a small, dark, cramped place with horse brasses on the wall and wood smoke in the air that stung the eyes. It was the last place on earth Lee would have chosen to go for a drink if it wasn't for the fact that he couldn't afford to be seen out and about. That had been one of Brandwood's stipulations. Still, every cloud has a silver lining and Lee made the most of the pub's one major advantage: in a gaff like that disappearing to the bog every few minutes would be put down to he and Jug Ears having had a dodgy balti rather than a wrap of gear. The old codgers nursing their halves and the stockbrokers sneaking weak G & Ts were not a suspicious lot.

A few locals cemented to the bar surreptitiously scrutinised them. Lee got a bad feeling and decided it was time to leave when, on the entrance of a particularly attractive female customer, Jug Ears got on one of the tables, started to howl and clutched his balls. Lee ushered him to the door without delay, grinning at the punters with a rigor mortis smile, Lou's words ringing in his head: 'Lee, you're not just letting yourself down, you're letting me, the whole country and your young admirers down.'

Lou had also added that Lee should grasp Brandwood's olive branch with both hands and go and visit Michelle who was energising herself for Christmas shop toil with a few days in Florida. Or, at least, that's what she'd said to Lee. 'Sort things out before it's too late,' Lou said. With eight days of freedom stretching ahead of him like an empty road this was the last thing Lee wanted to do. Usually he liked to have company, someone to have a gas with, but Michelle had been gone so long now, nearly a fortnight, that he'd got used to life on his own. It wasn't like he didn't want her back, it was just that he'd got used to not having her any longer. And somehow it seemed easier that way. He missed her bedroom tricks though. That was where it really hurt. All privileges had been withdrawn in the nooky department.

Those who knew the precarious state of the Sweeney marriage were choral in their unanimity: go see her, they said to Lee. Talk it through. Sort it out. You love her, she loves you – maybe there's some way to heal the rift. For Lee though, the real issue was that the problem had been ongoing for so long now that the rift *was* the marriage. On top of that it was difficult fathoming whether Michelle had club-classed it out to Florida because she was at the end of her tether, or because winter had raised its dismal head. Michelle couldn't stomach the cold.

Getting into the American spirit of things, so to speak, Lee pondered that very question over a half-dozen Jack Daniels and Cokes on the 747 en route to Orlando. Even Lee was embarrassed by the profligacy of travelling first class, making it a strict rule to apply himself to the miniatures in order to get his money's worth.

Lee enjoyed the company on the way over, even if it was an American geezer seated next to him. Property developer, he said. Lee offered a few opinions about property and investment (mostly stuff remembered from Lou, things he was doing with Lee's money, making it multiply). They had a good old yap. Lee came back from exercising the lizard to find that his companion had suddenly gone quiet. Strange. He gave him a nudge and the man slumped on to his side. Geezer has had a few too many, thought Lee. Typical Yank, talks the talk but can't take his booze.

He watched a bit of a movie and before he knew it they were circling over Orlando. Lee looked out the window taking in the dizzying flatness of Florida. He gave the Yank a nudge. Didn't want him to miss it. The man collapsed into the aisle.

A steward came running over, but was too slight to lift the stranded passenger, who must have weighed in the late teens. Lee unstrapped himself and lifted the geezer back into his seat and buckled him in. Fucking piss artist, thought Lee. If you can't handle it . . .

To his surprise Lee noticed that the steward was checking the geezer's pulse. After he'd finished he had a whispered conversation with a stewardess. The penny dropped: the bloke had croaked. Must have checked out somewhere over Greenland, thought Lee. The airline staff were quietly panicking about what to do, not wanting to upset their premium passengers. After all, none of them had paid ludicrous prices to have a corpse lounging next to them.

The stewardess smiled an I-know-you-know-what's-going-on-and-I'd-really-appreciate-your-keeping-your-mouth-shut smile. She snapped a pair of eye-shades over the man's eyes, pulled his safety belt extra tight and tilted the seat back as far as it would go. Lee supposed that they'd just sneak the body off after everyone else had 'deplaned'. Poor bloke. He'd told Lee he'd had a wife. Two kids. Lee was shocked. They'd had a good old blab. He had no idea who Lee was. Now he never would.

There was something about getting off a plane with a good half bottle of Jack Daniels inside him that always made Lee head straight for the car-hire pound. He was whisked through every available channel at the airport by servile ground staff whose job it was to ensure that he was not inconvenienced in any fashion. He loved it that airlines did that. That they give those who were richer, striving, already ahead of the pack, *extra help* just to stay in front of the howling steerage hordes. It made his day.

The bird at the Hertz desk eventually sorted Lee with a nice Beamer convertible (she'd tried to palm him off with red. He'd told her, in no uncertain terms, that he wasn't having any of that, and he ended up with something pukka, something silver). 'You're all set, Mr Sweeney. Have a nice day.' They all said that. It didn't matter whether they were black, white, Hispanic or Asian. They all said that and every time Lee wanted to marry them for it.

Another good thing about America, as far as Lee was concerned, was that they sold booze at petrol stations. Imagine that. Mainly beer, but Lee wasn't complaining. He was gasping after his flight, so the first opportunity he got he pulled into a Texaco and snagged a six-pack. Then he remembered that there were never any firelighters for the barbecue at the villa so he asked the geezer if he had any. He didn't answer Lee. Just asked if he was English. Lee said yes and asked if there was a problem. He got that a bit out there. A few people had an anti-English thing going because of Ireland. But he never put up with any of that shit. Thought they were all fucking Jack Charlton just because their great-great-grandfather came over from County Kildare when he was seven.

The clerk was from Pakistan. He'd heard Lee's accent and had fancied a chat about cricket. Now Lee knew fuck all about cricket; used to see all the cricket boys at dos, functions and that, but didn't really mix. Truth be told most of them were quite useful footballers. Didn't always work the other way though.

Anyway, Lee stopped to have a natter with this bloke and he was over the moon to be talking to someone who'd at least heard of Wasim Akram. Lee cracked a beer and the two of them got talking. He worked his way through a couple of cans and they eventually came to the conclusion that American sports were crap, which wasn't exactly news to anyone, but seemed like a good place for the conversation to finish.

Lee turned to see another customer, a young, attractive black woman approaching the counter to pay for her fuel. Feeling more friendly than he should be, Lee gave her a conspiratorial wink.

'Smile if you got it last night, darling,' he said. The next few seconds were a bit of a blur – the woman realising the gist of what he was saying and, being a public prosecutor, gathering her thoughts in order to summon the articulacy of her profession to heap derision on this cracker from the old country – Lee figured it was best to do a bunk as soon as he heard the words sexual harassment. He turned to see the clerk waving at him. He didn't want to get involved. Got back in the motor. He pulled on to the highway and headed for the villa. The sun was beginning to go down to his right, the roof was off the car (intentionally) and he was feeling good about seeing Michelle, when he heard a siren behind him. He put his foot down to pass another car and pull into the slow lane to let the cops go by, but they didn't pass, they pulled up right behind him.

'Pull over,' came a voice from a sci-fi movie. It was like the voice of the alien leader in a fifties B-flick. 'Pull over, driver, in the silver BMW.' Silver BMW. That was Lee. Fuck.

He'd heard all the stories about people getting shot by the cops because they made the wrong move, so he pulled the car to the side of the road and stuck his hands in the air. The voice came again.

'Driver, step away from the car. Keep your hands where they're visible.' He looked in the rear-view mirror. Two cops. Both white. Both weighing the same as two London coppers after a pub lunch. Both of them wore mirror shades like they'd seen too many movies about bad-ass cops on a mission to clean up the streets. Both had moustaches with traces of mullet creeping over their shirt collars. Both were bulked up and steroid-crazed, used to dealing with crack-heads and pistol-packing teens. Lee decided not to take any chances. He stood up on the driver's seat reaching his hands for the heavens. He shouted so there was no question of his not being heard.

'Don't shoot,' he declared, 'I'm famous.'

They checked his licence and ran through the obligatory particulars before asking the really significant question.

'Have you been drinking, sir?' said the blond one with the moustache and the shades and the muscles and the aggressive attitude. (Even if Lee hadn't been drinking their attitude was enough to make him appear to have been drinking.)

'Just got off a plane from London,' Lee said. 'The man in the seat next to me died. I might have had a drink just to steady my nerves, earlier on.'

'Then why are there four empty tins of beer in your car, sir?'

'Well, I got those from the petrol station, sorry, gas

station. Easy mistake to make even when you're not pissed.'
Lee grinned at one cop. He wasn't having it. The other cop
was checking the car over.

'Sir, we've had a report that this beer is stolen. As far as
we're concerned, Mr Sweeney, we're not only gonna bust
you for driving under the influence, you're going to be
charged with taking this liquor from the gas station back up
the highway.'

Up to the point they snapped the cuffs on Lee thought
that he might walk. Englishman abroad and all that. He
told them that he owned property in Florida, that he'd
invested in their beautiful state, but they didn't really seem
interested in all that. They pressed his head down when
they put him in the back of the car, just like he'd seen them
do in the movies and, because Lee was cuffed, one of them
had to transfer all his bags out of the boot of the Beamer
into the police car. Lee made sure that he remembered the
duty-frees. As they cruised along the highway Lee started to
breathe as heavily as he could, tried to up his metabolism,
tried to process the alcohol faster. If only he'd had some
Polos.

For Lee, that was the low point. Matters improved enor-
mously once aboard the US judicial system. Indeed,
everything he'd thought about American service was
demonstrated to be correct: he was processed by the police
and courts so fast that he was home in time for dinner, albeit
in a taxi. Imagine the fucking palaver back home. They
hadn't yet decided to ban him from driving, his lawyer –
young, stressed, Cuban with a painted tie from the Warner
Bros store – tried to wangle something by copping a dead-
passenger plea. Thought he might even get Lee off. Talked
to Lee about bringing an action against British Airways on
grounds of distress. Lee had tuned out at that point.

Lee clambered out the cab and the driver – Ukrainian,
got very excited about talking about football, kept on going
on about André Kanchelskis – screeched away from the
kerb, upsetting the serenity of Sherman Lakes. He stood at

the gates of his house. The sprinklers worked busily on the hushed lawn.

Lee loved the gates. Loved the simple fact that they existed. He loved that the gates had got guards and cameras and security buzzers and movement-sensitive lights and alarms. He loved that shit. There just wasn't enough of that kind of gear in England, although it was getting better. The gates helped Lee sleep at night, made him feel like the voices of doom inside his head might just be wrong. (He craved that they were wrong.) Some people couldn't understand the fascination. Lee could. He looked through the gates at his three acres of citrus groves and landscaped lawns and he just knew that when they invented electricity this was precisely the kind of scenario they might have imagined.

So he hit the buzzer for the villa. Felt the flow of energy beneath his finger, and waited. The shadows were beginning to get longer across the lawns, the sun still warmed his back, but didn't have the afternoon's intensity.

No one answered. He considered bunking over the gates. Thought better of it. Didn't know how quick those armed response guards might be. Just then he saw Raoul, the gardener, sloping across the lawn. This was his trademark: he was the anti-Lee, leaden of foot, never hurrying or changing his pace.

'Oi, oi, saveloy!' Lee shouted at him. Raoul looked over. His eyes were poor, but he knew who it was. There weren't many people with a voice like Lee's in Sherman Lakes. He ambled over. Same pace, took his time. Strange geezer. Cuban. Never came in the house. Took care of the garden and pool and disappeared at sundown. There was a dejection about him that Lee, despite his efforts, never managed to break through. Brenda liked to call him 'the pool boy' in front of people – something she picked up off some Yank soap opera – but Lee didn't like that. Geezer was in his sixties. You've got to have some respect.

'Señor Sweeney.'

'Raoul.'

'We expect you this afternoon.'

'Yeah, yeah, I know. There was a delay.'

'With the plane?'

'No, no, something else.'

Raoul nodded, satisfied.

'Listen, you couldn't open these gates for me, could you?' Lee said. 'Forgot me keys.' Raoul grasped the bars with both hands like some death row inmate feeling the limits of his bondage. He rubbed his hands together.

'Si, señor. No problem. But from the house only.' He stood there for a moment contemplating the gates like he'd never seen them before. Lee realised he was looking at him.

'Chop, chop son,' Lee encouraged him.

'Señor?'

'Look, Raoul, I'm fucking cream-crackered. Do me a favour and get in the house sharpish.'

Lee watched him trail back to the house. He always wore the same jeans – immaculately pressed indigo Levis. He was the last person in the world to wear jeans with creases in them, but boy did he take pride in those creases. A dirty bandanna hung out of his back pocket.

Standing there among his bags of tat and duty-free Lee looked up the road. A barge-sized 4 × 4 idled further down the road, its engine humming like some fire-breathing beast. It was called a Land Crusher or Terrain Buster or something. The windows were blacked out but, as it cruised past, he could tell the occupants of the car were clocking him, wondering about the strange figure standing outside the gates, his shirt-tails flapping in the breeze and his luggage piled around him like the remnants of some shanty town eviction. They were asking themselves the question that everyone in this place asked themselves when they saw a stranger: *Who the hell are you and what gives you the right to be in here?*

His attention was diverted when he heard a door slam and Michelle tottered out on to the bricked driveway. He was excited to see her. She had told him she was pleased that he was coming out – they'd have a nice few days together, she'd said – but he could tell that her anticipation was coloured by a slight nervousness about what kind of state he would arrive in. Still, he was looking good, had slotted into her sunshine queen meets lady of leisure mode quite easily. Lee knew there were a few clichés about footballers' wives and, frankly, Michelle embodied some of them. She was medium height, but always appeared a little bit taller because of her liking for mules ('They make me feel glamorous, like Jackie Collins,' she was once quoted as saying in *Home Woman* magazine when asked about her dress sense) which also always gave her legs the right shape. As it was early evening, and consequently the cocktail hour, she'd put on a pair of lightweight, loose-fitting trousers and a halter-neck top. She walked unsteadily towards Lee. Clearly the cocktail hour had started around lunchtime. This meant trouble.

She approached the gates with a disoriented swagger. Lee sat down on his suitcase, waiting for the worst. She leant against the gates, one of her tits poking through the gap.

'Lee, how lovely to see you,' she slurred. 'So glad you could make it.'

'Michelle.'

'Not that I was expecting you at lunchtime or anything, not that me, mum or Teresa spent all morning making a nice lunch for you or anything, not that in any way I should have expected you to have taken less than six hours to make it from the airport, a journey that usually takes no more than three-quarters of an hour . . .'

'Look, I'm sorry, Chelle, I got pulled over and I had to go and sort a few things out with the police . . . you know how it is.'

'No, Lee, I don't know how it is. I know how it is with you, how you manage to make a fucking dog's dinner of absolutely everything you ever do, but I don't really know how and why you manage to make such a mess of things, but I really wish I knew, I really do . . .' She was going to ramble on for a bit. Maybe even turn on the waterworks – pure vodka, Lee expected.

He butted in, trying to sound reasonable. 'Open the gates, Chelle, I'm knackered. I could really do with a drink . . . I've been in the nick for the last four hours and they don't even give you a fucking glass of water.'

'So, poor Lee wants a bit of sympathy does he? Well, here you go: poor old Lee, poor diddums. There you go. Feel better now?'

Lee put his head in his hands. His hair felt lank and polluted. Airplane hair. It was eleven o'clock at night in London and he was locked outside his own house in Florida with his shirt sticking to his back and a dull headache emerging just south of his hairline.

'Go and sleep it off, Lee. Go and get some shut-eye,' said Michelle. She'd taken a few steps back from the gate but was still holding on to the bars with her hands. 'Call me in the morning. I don't think it would be a good idea if you came in tonight. You know what would happen . . .'

'Yeah, I'd fall asleep within the next five minutes.'

'Sounds par for the course,' said Michelle arching her eyebrows.

'Chelle, stop fucking about,' said Lee. 'You know you'll only miss me. Come on, be a good girl and open up.' He was smiling now as if he knew her inside out, could see what she really wanted. He was trying to be persuasive, attempting the seducer's route.

'I'm not in the mood, Lee,' Michelle said.

'You never are,' Lee replied, bitterly this time. It was totally the wrong note to strike.

'Yeah – with you,' she said.

Silly cow. In his heart Lee had really been trying up to this point. He'd wanted to make a go of it, to smooth things out.

'Fuck it.' He stood up and approached the gates.

Michelle backed away. 'Michelle, don't be silly,' he said.

She started wagging her finger at him. 'You've got to learn your lesson, Lee, you've got to be taught how to behave, so I've decided your punishment – you're not coming in tonight.'

'You what?'

'You heard, Lee. You're not coming in tonight.'

'Areyoushaw? What am I meant to do? Where am I meant to go? You lost your mind?'

Lee rummaged among the duty-free and yanked a twisted Knickerbox bag from the mess. He reached inside and held up a black G-string and bra. She looked at him with pity in her eyes.

'Sometimes, Lee, novelty underwear isn't enough,' she said.

That's when Lee started to get really pissed off. She turned her back on him and started walking back to the house. He watched her bum twitching in those loose-fitting trousers. She was disappearing into a twilight of Ralph Lauren scented candles and seafood platters while Lee stood on the street like a chump, a prize mug kicked out of his own gaff.

This wasn't like Chelle. She and Lee had their differences, had a bit of a scream and a shout, maybe Michelle would chuck a few things at Lee and call him a bastard. And then she would usually forgive him, sometimes things might even get a little frisky later on if they had a couple of drinks. But this . . .

Then he saw her. Standing in the doorway – Brenda, Michelle's mum. Fifty-plus but done up like a twenty-year-old. Plenty of nip and tuck – which Lee had undoubtedly footed the bill for – and a permatan to boot (gratis his sunshine hideaway). Boot was the word, thought Lee. That woman was as tough as yesterday's steak. The outburst wasn't Michelle's style, it had Brenda's imprint all over it. This was down to her.

He grabbed his bags and slung them over the fence.

Michelle and Brenda looked over as they crashed on to the driveway. Lee kept one back. The one with the duty-free in it. He pulled out a bottle of Johnny Walker, unscrewed the cap, toasted the pair of them and headed off into the damp, earthy Florida night with the noise of crickets in his ears and Black Label in his veins.

Chapter Eight

There it was again. The noise.

Stop it.

Just got to stop it. Been going on for ages. Too much. Too much noise.

Jesus. Stop it. Just fucking stop it.

Lee stopped it.

'Lee! Lee! What's wrong with you? I know it's you. What's wrong? Speak up. What's wrong? Lee?!'

Lee pulled his sticky head from the pillow. Jesus. It was Brenda.

'Brenda?'

'Well, don't sound so bloody surprised.'

Lee leant back on the pillow, stuffing the receiver under his chin. There was less tension in his neck that way.

'But, I, how? What time is it?'

'Twelve o'clock, Lee. In the morning.' Lee tried to work out what time it was in England. What time it was in his head. Too difficult. His brain felt like it had been relandscaped.

'But how do you know where I am?'

'For God's sake, Lee.' Brenda's parade-ground bark made him pull back from the receiver. 'You called last night. Howling like a fucking banshee. Said you were going to kill yourself. It was keeping us up, so we turned the bloody answer machine off. We weren't in the mood, Lee. We'd had a long day. Anyway, you left an address. Hotel Flamingo. Said that's where we could find the body. Room thirty-six.'

'Well, the body's here.'

'I don't know who'd be interested in it, frankly, Lee, bar a few dog food companies.' This was Brenda's idea of a joke.

'That ain't very nice, Brenda.'

'Well, you should know by now that I'm not a very nice person.' Lee heard her exhale cigarette smoke into the receiver.

'You really blew it last night, Lee, you know that, don't you?'

'Well, I . . .'

'Well, you did,' she insisted, cutting through him. 'And if you ain't clever enough to work that out I pity you. Now you listen to me and you listen good, you've been pissing my Michelle around for long enough now and I'm tired of it.'

'Fuck's sake, Brenda. You know, it works both ways.'

'No, Lee. I tell you how it works. You turn up sober for once and we all get on. You turn up pissed and Michelle and me don't want nothing to do with you. It's pretty obvious. Work it out for yourself.'

'Chelle had had a few as well, Brenda, it weren't just me.'

'Look, Michelle doesn't know that I've called you, but I wanted to try and do what I can to make things work . . .'

'Well, that would be the first fucking time . . .'

'Enough of that, Lee. You and I are stuck with each other. Neither of us like it, but that's just the way it is.' Her voice broke off for a moment; she was stubbing her fag while expelling the last of the smoke from her lungs. 'You ain't putting in any effort, Lee. There's no willingness on your part. It's like you play football. Too bloody casual. I mean, what's Chelle supposed to think, for Christ's sake? You ain't seen the poor girl for two weeks.'

'Well, it's quite a lot of aggro for me to commute between London and Florida, Brenda. I know it's a difficult concept for you to grasp, but the money's got to come from somewhere. I am a professional footballer.'

'Professional piss artist more like it,' barked Brenda.

'Now I'm getting bored of talking to you, so I'm going to let you know what I phoned to say. Chelle is coming to get you. She left a few minutes ago, after her nails dried. So she won't be long. My advice to you, Lee, is to pull yourself together. Get in the shower, shave – have some breakfast if you're able to hold any food down – and get yourself together. You've probably got twenty minutes, depending on the traffic. Don't let everyone down, Lee.' And with that the line went dead.

Lee dropped the receiver and buried his head beneath the pillow. The bed linen felt rough, like it had been washed many times. He didn't want to open his eyes. There was still too much light. Jesus. Michelle was coming. He had to get his shit together. The pressure was on. Underneath the pillow he could make out the monotone drone of a dead phone line. But there was another noise as well. Music. Annoying, jangly guitar music. He pulled the pillow from his head and peeled back his eyelids.

Holy mother.

'Hi,' said the girl.

'Hi,' Lee replied. She sat on top of the acrylic bedspread wearing just a T-shirt, her long skinny legs crossed, milky against the chocolate brown of the textile.

'What we watching?' he asked for want of anything to say.

'MTV. These are the Eels. They're cool.' Fuck, thought Lee. She's watching MTV. I'm probably committing a crime just lying on this bed with her.

'You want a donut?' she asked holding up a waxed paper bag. 'I went over the 7–11 to pick up some stuff.' She spoke with the uplift of all American teens. Everything was a fucking question. Lee didn't need another question. All he had in his life were fucking questions. He had a question glut, an EC fucking question mountain.

'No, no, you're all right, love.' He was starting to feel nauseous. Michelle was on her way. 'Thanks anyway.'

'Sure,' the girl said in an offhand way. She pushed her

long red hair back from her face with the heel of her hand before starting to suck her fingers, hoovering up stray icing sugar. She had freckles everywhere – on her legs, her face, her arms – that made her seem younger than she probably was. Lee looked again. She had a frighteningly youthful appearance. An illegally youthful appearance.

'And we, er. . . .' he pulled a face.

'Sure,' said the girl.

'Oh my God,' he said hauling the pillow back over his face.

'Don't feel bad,' said the girl. 'I'm Lori. You want some coffee?'

'Like nothing else on earth.'

She passed over a tepid waxed cup.

'It's gone cold,' she said. 'Which is pretty cool. You can't taste cold coffee and that coffee was gross.'

'Thanks,' Lee said sipping the sludge. The milk had separated, leaving curling white trails on the surface.

'Don't feel bad,' she said, 'I picked you up. You were pretty wasted last night. I'd had a row with Slash and . . .'

'Slash?'

'My boyfriend, I wanted to get back at him.'

'What was the row about?'

'Oh, I'm like really getting sick of him dealing. He's, like, *totally* messed up.'

Great. Lee was in bed with what he assumed to be a teenager whose boyfriend was a drug dealer named Slash. Maybe he should just kill himself now to save Slash the trouble.

'And, Slash, does he live locally?'

'He lives in this motel.' Lori cracked up laughing when she told Lee this. 'Isn't that just, like, the *best*.'

'No, no, not really,' Lee smiled, but she was oblivious to his worry.

'You talk kind of funny,' she said. 'Did you say you were from Australia?'

'Probably,' he replied non-committally. The less she

knew the better. The less she knew the less there was for Slash to hunt him down.

'You were acting kind of strange as well.'

'How do you mean?'

'Oh, every time I went into the bathroom I'd come out and you'd be wailing something into the phone. It was real spooky. It kinda freaked me out.'

'Well, sorry,' Lee apologised. He slid out of the bed and looked for his watch. He looked over at Lori. On her left arm, precisely halfway between her elbow and her wrist, rested a Rolex Daytona with a stainless-steel strap.

'What time is it, Lori?' he asked innocently. She pulled the watch down her arm so that the strap hung loose.

'Twelve o'clock.'

She didn't get it. 'You know that watch of yours is just the same as mine,' he said testily.

'I know,' she answered. 'That's because it was yours, stupid.'

'Was mine?'

'Uh-huh.'

'Since when?'

'Duh! Since last night. Since you said you were going to give it to me because you were going to kill yourself and time had no relevance to you any longer.'

This was bad news. Lee put his head in his hands and kneaded his temples. The watch was gone. History. He just had to try and salvage what he could. Fifteen minutes. Michelle. Lori. Slash. Did he need a shower? 'Course he did. A transatlantic flight, a police holding cell and an adulterous binge tend to have that affect. He headed into the bathroom and jumped under a hot gust of water. He could feel it peeling back the sticky layer of filth that had accumulated upon him like a second skin.

He stepped out of the tub and looked for a towel. Lori, sweetheart that she was, had left each and every one of the standard allocation of four towels piled damp on the bathroom floor. He improvised and grabbed the only dry piece of cloth in the room – a washed-out flannel that had been laundered so many times that it felt like a loofah – and rubbed himself down. He clambered back into his septic plane-air-addled clothes and grabbed his wallet and all the necessaries. Lori sat there on the bed. He noticed a small seahorse tattooed on her ankle. She was engrossed in a Garbage video, donut icing sugar dusted the sides of her mouth.

'Well, I hope things work out with Slash,' he said. 'Say hi from me.'

'Don't you want your coffee?' she asked. 'You're leaving, right?'

'I'm fine,' he said.

'It's OK,' she said pointing to the wax cup. 'If you don't like coffee. It's gone cold. You can't taste cold coffee.'

'No, no, I like coffee,' he said. 'I just have to go.' She beckoned him towards her.

'I know that it was real nice of you to give me your watch, so I'm going to make a trade. You can have these.' She handed him a pair of glasses. The frames were shaped like a pair of daisies. Lee put them on.

'How do I look?' he asked.

'Really cool,' she said. Lee couldn't work out whether she was joking or not. Maybe it was ironic irony. She gestured Lee towards her. He sat down on the edge of the bed. She pushed the glasses back on his head and held his face in her hands.

'You know, I haven't been to college yet and I'm just, like, somebody who lives in a motel,' she said. 'But when you get back to Australia or wherever it is that you're going, you've got to promise me one thing – that you'll go see someone who can help you. You're a great guy, I mean, I've only just met you, but I can tell that. I'm a very intuitive person – everyone says that. But here's the deal: unless you do something positive, you're gonna end up in deep trouble.' She kissed him on the forehead. 'Now do me one other thing. On your way out, pay Eddie the bill for last night. He can be a little temperamental with people who don't pay.'

Lee backed out of the room. He was lost in her words, stunned by what she had just said and, to tell the truth, thought that he might just have felt the stirrings of something weighty. Better leave.

'See ya, Lori.'

'Sure.'

Lee went down to see Eddie who was watching QVC with a Marlboro jammed in his burger-padded face. More chins than a Chinese laundry. When he hauled himself out of his E-Z-Boy, Lee realised he was probably only in his early twenties; from the back his sweaty hairline made him look fifty. Lee asked if Lori had any outstanding bills. There was three weeks to pay, plus the value of a smashed TV. Lee settled up there and then. Cash, of course. Didn't want to leave a trail for the tabloid boys.

It was a hazy morning with a slight breeze. The sun would probably break through in a couple of hours. He slung his jacket over his shoulder and breathed deeply. There was a slight whiff of car exhaust, but mostly he could taste Florida air, a strange mix of the swamp and the sea. The dampness was the antithesis of English damp – it was the dampness of renewal, the dampness of life.

He saw Chelle's Lexus coming off the freeway and slipping through the circuitry of the road system before lurching to a halt. Another thing he'd noticed about America. It had quieter roads than England.

Michelle opened the passenger side window. Lee leaned in.

'All right, Chelle?'

'Been better. You?'

'Been better.'

She was wearing a grey sweatshirt, black cotton shorts and Nike trainers. No make-up. Her hair was pulled back from her face. The sun was beginning to take its revenge for her love of it. It was a cruel suitor. Her eyes were concealed behind dark wraparound shades.

'Want a ride then?'

'Where you going?'

'Going home.'

'Sounds good,' he said and slid into the passenger seat. The seat-belt alarm made a God-awful racket until he was settled. Michelle pulled back into the traffic and headed for the freeway.

'You smell terrible,' she said opening her window further.

'I just got out the shower,' Lee replied.

'It's your clothes. Probably your breath as well,' she said. 'Pass me a ciggy, will you? They're in the glove compartment.'

Lee handed her a single cigarette and a lighter with Orlando Magic written on it.

'So what happened to you last night?' she asked.

'Oh, the usual. Got locked out of my house by my wife and her mother . . .'

'Leave mum out of this,' snapped Michelle, her mood shifting.

'Leave her out of what?'

'Don't be clever, Lee. You turned up drunk last night. Then you storm off in a huff. Then, three o'clock in the morning, I'm fast asleep and all I can hear is you wailing into the answer machine like some psycho. It ain't on Lee, it just ain't on.'

They pulled off the freeway and headed into a manicured haven of golf courses, sprinkler systems and unscalable fences.

'Look, I don't want to argue,' he said. 'I've just got this to say. One. I wasn't drunk. Two. I didn't storm off. Three . . .' As they passed a petrol station his attention was distracted. Geezer getting out of a Jeep looked just like Colin.

'Did you see that, Chelle? Geezer looked just like Colin,' Lee said. 'Weird.'

'No, I didn't.'

'Number three ... well, I dunno, I must have been having a nightmare or something.'

'Rat-arsed more like it.'

They travelled in silence for a few minutes. After a while Michelle reached over and squeezed Lee's knee. He put his hand over hers and turned to look at his wife, a smile on his face.

'I still care,' she said. 'Maybe I don't always handle it the best way, but I still care.'

'I know you do,' said Lee. 'You've just got a funny way of showing it sometimes.'

They both laughed.

'We can get over this, can't we?' said Michelle. 'We can ride this out.' Lee felt sad her voice was fragile with uncertainty.

''Course we can love,' he replied more emphatically than he needed to. ''Course we can.' A sense of loss washed over him, a feeling of guilt that he could cause his wife such pain. After all, did he not still love her?

'I feel all right today,' he said trying to sound upbeat.

'Together, are you?'

'Yeah,' said Lee beginning to feel tired.

'Feeling strong and in control.'

'Yeah.'

'Got your head together.'

'That's right.'

'Then why have you got a pair of sunglasses shaped like daisies perched on your head?' asked Michelle.

She had a point.

Chapter Nine

He was never sure but he thought that he got away with the sunglasses. Just said 'Nice, ain't they?' when put on the spot, as if he'd known they were there all along. Said they had been left in a draw in his motel room. He'd meant to hand them in.

They rode in silence until they reached the villa and Michelle zapped the security sensor. Lee felt a flicker of relief when the gates folded inwards. As she drove the Lexus into the garage the sun broke through the clouds for the first time that day.

It appeared to Lee that Michelle had simmered down a bit. He'd meant what he'd said about working things through – it was more than he could stand to see her in pain. Anyway, he reckoned he just had to show willing, take her out for a lobster dinner and a couple of banana daiquiris and they'd be playing hide the salami before you can say trouble and strife.

When he thought about it, usually some time between his second beer and his fifth, Lee knew that he still loved her, but whether he had the energy and will to keep or deserve her was another matter. For Lee, Michelle was just a habit in a long line of other habits that he couldn't shake off. He didn't want a divorce, didn't want to hurt her. The truth of the matter was that he had no idea what he wanted, or even if he had a choice; things seemed just to happen to him and sooner or later Michelle would choose for both of them.

Often Lee thought that maybe he had married the wrong woman; this had nothing to do with Michelle, and everything to do with her mother. Before Lee met Michelle, Brenda was an expert in little more than bulk shopping, hair peroxide and daytime soaps. Lee always said of her that if she had been a swimming pool, she'd have been the shallow end, which wasn't the most graceful analogy, but conveyed his opinion clearly enough. Neither was it entirely fair, but all concept of justice and balance had gone out of the window as far as Lee was concerned when it came to Brenda.

She had had a hard life. She'd got pregnant, married and had Michelle all before her eighteenth birthday. Three years later her husband Paul was killed in a freak catering accident: a gas mains exploded outside the kitchens he was working in causing a tea urn to fall from a shelf and hit him on the head.

This left Brenda in her early twenties living in a semi in Walthamstow with a toddler. Fortunately Paul had had the foresight to take out life assurance, so Brenda received a tidy sum which she used to pay off the mortgage and tucked the rest away for a rainy day.

Fair play to Brenda, she had her head screwed on all right. If you looked at the photos of her and Michelle, mother and daughter are all smiles in every picture. Check out the album: Michelle on a donkey holding an ice cream, Brenda with a supportive arm around her waist; Chelle wearing her first Communion dress; Michelle starting secondary school looking spic and span in a starched uniform; Michelle receiving a poetry prize at school; Brenda and Michelle under a lush Christmas tree, a mountain of presents behind them. After the death of her husband, Brenda had wanted only one thing in life – the best for her daughter. She had wanted to do things right, and when her daughter blossomed into a looker – by general consent Michelle was the top sort in her class – Brenda took an interest in ensuring that any spotty Herbert with heaving hormones was put straight right away – there was to be no hanky-panky, otherwise there would be hell to pay.

Michelle invariably told Lee that she had never felt undermined or as if there had been undue interference in her life. She and Brenda declared that they didn't feel like mother and daughter, but more like best friends. Lee didn't doubt it. If he'd had his head screwed on right he would have realised when he took the plunge with Chelle that he was marrying Brenda as well. Other than their honeymoon (Seychelles) they had never been on holiday on their own. Since Lee had bought the place in Florida he had never been here with just Michelle. Sometimes he arrived and felt like he was walking into someone else's house – Brenda's house. Brenda's mantra was that she only wanted what was best for Chelle, which was fair enough. Coming from such a strong family background Lee didn't have a problem with that. What was more complicated was that he didn't know if Chelle knew what she wanted herself without the old dear getting to her. What really gave Lee the creeps was that they shared clothes. It was bad enough when sisters did it, but mothers and daughters? Well, to Lee, it wasn't normal. It wasn't natural.

So he knew when he got back to the villa that morning that he wasn't just going to be having a chat with Michelle (angry, but loving and reasonable), he would be taking on Brenda (uncompromising, no holds barred); a much less pleasant prospect.

Knowing that he would now have to brave the wrath of both his wife and her mother Lee began to feel a little confined, started itching for a bar. Michelle gave him a look when he got out of the car and, for a moment, he wondered if she might have sensed what was going through his mind. So he tapped the car on the roof and tried to play the family man by waiting for her at the entrance to the garage. She came out swinging her keys (she was always swinging things, something he still found sexy) and suddenly checked her watch (a Gucci 'timepiece'). Catastrophe. She was going to miss her hair appointment unless she left immediately. Lee would have to make his own brunch (Lee liked the way Americans managed to slip a meal in between breakfast and lunch). She dashed back into the garage before gunning the motor back up the drive. Lee wondered if she'd wave to him. She didn't.

He waited until the sound of the car engine disappeared before wandering round the back of the house. It smelt good on the north side of the villa; the sun rarely got there to whip away the scent of the flowers. Lee loved walking round there during the heat of the day, for the cool and the sweetness of the fragrance.

He opened the screen door and went through into the kitchen. The whiteness of the tiles and the units was blinding at that time in the morning, even though Consuela had pulled screens across the windows to calm the screaming sun. Lee was heading for the fridge for a Coke when the phone went.

'Yeah?'

'Lee,' came the voice. The same one. The one he kept hearing every time he picked up a phone. It was a smooth, slippery voice faintly kippered by tobacco. 'Is there something you forgot to do before you left London?'

Jesus. The money.

'I don't believe it,' said Lee, more to himself than the distant voice. 'Shit. I forgot. I'm sorry. Christ. Fuck.'

'Pretty words, Lee,' came the voice. 'But not good ones. For either of us. Now stop trying to expand your vocabulary and talk to me.'

'When I get back,' said Lee. 'I promise. It'll be there. Jesus. I can't believe I forgot.'

'This hasn't happened before, Lee.'

'No. And it won't happen again. Believe me. I'm sorry . . .'

The line went dead.

He'd been teetering on the brink of sickness all morning – the call was all he needed to push him into the realms of fully fledged nausea. The kitchen was too hot. He was being suffocated. He'd been wearing the same clothes for over thirty hours now. He felt like someone had rubbed meat stew all over him.

He pulled a Coke from the fridge and headed back outside. He drank most of the brown liquid in one go, still walking, and threw the empty can into some bushes. Sorry, Raoul. He kept walking, kept walking, kept walking until he dropped from sight into the cool blue of the pool. It was strange the way he entered the water; there was no large crash, just a curious quietness. The pool had swallowed him as if he'd been passing by unaware, like a South American frog grabbing an unsuspecting fly with its tongue.

His clothes became heavy. He didn't fight as their weight began to pull him towards the bottom. He was in a different world and the longer he was there the more he became convinced of his ability to breathe underwater. He stopped moving and lay there on his back looking upwards. He couldn't see beyond the surface, the world had disappeared from view, all he could see was a shimmering silver film gently rolling with the shifting water. It all felt so right. He felt good about the strange new place. He pushed the last of the oxygen out of his lungs to combat any lingering buoyancy. It felt like he might finally get some rest.

Time passed; he didn't know after how long, but eventually he sensed a prodding against his right leg. Clumsy but insistent, the force pummelled his thigh. He reached down and grabbed at it, eventually grasping an aluminium pole which ripped him upwards. He crashed through the silver film gasping for air. Beneath the water he'd not needed oxygen. There was peace down there, no need for bodily function of any kind. In the sunlight his lungs ached with pain trying to pull enough oxygen into his system to keep the blood from going static in his veins. He held on to the side of the pool, trying to fill his hurting body with enough life to sustain it.

He hauled himself halfway out of the pool so that he was

resting on his forearms. As his breathing eased it began to feel different, like his body was turning in on itself, and it began to feel like sobbing, like heavy, desperate hopeless emotion spilling from inside him. Its rhythm felt good, like he'd survived something that had overpowered him. It felt like he was a winner.

He heard the cicadas chirruping away and the sounds and smells of the world returned through the chlorine dimness. Opening his eyes he pulled his gaze up from the terracotta tiles. About a yard away stood a pair of brown feet, nails painted Kellogg's red. Lee looked up at their owner who returned his gaze with a look that was somewhere between shame and compassion. Like he was a mortally injured creature lying in the road that she was going to have to grind into the tarmac.

Brenda. Rescuing him as sure as mermaids breathed life into the lungs of wrecked sailors. He spat into the pool of water collecting beneath his chin to get rid of the taste of chlorine. Brenda padded off to get the skimming net and fished out one of his shoes, which was lying on the floor of the pool.

'Feeling better now?' she asked, as patronisingly as she could. 'Lee, I don't know what you think you were doing lying on the bottom of the pool, but if it was some kind of stupid stunt then you can just forget it. I won't put up with that kind of crap. It's not in my interest, it's not in my daughter's interest.' She checked her watch ostentatiously. 'Even you are unlikely to be bladdered given that you only got up at midday.'

Lee hauled himself out of the pool and stood dripping on the rough tiles. He was slightly askew on account of his wearing only one shoe. Brenda stood regarding her drenched son-in-law, her dry, tanned arms folded in front of her.

'Feeling better now?' she asked again. 'Got whatever it was out of your system?'

Lee pushed his hair back from his brow before tilting his

head to the side to shake water from his ears. 'S'pose I am,' he said. He actually did feel a little better. Some of the residue from the last two days had been stripped away. He'd shed some skin.

'You all right, Brenda?' he asked.

'You like making an exhibition of yourself, don't you?' she said. Her voice was cool, matter-of-fact.

'What did you get up to last night?'

'Watched some TV. Had a pizza. Few drinks. You know.'

'I know.'

'You'd better get dried off then, Lee.'

Without taking his eyes from his mother-in-law Lee unzipped his jacket, removed his shirt, trousers, shoes and socks and walked into the house wearing just his underpants, leaving a pile of wet clothes in an unwieldly mound. He looked at himself in the mirror as he dripped water on to the grey marble floor: unshaven, grey, wet. But that was all right – he could take it. He looked at his arm. At the top, just below the shoulder, he read: ellehcim. That's what he had written on his arm – ellehcim. She hadn't liked it when he'd had it done. She didn't like it now. Thought it was common. But it still meant something. Still meant she was under his skin.

Lee walked carefully through the kitchen and started up the stairs. He heard Brenda come into the kitchen and turn the TV on to some daytime pap. The voices cut through the still of the house.

'I never knew there were so many colours of the rainbow, Jim.'

'That's right, Carla . . .'

Lee reached out an arm and held the banisters firmly. He suddenly felt so tired that he had to stop climbing the stairs. He closed his eyes. Thought good thoughts for a moment. Collected himself.

Then the phone rang. Jesus. He didn't want to hear that voice again with its slick arrogance, its thinly veiled threats.

Please, God, no.

'Lee, phone,' called Brenda, her robust London vowels echoing in the still midday heat.

Lee walked back down the stairs and into the kitchen. As he entered the room he mouthed to Brenda – 'Who is it?' – not wanting to let the caller know he was there. Maybe he could get Brenda to tell them . . .

'I don't know,' Brenda bellowed, turning back to a cookery programme.

Lee picked up the receiver with dread in his heart. He would have to be careful. Brenda shouldn't hear this. 'Hello?' There was a silence before a voice – clearly distracted by something else – burst on to the line.

'Lee, it's Lou in London. How are you?' Lee could tell Lou was on speakerphone, reclining behind his desk, pleased with himself.

Before Lee could answer he continued. 'I have just had some great news. Some great news. I think you're going to be pleased. Very pleased indeed. I've just had a call from Dan Boyd at King Snacks and he's confirmed the deal.'

Lee didn't know what he was talking about.

'Lee, you're going to have a King Snacks chicken meal named after you! The money is knockout and all we have to do is one ad to support the promotion. We have finalised the wording, but it looks like your line will be something like, "I get peckish when I think of Sweeney's Chicken Pecks." What do you think, eh? Reckon you can handle that? Lee? Lee? Hello? Shit, maybe the speakerphone's fucked . . .'

Lee put the phone down on the counter without cutting him off. He didn't want to hear anything else, just wanted a shower. Just wanted to get some sleep.

He drifted in and out of sleep in the 'emperor size' bed Michelle had bought for them. He dreamed of Colin and Lou and Michelle and Brenda. They were all watching him play in a big game. He didn't know where it was, but every time the ball came to him he couldn't lift his leg quickly enough to kick the ball before he was dispossessed.

He stirred, opened his eyes and stared at the green bedroom curtains that flapped slightly in the breeze. He felt cold. The sheets were slightly damp. He didn't know whether this was because he'd flopped straight into bed from the shower, or because he'd had a fever. He could hear music playing downstairs; occasionally it was interrupted by big, booming, confident, rich-with-success American voices telling listeners about great deals on cars, furniture and shrimp meals. Lee wondered what it would be like to have a shrimp meal named after him.

He got up, put on some shorts and a T-shirt and went downstairs to the kitchen. He pulled open the fridge door. It was twice the size of the one in England – more like a warehouse, really. He tilted a couple of bowls towards him to see what was in them: grilled chicken and potato salad. He put some on a plate, pulled a tomato out of the fridge and started chomping on it as he headed outside.

Perhaps because he'd slept through the morning, he felt like he needed to get some rays on his back before he headed back to England. It was his third day off the charlie. He was beginning to feel good about himself. It felt like a novelty when, just for a few hours, his life hadn't been box office, hadn't been part of the entertainment industry.

Then it came back to him. The voice. The voice that always came. That never forgot. The voice that nagged and nagged and then went away when it was given what it wanted.

Only to come back.

He feared the voice like nothing else. Hated the hold it had on him. It was like a vice tightening on his head. He knew that he could only take so much before, inevitably, he was going to take the count. He wanted to make the voice happy, wanted to make it go away, to leave him be. But the voice only went away for a time, was only briefly satisfied. The voice always wanted more. For in the voice he heard what he feared most, the sound of his own impending destruction, the sound of his ruin.

He left his food baking in the sun and, with the maid watching, returned to the darkness of the bedroom.

Chapter Ten

Come and have a chat, they'd said. Come up and have a few minutes of our busy time now you're back in London. If Lee had had a choice he would rather have hung an anvil from his bollocks, but an invitation from the brothers was an invitation from the McKays, or the Twomacs as they were known.

Now Lee had always thought that brothers might at least share some common characteristics: similar builds, hair colour, maybe even taste, but the Twomacs were a living contradiction of this.

Meet Archie. Archie was a ringer for Burt Reynolds – and *Cannonball Run*-era Burt Reynolds with a chump-change syrup and Tango-orange skin at that, rather than *Deliverance*-era Burt. He carried himself like he was permanently on the nineteenth hole – blazer, beige polo neck, smart slacks, loafers. Archie was the one who did all the talking, filling the procedural emptiness with pleasantries and banter, repeatedly jumping up to fill your glass with vintage brandy that he kept in a decanter by the leather sofa in his office. He'd rarely sit behind his desk when conducting a meeting, preferring to get comfy on the sofa and have a cordial natter.

His brother Gerrard was another proposition. The story went that the secret of the McKay brothers' success in business was their good cop, bad cop routine. Archie softened people up, did the schmoozing, made the world feel like a safe place, assured you how much they respected your talents and intelligence, before Gerrard steamed in and screwed you into the ground. Gerrard looked a good ten years older than Archie, was taller and appeared slimmer, perhaps because of the broken-bottle-sharp Savile Row pinstriped suits that he always sported. His hair was grey, oiled and scraped back across his dome. Running across his forehead like a picture rail his thick, black eyebrows give him a sinister, patrician bearing. He always looked like he was scowling, and he rarely spoke. He'd look directly at his subject, like he could reach in and squeeze their minds, but he rarely uttered a word. When he did it was to growl rather than to reason, like a mean dog behind a chicken-wire fence. In meetings the Twomacs never looked at each other, never even exchanged a glance. Gerrard's snap was soothed by the Bollinger baritone of his brother. They might have had different styles, but they both pushed in the same direction. They knew each other's minds and Lee envied them that intimacy.

But what was really strange about the brothers, and what had made them notorious, was that they had married twin sisters. All four of them rattled about in a huge mansion, somewhere over towards Hertford. The pile had ten-foot walls enclosing the perimeter with signs barking 'Private Property – Keep Out' littering the place. When they bought into one of London's biggest football clubs the press were on to them like a shot, trying to scam up some kind of exposure, monster the wives, the usual sort of thing. The trouble was that there wasn't a lot for the rotters to write about, given that it was public knowledge that the brothers had married twins (admittedly spooky) and that their grotesque fortune came from stroke mags and dirty videos.

So why had they spent their flesh-procured fortune on a behemoth of a football club with huge overheads and a profligate wage bill that was an embarrassment even to those, like Lee, who were carting the money away? The answer to this was uncertain but Lee's theory, for what it was worth, was very simple: they needed something to do, both with themselves and their money. They had sold the majority share in Star Productions, the company they'd founded in the seventies, to an American porn conglomerate who were looking to get a foothold in the UK and European market for their out-of-town porn superstores. The brothers, as the sole owners of Star, had walked away with around £60 million between them as well as retaining a twenty-five per cent stake in the company.

Now, being the kind of guys who weren't going to be satisfied playing a couple of rounds of golf per week while keeping an eye on their annuities and waiting for a coronary, they decided to splash out. They mounted a hostile bid to drive out the Evans family – upper-class, Eton-educated bankers — who had been running the club for the past seventy years. A few bad seasons and fan unrest gave the family little hope of survival, and the McKays had been greeted as saviours by disgruntled fans mindful that in the modern game financial muscle usually translated into success on the pitch.

Which is why they had bought Lee.

As much as Lou had tried to convince Lee that it was he who was solely responsible for pushing the deal through, it was clear that the transfer would never have happened without the express involvement of the Twomacs. In fact, the moment the deal was completed Lee had been whisked off to the twins' villa in Marbella for an impromptu meeting. There he experienced a disconcerting, almost surreal, moment. As he had waited at the poolside table under a Martini parasol he realised that he was sitting in the place where some of the twins' most lucrative movies had been shot: he was, in effect, on set at Star Productions studios. *Double D Buttslam, Strap On Slags, Filthy Girls* . . . you name it, the twins' classics had all been shot here at their million-pound hideaway. It was then that Lee had realised that the brothers' reputation for thrift was wholly justified.

Lee's Marbella reminiscences dissolved as Wanda, the

Twomacs' matronly secretary, waved him through the ante-room.

'You all right, Lee?' she asked sorting a pile of papers on her desk. But before he could answer she was speaking into her headset. 'Lee Sweeney is here for your three o'clock.' She turned to Lee. 'They're waiting for you.'

This did not sound good. From what Wanda had said this sounded more like a mugging than a meeting. Lee ran a hand through his hair and knocked.

'Enter, enter,' came Archie's impatient voice. Lee walked in and saw him standing at the window, hands behind his back surveying the Wood Green skyline ('Look! Shopping City!') while Gerrard sat at one end of the brown leather sofa obscured behind an early edition *Evening Standard*.

'Hello, Lee, hello,' said Archie walking towards him with an outstretched hand. 'Thanks for popping by to see us. Gerry and I know that you're busy, got a big game on Saturday, so we appreciate your time.' Gerry? That was weird. Lee had never heard Gerrard McKay referred to as Gerry before. Bit like hearing Tony Blair referred to as Tonkers.

'Oh, it's no problem,' Lee said. 'Anything but.'

'Good, good,' said Archie, ushering him towards the seating. Gerrard had still to look up from his paper.

Then Lee felt sick.

He noticed the back page of the *Standard*: 'Exclusive – Sweeney To Quit', it said. There was a strapline: 'There's No Hope, No Ambition, says Lee'. Slowly his mind reformed the conversation of the previous night, words began to take shape, their meaning tingling in his mind, this time without the warm, comforting fuzz of alcohol. He'd been in a bar up West with a spar and they'd got talking to a bloke who seemed to know his football . . . He felt as if he'd stepped outside a hot room into a freezing wind. Unconsciously Lee embraced himself, trying to keep the cold out. The sofa was a good seven or eight feet long. He decided to sit at the opposite end from Gerrard to make it more difficult for the pair of them to make eye contact.

The leather creaked beneath his weight. 'Good, good,' said Archie to himself. It was his own private mantra. Abruptly he stuffed a white bowl of crisps beneath Lee's face. They were dusted with a reddy-orange powder.

'Salsa with mesquite Kettle Chip, Lee?' he asked. Lee politely declined.

'I know, I know,' said Archie. 'I find with the mesquite Kettle Chips that they flavour them so strongly that even if you've eaten some in the afternoon and then have your dinner and a couple of drinks, that when you repeat on yourself it's the mesquite Kettle Chips that form the predominant flavour.'

'That's right,' Lee said, smiling. 'Not nice in company.'

'But, of course, Gerrard likes his Kettle Chips – they're not as fattening as a biscuit, you see – so we tend to have them round the office. Kettle Chip, Gerry?'

Gerrard folded the paper, took the bowl from his brother and set it on his lap. He started working his way through its contents.

'Budge up, Lee,' said Archie. Lee looked at the two empty armchairs before moving into the middle of the sofa. He was now sitting between the McKays; the brothers framed him like a couple of bookends.

'So what snack products do you like?' asked Archie.

'Snack products?'

'You know, crisps, Twiglets, Wotsits, Hula Hoops . . . Or, don't tell me, Lee, your body is such a temple that you'd never think of defiling it with such junk.'

Lee smiled appreciatively, as if he'd been fingered as a professional athlete with a weakness for the odd Mars bar. Thank God they didn't know about the kind of junk that he usually defiled his body with.

'Well, I've got a deal with Honey Snaps, the cereal,' he said. 'Done a couple of ads, you know . . .'

Gerrard's hand suddenly halted its rhythmic passage from bowl to mouth. He turned his head to look at Lee.

'Why don't you endorse a product you actually use?' he asked. His voice was dry, there was no playfulness to it. Lee turned to Archie, looking for help. He just stared right through Lee, the same cheesy smile on his lips.

'I don't follow you,' Lee said.

'Surely if you endorsed Foster's or Smirnoff then people might actually fucking believe you. From what I'm told – and I'm told a lot of things – you're about as likely to eat Honey Snaps for breakfast as you are to walk past a pub.' He was totally deadpan. Lee could feel Gerrard's stare burning into his right cheek. Lee faked a cough to fill the silence.

'There you are. There you are,' Gerrard said. 'Professional footballer with a smoker's cough.'

'No, it's just a little infection I'm getting over.'

'The only thing I heard you're getting over is your leg,' said Gerrard. What was this geezer, a fucking comedian? 'Nice tan, as well,' continued Gerrard.

'Kirk gave me a week off, to rest,' explained Lee. 'Thought I was under the weather. We've got a place in Florida, you see.'

'Which we probably paid for,' said Gerrard, who abruptly went back to eating the crisps.

'Lee, I think what Gerrard is saying is that we're both a little concerned about you,' said Archie, pouring on the unction. 'We've had several chats with Kirk over the past few weeks and he's less than satisfied with both your attitude and application. He feels that there might be certain, er – how shall I put it? – distractions in your life at present which might be preventing you from focusing all your energies on the pitch.'

'Look, Lee, there's nothing difficult to understand about this,' said Gerrard stabbing an orange-dusted finger at him. 'We pay your fucking wages. We have your signature on a bit of paper in our safe. Until you're out of contract with this club we have you like that,' he cupped his hand to indicate his hairy fingers grasping Lee's plums, 'and if you choose to displease us then we have little choice but to squeeze as hard as it takes to get you back on track.'

'We've put a lot of faith in you,' said Archie with a smile.

'Fuck it, Archie, we pay his fucking wages,' said Gerrard. 'We own the bastard. He owes us.'

Gerrard was getting increasingly angry. Lee could see his chest rising and falling rapidly. Lee became worried that he might actually take a pop at him.

'Lee, we have made a significant investment in this club,' said Archie making it sound like he was being reasonable, 'and it is very much in our interests for this club to enjoy success. Consequently, a couple of good performances from the team over the next few months will see us reach the FA Cup Final, which would be wonderful for everyone associated with the club, from the players through to the supporters.'

'And us,' butted in Gerrard. 'Don't forget to tell him that it's good for us. That's all he should need to know. There's his motivation.'

'So what my brother and I are saying,' said Archie without missing a beat, 'is that we are concerned to see both the public revelations about your lifestyle and private life and the rumours and reports that we hear from within the club.'

Lee felt it was time for him to say something. 'Well, you shouldn't believe everything you read in the papers, or what you hear on the grapevine. I'm concerned to hear what you're saying, so I'm glad you've given me a chance to meet with you.' He paused, increasingly self-conscious. 'You can be assured that I'll be doing everything I can to bring success to the club. I understand that you're as hungry for it in the boardroom as they are in the stands.'

'Thirty-five fucking years, thirty-five years,' said Gerrard reciting the amount of time since the club last won a major honour like a mantra. The years hung like a millstone around the neck of the club. 'We were just young men at the time. Just starting out.' He was still agitated. 'If I hadn't come up with nearly twelve million quid of my own money to drag your flabby carcass back to this country I would seriously consider spending a comparatively small proportion of your transfer fee on having you dumped in the fucking Thames.'

This last statement seemed to require a laugh at the end of it. However, neither Twomac looked even moderately amused. Lee looked at Archie and pushed his lips up towards his nose as a I-think-it's-your-move kind of gesture. Archie took the bait while his brother continued panting to his right. Lee was worried Gerrard might lose his Kettle Chips all over his new Hugo Boss strides.

'Now, Lee, I don't want you to get the wrong end of the stick about our little chat, but I think it's worth bearing in mind that my brother and I have a very large network of friends who like to protect our business interests,' said Archie grinning like he was a game-show host. He started slowly rubbing the palms of his hands against each other. 'Let's just say that we're well aware of the fact that your off-the-field activities aren't always complementary to your profession. I hope I don't need to make myself any clearer than that.'

Lee raised his eyes to the roof, before narrowing them, as if searching to understand what was being said to him, before nodding slowly, like a truant caught pilfering from the corner shop.

''Course he knows what you're talking about, Archie,' said Gerrard, cranking himself up once again. 'What's the matter with you? Booze, drugs, birds . . . and the rest.'

Lee wondered what else he might be missing out on. He thought about questioning Gerrard for a moment, before ruling it out.

'What we're looking for, Lee, is a level of commitment from you,' said Archie. 'But what I'd like you to mull over is the fact that you need this club as much as it needs you. It would be an awful shame if, so near to the end of your England career – you found yourself struggling even to get into your club side. Such an awful shame.'

'You'll not be playing much international football if you're sitting in the fucking reserves, is what my brother is saying,' said Gerrard. 'And don't think we won't do it. You don't get your fucking act together we're going to sling you right back in the fucking stiffs.' He picked up the bowl of crisps and stuffed a handful in his mouth. It was his way of saying that the conversation was over.

'Right, I think that covers all the bases,' said Archie clapping his hands together, as if he were an instructor who had just inducted someone into the local gym. 'Lee? Have you got anything you'd like to ask us?'

'Not really, Archie. I'd just like to say that I'll make an effort to live up to the club's high standards.' Even Lee was embarrassed by the emptiness in his voice.

'Right then,' said Archie standing Lee up and moving him towards the door. 'We'd best press on. Thank you for your time and frankness, Lee. I'm sure we've made some progress.'

'Well, thank you, Archie,' Lee said shaking Archie's hand. He seized the door handle.

'Oh, I just thought,' Lee said. 'I do have a question.'

'What's that?' said Archie.

'Have you ever tried New York Cheddar flavour, Gerrard? If not, you should give them a go. They really are blinding.'

Chapter Eleven

On a superficial level the Florida excursion proved a success. The couple had done the right things during their days together, oiled each other's backs, exchanged intimacies by the pool, made each other laugh in bed. Yet in his heart, Lee felt only as if he were running through well-rehearsed and insignificant motions.

It was the voice that had done it to him, had reminded him of the dark possibilities of his life so that the crisp, cleanly etched reconciliatory blueprint that he had assembled in his mind became nothing but reminiscence in the bright, white Floridian light and the loamy expanses of the night, for every time Michelle looked at him with hope and enjoyment in her eyes it was all he could do not to tell her of the burden that made him feel further distanced from her, even more solitary, the faster he plummeted earthwards.

On the way back they had been ambushed by press reptiles who couldn't believe their luck at such a sighting while on a Heathrow Madonna vigil. The following day Lee studied the snatched pictures, looked for some clues that might aid him in pursuing a singular and obvious course of redemption, but there was nothing there. He looked at the photo and saw only what others might expect to see about him. There was no revelation.

That night, after kissing his wife carefully on the cheek and telling her that he might be back late, he went and picked up Colin. The brothers were due for a session to celebrate Lee's return and Colin was clearly taken aback that his brother had chosen to drive to the bar rather than get a driver to ferry them around. Lee had his reasons. He was going to dig himself out of the snake pit in which he found himself trapped. He had decided not to be beaten.

He summoned resolve, as if about to dive into water from a great height. 'I need to talk to you about something, Col,' he said.

Colin picked up a familiar note in his brother's voice. Lee was troubled, and Colin understood why. Lee was troubled by the Twomacs, troubled by football, troubled by Michelle and Brenda. Most of all he was troubled with himself. Colin knew the form. His eyes swivelled rightwards as far as they would go. It sent a sharpness across Lee's neck.

'It's all right, Lee,' said Colin playing dumb. 'It ain't worth worrying about. It's just a dip in form. It happens. Just keep your head down, keep plugging away and it'll come right. Stop feeling sorry for yourself. What about your poor brother?'

Lee was shaking his head, trying to tell Colin that he was wrong, that *everything* was wrong,

He began to feel sick at heart, depressed by his need for someone – anyone – to bear witness. The real tragedy for Lee was that, even as he was feeling his way back into some relationship with Colin, there was no one in his life with whom he could be totally honest – not Michelle, not his dad, not Jug Ears or King Tut. Not even a priest, though God only knew when he last made confession. There was only Colin. Lee thought when he was a kid that he was going to reach eighteen and suddenly everything would become clear. That his sense of realisation would become so keen that he would not only feel like he was cruising through life, he'd feel like he was riding it home.

He didn't know whether Colin was the right person with whom to share his secret – there was much about Colin that marked him out as furtive and mischievous. Yet, despite knowing this, like a man walking knowingly into a burning house, Lee made the decision that, no matter the inevitable repercussions, this was the man with whom he could share his dingy, bleak, concealed mysteries. Colin was the one to whom Lee would reveal the code that would take him to his out-of-the-way places.

Colin's easily soured temperament was something he'd grown used to, something Lee lived with in his professional life every time he encountered a crowd, for, among the rows of punters, the ranks of would-be Lees, the very things he did before them engendered extravagant anger, hothouse hatred. And Lee thought that maybe it was the same with Colin: he was facing a constant battle between loving and hating his brother.

Lee glanced over at his brother's watchful, sentry's eyes. And then he began to talk. He began to tell Colin everything. He just opened his mouth and words came out. At first they came slowly, like the first signs of spring after a cruel winter. The initial steps were tentative, and for good reason. He felt his way cautiously, hoping to cut a path through the thickly enmeshed layers he'd laid down over the years. Part time capsule, part foundation, it was the unseen, unmentioned fabric underpinning his life, and Lee was aware that he exposed and removed it at his peril, for his sense of what lay beneath and what might come after was slight.

The car barrelled back towards the A1, past the gorged City boys and riff-raff hitting the wall on their unemployment marathons, and all the time Lee's mouth was running, leaking inside the car, spilling words, exposing his secrets to sunlight.

And despite the fear, despite the discomfort of self-exposure, it felt good spilling his insides. Lee felt relief spreading throughout his system, like sunshine warming frosty spring soil. He'd never been much good at secrets. He was not bad at telling lies, but guarding secrets was another story. For the first time Lee could remember, Colin took words in with something approximating to attention. Like some halfwit with drool spilling over his chin, his jaw went slack and he sat and listened, as if in rapture, his stillness emphasising the shimmering, quiet, money-lavish of the car. The smell: calf's hide (Argentinian, apparently). The mood: the bright, slick tension of *now*, the buzz of the moment. And it made him remember why Colin was the only person he could tell, the way that he'd always thought of Colin as someone who offered warmth and protection. Lee had carried few friends through life and Colin offered consistency, some sense of intimacy.

This is what Lee told Colin: he told him the truth. He told him about what happened to him or, even more truthfully, what he'd done. After all, he didn't want to pretend that he was a victim; even in his most self-destructive moments Lee understood that you make choices in life, some of them good, some of them bad. Most of the time it didn't matter what he chose, the margin of difference made no odds. Other times the slimmest, seemingly insignificant detail could make all the difference in the world.

So this is how it went.

It was two days before the last game of the season in Italy. Two days before Lee returned to England, the deal sewn up. One of the Napoli lads, Antonio, approached Lee after training, asked him if he wanted a lift home. Lee didn't answer, thinking it was a joke; after all, surely Antonio was aware that the spanking new black Ferrari 355 glistening in the car park was Lee's. (If he didn't, thought Lee, he fucking should.) So Lee told Antonio that there was no need. He was all right. This didn't settle the matter. Antonio looked at Lee with a strange half smile and repeated his question. He said that he'd like to talk to Lee, there were a few things they needed to settle before Lee's departure. Lee thought he was talking about the players' pool, ensuring that Lee received his full entitlement. He looked at his watch. Michelle was in Florida; they had arranged to meet back in London when the Italian season was over. He had nothing to go back to the villa for bar a couple of bottles of Scotch and a bag of grass. If he was in the mood he could have had some gear dropped round to the villa, but he was hoping that he might be able to hold out for the evening, depending on how far he got with *Time Crisis.*

Antonio proceeded to show Lee what his red Ferrari 355 could do on the hill roads outside Napoli (strangely, it was pretty much the same stuff as Lee's own car could do). He gunned the red missile up to a high point on the road, a favourite with tourists, from where they looked out over the ragbag beauty of the city and the ocean. It was a popular spot with young lovers, who ascended the slope to map out their lives by grasping the feral beauty of the buildings, the tangled streets and lives teeming below.

Antonio turned off the engine and hushed the music. Lee felt awkward, realising that there was an angle being played. The two men sat alone and silent in the car watching the ocean. After a couple of minutes Antonio twisted so that his back pressed against his door and his right leg was hitched up on the seat.

The swivelling action put Lee on his guard: this man had something to say. Antonio spoke in English, something a lot of the Napoli players liked to do when they were with Lee as it gave them a chance to practise. Lee enjoyed still having some novelty value within the team.

'You like the car?' he asked.

'Not bad,' Lee replied. Antonio threw his palms out sideways in a gesture that suggested that he had missed the irony. He thought Lee was being a flash bastard.

'You like one just like this?'

'Suppose I could make a pair,' Lee said. 'Only problem is that I can only drive one car at a time.'

Antonio raised his eyebrows to the sky, as if Lee was being difficult to please.

'OK, let me tell you how you get one more car like this,' he said, his manner suddenly switching into a deal-clinching seriousness. He turned his head to look through the windscreen across the city. 'Saturday. Against Inter. We lose.'

'I suppose it all depends on whether we can break their defence down . . .'

'No, no, no.' Antonio leant forward and touched Lee's knee. He formed circles with his thumb and index finger on both hands, the way Italians do when they want to emphasise something. 'We lose. No question.'

Lee looked at him; it was a searching look more than a look of disbelief. Antonio suddenly seemed to regain his usual cocky demeanour, as if a difficult moment had passed. Transaction over.

'No questions. No problem,' he said, offering Lee no explanation, no hint of reasoning behind his scheme, as if there were a cause, but no effect. He reached into the back of the car and pulled a nondescript travelling bag from the shelf behind him. He put it on Lee's lap and told him to open it. Inside was a mess of green. American dollars crammed inside the leather without any care or attention. In movies you get it in a briefcase wrapped in neat bundles. That way you can count it. Lee looked at the money and shut the bag. He didn't look at Antonio.

'One hundred thousand US dollars,' Antonio said, turning to look forward again. 'Money enough for another Ferrari like this, eh?' His voice was flat, unconvincing. He started the engine. 'I hope that you are still happy here in Napoli. There is much to do, but you have made the people happy. They know that this season we are not going to win. We have one game left. We cannot win the Scudetto. We cannot improve our position. Maybe next year we can make them happier.'

They headed back down the mountain, this time at a slower, almost serene pace. At traffic lights local lads on scooters banged on the car roof, offered encouragement and tried to offer the two players insights into the way the team was playing. Lee couldn't forget the look of one of the boys. He was about eleven, clinging on to his elder brother who was revving his scooter as they waited for the green signal. He was staring at Lee intently, like he couldn't quite believe that the man he saw on TV wearing a light-blue shirt, a man whose image was plastered on flags and posters and pictures all over the city, could really be there sitting next to him. Lee winked, acknowledging that he wasn't seeing things, that they both knew there was something passing between them. And right before his eyes, as calm and cool and nonplussed as you could imagine, the kid winked back at him, as blasé as a milkman dropping off two pints of silver top and a dozen eggs. The scooter disappeared in a cloud of dust.

As they pulled back into the training ground Lee noticed Antonio glance at him apprehensively. He could tell he was wondering whether Lee could really be trusted, whether his serpent words had struck home, whether Lee had swallowed the bait. The car came to a halt. Lee pulled himself clear of the low-slung chassis. He walked to his car, Antonio's parting words echoing in his ears: 'You're not alone.'

Lee placed the bag on the bonnet and fished for his keys.

The sun cast a hazy light over the stadium on the final day of the season. Lee had slept well, but rose early to take in the city for the last time. Looking from his hotel balcony the city felt drowsy, untouched by the prompting of the sun's rays. Sunday, the only people up were old black-clad women, called to Mass by the pealing of ancient church bells.

He sipped coffee (a banned substance before games) and ruminated on his secret. One he didn't want to share. Something that only the coach, the president, Lou and a couple of people at his new club knew: this would be his last game for Napoli. Ever.

It had been a tougher decision for Napoli than for Lee. After all, he was bailing out, closing up the villa, being waved off by tearful staff and hot-footing it back to Blighty.

The last time the club sold a key player – to Juventus – there had been full-scale rioting. Ultras with scarves over their faces had battled it out with jack-booted *carabinieri* from the provinces. The president was put under twenty-four-hour armed guard after receiving death threats that the police took seriously in a city where death threats are issued casually. Only after Lee had been at the club for a year, and his antics had convinced and charmed the club's previously nonplussed and baffled supporters, did Alessandro DiSotti, the president of the club, feel relaxed enough to dismiss the burly monosyllabic men who shadowed him wearing wraparound shades and tiny microphones in their ears. You could say that Lee saved the man's life.

For Lee, that final day in southern Italy felt like that last day at school. It was over. The end of the affair. There was no way the team could improve its position and there was no one that could overhaul it. The players occupied an honourless no man's land: they had qualified for the UEFA cup, but for a team that had recently won back-to-back championships it was a minuscule peak to scale.

Lee boarded the team coach and leant against a window with his headphones on. No one minded anti-social behaviour before a game – it was understood that each player responded to pressure in a different way, but that day there was an uneasy atmosphere in the dressing-room. Usually an hour before kick-off players withdrew into clandestine worlds – mumbled their own private mantras, marshalled their thoughts, calmed their fears – but, as the season had crept to a close, when matters had been decided, a looser, demob atmosphere had begun to creep in. Yet the day that their performance had no bearing upon their league position, the atmosphere was like a morgue. Lee discerned players staring at him. Before he could acknowledge them, they looked away.

Coach Benazzi sensed the mood and proceeded among them having whispered Communion with the players as they went through their routines of undressing, dressing, massage and stretching. Lee was lying face down on the massage table, eyes closed, having his hamstrings kneaded when Benazzi arched down next to him and whispered. Lee knew he was enquiring not only how Lee himself was feeling, but was also hopeful that he might have the leaden atmosphere in the dressing-room explained. It felt more like the team were going out to try and avoid relegation than the formality of the last game of the season. Lee just nodded. He was fine. Honest.

Understandably, Benazzi thought that the mood was a result of the opposition, Inter Milan, needing to beat Napoli to secure their first Scudetto for several years, that the team's professionalism had got the better of its more frivolous instincts and that rather than treat the game as a glorified training session the team intended to have full bearing upon the result.

He was right about the last bit.

Emerging on to the pitch felt like surfacing from the depths of the ocean into stormy seas. The dressing-rooms in Napoli were linked to the pitch by a tunnel that ran beneath the running track. It was a narrow passageway lit by fluorescent strips that disfigured the flesh of the players, officials and coaches – they became green, sickly, hollow. To Lee the tunnel always felt more like a means of escape than a means of entry.

The Napoli players were given the signal to leave the dressing-room once Inter, crossing themselves, had left the relative sanctuary of the tunnel to enter the arena. Incited by fat men with bull horns the crowd was fevered. In the tunnel the players could taste the hysteria. They tried not to wrestle with it. No one talked. Talk was frivolous, unfocused. Some of the players fiddled with the drawstring on their shorts, others ran their hands across their faces and through their hair, as if trying to shake off any remaining vestiges of indolence. Most simply walked forward like somnambulists, their eyes glazed and deadly, a robot army on its way to war.

Napoli's appearance from the darkness was the signal for lathered dementia to break loose, as if the Pope himself were performing miracles. Thousands of tiny pieces of paper cascaded like snowflakes from the top tiers of the stands, fanatical fathers and sons bellowed, screamed and bawled; old ladies waved tiny flags, close to tears; the hard-core fans, the Ultras, brandished blue-and-white distress flares, their identities masked with scarves. The team broke out into a trot as it moved from the track to the pitch. Sometimes it was all Lee could do to stifle a grin: he felt so high on the noise that he could ride it. It was as if he was in the midst of the most intense manifestation of human passion on the face of the earth; the ardour was potent enough to light the whole of Europe. Even when still lost in whisky sleep this, to Lee, was like a cattle prod to the frontal lobe, a punch to the heart; he wondered if it was possible that he might get out of this place alive, he wondered if his nervous system would collapse under the flood of information. There were no shadows. There was precisely nowhere to hide.

But right in the middle of this sod's opera Lee was feeling all right. Not all right as in fair-to-middling, but *all right* meaning that he was feeling like doing the business, hoping that maybe today might be his day in the sun rather than out on the Special Brew tiles.

He trotted over to a certain section of the crowd to acknowledge a group of fans who always carried a Union Jack with them. Even when sections of the crowd had given Lee a bit of a hard time, this crew always carried this flag with them, a sign of support. Respect. That meant a lot to Lee. He gave them a nod and a wink and they gestured back.

Lee looked up and noticed the day's ref was this cantankerous old cunt with white, buzz-cut hair – like some cigar-chomping US army general from World War Two – who had booked him earlier in the season for an innocuous challenge on this niggly little weasel who'd been kicking him all afternoon. Lee surveyed his neatly ironed uniform and wondered if a man of order such as this was in on the scam.

The turf felt good beneath his feet, not too dry, not too springy, just lush and flat and begging for a ball to run across it. It was an unblemished day for football. Everything was in place. The coaches and mascots scurried from the pitch as if they'd heard a thunderstorm approaching. The crowd climbed to another level of derangement as the teams lined up waiting for the game to start. Napoli had kick-off. It was the last game of the season and the destiny of the Scudetto was in their hands. Or should have been.

The noise rolled over Lee, like an artillery bombardment, as the game commenced. He got an immediate touch as the ball was laid back to him. He looked up and saw Marco was in a little space on the left touchline. Lee tried to get the ball over to him, but caught it wrong and it sailed over Marco's head and into touch. The crowd whistled their disapproval. Lee turned his head and looked for Antonio, who was standing inches behind the man he was marking, looking directly at Lee. Lee felt his stomach sink. Antonio looked so fucking pleased with himself, like a dog with two cocks.

Inter were quick and organised and closed Napoli down quickly. They pressed hard – every time Lee got the ball he was hurried into making a poor pass or was hustled off the ball. His spirits dropped and it crossed his mind that he could hide for the rest of the game; maybe he should get lost and just think about what he was going to do when he got back to England (which was in precisely seven hours). His legs became heavier and he didn't seem to be able to get any purchase on the game. Sure enough the inevitable happened: Inter won a corner and Gonzales, this monster of an Argentinian target man with Samson-like locks, rose high above Antonio (who, strangely, had slipped and was recovering on the floor) to nod the ball into the net. The large contingent of Inter fans – in Naples hoping to witness a great moment in their team's history – went wild, setting off flares and waving enormous flags, while Napoli caught its breath. There were only twelve minutes gone.

Giuseppe, the captain, a terrier of a player who played in front of the back four, winning the ball and making surging runs upfield, put his arm around Lee. 'Come deeper,' he said. 'Come and collect the thing. That way you'll escape from that son of a bitch.' He nodded towards Lee's marker. One thing about Giuseppe: he was always one hundred per cent committed. Lee could guarantee that he would have nothing to do with the scam. Players put in different amounts of effort out on the pitch, but Giuseppe was never anything less than fully committed, rushing around like a rhino, leading from the front.

Lee watched him scuttle back to his position and the game restarted. It occurred to Lee that there would be absolutely no chance that Giuseppe would be involved in throwing the game, that if Antonio had tried to ensnare him in the deception he would probably have been decked and his beloved Ferrari trashed. Giuseppe was Neapolitan, this club was his life's great passion, his friends and family packed the stadium. He had three sons, all of whom he wished to play for the club. Lee watched him win another challenge that he had no right to, pull himself up off the deck, and suddenly found the ball at his feet. He had his back to goal, feinted one way and then the other and felt the sticky presence of his marker. He swivelled, brushing him aside and looked up for the front two players. One, intentionally or not, was too tightly policed to be able to do anything, but the other started a diagonal run ... Lee flighted the ball in between the two defenders, catching them flat-footed and the striker, Carlos, having no time to bring the ball under control, hit it first time. The Inter keeper flung himself to his left and tipped the ball around the post. The crowd were on their feet for the first time in the game. Carlos turned and applauded Lee, who knew then that at least two players were not involved in the scam. It came to him: he wanted to win.

The corner was the beginning of a sustained period of pressure. Napoli piled forward, and Lee realised that there were at least eight of them in the team who were playing to win. Even the ones he suspected of trying to throw the game were finding it difficult to sustain their intent: even if you're *trying* not to play well, there are certain standards of professionalism that pride will not allow you to sink below. Add to that the fact that silly mistakes were punished by merciless whistling and jeering from the crowd. Some of the lads had to bear it in mind that a really bad performance would precipitate a barrage of abuse from the home fans next season. Crowds rarely forgive, never forget. Most of the team would have to play in front of this mob next season.

The crowd were on their feet jeering one of the Napoli midfielders, Giovanni, who had put a stupid ball into touch. Giovanni backed off, following his man, and Lee gave him a dirty look. He smiled back at Lee with a mixture of arrogance and nonchalance. The away supporters roused themselves again. Napoli's period of ascendancy seemed to have come to an end. Inter took the throw-in and the ball went to their right-back, who was immediately put under pressure by Carlos, and tried to return the ball to the thrower who, by then, had moved into another position. Lee nipped in and moved quickly towards goal. He cut inside the full-back and moved in the direction of the near post (in these situations he could still hear his school coach's advice: 'Attack a post! Attack a fucking post!') looking for someone to move into space in front of him. Bizarrely, the Inter defenders were backing off; the situation was opening up. Lee was nearing the edge of the box when he felt his legs go from beneath him and a sharp pain shot up his right calf. He'd been nobbled by Inter's notorious Uruguayan centre-half, commonly known as

'The Cannibal'. He'd not received a shout of warning from his nearest team-mate. He'd have to watch that. The Inter players started arguing with the ref when he produced a yellow card, but he waved them away, told them to get on with the game. Carlos made a gesture to take the free-kick quickly, so Lee slipped the ball outside the milling Inter players. Carlos struck it sweetly across the face of the goal and inside the far post. The crowd went into frenzied delirium. The Inter players reacted by either hanging their heads or bitching at the ref. It was on the stroke of half-time, a blinding moment to score.

They had barely had time to restart when the ref blew up for half-time. The crowd roared: Napoli might only have been drawing, but scoring like they had gave them the psychological edge. The Neapolitan fans might have been resigned to finishing third, but they were savouring the prospect of stopping one of the hated northern Italian (and Milanese at that) clubs from having their day in the sun.

As Lee walked back to the dressing-room Antonio trotted past him. He put his hand tightly round the back of Lee's neck. 'Maybe you get injured in the second half?' he said before heading down the tunnel. Lee watched him disappear underground with a dry anger rising in his belly, an acid burn that rose into his throat. The fucker was really a shameful excuse for a human being.

In the dressing-room Benazzi raged on about the fact that the players all seemed to be asleep. Did they know which club they were playing for? And the least they could do was to show some passion . . . Exactly the kind of stuff that Lee would have expected. There was silence in the dressing-room, just the odd clatter of studs on the floor and the bullish sounds of heavy breathing. For no other reason than force of habit a couple of the players changed their shirts. Lee watched Antonio sitting there solemnly, occasionally pulling on a small plastic bottle of water. He sat with his elbows resting on his thighs, his head bowed, almost as if he was hoping not to be noticed. Like a camouflaged creature blending into its environment he seemed to be attempting to remain completely still, so as not to draw attention to himself. Giuseppe said a few words, asking the midfield to spread itself wider – throughout the first half Napoli were getting drawn into a dogfight in the middle of the park which they were losing. Then there were a few shouts of encouragement and slaps on the back from the coaching staff and they were up and out of the dressing-room.

Habitually, Lee was one of the last to leave the dressing-room, but that day he walked out of the door first. Giuseppe trotted up behind him in the tunnel and put his arm on his shoulder. He told Lee not to fret, that the chances would come. There was no way Inter could keep up the pace of the first half; they had flung everything at Napoli and must be psychologically damaged by the fact that they had enjoyed the majority of the possession but were, nevertheless, still effectively chasing the game. As they began to tire Lee would find himself in a bit more space.

Air horns sounded and the voices stirred as Giuseppe and Lee appeared at the top of the stairs. Lee could hear a few individual voices, some laughter, but mostly the noise was lost as he walked on to the pitch. Lee looked up at the sky; it was as pale as the blue of his shirt. A washed-out, bleached, summer colour that symbolised holidays and lazy days. A thin white trail had been left by a plane as it disappeared into the distant mountains. Within a few hours it would be Lee disappearing from this place, from these people. Three years of his life leaving only a vapour trail evaporating in the sky. He'd come for the money, that he could not deny. Jesus, he was *in it* for the money. But – and he still found it hard to fathom how he distinguished like this – not for the stinking money Antonio had given him which lay there, as if in slumber, beneath his bed, its value, in every sense, waning by the second.

The game recommenced and immediately Inter went for

the kill. Lee spent the first quarter of an hour just trying to dismantle the elaborate moves they were forging in the smithy of their midfield. It kicked off a couple of times between Inter's forwards and a couple of Napoli's stoppers. Every attack seemed to be the one that would put Inter ahead, with Antonio at centre-back and Alberto at left-back clearly lying down and waiting for the kill – it looked like it was there for the taking, if only Inter could finish properly.

Then, like thunder rolling from the hills beyond, the crowd started chanting: NA-PO-LI! NA-PO-LI! NA-PO-LI! An indecisiveness seemed to settle over the Inter players, as if the size of their task suddenly overwhelmed them, like they realised that their ambitions were beyond them. Lee knew the feeling – it was like being exposed, found out. They were impostors humbled beyond human reckoning before majesty, by the voices of a forest of zealots.

And that's when Lee knew that he couldn't be party to the fraud that was being engineered on the pitch, that during life's blur of engagement you have opportunities to redeem yourself, to drag the careering bus from the cliff's edge, to make a complicated life less complicated (or maybe more, depending on how you look at it). God knows he'd missed most of his chances to get ahead; but he wasn't going to let this one get away.

Gregorio, the right-back, collected the ball from the keeper and played it to Lee who set off up the wing. His legs felt as fresh and strong as the first half. He held on to the ball before knocking it into the space in front of him. The cross was too deep, but it was collected by Gianfranco, who played on the left side of midfield, on the other side of the box. He went around one Inter defender, headed for the line before laying the ball back to Lee on the edge of the box. There he stood, exposed and with nothing else to do but strike the thing. As it rolled towards him he sensed an impending double-footed challenge from the Cannibal, who was always the first to react in those kind of situations. Lee knew that he was going to have to hit the ball first time. He concentrated on making sure that his balance was right and that his head was above the ball so that he wouldn't drive the thing into row Z. As soon as Lee struck it he felt the sweetness flow through his leg, and he watched the unforgiving cleanness of its progress, the arrow-straight velocity, like some physics experiment on the purity of straight lines. The ball was rising slightly, heading for the top corner, the holy grail of goal scoring, where few goal-keepers are able to claw back the impending doom. Every-thing was silent, it seemed, except for the tearing of turf as the Cannibal's late challenge flew in. Lee was in mid-air, above the Cannibal's vicious, retributive studs, as he saw the ball crash into the back of the net. And when Lee landed everything seemed to fall in around him. He was leapt on by three team-mates and they crashed to the ground in a heap of blood-swept muscle and heaving lungs. The crowd sent up flares and fireworks into the sky, drums were being beaten, horns blown, and every man, woman and child seemed to be experiencing exactly the same feeling at exactly the same moment as he was: ecstasy.

The referee broke up the celebration. Most of the team congratulated Lee, but Antonio and two others either ignored him completely or offered only lame handshakes. The goal felt good: for once, maybe, he had done something right. It made him want another. He began to feel greedy, like a hunter after his first kill who has the smell of fresh blood upon him. The crowd were in fine spirits. Benazzi was sitting on the bench looking as tense as ever, his assistant making signs for the team to calm down and play possession football – there were still fifteen minutes on the clock. Inter drove the ball forward looking for an equaliser. With less than a quarter of the game remaining they had no choice but to throw caution to the wind and push for two goals. One of their forwards, a lumbering Swede, picked up the ball on the edge of the box, slid it outside, moved into the box and collected the return. He was heading towards the goal but there was no immediate danger. Then, out of nowhere, Antonio came sliding towards him and whipped both his feet away. It was a challenge of such ruthlessness that even the home crowd couldn't muster the *faux* consternation to complain when the referee pointed to the spot.

Antonio picked himself off the floor and threw his arms in the air when he saw the red card raised in the referee's right hand. The anger might well have been genuine: he would be unable to influence the game as a spectator. Despite the Napoli supporters' jeers the Swede slotted the ball home with ease, before plunging into the net, picking the ball up, running back and planting it on the penalty spot. Inter now had seven minutes to win the game and, potentially, the Scudetto; their supporters were hysterically urging them forward. It would have been hard to imagine such passion outside of a holy war.

Lee scrutinised the bench. Benazzi's demeanour was stoic, perhaps now resigned to the harsh retribution of fortune. He gave Lee a look that conveyed that he'd seen it all before. There were five minutes to go. One of the midfield boys dropped back to fill Antonio's position and one of the strikers filled his position in the centre of midfield. Napoli would play with a lone striker, Carlos, with Lee supporting from deep. From the kick-off Inter tore into Napoli like crazed men. Three times it looked like they had to score, but somehow a body or a hacking boot would put paid to their efforts. As soon as the ball was hoofed away they would regain possession. Lee huffed and puffed, trying to close the midfield down – how he wished his critics who dismissed him as a luxury player could feel his burning lungs – but was outmanned as Inter muscled their way forward. They gained a corner and pushed the entire team, bar one full-back, into the Napoli box. The ball floated over, the keeper grabbed it – nightmare! momentarily it popped loose – before he snatched it away from the flying head of an Inter centre-back. Lee headed into space. The keeper saw him and bowled the ball ahead of him. The break was on. Lee looked up and saw that Carlos had gone wide, followed by the full-back. Lee ran up the pitch until the full-back realised he would have to commit himself to a challenge. The defender drawn, Lee slipped the ball into Carlos's path. By this time another Inter defender had caught up with play. Carlos halted his run, pulled the ball back and looked for support. Lee momentarily dropped off the defender – as the Inter clogger moved backwards to provide cover, Lee moved in front of him and Carlos delivered the ball to his feet. Lee knew the defender would not be able to catch him; all he had to do was to slot it past the goalkeeper. He made up his mind to go for the far post. He drew his leg back and shot – lifting the ball delicately. It drifted past the desperate keeper, who flapped a hand and made contact with the ball which slowed and seemed to be drifting beyond the post. The keeper got up and pursued it, but wasn't quick enough to stop it. The ball crossed the line. Lee ran towards the crowd. He would always remember screaming at them, red-faced. He could never recall exactly what he said, but it was something like 'There you go! That's what you wanted! That's what you fucking wanted!'

Inter kicked off again but the task was beyond them. Napoli put the entire team behind the ball and spoiled. There was little Inter could do to break Napoli down, even playing, as they were, a man short but with now only two traitors in their midst.

The whistle went and the crowd erupted. Lee went and consoled some of the Inter players, who were sat on the turf, shattered and distraught. Their fans tried to give them a lift, by singing and waving their flags, proud in defeat. He peeled down his socks and loosened his shin pads. It struck Lee how hot it was inside the ground, how his shirt clung to his back and his hair stuck to his forehead. You think of your lungs when you're playing, and you think of your legs

– your precious legs with those fragile, complex joints – but you don't necessarily remember what's going on on the surface until you jump for a ball and the salt from someone else's brow stings your eye.

Lee looked over and saw Antonio consoling a couple of the Inter players, pretending to be the good pro, the anger gone from his body. He was the only player wearing a tracksuit following his sending off. Giuseppe, who had made a point of speaking to every Inter player, collected the team together for an end-of-season farewell to the fans. No one had left the stadium yet, and Napoli paraded around saluting their lifeblood, thankful it was all over, humbled by the way that they could touch people's lives. Secretly, in the knowledge that he would never be back in this place with these people, Lee felt a cheapness, a sense that there would always be a void inside him that needed to be filled. As the chemical flow in his body began to cease he felt blank. He could never believe how alone you can feel on a football field with thousands of people around you.

There was so much noise as they did their lap of honour that it was difficult to distinguish any pattern to the singing and chanting. But then, like it was coming from far away, as if it had been travelling across miles of ocean, growing in strength from its own resolve, confident in its own existence, the players began to hear a unified, definite roar. And all they could hear was Lee's name pealing round the stadium, two syllables of beefy English notoriety. And all he could think about as he looked into their faces as they brandished their flags and scarves in recognition, was that he had given them perhaps more than he'd given anyone before: ninety minutes of honesty, ninety minutes of passion, ninety minutes of *him*. Maybe they even knew it.

In the grand scheme of things he didn't think that was too bad.

Chapter Twelve

Colin waited for a moment before plucking a strip of chewing gum from a packet, unwrapping it, winding down the window and liberating it on to Euston Road. He chewed for a while.

'So you didn't throw the game?'

'No.'

'Despite the money.'

'Have you been listening?' Lee asked. Colin had an annoying habit of drifting off while people were telling him things and re-emerging at a given moment to offer a totally irrelevant remark. On this occasion Lee imagined that he might make a special effort; after all Lee had been talking about Colin's favourite thing: money.

'I told you Colin,' said Lee. 'I took the fucking money.'

'You took the money.'

'I took the money.'

'And you didn't throw the game.'

'I didn't throw the game.'

'But you took the money.' He said this flatly as if trying to work out, in his own mind, what the sequence of events had been.

Colin chewed rapidly, his lips slightly parted, before blowing a hole in the gum. 'Why are you telling me this?' he asked.

'Because I thought you might be interested,' Lee said. 'Because I wanted to tell somebody.' He swerved to avoid two icy teenage Chinese gangsters superpimping across the road. They glared at the Range Rover before breaking into smiles of recognition on identifying the driver.

'You're my brother,' Lee said.

'That's right,' said Colin. 'And if you can't tell your brother, who can you tell?'

Lee didn't answer the question – it was clear that it was rhetorical – although later he wished that he'd said something notable.

'A voice comes to me every so often, Colin,' he said. Colin swivelled in his seat to look at Lee, much as Antonio had done eighteen months before. Lee half expected Colin to try and wrestle the controls from him, as if rescuing a plunging jet plane.

'What are you talking about, Lee?' he said, as if patronising a very small, very stupid child.

'A voice on the phone.'

'Lee – this may sound a little odd – but have you gone completely fucking insane?'

'No,' said Lee quickly trying to express the import of what he was saying. 'No I haven't.' He thought then that maybe he had sounded a little overdramatic. 'Not that anyone, really, would notice. More than normal, I mean.'

'This is no joking matter, Lee, think about the bigger picture, your career . . . Think about the implications, think about the papers, think . . . Jesus, Lee, it's the gear and the puff, isn't it? There's been some fucking chemical reaction in your head, some fucking Chernobyl inside your skull and everything's gone fucking haywire. Jesus Christ . . .'

'He rings me every month.'

'Fucking hell, Lee . . .'

'Shut up, Colin,' said Lee firmly. 'Just listen, right. I'm trying to explain to you. It's to do with what I've been telling you. About Italy. About the money. A voice calls every month. Started when I got back from Italy. May last year. At first it was a demand, at first the geezer was heavy, my face was going to be beaten so badly not even my own mother would be able to recognise me . . . all that kind of stuff. Now he just calls up, tells me when to drop the money off.' Lee broke off for a few moments. His mouth felt dry. He licked his lips. 'But I tell you what, Colin, that calm, assured voice, Jesus, it scares the fucking shit out of me. Scares me worse than you can fucking imagine.'

'Jesus, Lee,' said Colin.

'It's the truth, Col.'

'You must be close to paying them off by now,' said Colin. 'It's almost a year and a half, I mean . . .'

'I paid them back the first fucking drop I ever made,' Lee said. 'They had their hundred grand back the first time I gave them anything. I was scared, see. Just wanted it to be over. Then the voice came on the phone again, nice and friendly, said that because of the misunderstanding they felt that it was only fair that we came to some sort of agreement regarding compensation. He's been calling ever since.'

'Mafia?'

'I dunno. S'pose. Maybe. Sounds Italian. Guess they must be the only people who would fix a football match. So every month I leave money for them in one of the lockers in Euston station. Number seven. Cheeky bastards. That's my shirt number.'

'How much?'

'Ten a month.'

'*Ten grand a month*? Ten fucking grand a month? Areyoushaw? Lee, *areyoufuckingshaw*?' Colin seemed upset for the first time since the conversation began. 'What the fuck have they got on you? You didn't throw the match.'

'I took the money, Colin. It took the fucking money. They sent me pictures, they sent me a tape of me and Antonio talking in his car . . . It got public, Colin, I'd be fucking slaughtered. Doesn't matter that I didn't throw the match. I can't prove that, can I? I can't prove to people that if I made a shit pass it was an accident and if I made a good one it was the best possible one I could have made.'

'Ten grand, Lee. Ten fucking grand a month, I mean, imagine what you could do with that, Lee, just imagine . . .'

'I'm sure Michelle could imagine.'

'She know?' asked Colin. There was a sly look about him. Lee took it to mean that he was intrigued by the lunacy of his position.

''Course not,' Lee said. 'You think I'm stupid?'

'Tell you what we do, Lee,' said Colin thoughtfully. 'This month we deliver the money, good as gold, then, when they come to pick it up, we ambush them and beat the living shit out of them. I could do that, Lee. I learnt that in the army. You can't let people take advantage of you, Lee. It just ain't on.'

'So we beat the shit out of some geezer who's been sent to pick up the cash. Where does that get us? Fuck's sake, Colin, that would only make them worse. Besides, I waited once, just to take a butcher's at them. Nobody showed. I reckon they're watching. I reckon they know more about me than I'd care to know.' Lee reached over and scratched behind his neck, something he did when he was nervous. This made him even more self-conscious.

'You've gone paranoid,' said Colin. 'You've lost it.' Lee couldn't tell whether he was joking, or whether he was serious. 'Remember that headline, what was it . . . ? "Vindaloony Lee's Booze And Curry Binge". That was it. Well, they were right. You've got to start doing something about sorting yourself out, Lee. It's all getting too much for you. I mean, I like a drink as much as the next man, but in your position you should think carefully about what you're putting into your body. Especially all that fucking charlie, I mean . . .'

'And who do I usually go drinking with, Colin? Who's always scored a tasty bit of gear. I can't fucking listen to you sitting there lecturing me, making out you're cleaner than a cat's arse . . .'

'Oh, stop your whinging, Lee. You're a fucking adult. Don't try and make out that it's your nasty big brother who's turned you into some kind of crazed drug fiend. You'd have been a fucking druggie with or without me. It's how *you* fucking deal with it that counts.' Colin assumed a child's voice and started mocking Lee. 'Oh, Mum, it was all Colin's fault. I was just playing quietly and he came along and smashed up my toys.' He changed back to his normal voice. 'You were a snide little bastard, Lee, always getting me into trouble. Fuck's sake, all the fucking things I did for you, all the times I stuck up for you at school, dug you out of trouble . . .'

'Yeah, like the time you gave my name to the police when you got nicked for arson . . .'

'I weren't thinking clearly . . .'

'The time you and your mates legged it when I was getting a kicking from Holly Park . . .'

'It weren't that bad . . .'

'The way that you and dad would never let me win at anything. The way you'd both pat me on the head, or hold me down on the fucking ground 'til I was spitting grass, the way the two of you would go off and leave me when we were out places, as a kind of joke . . . Dad spoilt you, Colin. He spoilt you fucking rotten. I remember the day you were put away and the whatsitcalled at the juvenile court said you were "a nasty piece of work". I remember dad crying. I remember he didn't speak for weeks. It was the same when you went in the army. You'd have thought you'd fucking died. He didn't speak to me for weeks.'

'He's my dad. What do you expect him to do, throw a fucking party?' said Colin exasperated. 'You're rewriting history Lee, you're only thinking of yourself, same as fucking usual.'

'He never treated us the same, Colin, and you fucking revelled in it. You never once tried to get him to show an interest in what I was doing. Remember how he used to come and watch you swimming? Would take you to all the galas and that? Remember? I was playing fucking county football and he was moaning about giving me the bus fare. If Mr Holland from school hadn't been willing to drive me around then I would never had made it as a pro. 'Course he comes to see me play now. It's good for him, ain't it? Makes him feel like the big man. "My Lee plays for England."'

'He appreciates what you give him.'

'I shouldn't have to buy him a fucking house for him to appreciate me,' shouted Lee, his voice deadened by the interior of the car.

'You didn't,' said Colin bitterly.

'I'm his son. I could afford to buy him ten houses. Twenty houses if I wanted. It ain't about that, Colin, and if you don't understand you're as bad as him.'

'You have got to be the most fucking self-pitying little fuck I have ever met,' said Colin. 'Everything comes back to you, doesn't it? What about all the shit mum and dad went through? What about me growing up in the shadow of a kid who loved having his arse kissed, who fucking lapped it up? You never knew what it was like to be normal, Lee, and – most of all – you've never known what it's like to be humble.'

Lee stopped the car.

'Get out now. Please,' he ordered Colin. 'This is doing my fucking head in.' He reached into his pocket. Peeled Colin off a big one.

Colin gave Lee a puzzled, threadbare look. Lee held his brother's gaze and thought, this is where fame's hit-and-get has landed you, throwing your own brother on to the street.

'Get a cab,' Lee said to him. 'I'm sorry.'

It might have made a difference to the way that everything turned out, kicking Colin out of the car like that, but Lee never regretted it. He didn't do it from spite or anger, out of hugger-mugger hubris, he did it because he didn't want Colin in his presence any longer; he didn't want a living reminder of his jaundiced past sitting there picking holes in his mind, gnawing at his juiced-out top-of-the-range present. Not in Lee's car he didn't. In some ways it had nothing to do with his Colin – he loved his brother, would do anything for him. but Lee didn't want to argue, couldn't face the conflict, would rather live with confusion than battle to resolution. He had unloaded what he had needed to and he felt both better and worse for it.

Lee didn't see Colin for a few days after that and it made him feel bad. First couple of times he called there was no answer. Then, third time, Colin's pal picked up the phone. Lee heard his voice change as soon as he realised who it was – he was being more welcoming than he might have been with any old punter on the phone. The Golden Glow of celebrity had given him a sunshine smile. He said Colin had gone away for a few days and, no, he didn't know where and, yes, he would tell him that Lee had called and maybe they could go out for that drink they'd been planning to have for at least a year now.

Maybe.

Lee knew that you had to keep an eye on those ex-army cunts. Always working an angle, whether it's trying to get a drink out of you or sizing you up for some grotesque humiliation, they were a feral lot, always on the make, always on the take.

Left to his own devices Lee settled into something of a normal pattern for about ten days. He missed his brother – wanted to apologise if he'd said anything painful, just wanted for them to go out for a big drink. Michelle and Brenda were in Florida, so he was home alone, rattling about the house on his lonesome. He turned up to training on time, played with a kind of lightness that he rarely found, even 'megged a couple of people. The gaffer told him to keep it all under wraps until Saturday, not to peak too early. Lee joked that he was feeling lucky that he was even peaking at all.

He looked back at Lee with a wry smile.

Chapter Thirteen

With Colin and Michelle out of the way Lee spent time on his own. The longer he was solitary the more he found himself drifting inwards, looking solely to himself for company, for his own counsel. This was not an unusual pattern for Lee. And when he found himself in such a state, his sense of isolation grew rapidly and people began to scare him. They scared him most when he saw them laughing at him, at what he was doing. He could see it in their faces – nervous, twitchy, trying too hard to agree that, yes, he was the funniest, most entertaining person they had ever met and that, by God, this was the most fun anyone had ever had anytime, any place in the history of where it's at.

That just made Lee worse. Made him head off to the bathroom more often, yell for the waiter to get him another pint double-quick-fast before he died of thirst.

It was lunchtime. Training over, Lee aquaplaned through the bristling December rain round the M25 to a silver-service-and-eighteen-holes country club hosting a charity golf tournament for leukaemia kids at which he was guest of honour. Lou had liked the sound of it; a consignment of other celebs had been engaged which meant plenty of snappers – the daily dandruff crowd, the clan of cable creeps. Lou had seemed a little distant of late. Lee had told him about the voice, the extortion, and could sense Lou panicking a little, told him not to do anything stupid, play along until they could come up with a plan. For the moment Lee's mind was elsewhere – wasn't he, after all, booked to tee off the first ball of the tournament, along with Jessica, the newest, hottest, Page Three stunna currently cashing in the quiet life as a restaurant manager in Southampton on the back (or front) of her 34DD 'megawhoppers'? To Lee, her lungs sounded like a burger meal.

The Range Rover was whipped away from him by some teenager with a skin condition. 'Don't touch the drugs in the glove compartment,' Lee said, giving him a wink. Double bluff. The kid thought Lee was joking. But he wasn't. It was locked anyway. Just a precaution. The kid laughed, pleased to have had some interaction with Lee Sweeney, something to tell his mates in the pub, brighten up a dull evening.

And Lee was keen to brighten up what might prove to be a dull lunch. For the past two weeks he hadn't put a foot out of line in training. With Michelle still sunning herself he was still caning the good stuff, but he was making sure the rest of his life wasn't turning to shit, didn't want the spiral to run out of control any faster than it was already. If he could only hold on tight enough, his thinking went, then it didn't matter how quickly he was rotating.

They had won their last three games on the spin. Lee hadn't scored, but had been held responsible for the team's renewed interest in the Premiership. The gaffer was still on Lee's case, but in a cooler prove-me-wrong kind of way. Lee was keeping him quiet, and he wanted it to stay that way. There was an England game coming up. It was only some poxy friendly, but already most of the papers were saying that he should be forgiven his misconduct and poor performances and get the nod. The only rider was that they reckoned no one else could do the job properly anyway.

Lee wasn't going to argue with that.

He entered the dining-room geared up for a big one. His favourite scenario: lots of food, drink and – most importantly – lots of people too pissed up and too freaked by his fame not to be part of it. In truth, the famous ones were the only ones Lee could really relax with, the only ones he didn't have to play court jester for. But the normal punters were more game, high on fame juice, pedalling hard with the high and mighty, floating along in the belief that life would be grand if they spent every workaday afternoon with football's Mr Barmy.

Flash. Flash. Flash. Lee with every grinning, bow-tied Tom, Dick and Barry. Lee with their glammed-up, glad-ragged wives, hair so teased and tortured it was crying out to be taken somewhere public and be executed. Lee didn't mind the posing, the clammy, excitable paws thrust in his and the boy-did-we-have-a-good-time grins that would adorn work stations, bar rooms and cork kitchen reminder blocks – be pressed under fridge magnets like butterflies pinned to a board – from Staines to South Shields. It didn't bother him. It was like being at your own wedding seven days a week – everyone wanted to touch him, make him momentarily theirs, to reach him with a pithy knockout comment that would stop him in his station-to-station tracks. Lee's mouth just went rigid after the first thirty or forty freeze-frame-pop-whirr-and-flashes; he tired of hiking his lips above his gums, exposing their sappy ivory whiteness once more and once more again.

After half an hour of this he sensed something different. The energy in the room suddenly changed. People started to look elsewhere – he was no longer the single pole of their attention. Grimacing through the bottom of his pint glass he witnessed her entrance. She arrived tanned and candied and lovely with the room fluttering and fussing in her wake. She sat down next to him and extended her hand.

'I'm so sorry I'm late,' she said apologetically. 'I was doing this promotion thing and, well, you know how it is.' Her voice was deeper and softer than he'd thought and she rounded her vowels out and ended her words properly, which he hadn't anticipated. (Lee had always imagined that if you squeezed her hard enough she'd squeak, like some plastic children's toy.) He'd expected the 'Sinner from Southampton' to be harsher edged, for her to have a sour, spoilt ugliness; but she was subdued and graceful in a slight and appealing way. She was wearing a black cashmere cardigan over a knee-length, body-skimming, A-line white silk dress. It came right up to her sternum. There was no cleavage.

That interested Lee.

He smiled. It didn't come out loony or money-maker like it normally did. It came out, well, *nice.*

On the other side of Jessica the old charity duffer who'd been blathering on to the woman next to him – some shoulder-padded triple-divorce survivor with plucked eyebrows, maroon hair and a saucy grin – introduced himself. Jessica broke off from rummaging in her handbag, dragging packets of tissues, lighters, gum and make-up on to the table, to shake his hand graciously. 'Pleased to meet you,' she said. 'I read the literature you sent over. You're doing great work with the children.'

Eventually she hit paydirt and fired up a Silk Cut. She crossed her legs, exhaled smoke and conjured a relieved smile.

'So what have I missed?' she asked.

'Well, other than Fergie dancing on a table with her knickers on her head and Ronan from Boyzone winning the gurning competition, not a lot,' Lee said.

She laughed. 'Looks like they're stuck with us,' she said mock dramatically raising her hands in a what's-the-world-coming-to gesture. As if to prove her point a couple of snappers appeared, like two alligators surfacing stealthily from a swamp, ready to chow down on a choice couple of morsels.

'Lee! Jessica! Come on now. Just a couple.'

Like good pros they cosied up, grinning like a couple of gormless kids having a school photo done under a silver umbrella. It was a strange sensation, being with someone else who instinctively knew the rules of engagement, was wise to what was required of them.

'Putcherarmarahnder, Lee!' shouted one of the snappers. 'Giveeranug, g'won!' Lee reached his hand round and gently rested it on Jessica's honey-coloured shoulder. Skin on skin. She was cool to the touch.

'You're that footballer,' she said, joking, still staring at the scrabbling snappers now frenzied at the prospect of a full-page showbiz splash.

'Which footballer?' Lee said continuing the joke. 'That footballer' was probably right, he thought. 'That' footballer probably summed him up.

'"Loony Lee's Cup Of Shame",' she said. 'You know: "That Footballer". Me on the third page – I hate the phrase "Page Three", but don't even get me started on that – and maybe a centre spread or a promotion, and you gallivanting about on the back page like a randy dog in need of castration.'

Lee had never thought about it like that.

'We're like a couple of bookends, you and me,' she said, gesturing a waiter over and ordering a Diet Coke. 'I really fancy a glass of wine,' she explained, 'but I've got to drive later on. Can I get you something?'

'Mineral water, please.' Strange. Lee didn't know where that had come from. It was like his mouth had become separated from his mind, like a headland cut off by a freak tide.

'Don't be soft. Diet Coke and a pint of lager please,' she said to the waiter. 'Unless you've gone on the wagon. I daresay that was an attempt to prove that you're not pissed.'

'But I am pissed,' Lee jokingly protested. 'I've been here for an hour. And because I'm pissed I've not got any interest in proving to you that I'm not pissed. If I wasn't pissed I'd be desperate to prove it.'

'Point taken,' she said. A seafood platter arrived for them both. Jessica stubbed her fag and seized a prawn.

'I thought you girls weren't supposed to eat much,' Lee said.

While chewing she cocked her head and offered him a look somewhere between a rebuke and annoyance. 'I thought *you boys* weren't supposed to drink much,' she said snagging another.

Lee laughed. There was a confidence about her, a shrewdness that he liked. She made him feel stronger, like their sparring was giving both of them sustenance in a world of bullshitters and sycophants (and just plain sickos). Lee felt the itch of chemistry.

He snatched another glance at her. Her hair was buttery blonde with a fringe. It was straight, and she folded it behind two cute little ears. Her candid eyes were hazel and her eyebrows were teased into a pair of question marks above her exclamation mark of a button nose. The top of her face was quite broad with high, fine cheekbones – but it tapered down to a sharp chin. Lee wasn't sure, but he thought she was only a little over five-foot two, her height impossible to distinguish on the page as she was usually concertinaed between a story about a lottery winner's love life ('Lotto Love Rat's Three In A Bed Romp') and freak rain ('Yes, It's Wimbledon Again, Folks!') awkwardly holding a beach ball, or riding crop, or newspaper, depending on the season: a living barometer of the nation's mood, a desire frozen on four-colour newsprint.

'So you've got to tell me the truth,' Lee said turning his shoulders towards Jessica. 'That story in the papers last week. How true was it?' He was referring to a story in which two male drivers on Marylebone High Street had reportedly collided while ogling Jessica. The story then detailed how she'd felt so sorry for the men that she'd signed their dented bumpers in lipstick. The paper had carried a picture of two men – one a balding West Indian with a big round hamster's face, and a white man in a suit with glasses in his late twenties – grinning sheepishly while holding up their bumpers, like two fishermen with a couple of prize pike.

'Well, if you want to know that,' she said leaning towards Lee conspiratorially, 'you'll have to tell me if the one about you was true.'

'Which one?' Lee asked.

'Don't be silly, Lee. You know.' She lit another cigarette and regarded him with the look of someone who'd just hung a picture on their living-room and wasn't quite sure it was in the right place.

Lee realised what she was alluding to. 'Me and Michelle you mean?' She nodded. 'Guilty as charged,' Lee said, and then regretted it immediately. It sounded too flippant, too hard. Bar-room bollocks. 'Well, we've decided to spend some time apart.' The story had been pure conjecture on the part of the paper, but was de facto truth; nevertheless, Lee couldn't believe he was being so brazen.

'So you can clean up your act,' she said. There was no hint of a question in her voice. It was plain, flat, sarcastic.

No one normally talked to Lee like that. No one just came out and directed words at him in that way. Usually he watched them scrambling to avoid the issue, fording streams, crossing valleys, reaching peaks, just to avoid crossing into the marginal area of his tabloid degeneration. It was not a border he usually guarded with any great exertion; people just generally chose to shy away from it.

'So I can clean up my act.' Lee grinned at his own crassness, feeling stupid.

'That's good.' Jessica nodded at a waiter who removed her plate. 'And *are* you going to clean up your act?' She said this in a short, clipped way and with the practised assurance of someone used to guiding conversations.

'I'd like to think so,' Lee answered.

'What a clever answer,' she said patronisingly. 'Full of intention, but without commitment.'

She'd got him there. Full of intention, but without commitment. A priest had said that to Lee once when he'd made some lame excuse about never coming to Mass.

'So tell me about yours,' Lee asked. 'I've shown you mine . . .'

'Not quite a huge, minging lie,' she said. 'But certainly a merging of fact and fiction.'

'So it didn't happen?'

'Not as you read it. What happened was that I'd just come out of this radio station and a few people were having a bit of a gawp. These two chumps were clearly not concentrating on the road because they were getting an eyeful of me and, before you know it, SMASH. Not a major one, just one tail-ending the other. No harm done. I jump in a cab and later this photographer from the *Sun* picks up both bumpers and tells the guys that he'll get me to sign them. So he speaks to Brendan, my agent, who *loves* the idea, he gets hold of some lipstick, puts the two guys together with the bumpers, gets the shot – hey presto, modern myth.'

'Makes you believe in Santa Claus and the tooth fairy, doesn't it?' Lee said laughing.

'Don't shatter all my illusions,' she said stubbing her cigarette. 'I've got to have something to believe in. Anyway, I wouldn't have signed the bumpers myself. Why waste expensive lipstick on a couple of saps?'

'You've just got to believe in yourself,' Lee said, knowing that this was an area in which he could find himself quickly marooned under questioning.

'Believe me, I know about that.' She was serious-playful again. Sexy. 'I didn't grow up dreaming of baring my knockers for the nation. You know what I'm talking about. I'm just giving myself a chance, just making the most of what I've got, just turning my body into money. Which is exactly what you do.'

Turning his body into money. Jesus, that was a frightening concept. Then it occurred to Lee. The mathematics of her body and his body, the celebrity maths of it all. Jessica plus Lee equals what? A multi-million-pound topless footballer? A booze-addled but brainy beauty? The possibilities were mouth-watering and endless.

'So how long have you got?' Lee asked, swept along by her candidness. She looked at her newly delivered plate of lamb – Lee could feel it gumming his teeth already – while

157

she considered his question and waited for a perspiring short man – one of London's swelling group of bottom-of-the-pile Eastern Europeans – to serve up buttered potatoes and collapsed veg.

'One, maybe two more years like this,' she said. 'Until I get a TV deal. I've had offers from shitty cable and satellite stations, but I want to hold out for terrestrial. Better money. Better shows. And I don't want to do some stupid game show or celebrity panel game. I'd like something like a travel show, or food programme. Maybe interiors. That's where it's happening now.'

'What about sport?'

'I'm all right on football, tennis, boxing, but I don't know anything about rugby, or cricket, or bloody golf. Oh, blimey, maybe I shouldn't say that here.'

'That's all right, most of them are too deaf to hear you and I'm in the same boat,' he said. 'Don't know a fucking thing about rugby or cricket. Doesn't matter though. No one cares about anything but football any more. Country's gone mad for football. It's different to before I went to Italy. It's all anyone talks about. Boring really. I hate talking about football. Don't like even watching it any more. There's too much of it on, for a start . . . Taken over, hasn't it? There's no fucking escape.' Lee said the last sentence like someone in a plane heading into the side of a mountain.

She laughed. 'We're all doomed!' she said, like Frazer from *Dad's Army*. It was beginning to flow, it was beginning to feel right. Lee ordered another lager. Jessica asked for a spritzer. Maybe she was warming up.

'So aren't we supposed to have that conversation now when we brag about how many Jacuzzis we've got in each bedroom and how we just don't know which one of our cars to drive?' she asked.

'My problem,' Lee replied with a straight face, 'is that I never know which one of my powerboats to water-ski behind.'

'My problem,' she said picking up the theme, 'is that I don't know which of my lakes on my country estate to water-ski on.'

They laughed and she turned away for a moment, distracted by the attentions of the charity duffer who placed his fingers lightly on her forearm, the way that old men do to pretty young girls who are young enough to be their daughters, because they know they haven't got a chance.

And Lee began to think that this woman was more like him than he cared to imagine, understood his world more than he understood it himself, had laid a finger on something close to his essence, a place far beyond his own reach, the worm at the bottom of the bottle.

Perhaps it was because they shared a world of contracts (co-signatories, witnesses, et cetera), of lives recorded on paper and celluloid – that made them both aware that at the end of the evening the theatre lights go out and everyone goes home. But it was more than this. The elements that stoked their fame and wealth could turn on both of them in an instant; they constantly teetered on the brink of a monstering: the pieces of paper they had signed offered them money and protection of a kind, but it was a protection that would, inevitably, expire.

A couple of photographers came over and asked Jessica to have her picture taken with a minted golf pro whose pearly teeth glowed from across the room. She smiled and told them that she might come over later, after she had finished eating lunch. The snappers ran off like two little boys who had been told that they might be bought an ice cream later.

'I don't feel like being her today,' she sighed wearily under her breath. 'Do you ever get that?'

'Wishing I was someone else, somewhere else?' Lee asked knowing exactly what she meant. 'All the time. Never when I'm playing, but other than that it comes and goes, but it's always there in the background.'

'You know what I wish, Lee? I really wish that I could leave the house just once without having applied my foundation, done my mascara and lipstick. I wish I could throw on an old pair of jeans and some mangy old trainers and go to the market and buy my fruit and veg. I wish I could cross the road without some bloke beeping his horn at me – and that's even before he finds out who I am.'

'You know what I wish?' Lee countered. 'I wish I could take a piss without someone asking me for an autograph. That's where men talk, you see, while they're having a slash, and every bloke who starts having a chinwag with me ends up drying off his hands and magicking a pen from somewhere and asking me to stand there with hot toilet air being recycled through the dryer and write out three versions to his wife, kids and best mate.'

'You should see what they ask *me* to sign,' said Jessica firing up another Silk Cut. 'I always say to them that I'd be lucky to fit all seven letters of my name on.'

Some idiot with a red jacket and a redder face got up in the corner and made some verbose announcements about the programme for the afternoon and evening. Lee looked over to the other side of the room at a rain-smeared window and felt reassured that there would be no golf played that day. Last fucking thing he wanted. He'd tee off the ball for the kiddies and then settle down for the duration. The man continued droning. Jessica was listening politely. Lee leant over to her.

'You know, I hope this doesn't sound funny, but I just want to say it before I get too pissed, but just sitting here talking to you I've really enjoyed myself and I just wanted to let you know that, I've had a really good time . . .'

'Give it a rest, Lee,' said Jessica firmly, but not unkindly. 'You're beginning to sound pissed already. Anyway, once we've suffered dessert and coffee we've got to start off this golf match, or game, or whatever you call it. I'm looking forward to that about as much as I am to getting my next bikini wax.'

'I had that once,' Lee said. 'Well not wax exactly, I was shaved. Hernia.'

'You tell the best stories, Lee,' she said drily.

So Lee did his duty: he went and met the cancer kids who scrutinised him; mild bemusement mixed with understated excitement was etched across their smooth faces. Lee tried to have a little chat with each of them. He didn't know whether they were shy or he was pissed and they didn't understand what he was saying. They just grinned blankly at him like they were embarrassed. He couldn't tell whether it was him or whether they were always like this.

The golf club captain – blue blazer with brass buttons, sensible grey slacks, 'Roger Strong, bloody nice to meet you' – led Jessica and Lee out to the first tee and got them lined up for the scrabbling pack. Strong, who, Lee noticed, had a bulbous lump on the end of his nose, started getting distressed by the antics of the photographers who were edging the cancer kids out of the picture in an attempt to isolate Lee and Jessica in the frame.

'Come on now, guys,' said Roger in a deep, military baritone. 'Let's not get silly. Play the game.'

Then Jessica turned and beckoned the kids closer. She picked up a small one and got the others round in front of her and Lee. The snappers sighed and whined, but none of them had the heart or bottle to try and do anything about the situation.

'What's your name?' Jessica asked the little one she was holding.

'Lauren,' answered the child.

'I've got a little girl just like you at home,' said Jessica. 'I hope that you're not as naughty as her.'

'What's her name?' asked the kid.

'Annette,' said Jessica. 'Her name's Annette.'

And with that, in a supernova of flashes under the grey Hertfordshire sky, Jessica placed her Goodyear lips against the little girl's head and kissed her.

That's professional for you, thought Lee.

*

161

'And that's the reason that some animals eat their young,' said Phil Crescendo. He sat next to Lee on a velour sofa in the bar area, sheltered from the thumping and wailing of the disco in the dining area. Phil had a large dark stain growing on the crotch of his trousers that caused him to keep looking down and grinning incredulously, like he couldn't believe the latest thing that had happened in his barmy, madcap world.

The stain was the result of his five-year old daughter having shoved away a glass of water that Phil had offered her. She was lying next to him in a bundle of tangled hair and crumpled tartan dress, drifting in and out of an uncomfortable, disturbed sleep. Her face, even when she drifted off for a few moments, was a resentful grimace.

'She looks well tired,' Lee said.

'Never should have brought her,' said Phil as if having learnt a lesson the hard way.

'Ain't she got school tomorrow?' Lee asked.

'Wouldn't have missed it for the world,' said Phil tapping his stogy on the edge of a large glass ashtray shaped like a golf bunker.

Phil and Lee had met about half an hour before when Phil had introduced himself as some kind of aggregates baron. After a couple of minutes' conversation it was clear that he considered himself to be a bit of a skirt junkie.

Lee sat for too long picking up some of what he was saying. Lee wondered if he might be a gregarious introvert: someone who liked the company of others but was quite happy to sit on the sidelines and listen to people like Phil crapping on about their exploits and achievements. Someone who, above all, is content just to listen, to pretend that he's not even really there. That was one of the things booze did for him. It helped him to sit with people like Phil without wanting to get away, to enjoy the company, to pass time without feeling agitated or fretful.

But now Lee was getting bored, other matters were beginning to preoccupy him, so he excused himself from

Phil – who said he was just off himself – and headed out to the front desk.

The receptionist was a middle-aged woman in a cream shoulder-padded blazer. She smiled and asked if she could help. Lee liked her attitude. He knew that he only had to ask and she actually *would* help. She looked like she had a couple of grown-up kids who'd left home and, as she liked to keep herself busy, she'd got herself a job at the hotel working the unpopular evening shift four days a week. She left a meal in the microwave for her hubbie who did voluntary work and had an allotment. She stashed away the money for holidays and occasional treats, like going down to London to catch a show with her daughter who was a high-flying buyer for the Burton group.

'I'd like a room for tonight, please,' Lee asked.

'Right, let's have a look,' said the woman. She put her glasses on and punched a couple of buttons on a computer terminal. 'Standard, superior or suite, sir?' she asked.

'Suite,' Lee replied.

Her eyes scanned the screen. 'You're in luck. We've got just one suite remaining.' She took his details and a credit-card imprint and asked if he had any bags. He told her that he was travelling light. She gave him the key and pointed the way, which was through an outdoor walkway and into another, newer building. Lee walked towards the room, trying to memorise the route, and then turned back, stalking through the lonely, public areas with their man-made carpets capable of repelling any liquid or solid flung at it, and headed back on to the dance floor, which was a shambles of gyrating limbs and torsos all tracking their own private rhythms.

He looked for Jessica. There she was tossing her hair around and laughing while she danced with a lanky bloke with a tan. He was younger than her, smiling a nauseating zipped-up smile, the sides of his mouth virtually touching his eyes as his mouth formed an enormous letter U. Lee pushed his way through the dancers earning himself an occasional 'Watch it . . .', 'No need . . .', 'Relax, you . . .' and approached her. With her eyes closed, lost in music, with what he imagined to be her fuck face on, she couldn't see him, so he tapped her on the arm and grinned. She looked a little startled. Lee said something into her ear.

'What?' she replied.

Lee repeated it. Jessica shook her head like she didn't understand what was going on. She was half smiling, friendly and willing to go along with the joke. Lee put his hand around her wrist and led her off the dance floor towards the dining area where men sat smoking cigars and large red wine stains ringed the catering grade white table cloths. Some of the centrepiece floral arrangements had been nicked.

She grinned up at him and pushed her hair behind her ears. She seemed impatient to get back to the dancing.

'What, Lee?' she asked.

'I've got to ask you something,' he said.

'What?'

Lee waited for a moment, rolling his eyes at his own stupidity, at his willingness to plunge head first into traps that he could foresee a mile away.

'Come on, Lee. Say it then.'

'Are they real?' Lee asked.

'What, Lee?'

'Are they real?'

She put her hands on her hips and turned her head momentarily towards the dance floor.

'Are *you* for fucking real?' she asked, staring him in the eye the way that only centre-backs did. 'Are you for real, Lee, that's the question.'

Lee sniggered, reached to touch her neck. She stepped back and raised her hand in the way a parent does when ticking off a kid.

'Don't be a clown, I've booked us a room,' he said, confused by how wrong this was going compared to how he'd imagined it while listening to Phil and-I'll-tell-you-another-thing-about-concrete Crescendo.

She could tell that he wasn't joking. She shook her head slowly.

'It's a shame, Lee. It's a fucking shame. It really is.'

Lee hadn't meant it to happen that way. He had wanted to reach her, he had wanted to say something that would really touch her, something that would make her his.

Lee just didn't know any longer. The bloke Jessica had been dancing with came over to see what was happening. Lee grabbed his arm.

'So tell me,' he said. 'You should know. Who's the patron saint of lost fucking causes?'

The man pulled away shaking his head; the two of them seemed to drift away from Lee on to the dance floor. And as they disappeared, Lee realised that in his heart he really didn't care. Really. He didn't need a lover. He just needed another drink.

Chapter Fourteen

Throughout his career, one of the ways in which Lee had managed to get through the grind of the working day was to view training as a social event. Things were mildly better for the club in the league, but Brandwood was still worried about discipline, was convinced that, at any moment, everything could turn to shite. The players never really discussed it but it was widely assumed that, as the newspapers reported, the Twomacs were on the luckless Brandwood's case.

After a lustreless midweek game in Liverpool the team was told, on arrival back at Luton Airport, that they would be expected at training the next morning. The players duly limped in, black-eyed and sleep-deprived, to be read the riot act. Lee could tell that most of the lads were finding it hard to stomach, felt like they were being treated like kids. But he could tell by the set of Brandwood's jaw that – really and truly – he didn't give a damn. He was just passing on the kick up the arse from upstairs. Brandwood stood there like Mussolini surrounded by his trusted lieutenants as he read out a list of offences that would incur fines.

1. Using a mobile on the team coach. £400.
2. Being late for training. £1000. Second offence, one week's wages.
3. Being seen out 48 hours before a game. One week's wages.
4. Missing a reserve team game, if picked. One week's wages.
5. Being late out for training. £400.

And worst of all:

    6. Putting on weight. One week's wages.

In his mind Lee sifted the gaffer's words before he sent him off to the fat farm the last time: 'Lee, unless you stop drinking you ain't going to have a stomach, you're going to have a fucking growbag.' One week's wages for putting on weight? He must have been out of his tiny mind. The players sensed that Brandwood was in no mood for any dissent so, after some stretching and a spot of five-a-side, they traipsed back to the dressing-room muttering to each other while the management team burnt holes in their backs with suspicious eyes.

'Treat us like kids and we'll fucking behave like them,' said Beno, one of the senior pros, to the rest of the dressing-room while bending down to untie his laces. He was a straightforward kind of bloke from somewhere up north – Lee never knew details like that. If you went to the boozer with Beno, when he was making a serious point, he would press his fingers on the table as if trying to strike a note on a piano.

Beno continued as he peeled his strip off, his voice echoing in the otherwise quiet room. A couple of the younger players ignored him, wandering into the shower. They didn't want to get involved. They were just happy to be in the squad.

The room was filled with tired, careworn men who just wanted to go home and get some shut-eye. It was the kind of moment when a captain might make a motivational speech. A voice piped up.

'You don't fancy the job, then you know what you can do!' It was Wayne, one of the black players standing stark bollock naked doing his well-thought-of impression of Brandwood. The tension collapsed like a curtain and the players fell about laughing. Wayne, enjoying the audience, continued. One of his favourite schticks was to cross

Brandwood with Bernard Manning.

'Let me tell you about my mother-in-law,' he said. 'My mother-in-law is such a bad cook that, when she's not looking, I give me dinner to the dog. Truth is the dog takes one bite and starts licking his arse to get rid of the taste.'

Everyone laughed. Wayne had a way of diffusing the dressing-room. He was one of those players who behaved like an animal when he was on the pitch – pulling hair, pinching, stamping, threatening defenders, lots of off-the-ball chat and psychology – but underneath he was desperate for approval from his peers. Wayne always played his heart out. If anyone from the opposition took a pop at one of his team-mates then he'd be in their face before they could take a swing. At that time there was a fashion for black players to give themselves nicknames. Because Wayne's surname was Marcos, he called himself 'The Boss'. Wayne 'The Boss' Marcos. Lee thought it sounded good.

'Tell you what though,' said Lee to Wayne, when the dressing-room had relaxed into the usual tomfoolery and banter. 'I went to this restaurant with Chelle couple of months ago in Florida and I could not believe the prices. I looked at the menu and I was "Areyoufuckingshaw?" They had steak on there, right, just steak with vegetables and some sauce – hundred dollars! I called over the waiter and I was "What's going on here mate? Was this a famous cow, or something?"'

Wayne stood up laughing and headed off towards the showers. He was naked, but always wore flip-flops in the shower. Hated the idea of getting verrucas. Highly-strung striker. 'You know what?' he said. 'It don't matter how much it costs I like my meat pink. I need to know it's suffered.'

'You sick bastard,' Lee said. 'There's hospitals for people like you. I tell you about that time . . . ?'

Wayne cut him off. 'Tell me later. Got to take a shower mate. Polish up my manhood.'

'That ain't a knob, mate,' shouted Mike Bates, the goal-keeper known for his taste in dodgy Versace shirts and his blasé attitude, 'that's a big clitoris.'

Wayne kissed his teeth and disappeared into the shower. Some jibes just weren't worth rising to.

'Oi, Wayne? What do you call an Indian lesbian?' shouted Mike. No answer came back. Just the waterfall rush of the steaming showers. 'Minjita!' shouted Mike to much laughing. 'Lee, you get into any trouble over that TV thing?' asked Mike.

'What was that?' asked Jim Baxter. He was the left-back, a smooth Scot and smallest man in the team at five seven. He fancied himself as a bit debonair, spent a lot of money on clothes, fancied a career on TV after he finished playing. He was always a bit aloof, but perked up if he got wind that anyone had been on the box. Lee knew Baxter hated the fact that he was always getting invited back on the box no matter how many times he fucked up.

'Lee was on this late-night thing,' said Mike, 'and the bird asks him if he had anything to say to people out there, so Lee goes "For anyone watching at home I'd like to say – get out of my fucking house!"'

Lee sniggered, recalling the incident. He hadn't really remembered doing it until the next day when Lou phoned to ask him what the fuck had happened – he'd had an irate conversation with a senior producer from the TV station.

'Thank fuck it wasn't this week,' Lee said, 'otherwise I'd have probably got fined a week's wages.' The room echoed with laughter and murmurs of assent.

He took a shower, smothered himself in a cocktail of colognes and potions powerful enough to kill cockroaches, dressed slowly and headed for the door. He thought he was the last one out, but he noticed that Roy Jones, the centre-back, was sitting there alone, a white towel wrapped round his middle. Jones was a lump of a man in his early thirties who just seemed to lumber on despite barely being able to train. His trademark ginger hair was always cut appallingly, like it had been done by a blind man with a knife and fork. His pale, white body was smothered with ropy swirls of orange hair. For a while the boys had called him Orang, as in orang-utan.

'What you doing, mate, trying to grow another shirt?' Lee joked.

'Yeah.' Jones laughed thinly, trying to get into the joke.

'You all right, mate?' Lee asked.

'Not bad, except for this damn knee,' said Roy in his deep musical voice.

'You've been moaning on about that knee for years,' Lee said. 'You always go "one more season, one more season, that's all I want". From what I hear you've been saying that for the last five years.'

'Well, I don't think there's any question of another season, Lee.'

'You seen a specialist?'

''Course. Says there's not much more he can do for me. Says the thing's as fragile as a house of cards in a fucking hurricane. S'pose I'll just have to get used to it.'

'You'll be fine,' Lee said. 'Just take it easy training.' He decided to change the subject. 'You playing golf this afternoon?'

'Do teenage boys like setting fire to things?'

'Cos you'd be better off getting yourself to a barber, do something about that carrot top.'

Jones threw his stinking kit at Lee. 'You're just a fucking gingerist.'

Lee didn't have time to hang about talking to depressed taffs. He had things to do. Business matters to take care of. Well, maybe not strictly *business* matters, more like money matters. For the past three weeks he'd been getting strange telephone calls.

Lee had got used to the regularity of the demands from the Italians. It felt like he could deal with it. On the first of every month, pretty much like clockwork, he'd come home from training and see the red eye blinking on the business line in what an estate agent might call 'the study', where Lee had computer games and a state-of-the-art B & O set-up.

Of course there was also said gear in the living-room as well, but sometimes Chelle wanted to have a little bit of P & Q, wanted to curl up on the sofa with a nice cuppa, spot of Sky Premier Movies and *Cosmo*. You don't want to be disturbed when you're in that frame of mind, do you?

But the monthly message pattern had been broken twice in the last three weeks by the appearance of a new voice. The new voice – pained, nervous – appeared on the machine, spelling everything out clearly, like it was asking Lee a favour. The normal voice was curt, businesslike and talked around the subject, saying something like 'Your friends are waiting in the same place at the same time, this month', or 'We'll be waiting at the usual place at the usual time', always clipped and hurried, no time to hang around.

But the new voice . . . Well, for starters he wanted the drop in a different place, this old abandoned air raid shelter in this little copse on the common, a haunt of drunks and pyromaniac teenagers. No problem, Lee thought, so he'd schlepped all the way out there and dumped the cash. But on the way back his hand slapped against his heart and he had a most God-awful feeling. He'd left the money in the wrong fucking place. If so, some old drunk with his toes poking out of his shoes might crash out there and wake up to find that under his mattress is a plastic bag containing ten grand wrapped in newspaper. Worse, kids might torch the place, stand around pissing themselves with laughter while tiny carbonised flakes of twenty-pound notes are carried skywards by the heat.

Lee had turned the car back and returned to the shelter. The money had gone. It was either a good thing, or a very, very, bad thing, he'd have to wait and find out which. The Italian would doubtless let him know in due course. He waited two days. There was no word. Lee assumed everything had run smoothly; after all, he thought, these were the kind of cunts who only called you when there was a problem, they didn't call up for a chat just to see how you were.

Five days passed and he'd gone for a couple of drinks after training, when he came home and ran up the stairs looking forward to a couple of games of *Abe's Odyssey*. He pressed the button on the machine expecting it to be Lou leaving some non-urgent message about some ad or interview when the voice was there again, painstakingly spelling out what it wanted in this stupid voice. It sounded like whoever it was was trying to do such an elaborate cover-up of his voice that he'd used all his brain power to do just that and was having difficulty thinking out the logistics. It gave Lee yet another place to dump the cash – in the hedge behind a pub car park towards Arkley. This new bloke was beginning to get on Lee's tits.

So he got back after training that day, after he'd run round the houses already that month for voice number two, to discover that the only message on his machine was him again wanting Lee to go back to the air-raid shelter. He said he wanted ten grand again, which was strange in itself because the other voice never, ever varied the amounts. It was just accepted that he'd hand over ten Gs.

Then it got weird. There was a message from the first voice telling Lee that he was to do the same thing that he did every month. There was no mention of the other payments, no suggestion that anything was unusual, he was simply to proceed as usual. He listened to the messages again. Their styles and content were totally different. The new one edgy and unsure of itself, the old one assured to the point of arrogance. He wondered what was going on, he wondered what more was in store for him, he wondered what the hell had washed up on his shore now.

Chapter Fifteen

'Merry Christmas,' said Colin standing at the front door holding two four-packs of Foster's Ice.

Lee hovered uneasily in the doorway. 'Merry Christmas,' he eventually murmured. 'Look, Col, I'm sorry about kicking you out the car. I tried calling, but you weren't around. You know . . .'

'All forgotten,' said Colin. 'You all right, bro?'

'Feeling a bit second-hand as it goes,' said Lee holding the door open for his brother. He was relieved. He wanted things to be right between them. 'Trained this morning.'

'I ain't being a bit previous, am I?' asked Colin, stepping indoors.

'No, no . . .' said Lee. 'Just that I'd sort of forgotten, you know, that you were coming.'

'Forgot, eh?'

They stood in the hallway, Colin staring at a screen print of a dolphin leaping from a sea bathed in a crimson sunset that hung on the wall.

'You like it?' asked Lee. 'Chelle picked it up in Florida.'

'Yeah,' said Colin. 'I told Chelle, already.'

'When?' asked Lee furrowing his brow. Colin started moving down the hallway towards the kitchen. 'We've only had it up two days,' continued Lee.

'On the phone,' said Colin. 'She told me about it yesterday when she and Brenda asked me over for lunch. Beer, Lee?'

'Yeah. Blinding,' said Lee following him towards the kitchen.

The white-tiled room was all steam and meat smoke. Michelle was slamming the basted bird back in the oven when Colin entered. She pulled off her oven gloves and gave him a peck on the cheek.

'Hello love, how are you?' she said. 'Merry Christmas. Shove the beers in the fridge.'

'You want one?' asked Colin.

'I'm all right. I'm on Bacardi and Coke. You want one, Mum?'

Brenda was rinsing some green beans in the sink, her arms brown against the white porcelain. 'I'll stick to the gin, love. Mother's ruin.'

'You were ruined a long time ago,' said Colin. 'We're talking Stonehenge ain't we?'

'Oh, Colin,' said Michelle, laughing.

'You watch it, you,' said Brenda affectionately, brandishing a wooden spoon.

'Come on then,' said Colin. 'Where's the mistletoe, I've been waiting for months for a kiss.'

Lee sat at the breakfast bar sipping his bottle of Foster's Ice. It occurred to him that had he made a joke connecting Brenda to Stonehenge the atmosphere may presently have not been so convivial. He put it down to Michelle and Brenda wanting to play happy families. Making an effort to smooth over the cracks in the family plaster work. Perhaps it was him after all, perhaps he'd clawed his way to a point too remote for his wife and mother-in-law to be able to fetch him.

He shifted silently on his stool; he was in a familiar place, somewhere he couldn't move. Maybe his brother was the key to them being able to play out a coveted life of domestic playfulness. Over the previous weeks Colin had spent a lot of time at the house. Michelle and her mother appeared to enjoy his presence which, accordingly, took the heat off Lee, for which he was grateful. But at the same time it made him feel that Colin knew things about women that he didn't, like Colin was a man with wallop in his shoulders. Lee thought maybe he could watch and learn, employ new wisdom.

He tried to tune into the banter fizzing before him, but his mind floated elsewhere. His thoughts were skittish at the best of times and, what with the Italians and Brandwood and the McKays on his mind, he couldn't quite bring himself to engage fully with the others. There was too much distance between them. He felt like the man at the party who shouts 'Conga!' and stands forlornly alone as he discovers that no one else is interested.

Still, it was good to see Michelle laughing. He remembered how he used to be able to do that. He used to make her laugh a lot. That was one of the things that had helped him to become a reasonable success with women. Lee had never been a great looker – he wasn't bad, he scrubbed up all right, as his mum said – but he once had a charm and humour about him that had helped him navigate a path to many a bed. Blokes know that. Blokes know that even if you're just average-looking, as long as you've got the chat you're in with a chance with the best-looking bird in the room. It's a great thing, a gift, to be able to give the chat, to make a room revolve around you, the women homing in on you as if drawn by some talismanic force.

Lee used to be able to do that, but now he sat in the kitchen watching his brother doing the same thing. *His brother*, who had always aroused suspicions in women on account of his unpredictability. In the past there had been a clumsiness about Colin that had caused women to shy away, to be watchful around him. But the army had changed him; ironically the institution had made him more adaptable, able to see what was required by different people to propagate intimacy and trust.

But the change made Lee suspicious, like he was watching some sleight of hand, and was trying to fathom how Colin pulled it off. Colin had learnt how to make people like him in the same way that somehow Lee – and he wanted desperately to reverse this – had unlearnt it. How he wished to be able to get people to tune into the frequency where they were really listening to him, where they heard what he was actually saying.

That Christmas, in his home with his family around him, Lee could not have felt more alone. He remembered once coming downstairs into the living-room when a child and Colin was riding around the room on their father's shoulders. He'd tried pulling at his dad's leg to attract his attention, to let him know that he too would like to be part of the fun, but to no avail: Colin and his father were unable to hear Lee above their own laughter. He waited for a couple of minutes, had even tried to fake laughter in order to join in, but he realised they were not aware of him, so he left the room. He climbed the stairs to his room, his cheeks red with humiliation, his heart aching with hurt.

It was a similar feeling to the one he was experiencing there in the kitchen. Like the shameful walk to the rear of a restaurant. He took another swig of his beer, whizzing the rest of the contents around in the bottom of the bottle. He watched his wife laughing at one of his brother's jokes. She caught his gaze.

'You all right, love?'

'Never better,' said Lee grinning. She gave him a half smile. She was enjoying herself, didn't want the atmosphere spoilt. He smiled at her and patted her bottom. She leant down and kissed him. Days like this didn't come around often enough. Lee took a shallow breath and remembered they had that in common – a sense of a family life being worthwhile, that family life, when it's good, is better than any other kind.

'You're looking tired, broth,' said Colin, sensing the change in atmosphere, tapping the right vein. 'You sleeping all right?'

'On and off,' said Lee. 'Not feeling too clever if I'm honest. Bit run-down. Had to fucking train this morning, like I said.'

'Heard you had a good game Saturday,' said Colin. 'Pity about the result.'

'Swings and roundabouts innit, Colin, swings and roundabouts.'

'Who's on the box tomorrow?' asked Colin.

'Arsenal Liverpool, innit,' said Lee. 'Fancy a score draw meself.'

'You reckon?' said Colin. 'You put anything on it?'

'You're fucking joking, ain't you?' said Lee. 'You think I want to go somewhere else where I can get in trouble?'

'Don't encourage him, Colin,' said Brenda, her face lost in a cloud of vegetable steam. 'If he gets going on that we'll have the bailiffs round before you know it.' Annoyed, Lee gave her a look, and was startled to discover her smiling at him. She was trying to make a joke.

'Seriously though, Lee, you look a little worse for wear,' said Colin. 'Something getting you down?'

'Nah, I'm all right, honest,' said Lee. 'It's nothing. We're under a bit of pressure and, you know . . .' He looked over at Michelle without meaning to; he could tell that she was listening.

'Tell you one thing though. Last Wednesday I had to go to the launch of this new computer thing, right, and guess who I ran into over there? Bobby O'Sullivan. You remember? One of them seventies heroes, like Best and Bowles and Worthington.'

'Played for West Brom and Leicester?'

'West Brom and Coventry City,' said Lee. 'Yeah, what made me think of it was what you just said.'

'What's he up to these days then?'

'That's the point – fuck all. Seems to spend all his time in the bookies and in the boozer. You'll never guess what – he's married a publican.' Lee and Colin fell about laughing. 'Can you imagine? Fucking hell, that's like Saddam Hussein marrying an arms dealer – bound to be trouble.'

'But doesn't she get pissed off with him?' asked Colin.

'You'd expect so, but apparently not,' said Lee. 'I mean, I think he knows he's on to a winner, so he lets her think she's wearing the strides. Tell you what though, he told me a terrible story. He was invited to whatsitcalled, that football restaurant in Leicester Square?'

'Planet Football,' said Colin.

'He's invited to the opening of that and he walks in and to get up to the main level you have to get a lift, right. And there's a massive bouncer guarding this lift. And old Bobby is strolling in behind that young Man United kid who everyone's talking about, Mark Sellars, right, and the bouncer just waved in the kid and Bobby gives him a smile and tries to get in the lift. The bouncer steps in front of him going "private party, private party" and Bobby smiles and tells him that he's invited and who he is, and the bouncer just keeps going "private party, private party", and Bobby looks up at Sellars, right, and gives him a grin and says "tell him who I am", meaning tell the bouncer, right. But the kid looks the other way. So Bobby starts giving him a bit of gyp, saying "who do you think you are?" and "you wouldn't have made the fucking reserves in my day", and the bouncer just pushes him. And Bobby's had a few, so he falls on the deck and he looks up just as the lift doors are closing and the kid goes to him: "The seventies are over." Imagine that! "The seventies are over." Talk about no fucking respect.'

'That is out of order,' said Colin. 'A bloke like Bobby deserves better. He never did anyone any harm.'

'Tell you what,' said Lee finishing his beer. 'When we play that lot I'm going to give him a fucking good kick, and while he's lying there I'm going to get in his face and go "Remember Bobby O'Sullivan now, do you?"'

'It's a disgrace,' agreed Colin. 'Bloke like that deserves better.' Lee looked at his brother. Something passed between them. Then it clicked: Colin was talking about him. Lee was the one being dealt the injustice, *he* was Bobby O'Sullivan. And, for a moment, everything was all right between them, like when you look at your arm in a certain light and it's tensed and looks golden and firm and like the hairs have been bleached blond by the sun and you wonder for a moment if it really is your arm because it looks so healthy and strong.

Lee considered the cracked geometry of his life, the strange shapes, smudged patterns, the distant voices coming through the ether, and he knew then that in some strange way he was coming to a journey's end. It was like finding a heap of stuff in the street that's fallen out of the back of a van. You just don't know what to do with it all so you walk away, leave it there in the street.

He felt Michelle's hand on his shoulder. It was resting, yet there was a firmness about it, like she was gripping; like she was holding on to him. For a moment it felt like they were standing shoulder to shoulder, as well balanced and content as any couple could be. He looked up at her and saw tenderness that made him shiver, for he had another woman on his mind – Jessica.

'You all right?' she asked, her voice barely louder than a whisper, her words only for him.

'Yeah, yeah,' he said. 'Everything's fine. Just a bit tired.'

She squeezed his shoulder as if trying to work some of the tension from his frame. 'Take Colin through, will you?' she said. 'I'm just about to serve up.'

'Yeah,' said Lee. The four of them were momentarily silent. He knew it was him who had to utter the next words.

'Anyone for a top-up?'

Chapter Sixteen

After the man at the security gate had given him the thumbs-up Lee pulled into the car park and looked at the sky. In London, unless you're driving across the river and you can look far into the distance, you can never see the weather coming. By the time you realise what's happening, it's upon you. The pale haze was being overrun by darker, pearl-grey cloud. He looked up, set the alarm and headed for reception. He checked his watch. Only fifteen minutes late. Not too bad. Anyway, it was a recording, so they could all wait.

He hated coming to these things on his own. If Lou had come he could have dealt with the creepy behind-the-scenes slaves, greenroom gophers and the cheery, chatty brood mares who administered slap in an overfamiliar manner. But that wasn't the worst; it was the moment when he had to go round shaking hands and being introduced to 'everyone' that really set his teeth on edge. As he said to Lou, when he was instructed to stop moaning, he knew it was part of the job but people didn't necessarily like every part of their job. Most postmen preferred a trolley run to a bag run, some wouldn't do a dog run. This was his equivalent of a dog run.

Anyway, wasn't it part of *his* job to take care of Lee at things like this? He'd come up with some piss-poor excuse about having some things to take care of.

Lee wasn't feeling too clever. The heavy Christmas pro- gramme had exhausted his reserves. To cap it all he'd caught a dose of a virus that was doing the rounds. It had laid him low, given him a fever and made his throat and joints ache. But it wasn't enough to get him out of playing. The way the gaffer was at the moment he'd have to report with two amputated legs to get out of that. And even then he'd probably have to sit on the bench.

Still, they were winning most of their home games, even if they were losing a few on the road. But not in the Cup. In the third round they seemed to have been touched by a supernatural force which had seen them survive a battering in a replay at Newcastle, but still sneak a lucky last-minute penalty to go through. No one was saying it in the dressing-room, but the lads wondered if maybe their luck was in, maybe their name was on the Cup. If so, nobody had told the gaffer, who was still whinging; existing, as ever, under a permanent state of siege. Maybe he thought that the Cup was his way of keeping his job, after some suggestions in the papers that the Twomacs were dissatisfied with the league performance.

Lee examined his trainers, which had an inch of mud around the bottom, like a pristine ocean liner with a rusty belt at its base, the legacy of this morning's half-hour trek across a deserted bit of farmland. The voice, the second voice, was leading him a merry dance these days, never suggesting the same place twice and seemingly taking delight in conjuring increasingly bizarre, out-of-the-way locations. Lee always felt more vulnerable in the countryside and kept checking to see if he was being watched as he crunched over the undergrowth and slithered among boggy ruts left by tractor tyres. He'd left the ten grand, as instructed, behind a stack of fertiliser. It had made him think of bank adverts about making your money grow. The first voice, its surety and consistency, he could handle, but he was beginning to really hate the second voice and its snide suggestions and capriciousness. He was beginning to have fantasies of getting hold of the second voice, of telling it to get the fuck out of his life. He wanted to tell it what it could do, he didn't give a shit any longer. Black thoughts had invaded his mind. The fear that had first motivated him now seemed like a small thing compared to the humiliation that he was beginning to feel.

It wasn't just the money, although that certainly hurt: what had started to get to him was the way in which it was beginning to take hold of his life, the way he thought, the way he acted. He understood all kinds of things about football. He understood all kinds of things about life; and both had taught him that if you allow yourself to be overrun, if you allow yourself to be bent out of shape and for things to take a semi-opaque course, then it can only be grim for you. Both Lou and Colin told him not to worry. It would go away soon.

So Lee met 'everyone' and was told that his lateness was 'no worries' by Kim, an Aussie bint with a hair wrap and blobby shoes that looked like a couple of Cornish pasties. Bet she got them in Camden Market a couple of hours after she'd deplaned from her Qantas 747, Lee thought. He was asked if he wanted anything to drink.

'Coffee with none,' he said. She gave him a look.

'Coffee. With. None,' he repeated.

'With no what?' she asked.

'Sugars. Coffee with no sugars,' he said. Jesus, this was going to be a fucking struggle. Kim trotted off and the director introduced himself as Josh. He was about twelve years old and posh. He never stopped smiling. Even when Lee was speaking Josh had a smile, his lips pressed tightly together, that made Lee think that he'd said something funny. He told Lee he was 'rilly, rilly excited' about the show and 'rilly, rilly excited' about having Lee on the show although, actually, he was more 'rilly, rilly excited' about what Chelsea were doing, what with their glamorous Italian imports. Lee tuned out. After a while he stood up, apologised for 'going on a bit', clapped his hands saying 'better get things moving then' and wandered out of the room. Lee put his head in his hands.

'By the way . . .' said Josh returning to the room. 'Oh, sorry . . .'

Lee tried to disguise his actions but made it look more like he was examining himself for nits. He decided to come clean. 'Bit of a headache,' he said.

'Right,' said Josh, laughing. 'Have you met Jessica? She's great.'

'Yeah. Few weeks ago. Charity do,' said Lee. 'Lovely girl.' He realised that was partly why he wasn't feeling the full ticket – the last time he saw her was the charity dinner. He was going to have to apologise, he wasn't very good at that.

'Yeah, super,' said Josh. 'I'll ask her to pop round and say hi, OK?'

Lee sniggered to himself when Josh left the room just to relieve the tension. He wondered where his cup of coffee was.

'Hello, Lee,' came a voice from the doorway. He looked up and there she was, the reason he found himself in this shitty-sweaty anteroom waiting to engage willingly in the exhausting siege of celebrity. He wouldn't do it for anyone but his sponsors. And he'd do it for Jessica.

'They taking care of you?' she asked.

'I'm being taken care of,' said Lee. 'How are you? How's it all going?'

'Well, it's not terrestrial,' said Jessica, shrugging. She walked into the room carrying a plastic cup of water in one hand and some papers in the other. She took a sip of water. 'Terrible throat,' she said.

'So have I,' said Lee. 'Lot of it about.' He could see that she'd been made up. Thick lines had been drawn to accentuate her eyes and lips, her hair was bigger than he remembered it. She'd been given a TV face.

'Lee, I need this to go well,' said Jessica. 'I hope you're going to be a bit more together than last time I saw you.'

'Yeah,' said Lee, embarrassed. 'I'm sorry.' Jessica waited to see if there was more. There wasn't.

'I'm going to be honest now, Lee,' said Jessica folding her arms. 'I didn't want to have you on the show, but I mentioned that I'd met you to Josh and, well . . . He's got a job to do, they're always shouting at us for ratings, so, well, here we are. I suppose I should say thanks for coming.'

Lee sat in his chair nodding to himself, trying to think of exactly the right thing to say.

'I bet you felt terrible the next day,' prompted Jessica. 'You were in a right state.'

'Well, you'll probably be surprised to hear that I made training,' said Lee. 'I wasn't too bad, as it goes. I suppose I'm a bit of a chunder-and-go kind of guy really. I bounce back. None of that lying around in a darkened room stuff.'

'Wish I was like you,' said Jessica. 'Sniff of the barmaid's apron I get a headache. Anyway, you can't mess about if you've got kids.'

'I wouldn't know,' said Lee.

'You'll find out one day,' said Jessica. 'That'll sort you out.'

Lee gave her a half smile. There was a difficult silence between them for a moment before Kim reappeared.

'Blimey! Sorry about that, Lee, I got sidetracked. White, one sugar, right? No worries.'

'Right,' said Lee, who couldn't be bothered to remonstrate. He sipped it and grimaced theatrically. Everyone laughed.

'This is Katie, who's doing your hair and make-up,' said Kim, gesturing at a plump, beaming woman in her forties holding what looked to be a toolbox. 'I'll be back in about ten minutes to get you, all right? Ciao!'

'I'd better run,' said Jessica. 'See you in a bit.'

Lee listened to her voice – professional, authoritative – in the hallway as Katie set about his mush with foundation.

'Not too much,' protested Lee. 'I don't want to be Tangoed. I don't want to look like Hansen.'

Lee was standing on-set with a sound man pulling a microphone through his shirt when Josh came running up to him. 'That was rilly great, Lee! Terrific stuff,' he gushed.

Lee looked over at Jessica who gave him a thumbs-up.

'Thanks, Lee,' she said. He couldn't tell whether that gesture was one of hers, or it was something that she thought TV presenters did. Lee looked at his shoes. 'Sorry about all the swearing,' he said. 'It's difficult, you know. You forget where you are . . .'

'No probs, no probs,' said Josh grimacing. 'We'll whip those out in the edit. Only wish we could use that line of yours. What was it? Oh, that's right, "Trousers are a real inconvenience when you want to take a shit in the back of a taxi."' Josh fell about while Lee grinned, pleased with himself.

'I thought that was disgusting,' said Jessica.

'It was only a joke,' protested Lee.

'So was that,' said Jessica.

The three of them started walking back towards the dressing-rooms.

'I was wondering,' said Josh to Lee. 'Saturday week, the Cup game against Chelsea, I was wondering if there was any possibility that you might have a couple of spare tickets . . .'

'No problem,' said Lee. 'Call me in a week and I'll sort you out.'

'If you're sure it's no trouble . . .' said Josh. 'That's wicked! You know, if you're ever in Notting Hill . . .'

'You want to come as well?' said Lee to Jessica, who was drinking yet more water.

'You know I don't like football, Lee,' she croaked.

'Only asking,' said Lee, hurt.

'Well, if there are any more tickets going . . .' piped up Josh. Lee gave him a look. The one he only usually gave defenders who'd gone right through him. Josh shut up.

'Well, I'd better scoot, Lee,' said Josh. 'It's going out tomorrow night at eleven on Image UK. You've got cable?'

'Satellite.'

'Hope you enjoy it. I'll give you a call about the game,' and he disappeared up the corridor leaving Lee and Jessica standing by a vending machine.

'Lee,' said Jessica. He could tell that she was aware that she'd upset him by refusing the ticket. 'I just want to thank you again for coming on the show. It really means a lot to me, I mean, getting guests of your calibre on the show gives me a crack at really getting something worthwhile . . .'

'What are you doing tonight?' said Lee.

'I, er, nothing,' Jessica replied. He could see she was taken aback.

'Then get a babysitter and meet me for dinner.'

'All right,' she said. She even sounded surprised at her own response. 'Where?'

'Nobu,' said Lee. 'You know it? It's Robert De Niro's place.'

'Metropolitan Hotel.'

'Eight o'clock.'

'Eight o'clock.'

She turned and left him standing there next to the glass machine stuffed with Walker's crisps and Pepsi. The Spice Girls peered at him with their Widow Twanky faces. Lee grimaced at them.

'What the fuck are you looking at?' he said.

He'd asked her out. For a moment Michelle flashed across his mind, but guilt was soon dissolved by a stronger brew of stubborn pride: it was the first thing he'd done in ages that he hadn't fucked up. Maybe that would come later.

Chapter Seventeen

Lee could imagine what it had looked like to Michelle. And it wasn't good. There, in Bizarre in the *Sun*, in full colour, him and Jessica sneaking out of the Met Bar, faces aglow like dazzled children on Bonfire Night. In the photo his hand was slightly raised as if trying to conceal his identity. In fact, he had just reacted instinctively to the pop of the flashbulb that had filled his face as he stepped from the door. Jessica looked downwards, probably only checking her footing in her perilous heels, as she teetered down the steps. But the picture only said one thing: guilt.

It wasn't Michelle's style to blow her stack. She'd done it all with class. He'd just come home after training and discovered the newspaper opened at the incriminating page; lying on top of it was a note reading 'Gone to Florida'. There was no signature. No explanation. Lee's guilt was assumed by the very assurance of Michelle's actions. It was a given. When he'd found it he hung his head and put his hand on a glass vase that they'd bought only the week before from Heals. It was as shiny and smooth as a toffee apple.

He wanted to talk to her, wanted to tell her that he thought that he might be getting better, that the helter-skelter of his life might be coming to some sort of conclusion and that maybe there were things they could do to make it all better. He wanted to tell her that he'd imagined a good future, imagined a good life for both of them. He wanted to tell her about the phone calls and the money and he wanted to tell her he was sorry. He wasn't quite sure what for, but he knew that she'd understand. He

187

wanted her to understand that Jessica was a good thing, how he loved her banter, admired her pluck. How he wasn't even sure he wanted to fuck her. Then again, maybe that wasn't such a good idea. He wanted to tell Michelle that he was still in love with her, even if he was still confused. Just being able to tell her would have been enough.

The tragedy was that they'd been making out all right over the previous couple of weeks. After Christmas lunch, when she'd heard Lee telling the story about Bobby O'Sullivan, she'd shedded her hardness towards him, as if she'd refound her empathy, aware of the potentially bad scenarios that could occur. They'd spent more time alone. For some reason Brenda had kept out of their way and Colin had disappeared up to Scotland to stay with an army mate of his. They were going shooting together. He'd promised to fill everyone's freezer with rabbit and pigeon. Nobody knew why.

So Lee and Michelle had done the things that they used to do: gone to restaurants, feasted on take-aways, they'd even rejoined the video club, sat and watched *The Bridges of Madison County* one night. On a *Saturday night*, of all nights. Lee had barely had a drink, just a couple of beers with his curry. Yet despite his feelings for Michelle, Jessica floated in the background, filling him with need. Just as the waves of feeling he had for Michelle crashed on the seashore so it was that he felt the undertow of Jessica dragging him elsewhere.

So when Michelle did a bunk there he was, alone again in the house with nothing but the TV and PlayStation to keep him occupied. That night he sat in darkness playing *Tekken 2* and drank a bottle of Absolut Citron. It was Michelle's. Duty-free. There was nothing else in the house. At first he'd chosen to be Lei Wulong because he liked his righteous fighting style and the fact that the assessment in the booklet said that 'Wulong has a reputation among our Triad and Sicilian business associates for being unbribable and intransigent.' Lee liked the irony of that as much as he liked Wulong's Kempo derivative fighting style. But as the night wore on and the vodka started to wear off, Lee changed character to Jack-2, the Russian Cyborg, because, as the booklet described, his fighting style was brute strength. Lee thought that maybe he was in a place where only brute strength would do. As the clock ran out again he rose for the first time in hours and traipsed to bed. He could think of only one thing: they were playing Chelsea. Chelsea, the west London glamour boys. Chelsea, who were only supported by thugs and glory hunters.

Maybe it was Jack-2 or maybe it was the vodka, but whatever it was, Lee played with all the brute strength he could muster the next day. Stamford Bridge is a very exposed pitch. Someone told him that they've sowed nylon in with the grass to keep the turf from tearing up in the winter. Anyway, they were one down within ten minutes, a good move, lots of pace, lots of runners moving in different directions . . . Lee knew in his heart that he'd lost his own man. Thankfully, he wasn't the one who'd scored. He looked over at Brandwood on the bench, sitting there with his hand wrapped round his chin. He seemed to be looking at all of them at the same time, and he seemed to be saying the same to each and every one: 'You are a useless shower of shite. Why are you wasting my time?' The Chelsea fans were loving it, thought they were on their way to Wembley. Lee couldn't believe the fuss they were making. He supposed that it was all they'd ever known – Cup success.

They got the customary bollocking at half-time, but it wasn't needed. The lads were barely listening – they all knew they were playing well below par, were aware that Chelsea were having to play out of their skins to stay in the lead. Their centre-halves were dodgy in the air. All it needed was a period of concerted pressure and once the breakthrough was made Chelsea'd collapse with the disappointment of failed ambition. And so it was, Brandwood broke into his first smile in weeks as his charges ran out 3–1 winners after a couple of goals early in the second half and the killer third from Lee only five minutes from the end as the blues desperately pressed for an equaliser. It wasn't a fair score, but sometimes it's a cruel game. Lee's performance was much admired, more for its unusual calm and control than for its tongue-lolling inspiration. Lee enjoyed himself for the simple fact that the team was playing well enough not to need him to play God every week. Although he didn't mind trying.

There was, however, one cloud on the horizon: after scoring the third goal Lee had decided to slide along the grass in celebration, during which he pulled a tendon in his knee, causing him to have to be substituted with only a few minutes on the clock. He would miss the next Cup game; but should be back for the semi if they survived the quarter without him.

After the physios and specialists had done their bit Lee was told that he wouldn't be able to train at all for at least a fortnight. Total rest was prescribed. Strange how things work out. He had a quick chat with Brandwood, who instructed him to take a break and recharge his batteries. On the way home, Lee called the travel agent and booked a flight to Orlando. He left that evening. There was nothing else to do if he still cared about his marriage.

Lee pressed the buzzer; he'd left his damn keys back home again. He'd called from the airport, but there was no answer. The machine wasn't even on, so he'd just headed over unannounced. Lee wondered what he might do next should Michelle not allow him entry. He shivered as he thought about all the guns in America. He worried that he might get shot. First he had to face Michelle.

He pressed the buzzer again. Moments passed. Maybe she was out, maybe she was with someone else . . .

'Yes?' came a voice. It was surprised and slightly annoyed, the voice of a person disturbed after having bought a plot of remote land in order to get some peace and quiet.

'Chelle, it's me. Forgot me key. Again,' said Lee trying to sound both commanding and penitent. He flinched as he heard the intercom go dead. He stood for a moment not quite knowing whether to wait and flag someone down, or to walk back to the security gate and call a cab from there. Lucky his suitcase had wheels on it. But then the intercom unexpectedly came alive.

'Lee,' said Michelle. Her voice was unsure of itself. 'What a surprise.' He was trying to detect her mood. She sounded confused, maybe less than ecstatic, but she didn't sound angry. Praise the Lord. Lee reached for the handle of his case to wheel it in.

'Well, open up then,' he said, disconcerted that she could see him while he was staring into an inch-wide video lens.

'Hang on a second,' she said and the buzzer went dead again.

As he was waiting to re-establish communication with his wife, Lee watched a duck fly over his house before dipping dramatically to land on his lush, sprinkler-enhanced lawn. It shook itself, as if it had just got out of the water, before waddling towards him quacking. Quaaak! Quaaak! it went, as if the house were its own and a wily intruder had been spotted at the gates. It momentarily flustered Lee and he turned and looked behind him as if he'd been caught in a place he shouldn't have been.

'Tell you what, Lee, how about if I grab my purse and come out,' said Michelle eventually, but it didn't sound like a question. It sounded like a command. 'I fancied getting out of the house for a bit. We'll grab a late lunch.'

'But . . .' Lee wanted to ask if he could just dump his bag first and take a quick shower, but she'd already cut him adrift in the compound. The only thing he could do was wait for her Lexus to drift by and pick him up.

The gates folded open and Michelle steered the car on to the road which, in the heat, appeared freshly laid. He marvelled that every time he picked either of his feet up a slight indentation was left by the soles of his shoes. Lee heaved his bags into the boot before running round the front. He went to grab the door handle and found himself staring directly at his wife.

'Shit – wrong side,' said Lee through the glass. Once inside the motor he sat back for a moment, tired and hot, and closed his eyes while the air-conditioning began to chill the moisture on his brow.

'You're not pissed, are you?' said Michelle. She sounded almost blasé – more composed than on the intercom.

'No, no,' replied Lee, disappointed that she could be so suspicious after all the effort he'd made in the preceding weeks. 'Only had a couple of beers on the plane.'

'So what are you doing here?' she asked.

'Well, I did buy the fucking house . . .'

'Come on, Lee,' she interrupted, patronising him.

'Done me knee ligaments, didn't I?' said Lee sounding tired of his hurting body. 'All my own fault, slid across the grass after scoring. Just my luck . . .'

'It's not bad luck, Lee,' said Michelle. 'It would happen to anyone else who slid on their knees. This stuff doesn't just happen to you, you know.'

'Feels like it's just me though.' Lee reached back for his seat belt having cooled down a little.

'So tell me why you're really here, Lee,' said Michelle. 'Don't tell me you just happened to be passing by. Orlando's a long way.'

'It's obvious, isn't it?' said Lee.

'No, it's not obvious,' said Michelle. 'That's why I'm asking.'

'I wanted to talk to you, you know, go through things with you.'

'Like what?' pressed Michelle.

'You know, us.'

'Us?'

'Us.'

'And what makes you so sure I want to talk to you about

"us"?' asked Michelle.

'Come on, Chelle, you're still my wife,' said Lee. He was beginning to whine.

Michelle burst out laughing, clearly for effect.

'What's so funny?' asked Lee, getting annoyed that his advances were being rebuffed.

'You,' said Michelle. 'What's happened to you since I've been away? You become one of them "new men" or something? "Us." I ask you? Since when have *you* ever been interested in *us*?'

'Michelle, I want to put things right,' said Lee, rather more desperately than he would have liked.

'Don't make me laugh, Lee,' she said.

'I'm serious,' said Lee. 'Serious as cancer.'

'Well, this is a turn-up for the books,' said Michelle. 'Get struck by lightning on the golf course did we? Been smoking some of your funny fags again?'

Lee folded his arms and set his eyes on the road. He would wait it out until they got to the restaurant.

In the time it took to finish the journey and be seated ('How are you today?' the maître d' had enquired as if they dined there every lunchtime, but hadn't waited for an answer before spiriting them to an oceanside table) the mood had changed from confrontation to sourness. Lee found it difficult to summon the necessary will-power to restart the conversation in the certain knowledge that he had a long and rocky road to travel before reaching any point that might be comfortable. Michelle sat smoking and staring at the waves lapping at the beach. Her body was almost twisted in on itself; her legs crossed tightly, her upper half virtually flush against her thighs. He watched her short, shallow breaths, inhaling and exhaling, like she was stoking herself up for something.

They ordered – she chicken and mango salad, which Lee knew she would barely touch since she had found her stride with cigarettes, while he went for the surf 'n' turf special. Then came the silence, the silence that Lee knew only he could break. She was waiting. He had an image of her concealed round a corner with a huge mallet above her head, Wile E. Coyote style, ready to bring the pain. He tried to put it out of his mind. It wasn't helping.

'Chelle, look, it's not what you think,' he said and regretted it. The hammer came down.

'Lee, the very least you can do for me is to come up with a line that most women on the face of the globe have not heard a million times before,' she snapped.

'At least I'm trying,' said Lee.

'Well done, Lee,' said Michelle.

'But you're my wife.'

'I'm not just your wife. I'm a person in my own right,' she said, putting down her fork. 'I don't just want to be known as Mrs Lee Sweeney. You didn't pick me out of page three like some of the other lads do.'

'I didn't mean it like that,' said Lee.

'Well, how did you mean it then?' she replied.

'That it still means something to me. That it's still important to me.'

'It's all about you, isn't it, Lee?' she said, firing up a cigarette. 'It's all about you. Suddenly we start talking about our marriage, and why? Why, Lee? Because for some unfathomable reason you decide that it's become important to you. Forget that for the past three years you've ignored it like a pair of old underpants you've left on the bedroom floor. Forget that I've had to pull your face out of your own vomit countless times, that I've had to drag your face out of slags' cleavages on countless others. Forget the fact that you spend most of your time lost in booze, or coke, or your fucking PlayStation.'

A couple of other diners looked over as Michelle's voice rose.

'All right, Chelle, keep your voice down,' said Lee. Even though he'd clocked them for Yanks, he never knew where the reptiles were. He imagined the headlines and winced. He tuned back in.

'Look at yourself, Lee,' she continued. 'You haven't even got any friends to speak of. You're on your own and if it wasn't for my mum and my mates I would be too. That isn't any way to live, Lee.'

'There's things going on, Chelle,' said Lee. He wanted to tell her everything, tell her about his pain and humiliation, his late-night terror. He wanted to tell her about the money. He wanted to tell her about his friend Jessica. 'There's been things happening, but I'm putting them right. I'm trying Chelle, I really am.'

'I know there's things going on, Lee,' said Michelle sounding tired. 'I'm not an idiot.'

'I know, it's . . .'

'And I'm not some kind of doormat neither.'

'You're wrong about all that, you know,' Lee said. He looked at her. He was trying to summon his most sincere look, something that would reach into her. It came out all wrong, like the kind of slow burn a middle-aged lothario with slick-backed hair and a five-year-old 911 might do in a Clapham wine bar if he happened upon a couple of un-attached women.

'Stop looking at me funny,' said Michelle. 'You're really getting on my nerves.'

'You should know the truth, Michelle.' He stopped for a moment and watched the water. Two seagulls were making a fuss about nothing much.

'There was a time, Lee, when I would have loved to know what was going on in that world of yours,' said Michelle, lighting another cigarette. She exhaled smoke and stared at the ocean as he turned his gaze from the water to his wife. 'Oh, yes. You can count on it. I really thought to myself, "My Lee, I know that I can turn him. I know that. All I've got to find out is how to unlock him."'

'Chelle . . .' interrupted Lee.

'I really thought it was that simple,' she continued, ignoring him. It was as if she were talking to herself. 'I thought it was like finding a key to a box. All I had to do was put it in and spring the lock. Then I'd be able to see. Then I'd know. But, you know, a couple of years ago I thought to myself, "I'm never going to find that key. I'll never be able to work it out for myself." I still had a little sneaking hope that maybe you might reveal it yourself, offer something up. But, as time went on I started not caring if you did or you didn't. It wasn't like I wasn't interested in you, didn't care. It was more that . . . I gave up hope.'

'You should never give up hope, Chelle,' pleaded Lee. He tried to reach his hand over to touch hers.

'Give me one good reason not to, Lee,' she said without bitterness. 'Just one.'

'Us, Chelle.'

'You don't understand, do you?' she said in disbelief. 'You really don't understand. I'm not giving up hope for everything. I'm not going to go off and top myself, throw myself over the white cliffs of Dover or something. I'm too damn strong for that, Lee. I'm too fucking good to deserve a fate like that. That isn't for me. I'm talking about us. I gave up hope for us. It was like trying to learn something over and over and over again. Day after day. You know what that's like? And none of it is going in. Eventually you've got to get up and walk away. You've got to get out of there just to keep your sanity.'

'I know what you're saying, Chelle, and, believe me, I'm going to try and put it right. Things haven't always gone the way I wanted them to.'

'I'll never forget, a few months back, sitting there at a game, and I hear these blokes behind me and one goes to the other, "Sweeney looks well, doesn't he? Nice tan." And the other bloke goes to him, "Yeah, he must have found a pub with a beer garden." And you know what? My first reaction was to almost start crying. I was so upset that my husband was being treated as some kind of joke. But then I started laughing, and I couldn't stop. And I kept laughing to myself for about five minutes. And mum came back to the seat and was asking what was wrong with me and I couldn't tell her.'

'What does that mean?' said Lee. 'I don't understand what you're trying to tell me.'

'I'm not trying to make a point, Lee,' said Michelle. 'I'm just trying to tell you how I felt. I'm not trying to tell you how you should feel or what you should do. I'm just trying to tell you what it's like to be me, because I know that you're not really interested in any other terms than how that effects you. I don't want just to be known as Mrs Lee Sweeney. I want to be known as me, I want people to want to be around me for who I am rather than trying to get a couple of free tickets for the Arsenal game off of me.'

'Well, that's not my fault, is it?'

'Oh, come on, Lee, talk to me.'

'Look, it's not like I planned it all out like this or anything. It's not like I tried to work things out this way. I'm trying, Michelle. I'm trying.'

Michelle lit another cigarette and stared out at the ocean. 'Oh, Lee, isn't it sad that still, after all this time, we still can't really talk?' The way she said this to him wasn't so much a question as a conclusion, and he felt sick at heart.

Michelle looked at Lee and in her face he saw something he hadn't seen in a long while, he saw regret and he saw a sadness that he could do nothing to alleviate. For, in Michelle's furiously blunt eyes, in her crooked, tense lips, he could see only quiet despair. But not the desperation of the recently pricked or haplessly broken, he saw the resolute despair of the bold. What he saw in them was acceptance born of a determination that her life might be different if she only chose to make it that way.

And this is what Lee realised: that Michelle had now crossed into a place in which she no longer saw herself as solely defined by her relationship with him. For years the balance of their pairing had rested on Michelle's willingness to rationalise, no matter what injustices and humiliations might be heaped upon her by marriage, that it was somehow worth the effort, that there were pleasures and compensations to be had outside of the thin times. Now, it seemed, her patience had evaporated and her imagination had extended its scope, achieving mastery over domains thought previously to be inhabited solely by wives happy just to have hit the jackpot.

As Lee watched her drain her Diet Coke through a straw, studiously averting her eyes from him, he was sick at heart that he had not pulled his head from the sand sooner. He had been too lost in his own battles to acknowledge her pain. If only she had shouted louder and earlier. But he knew her better than that. Her emotional make-up was more a complex canal system of differing routes and systems than a superhighway of rage.

He could protect himself from blunt attack, could fend off thumps and clumps and chumps. Heavy blows were nothing to him, an elbow to the teeth, a knee to the groin did not put him off his stride. She knew this. What drained him was the certain knowledge that her pain had been gradual but constant, a Chinese water torture doled out as simple routine. That he couldn't face, and was why, he realised, Jessica was present at the back of his mind – it was simpler to shed a relationship, to walk away from hurt and embrace the slick heat of new sex than it was for him and Michelle to reach marital resolution.

'And one final thing, Lee,' she said, dipping her fingers into a bowl of water with a couple of wedges of lemon floating in it.

'Yes,' he said, beckoning the waiter.

'I want a divorce.'

You think you know someone.

Chapter Eighteen

Lee remembered something else he'd heard about Bobby O'Sullivan. A few months before Lee had been invited on to a TV sports quiz, a late-night gag fest in which a couple of stand-up chancers brought the house down by mocking foreign players' names, a peppering of perfunctory baldy cracks and scoffing at sporting calamities. While the audience was catching its breath one of the chancers made a crack about O'Sullivan. 'Apparently he's in such a bad way that a rumour's started going round that he's alive and well,' he said. The audience fell about, as did the easy-to-please studio guests. But it did nothing for Lee. He sat there nonplussed, drawing a dig from one of the comedians. He just felt numb. There had been plenty of lager in the green room, of which he'd availed himself having arrived – phenomenally – in good time. The juice had made him feel a little fuzzy, like he was watching rather than participating. That's what canned lager does to you, fucking shite.

But the O'Sullivan crack just did it for him, it expressed exactly how he felt. It said everything and it said nothing. That Michelle had decided to end the marriage had, in one way, come as no surprise to him. Not in the sense that he had expected her to do it – he had always thought that it was possible for the two of them to dull the escalating throb of disaster – but in the way that, if he really thought about it, running through the full, grim history, any sane woman would have done the same thing.

Yet there was a part of him that found it difficult to comprehend the full effects of a divorce for the very reason that he had never stretched his imagination to what his existence might actually be like should Michelle no longer factor in his life. It was an inability to grasp her absence that had made him calm as Michelle had driven them home and they'd sloped wordlessly to their separate bedrooms, Lee with a bottle of Glenfiddich, Michelle with a single vodka and tonic and a copy of *Diana: Her True Story*.

Lying there, listening to the cicadas with the television on and the volume off, he'd spent a while trying to convince himself that she was acting a part, making the kind of gesture that a wife might make if she thought that things might be improved by upping the stakes. In some relationships this might have made some kind of sense: often in life things must get worse before they can get better. Yet, in the instance of Lee and Michelle, it made no sense whatsoever; Lee's mad-dogging had ensured that the stakes were already high enough. What he knew was that the situation in which he now found himself was a direct consequence of his own failings.

He poured himself another drink. He knew that he'd hardly been present during the four years of their marriage. He and Michelle often spent a lot of time apart because of his profession, but even when he was around – physically in the same place – he was inwardly elsewhere. Thinking back that night his heart ached when he remembered how he'd come home to find Michelle chattering away about whatever she'd seen or heard or done during the day only to be greeted by an unresponsive lunk of narcotically and alcoholically fuelled apathy. And it broke his heart how, after many years of simply not being able to get through, she had just stopped trying. What was worse was the privacy of her pain. Lee had barely registered it, other than in some blithe offhand way that made him feel relieved that he had removed himself from all engagement.

He hadn't recognised it, but that was the period during which Michelle had emotionally removed herself from the relationship, the time when she threw herself into her own business and found more reasons to visit Florida. It was also when Brenda had begun to spend more time at their house. Lee had always resented Brenda. It wasn't just that they didn't get on – he was big enough to realise that you don't get on with everyone in this life. It was more symbolic. In retrospect, Lee recognised it as a way in which Michelle had tried to break through to him. When they argued, which was rare, such was the extent of Lee's disengagement, she often accused him of making more effort with people outside the home.

Lee needed to feel that people loved him, regarded him as something special, so much so that he'd perform backflips and flick-flacks just to get them on his side. Someone had once said to him: show a man a woman with no sense of humour and he'll break his back trying to make her laugh. He'd never heard a truer word, and it was how he'd felt when he'd first met Michelle – she was the smart kid, the one who'd gone off to sixth form college, got herself some qualifications. She had ambition and she had a future and Lee liked that. He wanted to be with someone who knew her mind, someone who wouldn't be too clingy, who would have the confidence to let him loose to do his own thing. He could have had his pick of the permatanned nightclub girls rocking their slapper chic, but he had a hunch that a girl like that might not take kindly to him dropping off the radar on one of his extra-curricular jaunts. At that point in his life Lee knew that a relationship based on swapping a platinum Amex for blow jobs would have been more trouble than it was worth. In the final analysis he knew what he wanted – and that was a grief-free existence.

There had never been any grief with Michelle but, as time had passed, it became apparent that she had entered the marriage with few illusions, yet with an overambitious optimism as to how the relationship might develop. While never for a moment perceiving Lee to be anything other than a pleasure-seeking good-time geezer drunk on his own luck, she imagined that conciliation would make the questionable surmountable. More importantly, he had never doubted that she'd loved Lee; she'd loved him for as long as she'd known him and her feelings had never diminished, which says a great deal if you've been together since the age of sixteen.

She'd taken Lee on, warts and all, with the expectation that, like a crazed adolescent, he might mature into a calmer, more considerate creature. And even when mad-dogging he was almost obsessive about gaining her approval. He was never abusive towards her, even when drunk, and his public indiscretions were always accompanied by profuse and sincere apologies. Lee could put his hand on his heart and say that he had never once purposely hurt or upset Michelle. After all, did he not wish for nothing more than a quiet life?

Which was why, when he had seen the watch in the bathroom, he had picked it up and wondered how on earth it had got there. He had seen it before, had held it in his palm and studied the steady, precise movement of the minute hand. In a world in which many men sport watches that could double as tactical missile guidance systems, the object Lee held in his hand was as simple and authentic as timekeeping could be. He had looked at it countless times in clubs and bars, in shops and hospitals, even in his own home.

But his familiarity with the watch offered him no comfort. Quite the opposite, it brought upon him a sickness that reached right through him. The watch was his brother's. He had bought it just before he'd gone into the army. According to the vendor at the market it was a 1960s Commando watch. Lee remembered Colin being captivated by the idea that he was wearing a watch endorsed by an elite army force; that this watch would somehow accord him credence within the services, conferring him an entrée into an exotic, exclusive club. For someone as unsentimental and visceral as Colin it occurred to Lee that the watch held a strange power over his brother.

And now it held a strange power over Lee, for at once it told another story, offered another set of clues. Neither Michelle nor Colin had mentioned the fact that Colin might come and stay at the villa. Lee thought back to the day Michelle picked him up from the motel and he'd passed the gas station and seen a man resembling Colin, how when he'd arrived earlier in the day she must have taken him straight out to the restaurant because Colin was skulking in the villa. He closed his eyes as he silently articulated what he'd been thinking: his wife and his brother were having an affair.

Lee pocketed the watch before resting both hands on the cool marble sink and staring into the mirror. He tried to look through himself the way he might stare out of a window, tried to conjure strength by offering an impression of a formidable physical presence, a man of purpose with resolute eyes and a granite jaw. But no matter how hard he gazed all that came back was a hollow-eyed stare of someone beyond tiredness, someone just cruising until their tank ran dry.

He would not confront his wife. He would wait. Apart from anything else a showdown with Michelle was not what he needed at present. It would set him off again. And nobody needed that.

He turned off the TV and lay back in bed with the glass of Scotch resting on his chest. The dew from the glass felt good and cool. He listened for the television in Michelle's room. She was probably fast asleep. Michelle never lasted long when she read in bed. He smiled to himself. Maybe he couldn't make that assumption any more; after all, he clearly didn't know Michelle as well as he thought.

He would leave tomorrow, return to England. To what, he wasn't sure. The only thing he knew was that he'd be seeing Colin.

Chapter Nineteen

He had been a yard or two slow against Leeds in the Cup semi-final. Space, in every sense, had been difficult to find. He'd looked over at the bench a couple of times and seen Brandwood cursing him as he lost possession time and time again. But he didn't know he was in such bad shape until the penalty. Wayne jinked his way into the box, got past one of the centre-backs and was shaping to shoot when some Frankenstein whipped his legs from under him. It was clear cut, and though twenty thousand Yorkshiremen screamed blue murder at Villa Park, there wasn't a single protest from the Leeds players.

Lee stepped forward and placed the ball on the spot. He was trying to focus on the task in hand, trying to think exactly where he wanted the ball to go – top left-hand corner. Even if the keeper guessed right he'd be hard pressed to get a hand to it. But he didn't feel right, he felt weak, incapable of striking the ball with any kind of authority. He'd shut out the whistles and boos of the Leeds mob but there were other presences in his head: voices demanding money, his brother and his wife, the divorce, the Twomacs, Brandwood, the papers . . .

He started his run-up and changed his mind about where to put the ball – he'd blast it right down the middle; no he wouldn't, he'd do what he thought originally; but the keeper was moving to his right; maybe it would be better if . . . Lee stood frozen in the middle of forty thousand people and watched the ball sail a foot over the bar. The voices in his head were silenced by the delirium of the Leeds fans. Roy Jones gave him a slap on the back. 'Come on, son, pick it up,' he said.

The team dug deep, putting the Leeds goal under siege, but it was only a mix-up between the Leeds left-back and his goalkeeper that gifted Wayne a chance: a cross came over, both the keeper and the defender failed to put a name on it and the ball ended up spilling at Wayne's trusty right foot. One–nil. 'Sweeney's going to Wembley, his knees have gone all trembly,' chorused the fans, and they weren't wrong.

There was no way that Lee was match-fit. He kept looking over at Brandwood, expecting the gaffer to pull him off, but he just kept signalling for Lee to get stuck in. Maybe it was some kind of punishment, but Lee didn't know why he was being punished and why the gaffer might risk one below-par player in the trench warfare masquerading as a game of football.

As the rest of the players celebrated with the fans at the end of the game Lee marched up to Brandwood.

'Why didn't you pull me off?' he demanded.

'Get over there and say thank you,' said Brandwood gesturing to the fans. His face was cloudy despite the victory.

'You could see I was knackered. We could have lost the game.'

'Stop moaning, Lee, we won. Get over there with the rest of the lads.'

The fans gave a loud cheer when Lee threw his shirt into their midst; several children were bowled out the way by older men charging to grab a little piece of sweat-soaked history. They didn't care about the forces that were pulling Lee into a dark orbit, the violent undertow dragging him beyond safety. They just cared that he played a blinder in May. They just cared that they were going to Wembley. Wasn't that enough?

There were a couple of interviews after the game in which Lee went through the motions of imparting revelatory titbits that those who had just watched the game might have missed from their armchairs. Lee never really tried with these things, unlike some of the lads who fancied themselves as having a bit of a media career once they'd finished the game. He had two interview modes – the perfunctory and the cheeky, and he could see the terror in the interviewers' eyes whenever they realised that they'd got the latter version on their hands. Their grins became fixed and their eyes became those of a hostage watching his captor toying with a bowie knife. *You aren't really going to do that are you?*

A few kids came pelting across the players' lounge as Lee entered, each thrusting a pen and programme forward. The same thing happened every time; just as they neared him they came over all bashful and he would have to ask: 'You want an autograph, pal?' Struck mute, the kids would offer only an embarrassed nod of assent.

Lou was sitting in the corner nursing a ginger ale. He looked worried. But, then again, he always looked worried. Lee was confounded that even though his profession required a great deal of sociability Lou could never be bothered with people unless there was a serious purpose for interaction. Lou had no time for the affable oiling of the machinery of business, he simply expected it to be there for him to work his financial alchemy. Lou wasn't impressed by the glamour of the game, he wasn't involved in football because of the perceived status it gave him. For him it was simply a job, the way that he earned his crust, and Lee never begrudged him any of his money, for he thought that his agent earned an honest amount for an honest day's work.

'How are you, Lee?' said Lou. 'Drink?'

'I'll get it myself,' said Lee. 'You need anything else?' Lou raised his palm to say no. Lee forced his way with nods and handshakes through the throng and brought back a pint of lager.

'You smell like a whore's window box,' said Lou wafting the air.

'Cheers, mate,' said Lee. 'I was wearing it just for you.'

'Tough out there today?' asked Lou.

'Yeah. Feel like an old man,' said Lee only half joking. 'All washed up.'

'No, Lee, you're not all washed up. You're not washed up until you're wearing every item of clothing that you own. Then you're all washed up,' said Lou impatiently with a you-spoilt-footballers-don't-know-what-desperation-is voice. A flunky in a white shirt and blue waistcoat came and changed the ashtray between the two men.

'You bearing up?' said Lou. He was referring to Michelle's request for a divorce; although Lee had told no one that he suspected Colin had put the horns on him. He had wanted to face Colin, to have it out with him in person. He had tried to track him down, but his brother had remained elusive, disappearing on what he had told Lee were 'extended business trips with boys from the regiment' that Lee now suspected were something else entirely, although he had little idea what. Colin had talked of 'something big' happening. Surely he wasn't brazen enough to openly taunt Lee with his relationship with Michelle? Lee knew only from years of interpreting Lou's inferences and suggestions that 'you bearing up?' was about as intimate as the two of them ever got. Lou's eyes flickered round the room to check for prying ears.

'Haven't spoken to Chelle since I left,' Lee said. 'She's not called me or anything. I'm not really sure where we are.'

'I'll be blunt, Lee. It's a difficult one,' said Lou. 'You don't think she's got any intention of, you know, running to the papers with this, do you?'

'Chelle's not like that.'

'You sure?'

'Sure. She ain't devious like that.'

'Now, Lee, you can tell me where to go if you like, but I have to ask you something, OK? Understand that I'm interested on a professional rather than a trivial level, OK? We've got that straight?'

'Yeah,' said Lee taking a sip of lager.

'All right,' continued Lou wiping his palms on the top of his legs. 'Lee, you've been acting strangely for quite a while now and I wondered if it had to do with this Jessica girl that I saw you with in the paper.'

'What would you do if I said "yes", Lou?'

'Nothing,' said Lou. 'I'm just thinking that if all this gets to court we've got to be sure of our position otherwise you're going to get taken to the cleaners.'

'Lou, listen to me,' said Lee leaning forwards. 'How long have we known each other?'

Lou shrugged and turned down the side of his mouth in the way that he thought made him look like Robert De Niro. It was supposed to say, a long while, since time.

'Long enough to know each other pretty well, right?' Lee was beginning to speak more rapidly, his voice becoming more intense. 'I mean, sometimes I even imagine that our relationship might mean a little more than just business.'

'Of course, Lee . . .' butted in Lou.

'Shut up Lou, I'm not finished. So if you're such a caring, sharing kind of guy how come your first reaction when you hear the news that I'm getting divorced from the woman I've been with since I was a fucking teenager is to worry about what kind of money she's going to try and screw out of me?'

'I understand what you're saying, Lee, but I think you're being a bit over sensitive.'

'Listen to yourself, Lou. You're right, I have been a bit odd recently. I've been early fucking doors every fucking day of the week. But what does that tell you? That tells you I need a bit of help, not a shove into oblivion. I don't care about what happens in court, Lou. We're not there yet.'

'All right, all right,' said Lou trying to defuse the moment. 'All I'm saying is that if and when we get there you'll be glad that you're prepared for whatever happens. It ain't pretty in there, you know.'

'And why's that, Lou? Why's that? The answer, Lou, is

that undoubtedly Michelle will be represented by the same kind of fucking cold-blooded reptile as I've got representing me.'

'That's just my job, Lee. Don't curse me for just doing my fucking job.'

'And he's just going to be doing his job as well, Lou, and you'll both get paid handsomely and everyone will be happy. Michelle with her divorce, the lawyers with their fat pay packets . . . But what about me, Lou, what's going to happen to me? You ever thought I might be looking to you for something more than just legal advice? Divorces don't just happen like some kind of freak event. People make it happen, Lou, and every time it happens we're not just talking about statistics we're talking about people. People being fucked over. People being ruined. We're talking about real misery, Lou.' Lee changed his voice to do an impression of Lou: ' "It ain't pretty in there." What kind of a mug do you take me for?'

'Look, Lee, it's understandable, you're emotional, you're upset, it's come as a shock to you. You need time to come to terms with it all. Think about it for five minutes, Lee – what would I want to upset you for, Lee? Eh? Think about it for five minutes. That other girl I've seen your picture with, I only mentioned it because of the papers today – she was in it. Her ex-husband beat her up. He threatened her.'

'You what?' said Lee. 'When? What happened?'

'I don't know the details. It was just in the papers today. Her ex didn't drop the kid off when he was supposed to and he ended up hitting the girl when she confronted him. It wasn't too serious, but she's got a nasty shiner.'

'Bastard,' said Lee shaking his head and taking a deep breath. He stared at the wall for a moment, collecting himself.

Lou leant forward to Lee and put his hand on Lee's shoulder. 'She's trouble, Lee,' he said quietly. 'She's bad news. You want my advice? Don't go near her.'

Lee turned slowly to look at Lou. 'Thanks, Lou,' he said. 'That's really fucking helpful.'

Lou sat back in his seat, held his palms up and raised his eyes to the ceiling.

'Understand this,' said Lee. 'The world is a more complex place than you think. You can't always control where you go when you're following your heart and not your pocket. But you wouldn't understand that.'

Lou stood up holding his briefcase and leant in close to Lee. 'The real problem here is that you don't know what you're fucking saying, Lee. One minute you don't want to get divorced from Michelle, the next you're running after this other girl. You better get this sorted soon, Lee, because time is running out for you. And I know you know it too, I can see it in your eyes.' He turned to leave and then re-membered something. 'I'm going home. Don't give me a fucking hard time. I've been married for thirty-two years. Longer than you've been alive. I'm not the one getting a fucking divorce, Lee. Now I'm going.'

As Lee watched Lou weave through the crowded room he met the intrigued stares of a few journalists, the saliva virtually running down their chins in desperation to know what had just been said. Lee stared at them through the soapy dregs of his drained pint glass before making his way back to the bar.

Chapter Twenty

He was going to tell her. He was going to get to her this time. Maybe he'd even spill about Michelle and Colin. He needed a friend, craved intimacy, and he hoped that Jessica might just save him.

She'd agreed to meet him for a drink after he'd told her a lie; he'd told her that he'd been asked to present a chat show and he was looking for a co-host. Maybe she might be interested.

She'd answered as quick as a flash and it had made him glad, but also a little sad as well. So there he was, nice and snug in a corner of the Met Bar surrounded by gone-to-seed catalogue models and muggy, cigar-smoking City boys who were trying to land the honeys by lounging in club chairs, waving bull's-eyes and drinking reserve Scotch. And the place, and the desperate, marginal punters who were flattered to be allowed through the doors yet were trying to verify that they were where it's at, and the lie he had told . . . it all suddenly struck Lee as a bad thing. He waved at one of the waiters who made a point of ignoring him before taking his order.

'We don't do pints,' he said as if Lee had asked the dumbest question on earth. 'You can have a bottle.'

'Make it two,' said Lee. The bloke stormed off and Lee knew that the geezer was playing for the other side. He wondered why there had been no flicker of acknowledgement. But then you wouldn't expect that, would you? Not really. A feller like that.

Lee had got through one of his Beck's when the whole room – ever so discreetly – turned, as one, to stare at the blonde girl handing her coat to the attendant. It was a strange moment. The whole bar had simultaneously sensed a small tremor – like a big truck or train had passed by – and everyone had paused for just an instant to register what was happening. She turned round and the room became re-animated: Boom! Yes it was her! It was Jessica! Jessica March! Bravely out in public only days after she'd been brutally assaulted by her ex-husband. JESSICA'S TERROR: FIEND EX ATTACKS HER AND TOT the headline had run as Jessica had bared her bruised body for the cameras before exclusively revealing her love for three-year-old Annette. Lee wondered how much she'd got for the exclusive.

'Hello, darling,' she said to Lee. 'Don't get up,' before kissing him on both cheeks.

'Still horrible outside?' asked Lee.

'Revolting,' she replied. 'Kind of rain that gets under your skin.'

The waiter rushed over, his insouciance seemingly forgotten. 'Can I get you anything?' he simpered. Lee picked up a trace of a Scottish accent. He was tall, wearing fake tan and had dyed his hair a golden yellow and spiked it up.

'A dry white wine and . . .' she arched her eyebrows to ask Lee if he fancied another . . . 'another beer,' said Jessica, torching a cigarette. She didn't look at the waiter who skulked off, looking bored and angry again.

'I saw the papers,' said Lee. It was another lie, but not a bad one. After all, he *felt* like he'd seen the papers. Everyone had been talking about the incident. It reminded him of when a radio interviewer had referred to Lee's first autobiography *Call Me Mr Sweeney* and said to him off air: 'I've read the book, but not personally.'

'I couldn't believe the response,' said Jessica. 'I had no idea it was going to be such a big story.'

Lee took a sip from the neck of his bottle of beer. He'd left the glass untouched on the table. He wondered if the Met had been such a wise choice after the photo of him and Jessica last time. Then he realised that he didn't care. This was where top sorts were supposed to go.

'I mean, me and Brendan knew there would be some interest, but . . .'

'Who's Brendan?' asked Lee defensively.

'My manager . . .' The surly waiter slammed the drinks down. Jessica seemed not to notice his rudeness. 'But they all seemed to pick it up in their second editions. It was amazing. And inside all the women columnists were doing pieces on domestic violence and then the women editors were doing specials on that sort of thing as well and, you know, really I can't believe all the fuss there's been . . .'

'You sound like you're excited,' said Lee.

'Well, you know, it was a terrible thing to happen,' said Jessica blowing smoke through the side of her Cupid's-bow mouth, 'but I'm sort of used to Vince, he was like that all along. And at the end of the day I knew he was more bark than bite. I was more bothered about Annette. I mean, bless her, she doesn't deserve to have to go through that kind of thing. At her age and all.'

'So what did happen, exactly?' asked Lee. He sensed that she liked talking about the incident, liked walking centre stage, seeing how it felt staring right into the eyes of the audience.

'Oh, nothing that hasn't happened before,' she said. 'Vince got drunk, he came round screaming and shouting about me not giving him access to his own daughter. Then he banged on the door for a bit. I opened it and told him to shut up and piss off. He tried to get in the house.' She giggled slightly to herself. 'Well, staggered more like it. And as he fell forward, he landed on me, knocking my head against the door frame. I'm lying on the floor in agony with my eye swelling up and a pissed idiot on top of me and the Old Bill arrive. The neighbours called the police as soon as they heard the knocking and shouting. They know the form. Anyway, Vince is pinched and, within hours, I'm giving the exclusive to the *Sun*.'

'What about Annette?'

'Oh,' Jessica laughed. 'It was incredible really. She only slept through the whole thing, didn't she? I had to get her up early when the photographer and reporter arrived and she saw the black eye. She wanted to know what had happened to mummy, but I don't think she really knew what was going on. I made sure she didn't get to see any of the papers.'

Lee examined her eye. The bruise didn't look anything like as severe as it had appeared in the photograph. Jessica realised what he was thinking.

'Not that bad, is it? They put a bit of make-up on for the picture. Photographer was worried that the editor would do his nut that the damage wasn't bad enough. Can't even feel it now, really. Another one, Lee?'

'Go ahead,' said Lee finishing the rest of his bottle.

'You all right?' asked Jessica.

'Yeah, yeah,' said Lee. 'In a little bit of a dream-world really. Feel a bit washed out. Hard game yesterday.'

'Heard you won though. Sweeney's going to Wembley and all that.'

'Yeah, it's nice. Looking forward to it. Glad we didn't have to train today though. Felt well secondhand when I got up.'

'Bit of a monster one last night, was it?'

'Just a bit,' said Lee.

The waiter blithely tipped another round of drinks on the table before marching off.

'Do you think he's trying to tell us something?' said Lee. 'What's his fucking problem? Poncey little twat, if he comes over . . .'

'Come on, Lee,' interrupted Jessica. 'Give me the juice.'

Lee looked at her, baffled.

'The programme,' she said excitedly.

'Oh, right,' said Lee. 'Well, it's going to be a celebrity chat show on Channel 5. Late at night for an hour and they're thinking of asking me to present it. Me and Lou had a meeting with the producer last week and I was saying that I thought it would be a good idea if there was a co-host. Female one, and I mentioned your name, you know.'

'When you say co-host what exactly are you talking about? I'm not just going to be fetching guests for you, cos you know I wouldn't be happy with that.'

'No, no,' said Lee, emphatically. 'I've seen it in America when they have, like, the main bloke and his sort of sidekick and a lot of the programme is based around the banter between the two of them, you know.'

'Well I'd be happy to talk to the producers,' said Jessica. 'Can we set something up?'

'Sure, sure,' said Lee, 'no problem. I just wanted to sound you out first, you know?'

'Who are they?' she asked. 'Which production company?'

'I don't really know, you know,' said Lee. 'Lou deals with that kind of thing most of the time.'

'Well, get him to call Brendan, here's the number.' She put a card on the table. 'So, are you beginning to sort a few things out for when you finish the game then?' she said with a knowing smile.

'Well, I can't go on for ever,' said Lee. 'It's going to end some time.'

'Lots of people can't believe it's gone on as long as it has,' said Jessica, only half joking.

'Yeah, including me,' replied Lee.

They sat and drank and ate oriental bar snacks, exchanging uptown intimacies the way people do when they're sitting in a bar that's supposed to be the most happening place on the planet at that second and the clientele are nervously waiting to be identified as impostors, for the fatal tap on the shoulder that signals being frogmarched from the party.

Jessica looked at her watch. 'Oh, my God,' she said in an overly dramatic fashion. 'Look how late it is! Quarter past eleven. I can't believe it. I better be getting back. I've only got the babysitter until midnight. Best be off.' She picked up her cigarettes and lighter and leaned to give Lee a farewell kiss.

'Tell you what, I'll walk you to your car. Where is it?'

'Next door. Hilton car park,' she said. 'At eight quid a pop. Come on.'

The doormen wished them a nice evening. Jessica gave them a flash of her pearly white teeth. Lee had never liked doormen, had always felt that there was something cowardly about the compass of their power and chose to ignore their cheap sentiments. Still, Jessica probably made their narcissistic night.

She walked swiftly, pulling her jacket around her shoulders and shivering slightly. Her heels clicked on the pavement. Lee thought how much he liked that noise. What a treat. He was feeling good. The evening had been a success. They waited for the lift down to the car park in the Hilton. Jessica kept pressing the button.

'You know I told you about Florida and everything,' said Lee. 'Well, it's slightly more complicated than I made out.'

'Come on, come on,' said Jessica to the lift.

'Basically I went out there because Michelle thought that I was having, well, you know, that there was something going on between us.'

'Us?!' She laughed. 'What? That we were . . . Oh, that is hilarious. Well, I suppose not hilarious if you're Michelle . . .'

'She wants a divorce,' interrupted Lee. 'She wants it done as quickly and cleanly as possible. And there's more . . .'

The lift came. Lee slumped at the back of the metal box; the neon light above immediately changed his mood. A wave of nausea rolled over him. The high of the evening was fading and he was starting to feel as drunk as he deserved to be.

'Well, I'm sorry about that, Lee. I mean, I've been through the same thing and it's not nice. The only thing I'd have to say is that once you've made the decision you've just got to go for it. Don't hang around. The pain will only be worse.'

The lift door slid open and she stepped out. Lee grabbed her left bicep. She turned and looked at him, her eyes springing to life.

'What the hell do you think you're doing, Lee?' she said. 'Let go right now.'

'You and me, J,' said Lee. 'You and me. How about it?'

'Lee, you're hurting my arm. Let go. You're pissed and I'm going home.'

'Please, J, please. Just think about it. It would be great.'

A middle-aged couple appeared from nowhere and froze, clearly distressed at what they were seeing, but not quite sure how to react.

'Are you all right, miss?' asked the man. He was wearing a dinner suit, his thinning hair combed from the left side over the top.

'Fuck off, Bobby Charlton,' said Lee.

'We're fine thank you,' said Jessica firmly. She was looking at Lee not at the man. 'This gentleman is just about to escort me to my car and then I'm going home.' She tugged her arm from his grip and started walking towards her car while rummaging in her bag for her keys.

'Wait,' said Lee. 'Just give me an answer.'

'The answer is no,' said Jessica. The orange quarter lights on her car blinked to show that the alarm was off. 'What do you expect after this?' She was incredulous.

'Please,' said Lee.

'You've heard it, Lee,' she said, turning to face him. 'You've heard the answer. You can go back to the bar now and carry on drinking. I'm going home to my daughter.'

'But why?' asked Lee throwing his arms out. 'Why not?'

'Just think about it, Lee,' she said, exasperated. 'Just fucking think about it. What kind of an offer is it really? For a woman in my position? For fuck's sake . . .' She shook her head and opened the door of her Jeep.

'Oh, come on, Jessica . . . At least give me a reason.'

'I don't believe I'm hearing this,' said Jessica, slamming

the door. Lee put his hands on the driver's window. She wound it down. They were face to face. Their noses virtually touching.

'Think about it for one minute, Lee,' she said, suddenly calmer now that she was in the car. 'What's in it for a single mum, eh? Another relationship with an abusive alcoholic. Now there's an offer I can just about force myself to pass up.' She started up the car, the noise of the engine echoing around the stark, subterranean concrete.

'But I've never hurt Michelle,' pleaded Lee.

'And you think that I'm impressed by you telling me that?'

'I never hurt her,' insisted Lee, not getting Jessica's point.

'God, Lee,' said Jessica shaking her head. 'Maybe not physically.'

Lee felt the glass pull away from his fingers and he was left in a blue cloud of exhaust. He listened to Jessica's car clamber up the ramps towards street level then sat down on the oil-stained concrete and hung his head.

Chapter Twenty-One

This, he could not wait for.

Lee had woken with two rats banging cymbals inside his head and a sour anger burning in his heart. Michelle and Jessica could go fuck themselves. He was better off without either of them anyway. The two of them were nothing but a drain on him, a couple of parasites bleeding him dry. The way he looked at it, it was two tasks on his shit list taken care of. Good fucking riddance.

Now for number three. He'd got home and heard the voice, the first one. Firm, confident, demanding, in control. It left news. There was to be a change in the details: the money was to be left in a locker in Euston at nine o'clock the following night. Then that would be the end of it.

But there was something else that had changed: as he listened to the instructions Lee felt different. For the first time in two years the voice no longer had its hypnotic effect upon him. He no longer felt compelled and controlled by it. On the contrary he was angered. He wanted to find the owner of the voice and punish him for the fear and desperation it had caused him. The mystique had gone. As he worked his way through half a box of Crunchy Nut Cornflakes and three mugs of tea he listened to the unremitting pop culture bombast of *The Big Breakfast*. It was the perfect thing to blank out the everyday while he formulated his plan. Lee had never been one for revenge – he was either too pissed or too lazy to be a score settler – but this time he'd make an exception. This time he'd look into the bastard's eyes before he took him down.

He trained hard that morning. The gaffer warned him to go easy after a couple of rash challenges earned dirty looks and harsh words from team-mates. But he felt good afterwards, felt like he'd come through something. Most of all he felt clean, he felt as if he'd worked the hurting through.

Lee zigzagged the motor through the geeky Italians and Dutch drawheads in Camden Town. At one point a gaggle of Japanese – all vintage denim and haircuts culled from *ID* – unwittingly meandered in front of his bull bars, earning themselves a loud remorseless blast on the horn. Lee patted the plastic bag next to him. The silent interior of the Range Rover absorbed Lee's crabbed chuckle. It wasn't the sight of the Japanese, cowed and humiliated, rushing for the pavement, although that held a certain pleasure for him. What had descended upon him as suddenly as the blue-grey storm clouds that glowered above was the sheer fucking stupidity of the scenario in which he found himself. It was only now, he thought, that he could view the situation with anything resembling clarity, and the more intensely he considered it the more he felt belittled and compromised by it all. How could he, an international sporting colossus, a bully-beef British hero, have found himself so abused, so reduced in this way?

The answer had been fear. A fear of disclosure, a fear of being exposed, a fear of losing what he already had. He hadn't wished to find himself under the microscope, having his shirt collar inspected for signs of dirt in some bully-boy tabloid kangaroo court. Lee Sweeney just wanted to get on with his life, this life, without any bother. Lee Sweeney didn't want any trouble.

But now maybe he did. Not, you understand, to the extent that he wanted the whole thing exposed. He wasn't fucking stupid. No, what he wanted was to have this thing out with the dark masters that haunted his dreams, with the – he imagined – sinister executioners of the cowardly manipulation. What had happened with Michelle and Colin, with Jessica, even with Lou had altered the terrain of

Lee's life: he wasn't scared any longer, he was tired of the subterfuge and shadow games involved with playing along. There was to be an end to it. He promised himself that this would be the last time he traipsed around town with Tesco bags stuffed with used twenty-pound notes. All things came to an end, and it was about time this one fucking stopped.

Clutching briefcases and copies of the *Evening Standard* property section, the Nigels and Charlottes fled the city back to their B-road sanctuaries in Herts, Beds and Bucks, soothing themselves with survivor's exhalations as they settled aboard the 7.05; another day outlasted, the pension stoked just a little more, school fees assured for another strength-sapping term . . .

Lee had arrived early, dumping the Range Rover in the grim oxygenless car park. Sound and movement reverberated around him as the last dregs of commuters emptied out, leaving only the city residue. Suddenly his surroundings seemed to have been harnessed, made larger, more bold. The fumes from the taxis were more pungent; the noise of the engines more insistent; nobody seemed to be talking any longer, everyone yelled instead; the movement of people and machines was swift, decisive, aggressive. He tried to tell himself that it was just an underground thing, that as soon as he rose to a place where the light was not electric, his senses would contract back jagged degrees.

It reminded him of when he was playing and sometimes, out of the blue, the world would come into sharper focus and his mind and body would click and sharpen; when the whole schmear was somehow right. It was a miraculous place to be. He felt himself to be almost outside his body, for everything that he touched turned to gold, nothing escaped him, nothing was beyond him, he was master of his own destiny . . . Like when he'd first started to use cocaine, chasing that sudden energetic rush of omnipotence tinged with the willingness to make it all happen, to flood all around him with goodness.

The good stuff. Hadn't he heard that phrase enough over the last few years from free-wheeling dealers and money schemers? 'Here's some of the good stuff,' 'I want a slice of the good stuff.' Even Wayne up front had once screamed at him, one sodden evening at Hillsborough: 'Lee! Give me some of the fucking good stuff!' He'd wanted balls played into dangerous areas, angles he could turn to his own advantage.

Lee had had plenty of the good stuff: lived it, breathed it, horned and tooted it; even – sometimes – gave it. But he had never known good stuff that he anticipated with such relish as the eyeball-to-eyeball showdown in the offing at Euston, good stuff that still made him shiver with excitement, swoon with desire at the very prospect of receiving it. This – the confrontation – was something that was as unimpaired as scoring a goal, as finger-licking good as freakydeaky furious sex, more fun than drowning in a bath of champagne. This gave him a feeling which he hadn't known for too long – a feeling that he was whole once more; intact, unbruised. He felt that maybe his life might gain momentum again, like he might be slogging his way out of the valley.

He came up the stairs into the station concourse and tugged at his rudimentary attempt at a disguise – a baseball cap. Propped against one of the station's teepee-like franchise huts was a sack of rags with a human being inside. Lee only knew that there was a man inside because he saw a foot, enrobed in a blue ankle brace, courtesy of University College Hospital, poking from beneath a pair of sodden jeans. A can of Kestrel Extra Strength was, miraculously, propped upon his lap. As he heard the approach of Lee's footsteps, the man raised his hand – a limp, hopeless gesture – before tilting his head backwards, rolling his eyes, and mumbling something. Being, in some senses, a normal citizen, Lee's first instinct was to hurry about his business, slipping back into his stride, but something caught him and he turned to survey the man, much as tourists do when a dolphin is stranded on a beach, only without the frenzied attempts to keep the creature alive.

Lee's sharpened gaze registered a face of indeterminate age that had fallen, fallen so many times, at night, on to concrete and tarmac, that it had been physically remoulded by its history. The brows were as thick and deep as Cro-Magnon man, the eyes sunk deep like a baboon's. Along his forehead a black lattice work of dried blood held together his puffy, pickled skin. His jowls had collapsed earthwards, his mouth a slow gasping thing that occasionally belched sour noise. This was a face that had fallen so far that there was no reaching it. There was no rescue service for this kind of disaster.

'Are you all right?' asked Lee. He knew the answer, but thought that it was the least he could do. The tone of his voice, however, was unengaged enough for him to stroll off. So, after checking to see if there were any transport cops around who might actually *do* something, Lee walked away.

But the face stayed with him, for he knew that without his money, his status, his profession, his family, his wife – oh, Michelle – this was a face that he might wear. For everything that the drunk bore witness to was within him. Deep down he knew that he had choices, that he had places to go other than downwards; but just having the image in his mind was good enough for him to know that, as he balanced his way along the thin beam of success, there was another fate waiting beneath for him.

Trying to shake the face out of his mind, Lee walked towards the lockers. He noticed that his step had more bounce in it than usual, though whether he had installed that in his gait intentionally, or whether it genuinely reflected his mood, he didn't quite know. He was pleased that he had arrived early. It gave him a sense of ownership of the station, as if he were alive to every burger barn, mag shack and secret, stinking stall in the place. He opened the locker – number seven, his fucking number, the cheeky Eyetie bastards, as if they thought it was the only number he would be sure to remember – and slammed the bag inside.

Pulling his baseball cap down low he snagged himself a screwed-down stool in a Diesel Derek's – West Africans working the swine shift serving 'DoNuts' to drunks – and sipped at a bitter coffee that made his tongue thick. He was far enough from the lockers not to be spotted, but near enough so that the fucker would feel his hot breath on his collar the second he snagged himself the bag of cash.

The anticipation ran through his veins. He tried not to look at his watch; doing so would inevitably make the time pass slower. Eventually he cracked: it was half nine. The geezer was half an hour late. A bad thought crossed his mind – maybe they'd seen him? Maybe there would be no pick-up. He stood for a moment and considered feigning leaving the concourse, but thought better of it. They would come, they were probably just allowing him time for un-punctuality. He would just sit and wait. He would smoke the fucker out.

He waited and waited and waited. Eventually, once the pubs were turned out, there was another surge for the suburbs – balding men in macs belching lager and take-away curry, theatre goers, beer boys and good-time girls trundled, limped and raced across the station, all experiencing a moment of quiet confusion, their faces lapsing from Friday-night bonhomie to survival mode, as they stared upwards at the great board which dictated their safe homecoming that night.

And then, out of the crowd, came Colin, his hands buried deep inside a grey Berghaus fleece that he had zipped all the way to the top. He was whistling to himself, caught up in the Friday night let-down-your-guard atmosphere. Lee ducked behind a brace of doner-devouring clock punchers. Would you Adam and Eve it? What a fucking coincidence. Colin must have been out on the piss, on his way home after a session on the town.

Lee thought: maybe Colin hadn't been away after all. Just lying low. He pictured the watch. Michelle came into his mind and revenge boiled inside him. He couldn't do anything here. Not now. Too public. There would be a better time. He moved from his stool and started towards him: maybe Colin could help with his current situation, lend a little weight . . . Lee stopped. No. That would be a bad idea. Colin would go too far, Colin would cause a scene, make the whole thing go wrong. He checked himself. What the fuck was he thinking? This was the bastard who'd put horns on him. Lee stood, with people clicking and staggering past, and watched his brother walk away, duck behind a newspaper stand and head in the opposite direction from the platform that would take him to Hertfordshire, watched his head turn as he followed the progress of two pretty girls who had passed him, and saw him reach into his pocket and produce a key and – dear God, no! – stand, facing the lockers. Lee sucked air into his lungs; it was more like a sob than a breath.

And there he was, his arm reaching into the metal box, his back stiff and vulnerable. Lee thought of a nature programme he'd once seen in which a salamander dug deep into a turtle's nest to crunch his way through a batch of eggs, his chin slick with yolk. It was an image of such destruction, of decimation, malice, that it had stalked his dreams for weeks. The creature's cruel eyes were wired to a reptile's dead brain.

So here it was, not like he'd planned it, but nevertheless, it was time to act. By the time Colin had removed the bag from the box and closed its door, Lee was behind him. And only at that moment, when he was close enough to smell him, did he realise that he had yet to make up his mind what to do. Should he slap him about? Take him down with a double-dealing punch to the back of his neck? Demand an apology for his craven disloyalty and greed? Just shake his head and disown the bastard?

Lee placed his hand on his brother's shoulder. Colin whipped round, tense, drastically different from the carefree man who had just walked through the concourse.

'What the . . .' he said, his face wide open, scanning for information, judging his next move. It was probably something he'd learned in the army and it reminded Lee of the way that players sometimes looked when they realised they had no time and few options to do things. When he realised that it was his brother his look changed: his eyes opened, incredulous, while the rest of his face collapsed, hanging there as expressionless as a saddlebag.

Lee narrowed his eyes. 'It was you,' he said, his voice toneless and flat. 'It was you.'

Colin offered Lee a misty look, like he too couldn't believe that they had come to this, like he was shocked that he had fallen so low. Lee had expected his brother to swell his chest and make an attempt to bluff it out, but he just stood there and momentarily put his face in his hands.

'I'm so sorry, Lee,' he said. 'I really am so fucking sorry.'

'But Colin, I didn't think . . . I can't . . .' Lee was calm inside, but his mouth wouldn't obey his mind.

'You don't know how fucking sorry I am, Lee. I am so sorry.' He made a step forward to put his arms round his brother, but Lee stepped back. Colin, realising that Lee wasn't responding, pinched the top of his nose, like he'd just taken off a pair of glasses.

'I suppose this must be a shock, bro', suppose you want some explanation . . .'

Lee rocked his head firmly.

'Well, there's no fucking explanation, Lee. Nothing to say.' Colin was talking quickly now. 'I was stupid, I was greedy, I mean, what else do you want from me? What else do you want me to say? I fucked up, I was a prick and I don't expect you to forgive me. I don't expect it to come right between us, but all I can say is that there's no explanation other than the shoes. It was the shoes that did it to me, Lee.'

'What the fuck are you talking about?' said Lee disdainfully.

'You see civvies never notice things like that,' said Lee looking at the floor. 'You'd never have made it in the army, Lee. It's the shoes, you see. You're on the Tube and you look down at this row of blokes and their scuffed shoes and then right at the end you'll see a pair that'll bring tears to your eyes because they're like a pair of mirrors they've got such a shine to them. You could eat your dinner off the fuckers.

'And then you look up at the poor bastard wearing them: some old git who wakes up every morning at the crack of dawn but has nowhere to go but the Citizens Advice for a moan about the neighbours; twitchy old grouches doing shit jobs guarding building sites and supermarkets to try and keep them in Guinness; loners watching daytime TV waiting for a phone call from the kids that never comes . . . They might have spent, I dunno, twenty, thirty years serving Queen and country . . . Lee, it's enough to break your heart, it's enough to make you desperate . . . Lee, I had no choice.'

'Look inside the bag, Colin.'

'Not here, Lee.'

'Look inside.'

'Lee . . .'

'Open the fucking bag Colin.' Colin pulled open the inner bag and stared down at last week's *News of the World*. He smiled the smile of a loser. It was the first time Lee had ever seen it and he felt overwhelmed with sadness. This was his big brother piling on the pressure, adding to the madness.

'I thought it wasn't heavy enough,' he said and shrugged his shoulders.

Lee thought about Michelle, wondered why he couldn't summon the anger to face down his brother. He was too dumbfounded to explore his brother's moral crash-landing any further. Picking among the wreckage would offer too few clues.

'You can keep it,' said Lee, who turned and walked across the station leaving his brother clutching a plastic bag filled with newspaper while commuters tried to beat their way past him on the way home to the ones they loved.

Chapter Twenty-Two

Lee listened to the gravel being crushed beneath his alloys and thought of cereal; Rice Krispies generally, Snap, Crackle and Pop specifically. He was showered and deodorised and fresh out of the breakfast bar at home and he just couldn't believe the coincidence of it all, what with the partially digested snap, crackle and pop bubbling away in his stomach as he inched up the Twomacs' driveway as cautiously as a battle cruiser investigating new, uncharted territory. He had got home late on Saturday and thought there might have been a message from Colin. No dice. Lee was confused, isolated, didn't know how to take the next step, but he would drag the bastard down somehow.

He thought about Lou, wanted to ask forgiveness for his outburst at Villa Park the previous weekend, but somehow the week had crept past without him picking up the phone and offering an apology. Lou had been trying to help in the only way he knew how. Lee missed his clarity, his insight, the way he penetrated bullshit and offered advice that actually mattered.

Never tell a woman she's wrong when she says she's got nothing to wear. Lou had said that to Lee once when they were having a beer on Lee's terrace in Italy. They'd laughed about it – they often laughed when Lou doled out his charming, avuncular advice to Lee because it took them into a more intimate realm, one removed from their professional relationship. But mostly they laughed because they both knew that Lee had no intention of following any advice.

Which wasn't entirely correct. Lee had logged that

particular pearl away. He'd always wanted to use it: to sit silently on the bed toying with his car keys as Michelle ran around in her underwear rooting in her closet like an enraged truffle pig as daunting alpine stacks of Prada, APC and Miu Miu collected on the bedroom floor. He wanted to sit and not say a thing. Imagine that. Tapping his fingers with Michelle cursing to herself: how righteous would that feel? How annoyed would she be not to hear a single bleat about the time and how bad the traffic was going to be?

But it never happened. Michelle was the kind of woman who occasionally complained that she had nothing to wear, but this would be well in advance of any bedroom gridlock or closet capers. She would say it in a matter-of-fact way as if she were saying 'we've run out of milk'. The following day Lee would notice crisp, empty carrier bags inside the wheelie bin. No fuss. No bother. Just a new outfit.

Things had been different back then, back then in the life that he'd fucked up. And perhaps the worst thing about the gradual subsidence of their relationship was that over the years, months, days and hours of calamity he'd *known* – during every moment – that he was making a badger's arse of it all. He could try and pull the wool over Lou's eyes, make a monkey out of Brandwood, give Michelle some spin, but in the final analysis living with Lee Sweeney was the hardest thing of all; living with the impulses and the crack-brained, lathered dissolution was beyond tolerance.

It was like standing on City Road at five-thirty on a Friday night with the traffic lunging forward – all steel, oil and heat – only inches from flesh and realising that you're safe for the next six inches of concrete, but step beyond, into the grey realm of tarmac – and you're toast. And that's before you feel the Tube thumping under your feet, like a clandestine troll trying to break from beneath the pavement. For Lee it was obvious – they were coming at him from all sides. Like some manic shaolin master he could only fend off and block so many blows. Some of them would inevitably break through.

When people talked to Lee about learning experiences, when they offered loquacious anecdotes and shaggy dog illustrations to show how their lives had been altered, bent or reconveyed by the unplanned incident, the arbitrary moment, he had nothing to say to them, no pithy addition to the conversation, no wry grin of recognition. Things just seemed to happen to him, like he had stepped on to an escalator that gradually, steadily carried him further towards an inevitable, incontrovertible end. For most people, when they wanted to get somewhere, needed to arrive someplace, they had a plan, a way of reaching their destination. Lee didn't. He never had. He just sort of turned up.

The Twomacs lived in a large Georgian pile set in twenty acres of pastureland. If visitors narrowed their eyes slightly they might imagine they were living two hundred years in the past. Lee had always felt it a shame that the brothers had never seen fit to invest in any add-ons – garages, a tennis court, swimming pool. As he approached the house there wasn't even a barbecue area. There was no sign of any other cars in the driveway, no obvious place to stuff the motor, so Lee pulled up right outside the huge shiney black front doors. He rang the bell and waited. Above him, in some ivy, a couple of sparrows twittered a territorial war. It made him think of the birds outside his bedroom window a couple of months before. They'd never come back. He hadn't had to kill them.

The door was opened by a middle-aged Filipino woman. She nodded at him and stepped aside. Without a word being exchanged between them Lee realised that he was meant to follow her. They passed down a long passageway that reminded Lee of a posh hotel corridor – gilt-framed mirrors, ornamental tables with vases or lamps on them, the occasional oil painting of a horse or landscape. Plush, thought Lee. Plush but not showy. The first time he'd visited he'd half imagined the place would be all zebra-skin rugs, smoked glass and black leather – the fuck pad of a seventies era Bond villain.

They came to the end of a corridor. The woman stopped and knocked on a door. Without waiting for an answer she entered, held open the door and ushered Lee in. Lee cast his eyes around trying to make out his surroundings – the room was in total darkness, heavy curtains had been drawn across the windows, fingers of light escaping through the sides. In the corner of the room the blue light of a television cast further gloom into the space. It reminded him of being underwater, of the day in Florida when Brenda had fished him out of the pool. He turned, hearing the door close behind him.

'Lee,' came a voice. 'Glad you could make it.' It was Archie McKay. As his eyes adjusted to the darkness Lee could see the Twomacs were sitting on a sofa, their backs to him.

'What's the score?' said Lee walking round the back of the sofa towards the television which was tuned to a Test match from Georgetown, Guyana. 'Oh, don't worry,' said Lee, realising the score was in the corner of the screen. He approached it. 'Shit. 159 for six. It's all gone pear-shaped,' he said. He turned and looked at the brothers on the sofa. Both were wearing crew-neck jumpers with shirt collars poking out at the neck. Archie had a pair of tight, washed-out jeans on and a pair of tennis shoes. Gerrard was wearing olive-coloured jumbo cords and a pair of brown brogues.

'Sit down, Lee,' said Archie getting up. He went to a sideboard, picked up a glass and poured a measure of cognac for Lee who was settling into a tightly packed leather armchair. He took the glass from Archie. It felt heavy in his hands. Nobody said anything, they just sat in the darkness, lit only by the spectral glow of the television. Lee thought it was strange the way that men always watched cricket on television in the dark. There was no rule that dictated that it should be that way, but even when the day was beautiful and brilliant they would hide themselves away behind thick, heavily lined William Morris prints from John Lewis. It was one of the unspoken rules of manhood.

'Nothing like a Sunday afternoon with cognac and the cricket, eh?' said Archie. It was a general observation, but Lee knew that there was no chance of Gerrard answering, so he assented.

'So, Lee, how have you been?' asked Archie, taking a sip from his cognac.

'Well,' said Lee, wondering how far he should go, 'not so great.'

'Oh, why's that? I thought you played well yesterday. We deserved more than a draw,' said Archie. Lee detected a degree of artifice in his voice.

'Bit of trouble indoors, Archie.'

'Things not going so well with the old trouble and strife?' Archie's Scottish accent made him sound patronising when he used the London vernacular.

'You could say that,' said Lee. He looked at Gerrard whose eyes flicked away from him to the TV screen.

'You never know, Lee,' continued Archie. 'Sometimes these things can be patched up. Maybe the two of you just need a period to cool down. Things won't look so bad in a couple of weeks. I know how these things can happen: somebody loses control and before you know it both of you are saying things you don't mean. It can easily happen, Lee. There's no great mystery to it. Before you know it it's all got out of hand. You've just got to think of it in the bigger picture, you've got to think about your future in broader terms.'

'Yeah, maybe you're right,' said Lee. Then it struck him. What was he doing in this room, with these men, talking about his marital problems? He never talked to anyone about that kind of thing, let alone two blokes he hardly knew. Archie had left a message on his answer machine the day before. It had requested Lee's presence at Horton House the following afternoon. There had been no 'if you can make it' or 'let us know'. Lee's presence was expected.

'Business good?' asked Lee impotently, just trying to fill the darkness that was beginning to make him feel edgy.

'Oh, not bad, Lee, not bad,' said Archie, a self-deprecating smile playing around his lips. 'We're getting along, as they say.' Archie had started to roll his glass between his palms meditatively.

'And both your wives are . . .'

'HOWZATTT!' screamed Gerrard, his tree-trunk legs off the floor, arms thrown in the air.

Archie ignored his brother. 'Yes, they're very well,' he said. 'Thank you for asking.'

'For fuck's sake,' shouted Gerrard. 'The man was clearly leg before! Jesus. Have you ever seen anything like that?' He was addressing Lee.

'Sport's a cruel business,' said Lee.

'Tell me a fucking 'bout it,' grunted Gerrard, returning to his silent vigil.

'The thing is,' said Archie, 'that my brother and I wanted to have a chat with you about something and we thought that the best way to do it would be to invite you to our home. Not many people are invited here, you know, Lee. We like to think of it as a bit of a sanctuary in an increasingly insane world; so it's quite a compliment and a measure of our good will that we've asked you to come here today.'

Lee could feel his stomach muscles tightening. The cognac was beginning to taste sour. He was at the centre of the McKay web. A bad place to be.

'You see,' said Archie, slowly looking up from his cognac. 'It had already come to our attention that you are currently undergoing another, destructive, family dispute.'

Lee sat up, crossed his legs and looked at Gerrard. For the first time it appeared that he could see him as well as if it were daylight.

'Your brother has proved himself to be quite a burden to you since he left the army,' continued Archie eliptically. He was starting to use his left hand for emphasis, as if he were trying to persuade Lee of something.

Lee laughed and then checked himself. He was beginning to get a bad feeling. How on earth did Archie know anything about Colin?

'Been a fair amount of unpleasantness between the two of you, hasn't there?'

Lee didn't react, just sat there, as if waiting for a wave to break over him.

'Yes,' continued Archie. 'Not been a good time for the Sweeney family, you could say . . . Lee, my brother and I have got some things to tell you that might make you angry. We're quite prepared for that, it's a natural human reaction in some circumstances, but we'd like you to do one thing, we'd like you to hear us out, give us a chance to put our side of the story. OK?'

Lee nodded, as aware of his movements as a somnambulist. He knew when Archie stopped using the first person that the pleasantries were over, the business part of the conversation was starting.

'We probably know more about you than you'd care to think,' said Archie with a chuckle in his voice. 'So let's start at the beginning, shall we? OK. Now, you'll remember that when you were in Italy, and we did the deal to bring you back to England before the end of the season but we kept everything hush-hush. It all got a bit complicated, didn't it? That's right, the horse-trading that went on with the last match against Inter, we know all about that because, well, it was our money that was being spread around a little.'

Lee's jaw went slack. He took another deep sip of his cognac. He was beginning to see a pattern unfolding.

'Well, I'm sure you can understand that we weren't too happy about seeing our money go up in smoke like that thanks to you playing out of your skin. We'd gambled on being able to persuade you to do otherwise because we thought you might have lost interest in the team and the result by then. How wrong we were. And you, we presume, thought that you could run off with the money because it had been put up by some Eyeties and you were getting on a plane the same afternoon back to good old Blighty. You must have thought that you'd got away with it, must have thought that you were home and dry. Well, maybe not. The truth is, Lee, that we had Italian partners in our venture who required payment. They suggested rather harsher retribution . . .' He paused. 'Fortunately Gerrard and I were able to dissuade them of this. You were lucky, Lee, that it was Gerrard and I who were determining your fate. Those Italians really do have a nasty side to them.' Archie fell silent and turned towards his brother who, on cue, uttered: 'Pretty words, Lee. But not good ones. For either of us.'

Lee dropped his empty cognac glass on the floor. He left it there. He was too stunned to do anything else. *It was the voice*, it was the fucking voice that crept into every inch of his being, had haunted his thoughts and dreams and it was coming from a burly Scotsman sitting a couple of metres away from him who was too busy watching television to pay him proper attention.

'We can see from your expression that you're quite familiar with my brother's talent for mimicry,' continued Archie in an unassuming manner. 'Loves gangster films does Gerrard. Loves them. *The Godfather, Scarface, Good Fellas*, he's seen them all, as I'm sure you can tell.'

Out of nowhere Gerrard commenced an impression of an Italian-American that was somewhere between Brando's Corleone and De Niro's La Motta: 'I said to them, "Look at that! I've lost twenty pounds!" They said to me: that's incredible! I said, "You think that's something special? Over the last ten years I've lost nearly two hundred pounds!"'

Archie waited for the schtick to finish. He'd heard it before, but he was still amused by it. It was rare to hear Gerrard come out of himself. When he finished he continued to stare, glassy-eyed, at the television as if nothing had happened.

'You see, Lee, and, if I may add a personal note at this point,' said Archie, 'this is as difficult for me to tell you as

I'm sure it is for you to hear, everything you might have thought over the past few months hasn't been quite as it seemed . . .'

Here he paused. Lee sat and watched as Archie walked to the sideboard, collected the decanter of brandy, and padded over towards him and filled both their glasses. 'We probably both need another wee dram,' he said, replacing the glass stopper. 'You see, Lee,' he continued, 'this all goes back a long way. You, me and Gerrard go back a little further than you probably imagine.'

Lee took a loud slurp of brandy as applause rang out on the TV for another West Indian boundary.

'You'll remember your last game for Napoli. It was, of course, against Inter, and ended in an unexpected victory for the home side. Unexpected for many because Napoli had nothing to play for while Inter were hoping to capture the Scudetto. Unexpected for my brother and I because we had gone to great lengths to ensure that the result was of a certain nature, namely an Inter victory of at least a two-goal margin.'

Lee hung his head peering at the cream carpet through his amber spirit.

'You remember that, don't you, Lee?' said Archie without giving Lee an opportunity to answer. 'Because a certain friend of ours asked you to partake in a harmless enterprise that simply ensured that a business venture my brother and I had entered into had certain assurances. It was protection, if you like . . .

'The only problem was,' and at this time his voice took on the sour note of a loser, 'that we went to all that trouble to insure ourselves against any harm coming to our investment when one of the key operatives, who we thought had been rewarded more than handsomely, decided to take his own action, a decision that cost Gerrard and myself dear.

'You fucked things up for us, Lee. So we decided to fuck you up. A difficult decision, given your status as our employee, but one we've never regretted. An eye for an eye, as the Bible tells us. As you probably understand better than most, life is full of little ironies,' he continued, his mouth slanting upwards with an exaggerated smirk. 'Se-ren-dip-it-y. So now you're here.'

Lee was shaken, scared even. These men had harmed him, and were easily capable, might even relish, crushing him. He wondered what ruinous plans they had in store for him. There was no reason for them to play out their power fantasies with him, to call him here for . . . for what? Some kind of ritual humiliation? A punishment?

'What are you trying to tell me, Archie?' he asked, trying to mask his growing fear, trying to pretend he was not being manipulated as easily as Super Mario.

'All in good time, laddie,' said Archie, regaining the initiative, 'all in good time.' He looked through Lee who was trying to breathe some life back into his ailing frame. Through his frazzled nerves he felt something, a pressure on his shoulder. A muscle tensing. He reached up to knead the knot.

'Hello, Lee,' came a voice.

He whipped round trying to focus through the darkness. A familiar form began to emerge.

His brother.

Lee rose ponderously from his chair. He stared aghast at Colin before turning to look at the brothers who sat mute, watching his reaction like a couple of behavioural scientists. He felt nothing but blankness before outrage spilt into his limbs.

Silently he stepped towards Colin and swung through the gloom. The punch connected crisply with his brother's jaw. Colin's legs buckled and his torso hit the floor. He could only have seen it coming at the last moment.

Lee stepped forward and aimed a kick at his groin. Colin groaned and tried to cover the area, leaving his chest exposed. Lee moved closer and tried to stamp on Colin's ribcage but found himself magically transported away from the scene and deposited in the middle of the room. Straining to break free from his bonds Lee realised that he was in the bearlike clutches of Gerrard McKay.

'Leggo'ome,' shouted Lee, struggling.

'Come now, come now,' said Archie. 'There really is no need for that. We're all friends here.'

'Lefuckinggo,' said Lee, trying to sound in control, like he was issuing a threat. Gerrard relaxed his grip slightly but still held tight. Lee considered doling out a reverse head-butt but thought better of it.

Archie was helping Colin off the floor. His brother's body was limp, a string of drool hung from his lips.

'Dear, dear me,' said Archie. 'Dear, dear me.' He helped Colin into the armchair that Lee had previously occupied where his brother sat gingerly manipulating his jaw, his face to the ground.

'I'll fucking kill you,' said Lee to Colin who looked up and shook his head.

'Lee, behave yourself,' said Archie.

'Get him off me,' said Lee.

'Only if you promise to calm down and act reasonably,' said Archie.

'Reasonably?' said Lee incredulously. 'You cunts have been ripping me off, he's screwed my wife and you expect me to be reasonable?'

Archie turned sharply to look at Colin who raised his eyes quizzically to examine Lee.

'What you talking about?' he asked.

'Don't come it with me,' said Lee. 'Don't try and pull that shit. I know what's been going on.'

'That's more than I do,' said Colin wincing slightly.

'You've been avoiding me for weeks,' said Lee. 'Why you been doing that then? Then you turn up at Euston . . .'

'At this point I think I would like to intervene,' said Archie. 'Lee, Gerrard is going to let you go now, but you've got to promise to go and sit away from Colin and remain calm for the moment. All right?'

Lee nodded grudgingly and felt Gerrard's arms slacken. He flexed the shoulder and neck muscles that had tensed while he was being restrained before realising that his right wrist was injured. He tried to rotate it, but the pain was too intense. He trailed over to the sofa followed by Gerrard who sat next to him watchfully.

'Good,' said Archie. 'Well, I thought you might be surprised by Colin being here, but I really didn't expect . . .'

'The man's a slag,' interrupted Lee.

'Hear me out Lee,' said Archie. 'Hear me out. I guess this has all come as a huge shock to you – first of all discovering that it was my brother and I who were blackmailing you. Then to discover that Colin has been working for us in a trouble-shooting capacity . . .'

'I did it for you,' butted in Colin, addressing his brother. 'I wanted to make sure you didn't get hurt.'

'How could you do it?' asked Lee. 'You're my brother, it ain't supposed to happen this way.'

'Colin came to our attention by way of an association we maintain with a regiment of the Royal Infantry in which Gerrard served. It seemed that an association would be mutually beneficial as Colin seemed like an ideal candidate for what we had in mind as well as being an alumni of the regiment. I would like to add, Lee, that our arrangement with Colin predates our relationship with you by some months.'

Lee looked at his brother.

'I've been out for nearly two years,' said Colin through a swollen jaw.

'When Gerrard and I decided to gain our revenge it seemed that Colin might be the ideal person to ensure that everything ran smoothly – for all our sakes. And, as certain fears developed about you, he was equally well placed to intervene.'

'Intervene?' said Lee incredulously. 'Intervene? Does that involve fucking Michelle?'

Archie and Gerrard turned to look at Lee, clearly unprepared for this.

'You found the watch, didn't you?' said Colin.

Lee nodded.

'What did Michelle say when you asked her?' demanded Colin. His tone was aggressive. 'What did she say?'

'I ain't asked her,' said Lee. 'I wanted to have it out with you.'

'Well, why don't you ask her?' said Colin. 'Why don't you ask her why I was out in Florida?'

Lee was silent.

'I was out there because I was asked by your wife,' said Colin, who sounded angry. 'She wanted to talk about you, wanted to know if there was anything I could do to help.'

'Oh, yeah,' said Lee dismissively. Colin looked to Archie.

'Colin's telling the truth, Lee,' said Archie. 'We were concerned about your welfare and encouraged Colin here to develop a relationship with your wife and her mother to see if there was anything we could do to prevent you from destroying yourself. I can promise you that Michelle called from Florida. She and her mother wanted to talk but didn't want to return to the UK. Colin asked me if he should go. I said yes.'

'So you lot have been driving me mad with blackmail and then worrying whether I was going mental?' said Lee. 'You really wanted to help didn't you?'

'We had no intention of making the situation any worse,' said Archie. 'We may have miscalculated a little, which is why we want to settle matters now. However, I should add that we're of the opinion that, in general, our actions have had no other effect than encouraging a pattern in your behaviour that was already well established. Anyway, as I've already told you, the bottom line is that you fucked us, so we fucked you.'

Lee shook his head in disbelief. He was staggered by the self-righteousness of Archie.

'We're all worried about the drinking, Lee,' said Colin. 'We only wanted to make things better. Me, Michelle, Brenda, the brothers here . . . No one means you any harm.'

'You're joking, ain't you?' said Lee. 'Youravinalaugh. How can you be interested in my welfare when you've been ripping me off for so long?'

'Come on, Lee, don't be rash,' interrupted Archie. 'Think it through. I'm sure you didn't even notice the cash. Money isn't the issue here. The issue is trust. Now what I see here is a Mexican stand-off. We all know an awful lot about each other. Things that we'd like to remain private. Things that we'd like to keep between friends. There has to be a level of trust between us for us all to prosper, do you follow me?

'On a business level do you honestly think we would have done anything to harm you? To us you're an asset. We have an interest in you remaining at the peak of your powers, consequently it is in our interest that you don't drink yourself senseless. I should also add that we have ensured that there is absolutely no evidence whatsoever to link us to any allegations you might make public. It embarrasses me also to add that we have video and audio tape of your conversations regarding the Inter game and . . .' He picked up an envelope and waved it at Lee. '. . . a written deposition from a convicted Neapolitan drug dealer confirming that you were a regular purchaser of class-A drugs.'

Lee looked at Gerrard who nodded solemnly at his brother's words.

'Me and Michelle haven't got anything between us except for your best interests,' urged Colin. 'We're all just trying to do the same thing – trying to stop you from blowing up. All we want to do is stop the big bang. Wind your neck in, son.'

Lee looked at his older brother sitting nursing his jaw and wondered if the last of their relationship was squeezed out or whether the confusion he felt marked a fledgling re-conciliation. Exhaustion swept over him. He was too drained, too ragged, knocked prostrate by frenetic emotional zigzagging.

Archie approached him. 'I want you to understand that Colin had no other motivation than your best interests,' he said quietly, sensing that Lee was rushing downwards. 'Understand?'

Lee nodded.

'Then shake on it,' said Archie.

Colin rose from his seat and approached Lee offering his hand. 'I'm sorry for the pain,' said Colin. 'Let's be friends, yeah?'

Lee sighed deeply and took his brother's coarse right hand. It seemed like the right thing to do. Maybe this was the way out. Maybe Colin and the McKays were propelling him towards making the first steps towards putting his life right. The voice was over, finished. Maybe he could get on with his life now like everyone wanted. Maybe he and Colin could go back to how they used to be. A little hope was better than none at all. He breathed deeply and said to his brother, 'Yeah.'

Archie beamed. 'It's both an end and a beginning.' He slapped both of them on the back. 'Let's drink a toast. To family.'

Chapter Twenty-Three

Michelle waited nervously in the shop. She checked her watch. They were late. They'd said nine o'clock. It was nearly quarter past. She felt rough, thought she might be coming down with something. She grabbed an ashtray one of the shop girls had nicked from Mezzo following a bottle of Chardonnay and Malaysian prawn lunch and stubbed her Marlboro light. An image played through her head, a vision of a single chip strewn in a puddle she'd seen that morning. The oil from the potato had formed a mauve and green slick on the surface of the water. The image had gave her a bellyache.

She stared out the window watching harried commuters making their last dash for the office, cups of steaming cappuccino in their hands and papers tucked under their elbows. Hellish dispatch vans and livid cycle couriers hurtled up and down the street scattering those foolish enough to cross their path.

Busy Miss was situated on Bond Street. Michelle's eye for the classic and commercial had meant that the shop with its concrete floors, spare, industrial rails, concealed lighting and cool but flattering arm-candy staff had become popular with both girls about town and their style-conscious mothers down from the provinces on retail hit-and-runs. And although most punters were aware that it was Lee Sweeney's cash that had given life to Busy Miss it was equally well accepted that it was Michelle's eye for the classic and wearable of the European and American collections that had made it such a hit.

Because of this, Michelle had been drawn into an odd

realm of fleeting celebrity in which she was famous for not being stupid. For Michelle earning her own way was something she was proud of, and an aspect of his wife that Lee found hard to fathom, being a champion of the undemanding life. Which was all right with Michelle. Being the only one in the household who could read a ledger, follow a budget, talk turkey with an accountant, was just where she wanted to be. Especially with a divorce in the offing. She didn't like thinking that way, hadn't ever wanted to see the marriage end, she just couldn't see a way forward for it.

She had accepted that, for a couple of years, until she got herself back on her feet, the business would be her life and was secretly thrilled at the prospect. Now she just wanted to get on with it. After years of trying to conciliate and administer to Lee's needs she had simply run out of stamina and sympathy. The marathon grind of the relationship had taken too much from her already. And it wasn't like she hadn't tried. She had performed gymnastics of compromise and understanding, vaulting the truth where it might hurt, straddling beams of pain, scoring high for presentation, but with no impact on Lee.

Then his brother came.

She'd hoped that Colin getting out of the services might have helped put Lee back on the road to locating himself, but it had only served to make him worse, clouded his vision with self-pity. Colin had even come to Florida a couple of times, courtesy of Michelle, to talk to her and Brenda about Lee, to see if there was a way of saving him. Of course, Lee was never to know of this, it would only fuel his paranoia. As would his brother's perception of him – Colin's take on Lee was bleak, his diagnosis categorical. He kept using the phrase 'tough love'. With the mass of opinion from Brenda and Colin weighing strongly towards her sweeping her house clean, Michelle had taken Lee to lunch and dropped the bomb. Telling him she had felt dislocated, disconnected – her jaw moved, she formed words, but she found it hard to believe that they were her own.

It had been the Jessica photos that had moved Michelle to unburden herself. Until then things had been tolerable, sometimes even enjoyable. They had even started sex again, daily, until the paper had appeared and she realised that the improvement was just another upward incline on the Sweeney boom-bust cycle. Michelle had got angry and she had got drunk and she had woken one Orlando morning to find Colin in her bed.

She had fallen to Lee's level. Dissolved in a way she had never thought possible.

Accordingly, it was a lingering guilt that made her so prickly that morning as she waited for the television crew to arrive. She was always ready to publicise the shop, but when she had received a call from a producer on the *Jessica March Show* – an outpost on the margins of cable – she had refused point-blank to take part until it was made clear to her that the interview would take place at Busy Miss and would be conducted by a researcher.

So why the hell was Jessica March climbing from a Renault Espace outside her shop?

Dismay turned to anger. Michelle could handle it. She was ready for her.

'Look at that,' said Michelle, hearing footsteps behind her. 'I really gave him more credit than that. Blonde hair, slapper make-up, strappy shoes on a rainy day . . . Except for the boob job there wouldn't be anything on her. Seen more meat on a butcher's pencil.'

Leoni, Michelle's assistant, furrowed her caramel-coloured brow. 'And look at the length of her arms,' she said. 'Like King Louie, King of the Swingers.'

Leoni held the door open and a fresh-faced young man walked in, scanned the room, and approached Michelle.

'Josh Morgan,' he said. 'Pleased to meet you.'

Michelle didn't offer her hand. 'You told me that she wouldn't be here.'

The producer turned as if unsure who Michelle was referring to. At that moment Jessica approached offering her hand.

'Hi, Michelle,' she said. Gauging the moment, Josh slunk off and pretended to busy himself. Jessica's hand hung in the air.

'What the fuck are *you* here for?' said Michelle.

'The programme . . . I, thought . . .' Jessica kept smiling but her eyebrows suggested confusion. 'The programme. You knew we were coming . . .' She looked towards Josh, who was conspicuously having a conversation with the cameraman.

'You know what I'm talking about,' hissed Michelle.

'Well,' said Jessica uncertainly. 'I thought that it was about being the wife of a famous footballer, but . . .'

'Come with me,' said Michelle, turning and heading towards the back of the shop.

The film crew turned as both women clattered down the steps.

They reached the bottom of the staircase. The place was a muddle of rails and boxes of clothes. Jessica halted at the bottom of the stairs feeling that she was somewhere she shouldn't be. Michelle stood facing a work surface that supported a kettle and some mugs.

'What the hell are you thinking?' asked Michelle, seemingly calmer in the halogen-lit basement.

'Michelle, I really don't know what you're . . .'

Michelle turned round, hands on hips. 'Don't come the innocent with me, girl – you know exactly what I'm talking about,' she said wobbling her head – like the Puerto Rican women on *The Jerry Springer Show*.

Jessica suddenly hardened. 'Look, this is stupid. Either you explain what you're talking about, or I'm going to have to go back upstairs.'

'I'm talking about Lee,' said Michelle, her voice calmer, the anger gone.

'And?' replied Jessica.

'Come on,' sighed Michelle. 'Get with the programme.'

'Michelle, I don't know what it takes to convince you, but I have absolutely no idea what you're talking about.'

Michelle stared at Jessica – her immaculate but thick foundation, cherry lipstick, eyes a blueprint of carefully drawn lines – and realised that she was telling the truth. There was something too direct for her to be deceitful. However smart and ambitious she might be she was too straight ahead, too candid, to look Michelle in the eye in that kind of way and still be fucking her husband.

'You really don't know, do you?'

'I could take a guess,' said Jessica, 'but I'm amazed that you could think that way.' She raised her plucked eyebrows so high they looked like Mickey D's golden arches.

'I'm sorry,' said Michelle, losing the conviction that righteousness had offered her. This hadn't been about Jessica, it had been about her and the Florida false move. 'I don't know what I was thinking.' She took a cigarette from the packet and fired it up. Jessica realised she'd been clutching them the whole time, like a comforter.

'Look, Michelle, we've got to go up there in a minute and get on with what we've got to do. I'm not being funny, but this is my job . . .' she said softly.

'You know Lee though, don't you?'

'I hardly know Lee, but I think that I probably know him well enough to have some kind of idea what's going through your mind.'

'I've seen you together, in the papers,' said Michelle, blowing smoke out of her mouth sideways. It was a gesture of politeness. Jessica didn't look like a smoker. She had too much of a gym body.

'Yes, you have,' said Jessica. 'We know each other the way that people in the public eye know each other.' She smiled to herself. 'You know, one of the strangest things about becoming famous is that suddenly other famous people talk to you. People you've watched on TV all your life, people you admire, or you can't even put a name to.

They'll all come and talk to you, just the way that people who aren't famous always want some of your time. It's the strangest thing. Maybe it's like they feel you've already got something in common, or maybe they just think that they know you a little bit already . . . I'm going off the subject aren't I? All I'm trying to say is that nothing has happened between me and Lee, and neither will it.'

'It's not nice for me to have to talk to people like this . . .' said Michelle mournfully.

'You don't have to go there, Michelle,' said Jessica, cutting her off. The pair of them stood listening to the babble of the crew upstairs. 'There's really no need. No hard feelings, OK?' She gave Michelle one of her chipper everything's-going-to-be-all-right TV smiles. 'Let's get the show on the road shall we?'

'Michelle Sweeney,' started Jessica, 'you're the wife of perhaps one of the most famous men in the country. How do you cope with the pressure – both personally and as a couple?'

'Well,' started Michelle. Jessica was smiling at her encouragingly. The television lights had made her gloss-coated lips look almost ceramic, but Michelle was determined not to let even a glimmer of amusement play along her mouth. No. That would say to the folks at home: 'Yes, you're right Jessica! We're fantastically rich and successful! Sometimes we wake up in the morning and can't believe how lucky we are! But being famous isn't all fun, you know . . .'

'If I can take a phrase from my husband's book of quotations I'd say something like "we take every game as it comes",' she said.

Jessica giggled sycophantically.

'As far as I'm concerned fame brings both rewards and drawbacks and it's up to you how you respond to them. If you allow yourself to be spoilt by them, materially and in terms of the way that you perceive yourself, then it's your own lookout. You've got to try and remember who you were before all this stuff happened and hold on to what's inside you. Your values if you like.'

'So tell us,' started Jessica, who, Josh was quickly realising, was much better ad-libbing than reading from cue cards or question boards. 'How has the relationship changed you?'

'Well, Lee and I had known each other for a long time before we actually got married,' said Michelle.

'You were sort of childhood sweethearts, weren't you?' encouraged Jessica, remembering the research.

'Sort of,' winced Michelle. 'So it wasn't like I didn't know exactly who I was marrying when we tied the knot. It wasn't like when you hear about footballers who've met their wives when they've already been famous. I sometimes think how odd it is when girls marry players because of what they are and the lifestyle they have, rather than the person themselves.'

'Do people sometimes just think of you as Lee Sweeney's wife rather than an individual?'

'They might if I let them,' said Michelle, betraying her first smile. 'If people want to know me because of who Lee is then that's their problem, their hang-up if you like.'

'What do you do when you're not with Lee?' asked Jessica, sensing Michelle was beginning to tire of the questioning. The producer had had to work hard just to get Michelle to agree to a 'quick' five minutes.

'Well, I travel quite a bit,' said Michelle. 'I love being in warm climates, so I spend quite a lot of time at our place in Florida, which we're lucky enough to have. But when I'm in this country I run my own business, Busy Miss, here in Bond Street.'

'Tell us a little about your shop, Michelle.'

'It's a contemporary women's clothing store selling the best of the season's collections.'

'What's your role?'

'I'm a pretty hands-on owner,' said Michelle self-deprecatingly, 'so I like to oversee pretty much everything, from the way that customers are taken care of when they walk into the shop, to the purchasing of the collections.'

'Is it all *designer* clothing?' said Jessica, with the humorous lilt in her voice the way that women on daytime television pretend to be intimidated by anything that's not off the rack at C & A.

'Yes, it is,' said Michelle. 'But we buy very carefully, ensuring that we purchase only wearable, practical pieces.'

'Michelle Sweeney, thank you very much,' said Jessica abruptly. 'Thank you for giving us a glimpse of your life with Lee.' She turned to camera. 'This is Jessica March reporting from the West End of London. Now back to the studio.' She continued to look at the camera for a few seconds until Josh had given her a signal.

'That was great!' gushed Jessica, turning back to Michelle, who was already fishing a tiny microphone out of her cleavage. 'You were terrific. I'd never believe that you'd not done television before.'

'Went OK then?' said Michelle matter-of-factly. 'You'll get them to leave in the plug for the shop, won't you?'

'Sure, no problem,' said Jessica, smiling at her. Michelle could tell she was relieved that the thing was over.

'It's a fantastic shop,' said Jessica, looking round. 'I come in here a lot, you know.'

'Good,' said Michelle. 'The more the merrier, as far as I'm concerned.' She lit a cigarette.

'May I?' said Jessica reaching into her bag for a Silk Cut. Michelle watched, taken aback.

'I'm afraid that this is a non-smoking shop,' she said. She took another pull on her cigarette. 'Sorry.'

Jessica nodded, resigned to the fact that she was unable to charm her way out of this particular interpersonal cul-de-sac. The rest of the specky-techie crew with their Timberlands, tight jeans and Swiss Army knives dangling from their belt loops were all ready to go, their equipment stashed in metal boxes. The producer thanked Michelle loudly, told her she was wonderful and to watch the show tomorrow morning around ten thirty. Josh and the crew left, heading for the MPV, but Jessica couldn't resist one glance back over her shoulder. She arched her graphically enhanced eyebrows as a form of acknowledgement at Michelle, one last attempt to connect. But her eyes met only a stone-cold glare.

Michelle stood staring at the shop door for a few minutes. Leoni eventually appeared and handed her the Mezzo ashtray. The two waited silently, Leoni not wanting to break her boss's lingering contemplation. Eventually she had to speak.

'Shall I open up properly?' she asked. Michelle nodded as Leoni pulled open the blinds and put Cassius on the stereo. Feeling thirsty she decided to go downstairs and fix herself a glass of water. She'd make Leoni a coffee while she was down there. She filled the kettle and contemplated her empire. She smiled to herself. It was enough for her. It was a start.

Chapter Twenty-Four

He had just rescued the ambassador from a crew of kidnappers of indeterminate racial origin, when the doorbell went.

'Bollocks!' shouted Lee throwing down his moulded firearm. 'Why now? Why fucking now?!' Postie would regret this; Lee would never sign another ball for a charity raffle, or donate a strip for a kid's cancer op again. As he got to his feet he collided with the coffee table knocking a bottle and a semi-full glass of vodka which splashed on to the floor and formed a dark shape on the cream-coloured carpet.

'Fuck!' shouted Lee leaving the mess where it was. He caught himself for a moment. Two pizza boxes were strewn on the sofa, their lids open. Smeared plates and numerous mugs in varying states of bio-development littered the coffee table, the glass top of which was ringed with half a dozen coffee circles imprinted from the bottom of mugs. Lee checked for a moment and stared – the rings formed the Olympic ensign.

Cursing under his breath, he stumbled along the hall to the front door.

'All right, bro?' said Colin.

Lee nodded his head slowly as if recalling someone he hadn't met for years.

Colin stood on the doorstep, his hands planted in the pockets of his jacket like he was a bank robber hiding a couple of pistols. He coughed and brought out a fist to cover his mouth.

'Came over to see how you're doing, you know, talk

253

things over. Make sure everything's cool between us.'

Lee shrugged. Stuck out his bottom lip. 'I'm not so bad,' he said.

Colin smelled the alcohol on him. 'You sure, bro?' he said. 'Archie and Gerrard thought it would be a good idea as well.'

Lee didn't like hearing that. There was no need. It broke the intimacy between them. 'Oh, that's right,' said Lee. 'Your mates the McKay brothers.'

'Come on, Lee,' sighed Colin. 'I thought we had all this out the other day? The Twomacs had to pay off their Eyetie partners who, in case you've forgotten, wanted to have you taken out. The brothers, they didn't like getting turned over like that. They hired me to make sure that everything ran smoothly. To make sure that you didn't get hurt. Come on, Lee. You think I would get involved with something like that without knowing that everything was going to be all right?'

Lee didn't answer. Twisted and fucked, he felt like he'd been beamed down with the transporter settings a bit off.

'Come on, Lee,' said Colin. 'Let's try and sort it out, eh?' He reached up and rubbed his jaw, as if reminding Lee that he had already suffered.

Lee took a deep breath. The April air tasted fresh and clean; it had yet to be fucked by the summer, the pollen and pollution, turned into a virus-laden soup before the bonfires of October and gunpowder of November. It calmed the jumpiness he felt at the very core of him, beneath his breastbone. For the previous few days he had felt as if there had been a candle burning in the centre of his torso. It reminded him of when he was a kid and his dad took him down to the allotment; there were bonfires there that were lit at lunchtime by old men in casual shirts and were still burning at dusk.

It burnt slow and still inside him and there was only one way to put it out.

'Fancy a drink, Col?' Lee asked.

*

'Fucking hell, Lee,' said Colin. 'You got squatters?' He held his hands out, palms angled to the side to emphasise the question. Colin was twitchy around mess; in some way it offended him personally. It wasn't on.

Lee ignored him, sitting on the floor with his hands wrapped around the PlayStation handset. He held it delicately like he might cradle a bird. Colin eyed him warily – he had yet to hold his brother's attention since he had entered the house. Lee was wearing nothing but a pair of Swish! tracksuit bottoms. He was unshaven and, totally uncharacteristically, his hair was unkempt. It looked like a hanging basket outside a pub in a bad part of town.

'You smell awful,' said Colin.

'Didn't shower after training,' said Lee, disinterested. 'Came straight home. Haven't got round to taking a shower yet.'

'Look at all these fucking cans,' said Colin gesturing at the room like a disappointed father inspecting his errant teenage son's bedroom.

'It's the beer I'm interested in,' replied Lee without taking his eyes from the screen. 'The can just comes with it.'

'Fuck's sake, Lee,' said Colin. 'What happened to the cleaner?'

'Ask Michelle,' replied Lee, abruptly.

'She in Florida?' asked Colin.

'Her mum's,' said Lee. 'We're not talking. Or she's not talking to me.'

'I've never seen the place like this . . .' said Colin. He looked disgusted at the pickle of pizza boxes, mugs, glasses and unemptied ashtrays – he had already clocked the Rizla packet with the strip of packaging removed as well as one of Michelle's make-up mirrors that seemed to have been left incongruously on the sofa. This was Lee gone AWOL again, Lee as they'd come to know him at intermittent stages of his life. It was the Lee who couldn't find a way out of himself, a Lee who had turned inward to such an extent that the rest of the world was no longer something with which he interacted; it was two-dimensional and judgemental, passive yet too threatening to be tampered with.

It was the Lee Colin remembered from childhood, the one who switched off when all around him was tension and expectation, the Lee who discovered from an early age that the only way to preserve any essence of himself was to disengage, to remove himself from the material world. The Lee who preferred the world blurred and muddy, who avoided the sharp edges of life where definition and conflict might arise. It was the Lee who never wanted to get involved: tell Lee that he had a drinking problem and he'd grizzle that, at that moment, he didn't need the hassle; point out that he wasn't able to take responsibility for his own life and he'd slaughter you for getting on his back.

Without his brother noticing, Colin passed into the kitchen, rooted around for a bin liner, and returned to stuff pizza boxes and lager cans into the black bag. After he'd done all that he could Colin stood and watched his brother sitting, utterly absorbed by the dancing electrical images upon the screen, and all he could think of was Lee letting him down, from the very beginning, from when they were kids – Lee backing off when Colin looked towards him for a bit of moral support when charged with some schoolyard misdemeanour; Lee hedging his bets and never allowing loyalty or blood to cloud his relationship with even casual friends; Lee the attention magnet at home, the boy who was, in his own father's words, a 'bit special'. How Colin longed to be a bit special, to garner the rapt, complete attention of his family. He could not complain about the love he got, he had never felt deprived, but it was an everyday love, the kind of love that only the most cold-hearted of parents could deprive their child of. What Colin craved was the pink-cheeked bonhomie that he witnessed whenever adults were around his brother – he remembered it well, it was almost as if they were *in love* with him, men and women.

But Colin had learnt how to remedy this. He had shown how the simple artistry of Lee Sweeney could become not a thing of joy, but a commodity upon which all who came into contact with Lee might project their desires, needs and frustrations.

'Where you been?' asked Lee. 'Haven't heard from you for a while.'

'Been away,' said Colin.

'Doing what?'

Colin regarded him warily. 'This and that, you know . . .'

'No.' Lee continued to play the game.

'Some business,' said Colin, reluctantly.

'That thing you were talking about?' Lee put on a mocking voice ' "Something big?" '

'Yeah.'

'That a McKay thing?'

'No. I'm in with a couple of pals from the regiment.'

Satisfied, Lee let the conversation lull. Colin moved towards Lee. 'Here,' he said.

Lee reached his right hand back without taking his eyes from the screen. Colin put a large wrap of gear into his palm.

'Thanks,' said Lee. Without looking at it he placed it on the floor next to him.

'Don't tell the McKays, yeah?' said Colin. 'About the business or about this.'

Lee nodded.

'Let's keep it our thing – you and me,' said Colin. 'Trust, remember?'

'Kiss me,' said Lee.

'What?' said Colin.

'I like to kiss when I'm being fucked.' Lee smiled a crooked smile that was so run-down that even Colin felt done for.

'You've got to sort yourself out,' said Colin. His brother ignored him. 'I mean it,' he continued. 'This is no fucking good to anyone.'

'Yeah, yeah . . .' drawled Lee.

Colin sighed theatrically. 'It hasn't been easy for me,' he said. 'You know that, don't you?'

'Sure,' said Lee, with no feeling.

'Getting a job and all, it ain't easy,' said Colin. 'Especially if you're in my position. Remember the shoe man?'

Lee put the console down and looked at his brother. Had he come round just to have a fucking moan? Lee didn't want to hear it.

'The McKays didn't tell you everything,' said Colin. 'I didn't leave the regiment. I was kicked out.'

Lee chuckled to himself and shook his head as if nothing could surprise him.

Colin stared at his hands. 'You meet people in the army,' he said by way of explanation. 'And sometimes you get carried along . . . When I was in Germany we used to go out in Hamburg and Amsterdam. Clubs and that. I got involved with things and people I came across. I shifted a bit of stuff around, nothing major. A couple of the boys were bringing loads of gear back on the ferries and getting rid of it over here. They got caught, sent down for an eight stretch. The MPs knew there was more going on so they did random tests – thought they'd weed out the bad apples. They got a fucking shock. Twenty-one of us tested positive out of 250 in the battalion. They discharged the lot of us.'

'Dad know?' asked Lee.

'' Course not, said Colin.

'You've been away a lot,' said Lee elliptically.

Colin gave him a look and Lee understood right there in what kind of 'business' Colin had ended up. There was silence. 'I don't want to hear anything more about it,' said Lee. 'I think you should back off. It ain't good for me to be around you.'

Colin surveyed the room and raised his eyebrows.

'Keep away for a while, Colin, all right?' said Lee with a calm firmness. 'Everything's cool, just keep away.'

There was stillness. Colin considered his brother's words before getting up and walking into the hallway. More words would have been pointless. Lee trailed raggedly behind.

'We're still brothers, Lee,' said Colin. 'Despite everything. Before I go I just wanted to tell you that. We're still family. Remember what mum used to say, God rest her soul.'

'Don't mention her,' said Lee, angrily opening the door. 'She wouldn't like what you're doing. We might still be brothers, but everything's changed.'

'And she'd be fucking heartbroken to see the state of you,' said Colin, with feeling.

Lee looked right through him.

'We can sort it out,' said Colin.

'Maybe,' said Lee, his voice reedy-thin and lacklustre. 'Maybe we can.'

He closed the front door on his brother and gulped air, trying to catch his breath. Colin was mixing it with the big boys, using his trips for the McKays as cover. He fought to distance himself from the quiet simmering of his brother's intrigue, told himself not to be corroded by its pernicious contrivance. As his mind reeled he committed himself to one intention – he would not set eyes on Colin again. It was vital to his outlook: one less problem to contemplate, one less person to twist him into ugly shapes.

Chapter Twenty-Five

Lee sat among the debris in the living-room waiting for Michelle to call. Despite his state of readiness he eyed the phone suspiciously when it started to chirrup. The answer machine kicked in: it was the second voice leaving another set of ham-fisted details. Lee giggled to himself, his head rocking back and forth in an exaggerated nod. A spliff fizzled in an ashtray by his side and Croc had just collected another crystal. Life was sweet. He took another gulp from a bottle of Vladivar and pressed the 'go' button. Prepare to do battle. The other voice, the assured one, had gone now. He had cracked the code, a chimera of Colin and Gerrard. A fucking pantomime horse of two nutters.

But the second one, the one that didn't really sound like it was one hundred per cent convinced by what it was doing, was still coming. After the events at Euston it was a revelation to Lee that this voice had no *right* to be taking his money, it had no claim upon his nervous energy. Newly anachronistic, it was a curiosity to Lee, an oddity. Something to be cleared up.

He thought it was time he discovered the owner of the irresolute voice.

Within his vodka-inundated mind he made a note of the details: a lay-by on the rural suburbia that flanked the A1081. If he followed a footpath he would come to a disused piece of farm machinery. If he reached beneath he would find that there was enough room to place a plastic bag chock-a with cash. Leave the money at two o'clock, it said, which was nicely timed for an après-training detour. Lee logged it. He'd be there.

But his mind was elsewhere – and it wasn't on Croc. Lee had been waiting for a call, for a pulse of electricity to light him up. He had not spoken to Michelle since he'd left Florida, and now he searched his mind for fresh memories to service his morose sentimentality. He knew she was back in London, he saw her – amazingly – being interviewed by Jessica on TV. He had been sitting in the dark drinking beer when the image of his wife happened upon the screen. His reaction had shocked him more than he could imagine. He had sat transfixed, too startled to press the mute button to regain the volume – his favoured manner of watching TV was on his own, in the dark, with the volume off and a skinful of beer.

It was how Michelle often found him (and left him) when she was at home. When she appeared on the screen (Lee noticed that they captioned her 'Michelle Sweeney, wife of footballer Lee' – she wouldn't have liked that) it had felt intimate to him in a way that he couldn't understand. With her face filling the thirty-six inches of his television screen, she was larger than she was in the flesh.

'Hello, darlin',' Lee had said, as softly as if he were talking to a sleeping baby. 'Been a long time.' Michelle moved her head to the side. She was listening to a question. She smiled and delivered a rapid response, as if cracking a joke in reply to one of Jessica's questions. She looked confident, she looked in good nick, on top of her game. Lee moved closer to the television, a couple of beer cans ringing metallically hollow against each other as he slid across the floor. He reached out to the screen and traced his finger down the outline of her hair.

'You're looking good, girl,' he said. 'You're looking fine.'

The image suddenly changed. Cut to Jessica laughing at one of Michelle's comments. Lee snatched his hand back from the screen, recoiling. He frowned. 'Bitch,' he said angrily. His voice was slurred, its inflection skewed. 'What you done with my girl, with my Michelle?'

As if in apology Michelle returned to the screen. She was

smiling gently, her mouth open slightly, her teeth pro-
truding from the bottom of her lip. Lee smiled back as if
she had her eyes fixed on him. She reached up to push her
hair behind her ears.

'That's my girl,' he said, his eyes filling with tears. He
reached out his hand again and tried to cup her cheek. The
static from the screen fizzed beneath his palm, although he
was oblivious to it.

And then, as suddenly as she had appeared, she was
gone, disappeared into television ether to be replaced by a
grinning anchorman who couldn't have been happier that
the show was over and it was time for him to jump in his
Rover and hightail it back to Berkshire where it was safe
and clean.

Lee fumbled for the off switch. The image drained from
the screen and the machine squealed as if it had been hurt.
Lee sat in the darkness. 'When you coming home, darling?'
he asked. He stared into the television, made out his own
image in the grey-green screen and he felt further from her
than he'd ever been before. He spoke, then caught himself
as if he were revealing a secret that should not be told. Then
it spilt out.

'When you coming home, sweetheart?' he asked. 'When
you coming home?'

Lou saw him coming but he didn't run. He hung his head,
defeated by his own stupidity, ruined by his gotta-have
greed. He put down the plastic bag on the rusty machinery
and waited for his approaching client. As soon as he'd seen
the movement in his peripheral vision he'd known who it
was, something about the way Lee walked, the swagger of
it. He was about twenty yards away, wearing his training
outfit. Lou could hear nylon waterproofs rubbing together.
The only other noise was the soft rustle of rain – constant,
but light – falling on the crops that filled the field. Lou had
no idea what kind they were – wheat, or something, but he
liked the colour of them on such a bleak day.

Lee paused about five yards from Lou, nodding to himself. Lou didn't know whether this was to show that he had been suspected all along, or whether it was the nod of the victor, the triumphant hunter facing his prey. Lou lit a cigarette and waited for Lee to speak; it was too much to ask for him to lead this conversation the way that he usually had to. Lee looked tired. He was unshaven and there was a darkness, quite literally, about him that Lou didn't recognise. The exhausted and the broken are more usually pale. Lee could see that Lou considered this an ending of sorts, for either one of them, maybe even for both.

'Gis a cigarette, Lou,' said Lee.

'You shouldn't be smoking,' said Lou reaching into his pocket. He threw the packet and lighter to Lee; it seemed too intimate to simply hand them over. The two men stood smoking in the rain. Lou watched the clouds of smoke billow upwards and outwards.

'So,' said Lou. 'Surprised?'

Lee smiled, looked into the mud beneath his feet. 'Hard not to be at the moment, but when I sit down and think about it I'm sure it will be all too fucking obvious.'

'Surprised that it went on this long,' said Lou. 'I thought you'd come after me before now. I mean, I'm not under any illusions, I know that I was no fucking good at it.'

'If the other lot hadn't been so fucking good at it then I might have been a bit quicker,' said Lee.

Lou rummaged in his pocket for a hanky.

'So that's why you said not to go to the police about the other lot, was it?' asked Lee. 'No wonder you asked me so many questions about how they went about it.'

'Well, at the time, no. Not really,' said Lou earnestly. 'I wanted to think it through. Wanted to see what the options were.' He watched a pair of birds take flight.

'So you came up with this.'

'Yes.'

'Proud of yourself, Lou?'

'I should ask you the same question.'

Lee took a step to the side. Lou noticed that enough water had gathered upon his face for a drop of rain to be hanging from his chin.

'So who were the other lot then?' asked Lou. He wanted to know.

'The McKays,' said Lee.

'*The McKays*?' exclaimed Lou. 'Why?'

'Revenge, Lou, revenge.'

'For Italy?'

Lee nodded.

'What? It was *their* fucking money?!' said Lou incredulously. 'Jesus fucking Christ.' His laugh rolled across the silent field. 'That's fucked-up,' said Lou. 'It ain't like they need the money. You want to watch yourself. They're nasty bastards. They'll fuck you up if you cross them.'

'I know,' said Lee.

'Pride thing, was it?'

Lee nodded, not wanting to go through the details of the matter once more. 'The money's not important,' said Lee. 'It used to be, but not any longer . . .'

'What are you talking about, Lee?'

'Colin.'

'Colin what?'

'Colin was doing their dirty work for them. He'd been out of the army for two years, been on the continent. He'd been working for the twins doing the pick-ups of the money for six months before he bothered coming to see me.'

Lou crushed his cigarette butt into the mud. It fizzled slightly before dying. 'Then there's me,' he said.

Lee shrugged. 'I can't pretend I ain't hurt,' he said. 'You were like a dad to me for so long. I suppose I'm just beyond it all now. Anyway, at the end of the day you're a money man.'

He turned to go as if he'd had enough. Lou stepped towards him, irritated at Lee's reaction. That was it? He was his friend and he had betrayed him, stolen his money, humiliated him, and this was his response? A shrug of the shoulders? What about all their time together? Did it mean nothing to him?

'You never deserved me anyway,' said Lou. 'You never deserved any of what happened to you. You didn't deserve Michelle.'

'You what?' said Lee turning.

'You've fucked it all up Lee,' said Lou. 'And you fucked it all up yourself. It was the one thing you didn't need any help doing.'

'You're out of your tiny mind,' said Lee.

'Oh no, no, no, Lee,' said Lou. 'Wrong again.'

Lee ran his hand through his wet hair. It stuck up in clumps, like seedlings growing from bare earth. 'You know what you told me once, Lou?' he said, his voice gentler, more brittle. 'You said to me, and I can't remember exactly when, I can just remember the phrase . . . You said to me, "if this all goes well we'll be wiping our arses with fifty-pound notes". I remember us laughing at that . . . Well, you know what, Lou? You know what? We can both do that now, easy as we like. No big fucking deal. And you know what? Now that we've got it all . . . I don't give a fuck, Lou. All the schemes we came up with, the planning and plotting and jockeying, it was a waste of time because look where it's got us, look where we've ended up. Two people standing in a fucking field shouting at each other.'

Lou waited. He swallowed uncomfortably. 'I know that, Lee,' said Lou. 'I never thought any different. You've just got to insulate yourself from it all. Some people learn that early on, other people don't get it 'til they've been stung so bad you can barely recognise them. You've got to stop yourself from getting hurt by all the shit that's out there. That's all there is to it. Don't take it personal. And believe me, Lee, there's no more shit out there for you than for anyone else.'

Lee sighed. The pair of them were catching double

pneumonia and Lou had the cheek to give him a fucking lecture?

'Whatever I got, Lou, it was because of me. It was because of what I could do. It's like someone told me – I turned my body into money.'

'Very profound, Lee, very profound,' said Lou, patronisingly. 'But did you ever stop to think for a moment what it might have been like if you hadn't behaved like a fool? If you hadn't tried, every day, in some small way, to belittle everything that you've been given? You reckon most of the players the world over would have treated your gifts the same way? As if the world owed them a fucking living? You threw it away, Lee – you were given something precious and you chewed it up and spat it out. Yeah, you're self-made all right. You're a self-made midget. And that makes me so sad. You don't know how sad.'

'You think it's easy, eh?' said Lee. 'You think it's easy being the famous Lee Sweeney? What if I didn't want what I'd been given? What if I didn't value it? There's nothing to say that I have to behave in a certain way, do things like everyone else wants them to be done. I've spent the last fifteen years of me life doing what other people want me to do – mum, dad, Colin, coaches, managers, fans, journalists, you, Michelle. And what about me, eh? What about what I want, who I am?'

'I don't think you even know any longer, do you?' said Lou. 'I don't think anyone would recognise you. What about Michelle, eh? She happy with what's going on?'

'Don't ask me,' said Lee despondently. Lou read this as flippancy.

'Just show some dignity at least, show some fucking self-respect. Michelle was the best thing ever to happen to you. She was the one who was there from the start, when you were just a youth sweeping out dressing-rooms and cleaning boots. She never knew that football was going to work out. She never expected anything. 'Course when the good life came she was pleased to greet it, but it was never

266

what she was about Lee, it was never who she was. She only ever wanted you, Lee.

'She was bound to leave you sooner or later. She cared about you too much to watch you hit rock-bottom and keep digging. Think about it, Lee. Can't you fucking see? She left you because she loves you, because she can't watch what you've become. She left you for the oldest reason in the fucking book – you're not the man she married.'

Lee looked to his left, into the distance. He couldn't bear to meet Lou's stare – he had set his jaw the way he did when he was angry. There were tiny whispers of steam rising from his head.

'So I'm all washed up, am I?'

Lou tutted and shook his head. 'You don't fucking get it, do you, Lee?' he said. 'You just don't know anything, do you? I told you before. You ain't washed up until you're wearing every piece of clothing you own. Get a fucking grip, Lee. Just get a fucking grip.'

He raised his shoe from the sticky mud, looking down as if he was worried he'd trodden in something unsavoury.

'So what are we going to do?' asked Lee.

'We?' questioned Lou. 'I don't think there's any we about it. You're on your own on this one, mate. I ain't getting my percentage.'

Lee turned up his collar. 'Keep the money,' he said. 'It's real. I don't know why – force of habit, I suppose – but I got the ten grand out anyway. You have it.'

With that he turned and started across the field. He didn't follow a path; instead, with difficulty, he navigated his way through the green shoots that reached upwards towards the sky.

'Lee!' shouted Lou. 'Lee! Take the money! I don't want your fucking money. I'm leaving it here. It'll just be left here. Lee! I'm leaving the money.' Lou turned and ran back the way he had come a few minutes earlier. In his haste he slithered and slid his way along the chocolate-coloured pathway. It was as if he were running from a ticking bomb.

He turned to see Lee climbing over a fence on the other side of the field before his blue nylon training top disappeared. Lou continued running back towards the lay-by. He turned and looked at the drenched plastic bag sitting on the rusting plough before climbing over a stile and clambering into his car.

It was still sitting there twenty minutes later when he went back to get it.

Chapter Twenty-Six

It was as if he were falling, plunging from a great height. He imagined it to be somewhere hot, a vast place where his cries would be lost on the wind; the Grand Canyon, somewhere like that. He thought about walking along a thin track, carved from the rock, just wide enough for a man and a mule. He thought about struggling up the track – it was hot, silent save his own footsteps – and losing his footing, feeling his equilibrium shift violently, the last desperate gasp, of trying to claw his way back to solid ground; and thereafter the certain, almost liberating, knowledge that it was all over.

He couldn't imagine what the rest of it would be like, the fatal descent. He just had an image of himself with blue skies in the background falling into the canyon, heading for earth passing from shade to sunshine, shade to sunshine. That was him, the man falling, the man going from darkness to light, from light to darkness with the shape of his shadow heading inexorably towards him.

A bluish strobe of lightning flickered across his face as he waited for the door to the McKays' house to open. The rain beating on the gravel was so loud that it sounded like another car was approaching. He'd finished with Lou and returned home to discover a message requiring his presence at McKay Towers. The housekeeper answered the door without a sound and ushered Lee into the hallway.

'You like a towel?' she asked, looking him up and down.

'I look that bad?' asked Lee. The housekeeper shrugged. It was no loss to her if he wasn't interested. She started off down the hallway with Lee, dripping, following close behind. After the gravel the carpets felt as springy and thick as moss. Archie opened the library door before the house-keeper reached it. A sunshine-smile spread across his tanned face matching the Côte d'Azure sportif look of his pastel-coloured clothes. Archie's message was this: it might be torrential rain for most people, but for him there was perpetual cheer, constant success.

'Thank you, Elaine,' he said. He opened his arms like a game-show host. 'Lee, you made it! Is it still raining outside?'

Lee ignored him, passing directly into the room. Archie was still chuckling at his own joke as he closed the door.

'Drink, Lee?' said Archie, heading towards a sideboard upon which several decanters and cut crystal glasses sat in an enormous silver tray. 'By God, man, you're soaked through. Take your jacket off, at least.' Lee felt the damp upon his shoulders and shivered. He sat down on the edge of a sofa.

'Large Scotch, Archie,' he said, nodding towards the drinks.

'Right you are,' said Archie. 'Something to warm the cockles, eh?'

Lee sat waiting for his drink. He listened to the ticking of a clock on the mantelpiece and the splashing of Scotch in glasses.

'I have to apologise for the absence of my brother,' said Archie, handing Lee a glass. 'He's had to go to Singapore for a couple of days on business. He sends his best wishes.'

Lee thought that there was no one in the world less likely to send his best wishes than Gerrard McKay.

'So, Lee, I think it's best that I cut to the chase, don't you?'

Lee sat impassively, sipping his drink. Archie wondered if he was even listening to what was being said. He sat down in front of Lee on the edge of the coffee table, hands clasped together. He looked up at Lee expecting something to be said. Lee sat unblinking, toying with his whisky.

'It's like this, Lee. Gerrard and myself lost a considerable sum through this whole fiasco. If Gerry or the Eyeties had had their way you'd have got a good coating. And, although I don't always subscribe to the same school of thought as my brother, there, I admit, have been times that I've imagined your face meeting immovable objects.' He paused for a moment. 'We McKays don't forget. We don't forgive.' He leant forward and took Lee's glass from his hand gently. 'Top up, Lee?'

Lee assented. Archie didn't say another word until he was reseated.

'We've had an idea, Lee, that will put us right back on track. We'd like you to help us as a gesture that you're desirous to get back on level terms with us. We're giving you a chance to get off our shit-list. And, believe me, Lee, you really don't want to be on that. We're from Govan, Lee. Glasgow. We don't fuck about like you cockney cunts.'

Lee raised his eyebrows. He felt his skin tingling red as his heart bounced within his ribcage. There was steel in Archie's tone.

He continued. 'That way we can all put this sorry mess behind us. The Cup Final, Lee: we must lose by at least a two-goal margin.'

Lee opened his eyes wide; they burnt from being starved of fluid.

'Yes, Lee, a two-goal margin. I'm sure you know what Gerrard and I have done, and I'm sure you can guess that we got extremely handsome odds given that we are hot favourites to beat a struggling First Division outfit of journeymen cloggers.

'You may well ask yourself, Lee, why my brother and I, as the sole shareholders in the club, might want it not to be successful, to prevent it from entering European competition next season. It is a good question and a fair one. All I can say to you is that Gerrard and I are experienced businessmen and we have our reasons.'

'You want me to throw the Cup Final,' said Lee. 'You want me to swallow.'

'There is the matter of bonus fees to be paid to individual players whom we judge to be deserving of them, if you see what I'm saying. We estimate these bonuses should come in at around £100,000 per player. We estimate that one or two other key players – those who can genuinely influence a game – may join you in the venture.'

Lee sat and shook his head laughing quietly to himself. He looked up at Archie who stared back with empty eyes.

'It's a mad, mad world, Lee,' said Archie patting him on the shoulder. 'Get something out of it while you can. Be sensible. You mess us about again and we'll fuck you up so badly you'll wish you'd never been born.'

Lee cupped his hands around his chin resting his fingertips on his eyebrows. The gesture offered some small measure of shelter.

'It'll take a little time to sink in, Lee,' said Archie. 'Go home and get some sleep. You'll feel better about it in the morning.'

'All I'm trying to do is just hang on,' whispered Lee.

'Sorry?' said Archie leaning forward, smiling, thinking that Lee had cracked a joke.

'I'm going football crazy,' said Lee to Archie.

'Don't be stupid, Lee,' said Archie. 'You were always a fucking nutter.'

In Archie's eyes he saw a sort of escape, a way to work his way free from the place he was in. It was just another game. It was just someone else wanting a part of him.

He got up to leave the room, moving slowly but purposefully. He didn't want to sit and listen to this any longer.

'Get some sleep, Lee,' said Archie. 'Think on it. One thing though – you fail us, you fail yourself, you've no future. Not here. Not in this lifetime.'

But Lee couldn't hear him. He was in another place altogether.

Chapter Twenty-Seven

Lee heard Michelle slide the door chain free and snap the Yale. She would know who it was, would have been expecting him. Maybe part of her thought it better to ignore the chime of the bell, sit in darkness, pretend she wasn't at home. Lee would never know . . .

But it was too late for that. There would be no more evasion, no more fly-by-night dodging and ducking. Only words. The right ones. Despite everything Lee still understood some things about his wife: she would know what it was that she had to say to him, she would just have to engineer the means of communication for someone who had stopped listening. Lee knew that she would only get what she needed to get done if she found the right tone, the one that was steady, rich and calm. Lee was seduced by it, came with it, gave in. She would determine not to use the shrill one that made Lee as jumpy as a cage of lab monkeys. He heard her take a steadying breath and imagined there to be one thing on her mind: she would use the voice. She would cosh him with it.

There he was on her doorstep, unshaven and bedraggled, polluted by his conversation with Archie McKay. His waterproof had turned a shade darker because of the rain. Water hung from his chin. His eyes flickered towards her before looking down. He could see it in her furtive eyes: it was all she could do not to take him in her arms.

'Can I come in?' he mumbled. It was a question.

''Course,' she said keeping her tone steady, controlled. The two of them stood in the hallway beneath a painting of St Francis that Brenda had got from the back of *Sunday* magazine. (The same issue, coincidentally, that had featured Michelle's very own recipe for brownies.)

Michelle was wearing a black cardigan and an old pair of cotton Swish! tracksuit bottoms that Lee had given her. He looked at her sheepishly. He noticed that her feet were brown and, unusually, there was no nail polish on her toes.

'Take off your jacket, Lee,' she said firmly. 'You're going to catch your death.'

Lee dragged the waterproof off – the dampness made it cling to his frame. Drops of water fell on to the pink carpet turning it red, like splashes of blood.

'Come through,' said Michelle leading Lee into the kitchen. She put the kettle on. 'Better get something warm inside you, eh?'

Lee didn't say anything, just perched on a stool at the breakfast bar. Michelle folded her arms and cocked her head to the side slightly.

'So how long has it been this time, Lee? A day, two days? Three?'

Lee smiled on one side of his face and swung his head in an arc from the middle of his chest to his shoulder.

'I'm just glad I don't have to watch it any longer,' continued Michelle.

'You're watching it now,' said Lee.

'It speaks!' said Michelle mock dramatically. Rain momentarily beat against the leaded kitchen windows. She reached into a cupboard and pulled down a couple of mugs and a box of PG Tips.

'You haven't got anything stronger?' said Lee elliptically.

'No, Lee,' said Michelle. 'There's no booze in the house. Not any more.'

'Not ever,' said Lee mocking her.

'Not for you,' said Michelle.

'Fucking hell,' said Lee running his hand across his face from chin to forehead. His hands were filthy. Michelle noticed that a couple of the knuckles on his right hand were bloody.

'What happened to your hand?'

Lee held his left hand in front of him focusing his eyes.

'The other one, dummy,' said Michelle. Lee stuck out his bottom lip. 'I don't suppose you know, do you?' said Michelle dismissively.

Lee tried his winning smile. No dice. She was using that voice. The one that pleased her, that made her feel in control.

'I've no idea,' said Lee.

'That's handy,' replied Michelle. She did an impression of him: 'I don't know, nothing to do with me, must have been someone else.'

'That tea coming then?' asked Lee, annoyed.

'That's right, Lee – your marriage is up the spout, your career's all over the place, you're drinking for England instead of playing for it – and all you can think about is a cuppa.'

'Don't start all that shit,' said Lee, his head sagging towards the breakfast bar.

'Don't worry, Lee, it's too late for all that, we're too far gone. I just wish you'd have the honesty to acknowledge where you are, to be honest – not even with me – but with yourself.'

'Oh, you're the honest one, are you?'

'I'm honest enough to tell you that I need you to set me free,' said Michelle suddenly. She stopped herself for a moment. 'Lee, I need your blessing to walk away from all this.'

Lee exhaled quickly and shrugged, a gesture that conveyed exactly what it meant – that he could find no words to express himself.

'I don't know,' said Lee.

'You don't know what?'

'I don't know much . . .' his voice trailed off. Michelle waited for a second, trying to work out whether this was Lee trying to genuinely communicate or whether it was merely whisky words.

'I know it might have come as quite a shock to you when I told you in Florida – it would come as a shock to anybody. But I think enough time has passed for us to be able to make some decisions.'

'So what have you decided, Michelle?' said Lee sarcastically.

'I don't need to decide anything, Lee. It's simple. It's over. The only decisions we need to make are about the future, not the past.'

Lee started giggling to himself, his body convulsed in a spastic shake.

'What's so funny, Lee?' asked Michelle. She was beginning to feel angry. In some ways that was good – it liberated her, made her sure that she was doing the right thing.

'I don't know,' said Lee. 'I don't know what's wrong. You do, though. That's where we're different. You know exactly what's wrong.'

Michelle sighed. It was going to be so much harder with Lee in a shadowy, remote mood. 'Come on, Lee,' she said. 'Do I have to spell it all out? Do I have to? All my life I feel like I've been giving you the answers to questions you should have known.'

Lee tugged at the lobe of his right ear nervously.

'I loved you so hard, for so long without getting anything back that maybe it just all got used up. I spent it all and I fell out of love.' Michelle said it in the most matter-of-fact way that she could muster – as if only a total fool wouldn't understand why. She said it without malice.

Lee looked down at his soggy trainers.

'For me,' said Michelle, 'love is like a fire – you've got to keep feeding it. It can't just go on for ever without some-thing to nourish it.' She stopped momentarily. There was a new sadness to her voice, as if the words that she'd rehearsed were passed and she was suddenly realising the import of what she was saying.

'You never gave me anything back,' she said.

276

'You know I always loved you,' said Lee.

'How?' replied Michelle. 'How would I know?'

'You could tell,' said Lee. 'It's just there.'

'Maybe it's like that for you, Lee, maybe you see things that I can't make out, but for me there was nothing but space in our relationship that we didn't know how to fill. I tried to move into it. Tried to throw myself around to fill it up. But the only thing I ever heard back was an echo. My own.'

'The sound of one hand clapping.'

'What's that?'

'I dunno, I must have seen it somewhere.'

She put her hand on his. 'We've been together an awful long time, Lee,' she said, losing the voice that she wanted. 'Sometimes things come to an end.'

'Is that what you want?' said Lee holding her gaze for the first time that evening. 'Is that really what you want?'

Michelle bit her bottom lip, her eyes clouded over but she never took her eyes from Lee.

'Yes, Lee. Yes, it is,' she said.

'But what about me?' said Lee. 'What do I get out of it?'

Michelle shook her head. 'You don't always get what you want in life – there's not always an upside . . . Lee, I can't make the world right for you. I tried for ten years, for longer, to make the world a good place for you, to smooth out its rough edges, to hide the stuff that you didn't want to see. Most of all I tried to get you to take a look at yourself, to discover what it was that you'd become. And you know what? After a while I realised that you didn't even know that I was there.'

'I saw you every day, didn't I?'

'I'm not talking about that.' Michelle drummed her nails on the kitchen counter in exasperation. 'I don't know, maybe it wasn't even your fault. You live a life where everything revolves around you, where everywhere you go people want to know you, where everything you say is funny . . . The drinking, Lee, my God, the *drinking*.

Maybe you thought that you were doing it to relax yourself, to have a laugh . . . But we'd be out there in the middle of a party or whatever and I'd look at you and I could see that you'd shut down for the evening. You could be among all those people but all you wanted was the drink.

'Maybe you lost yourself, Lee, maybe you forgot who you were. One thing I know is that you forgot who I was. I wasn't Michelle any longer, I was your wife, the trouble and strife waiting at home with a rolling pin to cramp your style. That's how you thought of me.

'Well, maybe I asked too much of you. Maybe I expected just a little more, or maybe your standards just turned to shite. Whatever. All I can say is that it's beyond me these days what's going on in your head. In my darkest moments I think that even you don't know. I've decided to stop being responsible for you. It's too much, Lee, it's too fucking much.'

'What about Colin?' said Lee, his voice flat and clear as an early spring morning.

It caught her unaware. Despite his state Lee had lost none of his talent for a counter-attack, for spotting weakness and exploiting it. Michelle swallowed. He tried to read her face and could tell that she had no idea what he really knew. He had listened to her being open and honest and revealing her innermost feelings to him, but . . . He watched her trying to compose herself, to regain her footing as she passed from honesty to defence.

'You mean . . .'

''Course.'

'It was, well . . . Jesus, Lee, I don't know . . . I don't know what to say.'

Lee didn't help her out, just sat there waiting for his wife to compose herself. She dabbed at the corner of her eye with a tissue that she magicked from her sleeve, the way he'd watched women do all his life.

'Don't give it the waterworks, darlin',' said Lee. 'You're a big girl now, remember. You're taking responsibility for your own life, not just looking after that overgrown kid of a husband of yours, eh?'

'It was a mistake,' said Michelle defiantly. 'It never should have happened.'

Lee stood up: his brother had lied to him, looked him in the eye and betrayed their relationship as if it meant nothing to him. He drew a pattern in the condensation on the window before turning and throwing a punch in the direction of the wall. He pulled his fist back at the last moment, remembering the condition of his right hand.

'Don't, Lee!' cried Michelle. They both stood there in silence shocked by the electricity of the instant and listened as footsteps came down the stairs. Lee stood, his chest rising and falling as he breathed. Brenda appeared at the kitchen door. She ignored Lee.

'Everything all right, darling?' she asked Michelle softly, as if she didn't want Lee to even know that she was there. Michelle nodded assent, her eyes red with tears.

'You've got to understand, Lee. We were both worried about you . . .' said Michelle finally.

'Colin? Worried? About me?' said Lee sneering.

'He came to Florida to talk.'

'Why didn't you tell me?'

'Come on, Lee. For fuck's sake, you were so messed up no one knew what the hell to think. No one knew what to do with you.'

'That time when you wouldn't let me in – he was there, wasn't he?'

Michelle nodded slowly and not without guilt.

'So you fucked him.'

'Oh, come on Lee, make this easier for both of us . . .'

'Why the fuck should I make this any easier for you, eh? Why do you deserve to have anything but fucking contempt from me?'

Michelle answered quietly. 'I asked myself that question every day for the last five years, Lee. I asked myself why I should deserve anything but contempt from you. And you know what? I worked out the answer on my own, without you bullying or ignoring or humiliating me. I worked out one thing, and it's the one thing I'm going to hold on to for the rest of my life: I *deserve* better than that. I deserve to be loved.'

Lee stood silently, not meeting Michelle's gaze which burnt into him with self-righteous anger.

'So you decided to love Colin.'

'Don't be stupid, Lee. I don't love Colin. I've never loved him.'

'But you fucked him.'

'Yeah, I fucked him!' shouted Michelle, incensed. 'Is that what you want to hear, Lee? I fucked Colin. I fucked your brother. It's not true, but that's what you wanted to hear. There, better now?'

Lee turned and took a couple of paces away from the table lacing his hands behind his head, like an athlete trying to open up his ribcage, trying to pull in more oxygen.

'You got me to say it. You don't know if it's even true. What are you going to say now then, Lee? That I'm a slag, that I'm a no good conniving bitch? That's what you're thinking, isn't it? Eh? Like you've never played away from home . . . You treat me like I'm dirt, like I'm barely visible, you screw any slag who flutters her fake eyelashes at you and you have the cheek to point a finger at *me*? For Christ's sake, there are women out there wearing tops saying "I slept with Lee Sweeney and all I got was this lousy T-shirt". I tell you what, Lee, before you do any kind of finger-pointing you take a long hard look at yourself. You take a look in the mirror before judging me.'

'You and Colin,' said Lee eventually. 'I should have seen it coming.'

'That's bullshit, Lee,' said Michelle. 'Your sense of reality is so fucking screwed up by booze you don't know what's happening from one moment to the next. All you do is keep the lies coming, keep the deception cooking, keep everyone fooled – because the moment you stop believing in just one little part of that big fucked-up picture of the world that you're carrying around in your head, then the whole thing comes tumbling down.'

'You don't understand, do you?' said Lee.

'It's you who doesn't understand. We're over, Lee. We're over.'

Lee snatched at the mug of steaming tea in front of him and drained it in one go. A sliver of browny-orange liquid slid down his chin. Lee left it to dilute in the layer of moisture that remained on his face. He rose from the table.

'I've got to go,' he said. He moved towards the door but turned and looked right at her. There was an intensity about his gaze that could almost pass for clarity. Michelle bowed her head and listened to the front door close. He knew that there was nothing more that she could say to him.

Chapter Twenty-Eight

Lee had a plan: that night he got in his car and, vigilant and unfamiliarly cloudless, he drove, finding himself drawn to the M1 and pulled northwards, without deviation, passing through the industrial-lite navel of the country and up, up to Leeds, near the top of his footballing universe. He pulled off the motorway at Leeds, knowing there was a Harvey Nichols there. He looked at his watch, it was four a.m., and Leeds was shut so he swung around and steered for home, with the sun creeping from his forearm to his face, mercifully awakening as the alcohol thinned in his blood and the rays warmed his skin.

It was hushed in the cab of his car, but he was not alone. Michelle and Colin rode with him alongside Lou and the McKays, and there was plenty of room for Jessica, even though she wasn't returning his calls. They cluttered his mind, making him wonder how it had all come about, how the contours of his life had become so misshapen, how his history had become serrated, how it had all happened to *him*.

But when he got to Northampton and the early commuter traffic made its appearance – the vanguard of reps in souped-up Vectras with freshly ironed shirts pendent in the back, company directors making an early-morning dash for the office to lever a conference call with Tokyo, Mondeos and Almeras lunging for the early shift at the warehouse, supermarket or hospital – there was a singular moment. He remembered he had a ready-rolled joint in the glove compartment, which he opened. He glanced inside at the wizened object. It had been lying dormant in there for a couple of weeks at least. What a waste. Although the sunshine and the movement of the car had relaxed him in a way that sleep never did he yearned for a smoke, yet something within him wouldn't allow him to fire up.

What was peculiar was that his abstention didn't mask a feeling of deprivation, of not being able to do what he wanted; it was simply a matter of deciding not to. Today, *he decided*, he would not smoke. He liked the feeling, there was nothing self-righteous or censorious about it – it was what it was: a decision. The ability to make choices, to realise that he had options other than the withered selections he had already made was something that had been missing from his life for so long that rediscovering it was liberating. It felt good cruising past deadwood straggles like Hemel Hempstead and Luton staring at the blunt, knowing that its sweet, cryptic secrets would never unfold within his lungs. Likewise, the ideas – the plans – that had been fattening in his mind began to feel more coherent, more compelling.

He got off the M1 at Junction 2 and rolled round the North Circular eastbound trying not to let the stodgy, constipated London traffic spoil his mood. As he crawled through the suburban prairie of mock Tudor semis he gripped the wheel tight, turning up the radio – Chris Evans, clatter to keep his mind engaged as fatigue kicked in – trying to ignore the slight tremors in his hands. The sun was high in the sky early; London was dusty pink, on edge, nerves raw already.

Wood Green. He remembered it from when he was a kid. His mum took him shopping there. They got his school uniform every year from British Home Stores; there was a restaurant upstairs where they would have fish and chips and limeade that was so full of preservatives and chemicals that it made him wheeze. He still went back for a second glass though. It was different now, the high street was dominated by a revenue-per-square-foot Shopping City that made the streets feel abandoned and ghostly after dark when garbage-food wrappers whipped around stragglers' ankles like malevolent rodents.

And Lou also remembered it back in the day; before the jaggedness set in. He'd had his office, upstairs from a dry-cleaner's – the heat in the summer! – since 1970. The office had seemed smaller, cleaner, neater. It had not felt like a place where bad things would happen. Now, well, who knows? He had not heard from Lee since Lee had tumbled him. As far as he knew he still represented Lee Sweeney and, until he was instructed otherwise, he would, paradoxically, continue to act in his best interests. So he got on with the everyday stuff – the phone calls and meetings and paperwork – resolving to keep his head down for a bit. See how it all wound up. And if the truth were told he missed Lee in a way that he would never have thought possible. In his heart he hoped that matters might be put right between them – he had behaved awfully, he knew that, but there was too much history between them for it all to be put to waste. Lou was too sentimental to shut someone he had known since time out of his life.

The phone rang. Lou answered while washing down a handful of Pringles with a cup of black coffee.

'Lee's here to see you,' said Esther, her voice tilting upwards at the end like a question. She knew nothing, of course, other than that Lou liked to conduct his meetings away from the ragged office. A client coming to see Lou, well, there was something.

'Lee?' said Lou, reflexively reaching to his throat to loosen his tie and undo his shirt collar. 'Lee Sweeney?'

'You only have one client called Lee,' said Esther, her voice a terse whisper, disorientated and fed up with having to talk in a clandestine way in a pygmy ante-room that was packed with two bodies in it.

'One minute,' said Lou. He put the phone down and scanned the office. He wanted to do something – either finish a piece of work, or make a phone call or tidy some papers – anything to make it seem as if this were a normal day in a normal office with a normal client.

He swallowed another mouthful of the lukewarm brew, shuddering to help the brown slop slip down – he just needed something to relieve his sapless throat. He buzzed the nettled Esther, and Lee entered his office gingerly, but without knocking. It was as if he were visiting a tomb that had lain undiscovered and untouched for hundreds of years.

'Lee,' said Lou clumsily. He approached him but didn't offer a hand. Somehow it seemed wrong. They both stood awkwardly for a moment.

'Please, sit down,' said Lou clearing files from the only other chair in the room, a high-backed dining-chair that had been left in the room by its previous occupants.

Lou retreated behind his desk and searched among the debris for his cigarettes and lighter. He fired up a fag and regarded Lee through the smoke: there was a staleness about him, his clothes were lived-in, he smelt curdled and his hair was neglected. But when he looked into Lee's face he saw something else; granted Lee looked tired, exhausted even – there were dark circles beneath his eyes, he had several days' stubble masking his chin – but there was something different about him. By force of habit Lou checked for the tell-tale signs of drink, but Lee seemed clean; there was no evidence that it was alcohol that had thawed him out, made him appear so calm.

'Still wiping your arse with fifty-quid notes?' asked Lee.

Lou smiled. Relief spread across his face. 'You know me, Lee, I've never even seen a fifty-pound note.'

There was a pause.

'You went back for the bag, didn't you?' asked Lee.

Lou looked into the corner of the room.

'I knew you would,' said Lee, satisfied, a smile tugging at the side of his mouth.

'If I hadn't the fucking thing would still be sitting there,' said Lou, embarrassed.

'Well, at least it's found a good home,' said Lee.

'So what now?' said Lou. 'What about us? Am I still to represent you?'

'I didn't come here to go through that,' said Lee cutting him off. 'There's no point. I'd only have to find some other shyster and, frankly, I can't be bothered with all that now. I don't know where it's going to get me other than nowhere, if you see what I mean. You've made me lots more money than you've cost me over the years. I'm not going to get myself worked up about it.'

Lou swelled, pleased with himself, satisfied that Lee had acknowledged his achievements.

'I'm disappointed though, Lou,' said Lee. 'Upset even. I thought that we had more going for us, hoped our friendship might amount to something. Well, maybe it did for me, evidently not for you. I'm sorry about that, Lou, I'm awfully sorry, but there it is.'

Lou had planted his elbows on the desk and was opening his thick hands like a man estimating the size of a fish. A cigarette smouldered in his right hand. 'Lee, I realise that what I did was awful – unethical and immoral,' he said. 'I betrayed a friend. I know that you can't ever forgive me, but I hope that our history might count for something. I feel terrible. It's driving me meshugge. I know that it won't change anything, but I want you to know that I'm sorry.' He looked intensely into Lee's eyes to try and convince him that he was genuine, but pulled back, worried that Lee might think that this was just some deal-clinching technique.

'Did you ever believe in me?' asked Lee. There was no weight to his words. No agenda. It was a genuine question.

'Yes, Lee,' said Lou, honestly. 'I did believe in you. I believed in you for years. There was never a moment when I didn't remember that I was representing the best footballer in the land, maybe even the world. And I'll never forget that, Lee, I'll never forget the buzz of watching you working a midfield like a gang of gyppo pickpockets at a fairground. People didn't know that they'd been mugged off before it was too late.' He paused and sighed. 'I thought you might even come good when we brought you back here. I had that much faith, Lee.'

'And now?' asked Lee.

Lou opened his hands. 'Look where we are, Lee. Look what we've come to . . .'

'Do you still believe, Lou?'

The older man looked at his hands that rested palms-down, on the desk.

'Well?' said Lee.

Lou swallowed and looked at the ceiling.

'Lou?'

'Yes, Lee. Yes,' said Lou finally. 'On your day I still think you're unstoppable.' He looked at Lee, his eyes flat and close. 'I mean it,' he said.

'Prove it,' said Lee.

'You what?'

'Prove it – put the money on us to win the cup by at least two goals. With me scoring at least once.'

'What are you talking about, Lee?'

'A bet. You've got the money. You took it off me, so use it. Show me that you've still got faith in Lee Sweeney. Show me that there's still something between us.'

Lou looked at him. He tried not to appear suspicious. How was he to know that Lee was telling him the truth? How could he be sure that this wasn't some kind of elaborate revenge scenario? He couldn't. He just had to wait. He had to have a little faith.

Lee folded his arms. 'So what you going to do then, Lou? How do you feel about this one? Do you feel lucky?'

Lou began to smile.

Jug Ears was serving a round of lager tops – a welcome break from doling bottles of premium product and glasses of Australian Chardonnay – when the phone went.

'Hello, Corks,' he said in a voice that told the caller that he was polite and fair but busy with the Friday lunchtime office fugitives and would appreciate brevity.

'Is Jugs there?'

'Speaking.'

'Jugs, it's Lee.'

Jug Ears's tone changed dramatically. 'Oi, oi, saveloy. Where the fuck have you been?'

'How's it all going, mate?' asked Lee.

'Brilliant,' said Jug Ears. 'We've just had to take on someone else to cope with lunchtimes. It's fucking mad here most days.'

'Wicked,' said Lee. 'Chuffed for you.' He paused. 'Look, Jugs, I need a favour.'

'What *now*,' replied Jug Ears, joking.

'There's a pair of Cup Final tickets in it for you,' continued Lee.

'Now you're talking. Royal Box, yeah?'

'I'll stick something up your box,' said Lee.

'So what's the scoop?'

'It's a bit complicated, but I need you to place some bets for me . . .'

Chapter Twenty-Nine

There was a wall in the Brook Beech Hotel – a haven of nine-hole golf, high-cholesterol business lunches, corporate hospitality and staff with false bow ties, just off the M25 – that displayed nothing other than signed football shirts and pendants. All the greats were there – Arsenal, Manchester United, Liverpool – as well as some foreign teams: Nigeria, Holland, Mexico. All had hunkered down at Brook Beech as a prelude to Wembley appearances, their low-key preparations marred only by having to pose for photographs with the unctuous owner of the gaff.

Lee had stayed there before, several times. He knew he had because there was a signed photo of him and the owner on the wall. Back then the booze had tended to blur everything; what he actually recalled was having dry heaves for breakfast while suspicious coaching staff observed him side-step solids between trips to the toilet which were excused as a stomach upset.

It was the night before Cup Final, a balmy Friday evening in May with just enough warmth in the air to make knitwear unnecessary. This time, Lee thought to himself, his stay at Brook Beech would be different. Tomorrow morning he would eat a full breakfast, he would mop up a lake of HP sauce with a piece of crusty bread and wash it down with a cuppa. For two weeks, since he last saw Michelle and got Mike to place the bets for Lou at bookies throughout the Home Counties, he hadn't had a drink. The sickness had stopped after a week and he'd regained his appetite. But he slept only fitfully; he remembered how much easier it was to disappear into darkness when he'd had a skinful. It was a strange thing giving up drinking – it wasn't like he suddenly felt a lot better. He possessed a certain clarity now, but he was having to face the world without the cushioning of liquor, which was a different kind of proposition altogether. It just made things appear different. A paradox similar to the way that drink had made him come out of himself but go into himself at the same time.

But even though there was none touching his lips the drink never went away. It was a part of him all the time, present in his conscious and unconscious. They'd had dinner and a team talk – Brandwood's usual tub-thumping, blood-curdling call to arms – and a movie had been set up on a jumbo screen (not that jumbo, not much of a screen) for the lads to watch. Some had drifted up to their rooms; others, mostly the younger players, hung around talking, not wanting to be alone.

The sun had disappeared behind a fugitive piece of woodland, the sky the colour of tinned salmon, when Lee stretched his arms and decided to go to his room and watch a movie in bed. He was tired but it was a restful tiredness, as if his body had gone into itself, was regenerating itself, rather than the sheer drop-to-your-knees knackeredness he'd felt over the previous weeks and months. A movie might do the trick, settle him down, put the game out of his mind. He'd noticed that *Godzilla* was on Sky Box Office. He'd avoid that. It would remind him too much of Brandwood.

He padded down one of the interminable carpeted corridors on his way back to his room. Outside, guests from a wedding reception that was unfolding in another wing of the hotel were following burnt-orange koi which drifted lazily in a cloudy, lily-strewn pond. He stopped momentarily to watch. It was the kind of thing he never used to do.

When he turned back to continue his walk there she was.

Jessica. He looked at her like he might view a hologram, trying to work out the trick, trying to decipher how it was all put together. It didn't make sense.

'My God!' said Jessica incredulously. 'Lee!' She slipped her hand in his and kissed him. As her cheek pressed against his he noticed how his skin felt unexpectedly soft since he'd started to shave daily.

'What are you doing here?' she asked pushing the strap of her bag up her shoulder. Lee was confused. The last time they'd been together was in the car park when she'd given him a knock back, yet she was behaving as if it had never happened.

'Cup Final hotel,' he said clasping his hands in front of himself. He never usually carried himself this way. Alcohol, kindly, had often dictated the arrangement of his limbs. It felt strange. Awkward.

'Of course,' said Jessica. 'Tomorrow, isn't it? How could I have forgotten that?'

'Well, it happens,' said Lee. 'I've forgotten games that I've been playing in.'

She looked at him as if he were trying to tell her something, an inquisitive look, like she didn't quite grasp what it was that she was supposed to understand.

'Fancy a drink?' she said, grasping his arm.

'No,' said Lee a little too quickly. 'I mean, I was just off to bed – big game and all that. Why didn't you return my calls?'

'Come on,' said Jessica, ignoring his question. 'Just one won't hurt you.' She was trying to sound playful, winning, but there was an inkling of desperation in her voice.

Lee freed his arm. 'I really can't,' he said. 'Maybe some time next week.'

'Just one drink?' said Jessica. 'One little one.'

'It can't be done,' he said determinedly.

'All right then,' said Jessica. 'I need a favour . . .'

'I don't have any tickets left I'm afraid,' interrupted Lee.

'No, not that,' she said, smiling. 'I didn't even know the

game was on, remember? No, something else. You see, I've got some friends coming over, they live in France and they wanted to stay in a hotel nearby. I just wondered what the rooms are like.'

'They're fine, you know. Not massive, but they do the job. Clean.'

'Can I take a quick look?'

'Well, I was going . . .'

'A really quick one. Then I'll be out of your hair.'

'I really . . .' said Lee, exasperated.

'Please.'

'All right then, you've got to be quick though.' The interaction with Jessica was beginning to erode Lee's drowsiness. He was mildly narked that it was going to take him time to re-establish the necessary frame of mind for sleep.

'I'll be just two ticks,' she unexpectedly said rushing off down the hallway. 'Got to visit the little girls' room.'

Lee looked back out the window. He was irritated that he'd let her do this to him, especially since she hadn't told him why she had never called him, and resolved to kick her out of his room as quickly as was polite. He went back to watching the wedding guests admiring the pond.

A couple of minutes later he heard Jessica coming up the corridor. He knew it was her by the sound of her body rubbing against her clothes and the quick, slightly heavy way that she walked in her heels. He turned to her, she flashed a smile, but he didn't see it – all he could take in was the bottle of whisky she was grasping by the neck.

'I was just off to visit me dad,' she said. 'Thought I'd take him this. He's partial to a wee dram.'

Lee took his eyes from the bottle and looked back at Jessica. His mood had changed, his heart was beating a little faster, the juices were beginning to flow. He rubbed his palms together slowly as if trying to remove a bit of stubborn grease.

'Are we off then?' said Jessica.

'Right,' said Lee, after a beat. He sounded preoccupied, like someone trying to listen to two different conversations.

The hotel had been built over a few years in lots of different stages – getting anywhere involved a journey through the architectural histories of the early part of the century as well as the seventies and eighties. 'English heritage meets contemporary elegance' is how the brochure described it. A bloody nightmare is how Lee thought of it as he and Jessica headed towards the modern annex the team had been allocated for their own, and other guests', privacy.

He opened the door and Jessica swept in, dumping the bottle and her bag on the desk that was situated next to his bed.

'Very nice,' she said. 'Nice colours. Modern. Very plush.'

Lee opened the curtains and a window, felt the early evening float in. He switched on one of the bedside lamps.

'You mind if I take a look in the bathroom?' asked Jessica. 'Don't worry, I'll keep all your secrets to myself.'

Lee switched the TV on and immediately regretted it – the noise made the atmosphere more sociable, like it was OK to talk.

Jessica came out of the bathroom pulling a cord to switch the light off. An extractor fan remained on. 'Nice, very nice,' she said. She walked towards the bed and tested its firmness. 'How's this?' she asked.

'Not bad,' said Lee.

'Mind if I try?' she said lying down. 'That's good. I need a firm bed, you see.'

'Right,' said Lee. He said nothing else hoping that Jessica would take her cue.

'I thought you footballers were supposed to share rooms,' she said turning towards him and lying on her side. He watched as her hips and upper body formed mountains, her waist a valley and her legs a gentle slope.

'Some do, some don't.' He glanced briefly at the bottle

of whisky. Jessica caught the look. 'It depends what you want. I've got it in my contract that I don't have to share.'

'Tell you what,' said Jessica. 'We'll just have one drink – to wish you luck – and then I'll be off.'

'I'd really rather not . . .'

'Just one. Come on. Don't let me drink alone. It's no fun.'

How wrong you are, thought Lee. Drinking alone is the best – it's when you're able to drink exactly how you'd like to drink. There's no one there to give you dirty looks, or tell you to take it easy. Drinking alone is the best kind of drinking, the truest kind of drinking.

'I mustn't,' said Lee.

Still sitting on the bed Jessica reached over for a couple of glasses that were resting, face down, on the bedside table. Lee heard the metal cap snap as Jessica twisted the lid off. Then he heard the liquid splashing in the glass, as sweet as a hymn to a priest. Dear God . . . She handed him a tumbler. He took it and sat next to her on the bed. She took a sip without taking her eyes from him. She smacked her lips. Lee held the glass in his hand, frozen by the intensity with which she was looking at him.

'Go on,' she said. She put her glass on the side and reached for his leg, running a manicured hand up his thigh towards his crotch.

Lee stood up. 'You'll have to go,' he said.

'What?' said Jessica. She put her hand to her chest, momentarily startled.

'I mean it,' said Lee standing up and pointing at the door.

'Come on, Lee, it's just a bit of fun,' said Jessica. She lay back on the bed and took a sip from her glass. Lee glared at her. She looked back at him before extending her arm, as if trying to drag him to the bed with an invisible cord.

'This isn't you,' said Lee. He saw the glass of whisky in his hand, stormed into the bathroom and tipped the liquid into the sink. He ran the tap, rinsing the glass and the bowl.

The smell of it made him feel nauseous.

He came out of the bathroom and looked at Jessica. She was lying on the bed refilling her glass. Her eyes burnt with anger.

'What the fuck are you doing?' said Lee.

'Relax, lover boy, I'm just having a drink,' said Jessica, her voice dry. 'You of all people should understand that.'

'I don't understand,' said Lee.

'There's nothing to understand,' she said unconvincingly, turning away from him.

'What the fuck are you trying to do to me?' said Lee angrily.

'We were just having a drink,' said Jessica bitterly. 'And you went and ruined it.'

'Went and ruined what? What are you talking about?'

'I'd better get going,' said Jessica getting up from the bed.

Lee grabbed her by the wrist.

'Don't try that shit again,' said Jessica. 'Let go.'

'Not before you tell me what you were trying to do to me.'

'Let me go,' said Jessica icily. Lee dropped her hand as if it were contaminated. Jessica reached for her bag.

'You want to kill me, is that it?' said Lee.

Jessica smiled to herself. 'Not quite,' she said.

Lee cocked his head to the side wanting her to say more.

'Let's just pretend this never happened, Lee,' she said straightening her hair. 'It was all a big mistake, a misunderstanding.'

'But I don't think it was, Jessica,' said Lee. 'I don't think it was at all. And you're not leaving this room until you tell me what's going on.'

Jessica sighed. Her face dropped. 'Look, I know you deserve better than this, Lee, believe me. But I didn't have a choice.'

'Try me.'

'I like you, Lee. Really.'

'And?'

'I feel really bad.'

'Go on.'

'It stays in this room, all right?'

'Yes.'

'You promise?'

'I promise.'

'I owe the McKays a favour . . .'

'A favour.'

'A film. I did a film. Nothing too awful, just a bit embarrassing, but I was young, and they've sat on it for years, promised to keep shtum . . . I knew there would be payback one day and I suppose this is what it was.'

'What was it?'

'Don't make me . . .' she said looking the other way.

'Say it.'

'For fuck's sake, Lee. What do you think it was? It was to get you fucked up. To get you so fucked up that tomorrow would be nothing but a blur for you. I don't know anything more than that. I was told a bottle of whisky and a couple of grams of coke would do the trick. The other stuff was, well, discretionary.'

'Very discreet, yeah,' said Lee. He put his index fingers on his temples. 'Fucking McKays,' he said. 'They're out to fucking kill me.'

'They're heartless bastards,' said Jessica. 'That's a fact.'

Lee felt a wave of terror surge through him. He thought he might throw up. 'Just wait there a minute, will you?' he said.

He went into the bathroom, splashed cold water on his face and rested his cheek against the tiled wall which was strangely tepid rather than the cool that he'd been hoping for. He looked in the mirror and tried to remember who he was.

There was a knock on the door.

'Lee? Lee? Are you all right? Lee? What's going on?'

He turned off the faucet and opened the door.

Jessica stared at him. 'Jesus, Lee, you've been in there for ages, I thought something terrible had happened . . .' She ran a hand through her hair embarrassed at her own words. 'Look at you, you're all covered in water.' She pushed past him into the bathroom and took a towel off the rail. She draped it over his shoulders. It was a bulky white hotel towel – too luxurious to be easily stuffed in a suitcase.

'There you are,' she said trying to dry his hair.

'I'm fine, I'm fine,' said Lee.

'I like you, Lee,' said Jessica eventually, 'but you need to get some help.'

He remembered the girl in the motel in Florida the night that Michelle had refused to let him in the villa and what she'd said to him. He remembered the feeling more than the words, the symptoms of waking up. For too long he'd not known what it was like to wake up and not to dry heave, to think that the world was going to end at any moment. He recalled waking up next to a girl a couple of years before, perhaps he even knew her. He remembered trying to think, but not too hard. It hurt too much. Trying to piece the lost hours into a semblance of reality, or what passed for his reality. It was always too difficult, so hard that he always stuck with what he had. It was easier that way.

'You say the nicest things,' said Lee.

Jessica smiled before going to fetch her things. Lee rested his body in the door frame of the bathroom. She returned brandishing the whisky bottle. 'I think I'll take this,' she said with a self-deprecating smile. 'I think I'll be needing it tonight.'

Lee smirked. He remembered how much he liked the way she made fun of herself.

'Good luck tomorrow,' she said, before kissing him softly on the lips. She opened the door to go before turning and saying: 'I suppose I should say that I'm sorry, but something inside is glad this happened, but I'm not sure why.' She smiled an embarrassed smile before closing the door.

Lee rested against the wall in the hallway for a few moments before sliding down on his haunches. He remained like that until his legs went numb and his tears dried.

Chapter Thirty

'Slow down,' said Lee. 'You're driving like a nutter.'

A cigarette plugged between her lips, Jessica muscled her Jeep past a monolithic Volvo estate towards Redbourn. She flicked some ash out of the open window. It blew straight back in. Her sunglasses sat on her head like an Alice band, keeping her hair out of her eyes as the wind rushed into the car.

'I can't believe I'm doing this,' said Lee.

'Stop fretting,' said Jessica. 'We'll be there soon. You'll get back in time.'

She'd returned to his room the night before, about an hour later. Although he'd not willed it to happen he hadn't fought her off after he'd spied her through the security viewer. She knew he was looking at her as their gaze met through the glass prism. It turned Lee on, her not being able to see him. He opened the door and let her in.

'You forget something?' he asked trying to conceal his swollen, tear-stained face.

'Only you,' she said arching up towards him. As they kissed he wrapped his arm around her waist. It was good to feel the warmth of another against him. He could still taste the salt from his tears at the back of his mouth. They kissed long and hard. Her hand reached down for him and felt his excitement. She pushed him down so that he was seated on the bed and pulled off his T-shirt before undressing herself. She stepped out of her underwear and pushed him back on the bed.

Inside her he felt good, wholesome, different: it was the first sober fuck he'd had in fourteen years.

Lee closed his eyes, drew the warm May air into his nostrils. He wondered if they'd noted his absence yet. He was hoping to slip back into the hotel without any fuss, knew there would be a price to pay should he be discovered. He could just imagine the scene:

Brandwood eyed George, one of the club trainers.

George looked back at him sheepishly.

'This is a fucking joke, right?' said Brandwood. A thin slick of jam trailed across his cheek. George focused on that rather than looking in his boss's eyes. The news was too ugly for that; you'd have to be some kind of cold hard fuck to be able to search too deep within Brandwood at that moment, to see the desperation, the anger, the resentment . . . Most of all he saw a kind of resignation, a sense of inevitability that shadowed his face. 'You ain't serious,' said Brandwood.

George said nothing. His eyes settled on a teapot on the breakfast table that Brandwood shared with some of the coaching staff. The chrome on it had been eroded by over-use. Nobody else spoke, all of them unsure how Brandwood would react.

Brandwood took a nonchalant sip of his tea. The colour of the cuppa matched his skin.

'Well, fuck him,' he said finally. There was movement at the table. Nervous energy let loose. Someone reached for the marmalade. 'We'll do it without the cunt.'

George sat down next to Brandwood. 'Where the fuck can he be?' he asked.

'No idea,' said Brandwood folding his arms. 'Saw him about nine last night going to bed. He looked all right, you know. He looked calm.'

'Lee? Calm?' scoffed George. 'And my arse plays the banjo.'

'I mean it,' said Brandwood. 'I watched him go. He even walked differently. I thought to myself how together he was, how focused. I mean, come on . . . Lee? Focused?'

'So what are we going to do?'

'There's not much we can do. Get someone to call his mobile – you never know, maybe the idiot's gone for a walk or something – otherwise I'll tell the rest of the boys when we have the get-together before we leave. I don't want the fucking press knowing, so don't tell anyone else. When we're on the coach we can make up some excuse about him not wanting to go on the coach, superstition or something. Or a bet. Or that he forgot to bring the boots he's scored in every round with. Some shit the press will believe. Something that sounds like Lee.'

George nodded knowingly.

He had no understanding why, but Lee knew that there was only a certain speed above which it is safe to travel on a horseshoe gravel drive. Momentarily he turned and looked at Jessica as they sped towards Horton House. He wondered at what point she would decide to hit the brakes. Eventually she pressed hard upon the pedal and the car came to a halt after ploughing a groove deep enough to plant watermelons in.

She turned and looked at him. 'Now what?' she said.

'I hate to tell you,' he said. 'But this was your idea.'

'Yes, you're right,' she said after a beat. 'Let's go.'

Lee laughed to himself. He didn't want her to see him, didn't want to thin her resolve.

The door was answered by the housekeeper who was almost knocked over by Jessica launching herself into the hallway. 'We've come to pick something up,' said Jessica. 'The brothers sent us . . .'

'They are not here,' said the housekeeper, unsure whether to be indignant or whether the pair of interlopers were, in fact, on the premises with the brothers' blessing. 'Please sit. Let me phone them.' Her tone was conciliatory, although her English was becoming laboured.

'They said just to nip in and pick it up,' said Jessica.

'Please,' said the housekeeper. There was panic in her voice now that hinted at worry for her job, her immigration status. She gestured at a couple of armchairs in the hallway. 'I will call them.'

'It'll only take a minute,' said Jessica shooting off along the corridor, her clothes snapping with her movement. Lee exchanged a sympathetic look with the housekeeper before heading after her. The housekeeper followed them for a few steps before cutting her losses and searching out a phone.

By now Lee was vaguely familiar with the layout of the house but, it seemed, nowhere near as familiar as Jessica who deftly weaved her way through the intricacies of the house like a shuttle passing through a loom. Snaking her way commandingly, Jessica entered the library by not so much opening the door as knocking it down.

'Here we are,' she said. Lee could hear that she was slightly out of breath. 'In the lair of the beasts. What you reckon, Lee? Fifty grand well spent?'

'What?' asked Lee.

'The library,' said Jessica. 'They had it built. Spent fifty grand on all this wood.'

Examining the room Lee took in acres of hardwood panelling, interrupted only by shelves of leather-bound books. It was not like any library he had seen before, although he would hardly classify himself as being know-ledgeable about such places. For a start it was immaculately clean. The Filipino housekeeper obviously put in double time on the dusting. Secondly, it smelt different. The aroma of the passage of time, of paper, print, binding materials was absent; instead it smelt of Glade plug-ins. Lee put his hand on the back of the leather club chairs. There was no give in it. It was like they had never been sat in. On a coffee table – green leather top, huge crystal ashtray in the middle – sat this month's *Golf Digest*.

'How did you know?' asked Lee.

'What?' said Jessica. He could tell that she understood exactly what he meant. She caved in eventually. 'I didn't tell you everything,' said Jessica.

'And you don't have to,' said Lee raising his palms. He

looked at his watch. 'Come on, we've got to get moving. I don't want to get caught here.'

'Look, a long time ago, I had a thing with . . .'

'Archie,' said Lee completing her sentence, wanting to spare her. He waited for her to assent. Lee rolled his tongue along his bottom set of teeth. Silence.

'Gerrard?' he said eventually.

'Sort of,' said Jessica. He knew there was more.

'Both?' he said. He let out a small, involuntary laugh.

'Yeah, big joke, eh, Lee? Hilarious.'

They stood in the room staring at each other. The antagonism passed quickly.

'There's half a fucking rainforest in here,' said Lee trying to draw her from a crabby mood. 'We get caught . . .'

'Right,' said Jessica, 'you start over there.' She gestured to the far end of the room.

'Start what?' asked Lee.

Jessica put her hands on her hips. 'Cooking breakfast,' she said. 'What do you think? Searching for this fucking video.'

'Where?' asked Lee.

Jessica plucked one of the leather-bound objects from the shelves, opened it and pulled out a plastic oblong which she waved at him.

'You didn't think they were real books, did you?' asked Jessica.

'What do you think I am – stupid?' said Lee sarcastically.

'As if,' said Jessica clambering on to a chair and pulling video cases down from the top shelves. She opened them briefly, and checked the label before discarding case and video on the floor.

'They're not all skin flicks,' said Jessica. 'They love De Niro, Pacino, all that boys' stuff.'

'What am I looking for?' asked Lee.

'*X Plates*,' said Jessica quickly, 'and make sure it's got "master" written on it. They keep one of each.'

'*X Plates?*' said Lee.

'It's about a driving school,' snapped Jessica.

'Of course,' said Lee.

'It's not horrible or anything,' she said. 'Discreet really. Just a bit embarrassing now, you know.'

He walked to the middle of the shelves, pulled out a box, examined it and then discarded it on the floor. He moved four feet to his right and did the same thing.

'Lee!' said Jessica irritably. He thought she might even stamp her foot. '*What* are you doing?'

He ignored her and reached on to one of the lower shelves and pulled out another case. He pulled out another, and another . . . Jessica frantically worked her way along one of the shelves.

He tapped her on her hip holding a cassette nonchalantly.

'Is that it? Is that it?' said Jessica jumping down from the chair. She examined the label and smiled before hugging Lee. 'How did you know?'

'It's alphabeticised,' said Lee.

'Duh!' She laughed at herself. 'Jesus, I was in such a state I wasn't thinking clearly . . . Thanks, Lee.'

'Come on, let's go,' he said. 'We can't have long.'

When they got back to the hallway there was no sign of the housekeeper. Lee thought he could hear her yapping on a phone in another room. Lee felt strangely sedate. It was then that the door swung open, flapping loosely like a broken bird's wing. Lee looked into his brother's eyes.

'You're up early,' said Colin. He was popping beads of sweat; must have broken his neck to get there. Lee looked at him impassively, more taken aback than cool.

'Shouldn't you be somewhere else?' said Colin to Lee. 'Always in the wrong place at the wrong time, our Lee.'

'We're leaving now, Colin,' said Lee.

'I don't believe that we've had the pleasure,' he said extending his hand to Jessica. She drew back and wrapped her arms around herself, clutching her bag just below her breasts.

'So, breaking and entering,' said Colin. 'Or is it trespass?

Burglary? Theft?'

'Come on, Lee,' said Jessica moving towards the door. Colin held his hand up theatrically, like some kind of traffic policeman meets a matador.

'Stop, right there,' said Colin. 'Get what you came for?' Jessica looked towards Lee.

'We're leaving, Colin,' said Lee.

'Pick a window,' said Colin. His face suddenly brightened. 'Do you remember that Lee? From school? You're leaving – pick a window?' Colin sniggered to himself. The question was rhetorical. Colin closed the door behind him. The hallway fell into a kind of twilight.

'This is you now then, is it?' asked Lee. 'The McKays' bum boy? No job too small or dirty?'

'You two have a good time last night?' asked Colin. He put his hands behind his back and craned his neck towards Jessica and mouthed, 'Did you get the job done?'

'Why are you such a dickhead?' said Jessica. 'Aren't you depriving a village somewhere of an idiot?'

Colin ignored her. 'Feisty, eh?' said Colin to Lee. 'Like them like that, don't you, bro?'

'You were in on that stunt as well?' asked Lee.

Colin nodded smugly. 'Indirectly,' he said.

'I was right about you all along. You really are fucking scum, aren't you?' said Lee. 'We're going to leave in a minute. But first I want you to give me a straightforward answer to a question.'

Colin wiped sweat from his forehead, disinterested.

'What's going on with the Twomacs?'

'Wouldn't you like to know?' said Colin. Lee waited. He was counting on Colin's vanity – his brother loved showing people that he was in the know, that he was one up on them. 'That really would be telling,' said Colin.

'So tell,' said Lee.

Colin waited for a moment, but Lee knew that he was going to spill. The drama of the moment was pure Colin. 'Well, Lee. You of all people know that the brothers are gambling men. Of course, there's gambling and there's gambling – there's going to the bookies and there's what, in the City, they call investing. Put simply the brothers realised that the season was turning to shit, hence they were likely to take a loss on the year's trading and the share price of the club. Never ones to take it lying down,' he looked pointedly at Jessica, 'they decided to indemnify themselves against the club's failure. Hence they took what we can loosely call a bet, but in the City they'd call it a position.' He eyed Jessica again. Lee struggled not to say anything; he didn't want to break up the story.

'Their position was, and still is, that the club's price would be lower than a certain point when trading starts next Monday. Hence, if the game is lost today, following a disappointing performance in the league, with few tangible assets or even cash and no Europe next season, and the possible exodus of an ageing star player, namely you, then the price goes tumbling down to a point where the brothers cash in.

'Your friend Jessica here was supposed to ensure that you didn't, shall we say, live up to your full potential. Maybe you did, but only she knows.'

Lee didn't react. Didn't want to give Colin the pleasure of having got to him.

'I think we'll leave now,' said Jessica moving forward. Colin stepped to the side allowing her to open the door.

'There's no point in me trying to stop you,' said Colin looking at Lee. 'You ain't playing today anyway. Brandwood will do his nut when he finds out you've gone AWOL. Talk about a final straw . . .'

He put his arm across the door frame just as Jessica was attempting to exit. 'Er, I think you've forgotten something,' he said extending his other arm. 'The brothers told me all about your acting debut. It sounds very promising. I'm looking forward to watching it. Such a pity if the master tape had gone missing. Let's not get plod involved, shall we?'

Lee watched, horrified, as Jessica reached into her bag and gave Colin the cassette.

'Thank you,' said Colin retracting his arm.

Then it was just the two of them.

'The brothers are very disappointed about this,' said Colin. 'They are going to want to talk to you about it.'

'You don't even know what disappointment is,' said Lee. 'You've sold your fucking soul. It's all turned to shit for you.'

'Don't be so sure,' said Colin meeting his brother's eyes.

'I'll be seeing you,' said Lee, still boring as deep into his brother's eyes as he could, while he walked to the door. He wanted to punch him – revenge for Michelle – but he restrained himself. He had something in mind that would hurt Colin far worse than that.

'Yeah,' said Colin. 'And I'll be seeing you.'

Lee had barely closed his door when the Jeep's wheels spun and it shot off down the drive. Lee felt ashamed.

'I'm sorry,' he said. 'I'm sorry about that.'

'Don't be,' said Jessica.

'But the film,' said Lee. 'You had it in your hands and now those bastards have got it again.'

'Wrong,' said Jessica. 'I think your brother might be a little disappointed with his evening's viewing. He hasn't got it. When we were going through all those boxes I found a copy of *Pretty Woman*. Love that film, fancied seeing it again, so I slipped it in my bag . . .'

'And now Colin's got it.'

'Precisely.'

'Fan-bloody-tastic.'

'You know what, Lee?' she said opening the window. 'Colin's going to have to get up pretty early in the morning if he's going to catch us out. Now let's get you to Wembley.'

Chapter Thirty-One

It was one of the hottest Cup Finals on record. An average of 28°C. There's nowhere to hide in a Cup Final, although it's not unknown for players to go missing, not unheard of for the cocksure and experienced to go AWOL – though rarely in the way that Lee had. More commonly, on that vast pitch, in the heat, and overwhelmed by the occasion, teams can simply wilt.

Lee had watched from the bench, sitting behind Brandwood. The gaffer's neck turned an intense shade of pink during the course of the first half, but whether it was from the sun or the performance of the team Lee didn't know, although he suspected the latter. Ipswich were making a go of it, lifted by their fans – all face paints, balloons, banners and cheeky chants – who were making more of the day out than the metropolitan fans who were not unused to visiting the home of football. As the half wore on the cries and chants of the London fans became increasingly belligerent; a sourness crept into the west end of the ground cast, as it was, in shadow.

When the teams had been read out before the game the biggest cheers had come from the Ipswich fans when they discovered that Lee had been relegated to the bench. The Londoners countered by singing 'One Lee Sweeney/There's only one Lee Sweeney' but it was half-hearted and troubled more than anything else.

Walking from the tunnel, into a blanket of sunshine and noise, Lee felt a pang of regret. This, after all, was what it was about. Glory. An Ipswich balloon bounced off his head, and his senses tried to take it all in. It was difficult to know where he should turn his attention. He was the last man on the pitch, relegated, as a substitute, to the back of the procession. Most of the players searched the stands for family and friends, offering half-moons of teeth, high on the intensity of it all, as excited as the punters to be there. Lee didn't look into the stands, he had no one to search for, to make contact with. He was on his own, had given his ticket allocation away to one of the lads so his grandparents could come over from Guyana.

They stood in lines, keyed up, wanting to get on with it, and met the nobs. One of the chinless wonders, popping with sweat in a woollen pinstriped suit, had bent down to him and said, 'Injured, are you?' Lee had stopped chewing his gum for a moment and nodded.

'Not quite one hundred per cent,' he said. 'It's a groin thing.'

'Yes, I know about that kind of thing,' said the flushed chinless wonder giving him a wink.

Then they were off. Lee certainly was. Making his way regretfully to the bench, almost embarrassed to be lumped in with the stiffs who couldn't quite make the grade. When watching the final in Italy two years before Lee picked up a tip about sitting on the bench at Wembley – never pick your nose; there will always be a camera there to spot it and a director mischievous enough to transmit the humiliation.

Jessica had dropped him outside the gates of Brook Beech. He'd wandered through the grounds and back to the hotel just as the players were assembling to get on the coach. Lee had claimed that he'd gone for a walk to collect his thoughts and had forgotten the time. Brandwood had stepped close to him, probably to sniff his breath, and shaken his head.

'Just get on the fucking coach,' he'd said. 'Don't bother putting on your suit. There's no time.'

Lee had tried to apologise some more but had found himself talking to the gaffer's back, which was pretty much the view that he got of the game.

The team was finding it difficult to penetrate the game. The midfield was huffing, puffing and perspiring but not making inroads into the Ipswich half. At the back they were jittery, the centre-backs ruffled by the pace and movement of the opposing front line. The First Division team were creating the better chances, passing the ball more sweetly, finding the time and space to dictate the pace. The aristocrats were beginning to look stupid.

And then the goal came. A simple affair really – a move was broken up on the halfway line and Ipswich counterattacked with pace and enough options to panic the centre-backs. The ball was put wide before being crossed with pace – a flick from a striker at the near post took it past Mike Bates, the keeper. Pandemonium erupted at one end of the ground. Lee couldn't find the right emotions, just kept looking at the pitch thinking how green it looked in the sunshine. It contrasted nicely with the pinkness of the gaffer's neck.

Then it got embarrassing. Some supporters near the bench started shouting over at Brandwood. 'Get Sweeney on', 'Let's get fucking Lee on', 'Come on, Brandwood, we want Sweeney.' Nobody on the bench said anything but they all heard. There was absolute stillness among the staff whereas the Ipswich bench was hopping around like someone had put itching powder in their trousers. Brandwood acted like he couldn't hear the barracking, but the slouch in his back suggested a man who was hating himself for his own stubbornness.

The whistle went for half-time after a further period of Ipswich pressure; four corners in five minutes seemed to suggest that a second, killer, goal was on the cards. Town went off to frenzied support, fans on seats pumping their arms, shirtless fat lads beating their bellies like bass drums. This, they sensed, was their day. At the other end, where the goal had been conceded, the Londoners looked nervously at each other, waved their arms in encouragement, but were mostly too stunned to do anything but watch sulkily.

Brandwood slammed the door as the last of his players entered the dressing-room. He delivered a bollocking of epic proportions. Having had enough for the day Lee skulked at the back trying to become invisible. Then he heard his name mentioned and the kit man slung some gear at him. He was on.

Stepping on to the pitch Lee looked up into the stand to his right and searched the royal box. This is where the brothers would be glad-handing and greeting the dignitaries and officials, crying their crocodile tears about their boys being a goal down. Archie would be in his element; unctuous and smug, beyond pleased to find himself in such lofty company.

Eventually he found them, Archie and Gerrard, sitting in matching blue blazers wearing club ties, their tanned faces watchful, suspicious and aimed directly towards him. He could see Archie trying to fix upon him, to com-municate across distance, an intimate moment in such a public place; there were millions of people across the globe watching, yet none of them could see what was going on between Lee and Archie.

Lee spat on the grass and jumped on the spot, his knees nearly touching his chin. He clapped his hands shouting to those around him. He wanted to send a message to the McKays, he wanted to make them suffer, he wanted to let them know what it was to be losers again.

The noise built, the London supporters roaring the team on, enthused by the appearance of Lee. This, they sensed, was some kind of hope. The game resumed and Ipswich went straight on to the attack. The boss had clearly told them that one more goal would see them all right; go on the offensive rather than try to protect a slender lead.

Although he'd played at Wembley nearly three dozen times Lee always found the first five minutes difficult, terrifying even. The size and atmosphere of the place de-manded a big heart and Zeppelin-size lungs. There was nowhere to look but at the pitch and the crowd. The only way to see the sky was to look directly upwards. Lee found himself spending the first five minutes just trying to tune into the rhythms of the game, trying to decipher its pace and atmosphere.

But the longer Ipswich went without scoring the more the initiative moved away from them. The Ipswich midfield was tiring a little, there was more room to move the ball for the opposition. During the first ten minutes of the half Ipswich found it hard to gain possession: two of them were booked for late challenges, one on Lee himself as he was making a diagonal run towards the right side of the box. The free kick was nothing – just lofted in the air towards the goalkeeper, the kind of ball that always made Brandwood say 'that'll probably come down with fucking ice on it'. The Ipswich keeper came for it unchallenged; he had one leg pulled up beneath him, the other trailed beneath. It was a no-pressure situation to such an extent that he took his eye off the ball looking to distribute it as quickly as possible.

And that was his undoing. Wembley is a cruel place, stakes are high and it was almost embarrassing when the keeper fumbled the ball before flailing around on all fours trying to collect the thing while it ricocheted around the box before, eventually, the Ipswich net bulged with its weight.

Lee joined the mêlée of his team-mates, a huge white beast with limbs skewed at crash-victim angles, mouths agape like a pack of feeding animals. But he could not resist a look at the goalkeeper who seemed to have diminished in size, his huge gloved hands now appearing comical rather than practical. Like every other player on the pitch Lee felt a sense of relief – not that his side had equalised, more that it wasn't him who had made the calamitous blunder by which the game would be remembered, the subject of a hilarious round of sporting absurdities on *They Think It's All Over*.

And so it was that the tide turned. The Premiership side

sensed the fear in the opposition's hearts, their sense of belief and resolve weakened like their legs. The Premiership side pressed forward realising that they had only to seize the moment and press home their advantage.

And no one was surprised when it was they who took the lead midway through the second half after a lightning swift exchange of passes which saw Wayne clean through before rounding the hapless Ipswich goalkeeper and slotting the ball neatly home. Lee wondered for a moment which of his team, if any, were in the pay of the McKays. If there were any others they were finding it pretty hard to disguise their lack of enthusiasm.

The inevitable happened and Lee scored a screamer from the edge of the box. It was in the dying moments when the London fans were nervously celebrating victory that the ball was pulled back to him on the edge of the box and he let go with all his might. This one was for the McKay brothers, he thought, and he wanted to break the bloody net.

As the nation watched Lee stagger up the steps to the royal box, buffeted by pats on the back from enthusiastic spectators, saw how he victoriously offered his hand to both icy McKays, and took his turn in hoisting the cup above his head, no one would have thought it possible that he would never pull on a football shirt again.

At that moment, despite a grin as wide as the twin towers, only Lee knew that it was over. Like a relationship gone bad. He was finished with football.

Chapter Thirty-Two

The result did not please the McKays one bit. They had glowered at him from the royal box and afterwards in the hospitality area they delivered him more frosty looks. They left as early as was polite to be chauffeured back to the hotel. Before departing they had shot meaningful glances towards Lee that suggested this was far from the end of the matter. This was no surprise to Lee. They were not meant to enjoy it. For him that had been the point of the game.

Point proved.

There was a dinner at the hotel at which most of the lads were pissed. He sat trying to smile, but as soon as he caught one of their shiny, celebratory faces in his gaze he had to look away. It was like watching video footage – they were in a different time and place to him. They looked squeezed out, like they'd come through something together with their frog mouths pouring forth jokes and songs in direct proportion to the alcohol that was consumed.

In the middle of it Lee was silent and alone. It reminded him of when he was drinking, how he would either find himself as a hurricane lashing through the party, or alone, unable to drink at the rate he wanted, aware of the looks he attracted whenever he returned to the bar; nursing his drink anxiously, hoping that someone would offer him another one; not being able to converse for the yearning of placing his fingers on another, fresh glass.

A waiter went past with a tray of drinks. Lee beckoned him over. He ordered a beer. The party went on around him. The beer arrived, drops of condensation dripping on to the white tablecloth. He would keep it there, he would look at it but he wouldn't touch. This would be his temptation, his marker, and if he picked it up it would surely kill him; he knew that he could no longer live a drinking life, but could he live a life without drink? The question pressed down upon him as he traced patterns in the condensation beaded on the green glass.

There was a tap on his shoulder. He surfaced from his meditation. The room had quietened. The noise was more orderly, less raucous. He turned in his chair to see Gerrard McKay standing behind him. As he proceeded about the celebrating room Gerrard's face had been more open than normal; his mouth might even have yanked itself into a smile . . . But then Lee looked again: Gerrard's eyes were steel grey, unblinking, as relentlessly bleak as the London sky in February.

Lee saw Archie coming up the row of seated players patting backs and shaking hands, like a politician doling out affably inconsequential salutations. His hand eventually dug into Lee's shoulder.

'Here he is, here he is,' said Archie, his fingers working their way sharply into Lee's shoulder. 'The man who scored in every round.' His face was too creased for the smile to be genuine. 'What a game,' said Archie. 'What a game.' The room had begun to disengage from the brothers' presence. The noise level began to climb again.

'Lee, would you mind popping outside for a moment?' said Archie. 'There's someone who'd love to meet you.' The brothers ushered him from the room with jovial smirks still plastered across their faces. Once outside their expressions altered. They didn't speak. Lee was shoved into an office, the heavy panelled door slammed behind them.

'What the fuck do you think you were playing at?' shouted Gerrard. 'Do you take us for a couple of fucking mugs?' It was clear that he'd been holding this in for some time. He stepped forward and hooked Lee in the solar plexus. Lee, surprised, did nothing to cover himself.

'Is that what you think we are? Fucking mugs?' shouted Gerrard.

'So where's your little friend?' asked Archie. 'She allowed you out on your own?'

'We just took what was hers,' said Lee. 'We didn't touch any of your stuff.'

'My *Wild Geese* video is fucked,' said Gerrard, his voice deep and hurt. 'Someone trod on it.'

Lee felt himself being guided into a chair behind the desk. Archie grabbed his chin.

'You tell her to keep her fucking video,' said Archie. 'Tell her she's got a fat arse anyway. More crack than fucking Brixton. It's you we want to talk to, Lee. It's all about you.' Archie was talking faster than normal. The assured suaveness was gone from his voice. 'We've been good to you, Lee. We've been really good to you. Haven't we? Eh? Haven't we? Put up with all the drinking and fucking about? Suffered as you took money from us in Italy? And what do we expect from you in return? A little bit of help, a bit of respect, we hope that you'll keep your side of a bargain. We ask you to swallow, just once. But, oh no, not you.'

'You're a fucking loser, Lee,' said Gerrard. 'A fucking loser.' Archie gave his brother a bemused look.

Lee held his stomach. He couldn't fathom it, but he was laughing. Gerrard had the audacity to call him, who could still taste the metal of a winner's medal in the Cup Final that afternoon, a loser.

'Why's he fucking laughing?' Gerrard asked his brother.

'I'm laughing at you clowns,' said Lee. 'Listen to you. Like Abbot and Costello, you two. Have you no sense? Why the fuck did you bet on your own fucking team to lose? Are you mad?'

'It's not up to you to question our motives or actions,' said Archie. 'We pay you, that's all that matters. We pay you fucking good money.'

'You ripped me off,' said Lee. 'You took me for a mug and ripped me off.'

316

'Watch yourself, Lee, just watch yourself,' said Archie. 'You might be an investment for us but it would bring me an awful lot of pleasure to see you on crutches, to see your career end with months of repetitions and rehab. We know people, Lee. We're clean as fucking daisies us, but we know people.'

'I'll fucking do it myself,' said Gerrard. 'I'll crack his fucking kneecaps.'

'This ain't to do with the money,' said Lee. 'This is to do with what you had coming to you. Payback. You're the fucking mugs. You think you know Colin,' said Lee. 'You think you know my brother? Let me fucking tell you . . . You seen him recently? No, probably not. He's too busy working for you in Amsterdam and Hamburg, dealing with the contacts over there to ship smut over here. You know the score? Where d'you think Colin gets the money for a brand-new motor from, eh? From the money he's earning being your errand boy? I don't think so.

'Maybe it's something else. Maybe it's because of other deals he's doing there in Amsterdam. Maybe it's because of other things he's importing into the country in your containers, in your vans. You getting kickbacks for that? You getting your slice? You like the idea of customs and the drug squad sniffing around your lovely, clean, legitimate business?

'What's that stink, eh? You can't even smell it and it's under your own noses. Colin was court-martialled from the army, you mugs. They never managed to stick dealing charges on him, maybe they never wanted to create a fuss, bad publicity and all that. What do you think he was sent away for in the first place? Colin had always dabbled, always been small-time – but you two have given him the chance to go big time. And he's robbed the pair of you blind, right under your own noses.'

Lee stopped and listened for a moment. He could not believe what he had just said. There it was: he had betrayed his own brother and, no matter how badly Colin had treated him, he could never forgive himself for that. His mother deserved better.

'Colin's nothing without us,' said Archie.

'You tell him that,' said Lee.

'Well, well,' said Archie. 'Payback is a bitch.' He was suddenly calmer, trying to regain mastery over the situation. 'How's the wife, Lee? Michelle all right?'

Lee straightened up. He was listening. It was like a flash had run up and down his spine.

'You see,' said Archie. 'You and Colin seem to share one thing in common, one thing that Gerrard and I could never understand – and that's a liking for discussing family business with outsiders.'

He paused, enjoying himself. Lee waited, his body tensing after the shock of the punch. 'You see, you've probably heard the phrase "I fucked your wife" uttered from every ugly terrace in England. But what you don't know is that the voice uttering it was that of your brother.'

Lee's face clouded. He visualised the different ways in which he was going to make Archie pay for this.

'How do you feel about that, Lee? I mean, letting your brother fuck your wife really is beyond the call of duty.'

Lee blotted them out. It was a lie. He wouldn't give them the pleasure. They couldn't hurt him. They couldn't reach him any longer. He was beyond pain.

Chapter Thirty-Three

Click. *You have two new messages.*

'Lee, it's Lou. I took your advice. I took the bet. You came through for me. Jesus, Lee. You've still got it. You can still do it. I know this is the start of something big for you. I know it's going to work out. I'm so proud of you, mate. You don't know how proud. I'm going to Portugal with the family for a couple weeks, but we'll meet when I get back. Thing is, the money I just made, I'm thinking of jacking it in, moving out there, you know, learning some golf maybe. But, if you want, if we can work something out, I'd really like for us to, you know, try and carry on. It means a lot to me. You mean a lot to me. If we move out to Portugal you'll come and visit, won't you? You will, Lee, won't you? We'd love for you to come out. Liz would and Nathan would. Look, I better get going. Take care of yourself and thanks, thanks again. I knew you'd come through. I never had a doubt.'

Click.

It was his dad who brought him home the day after Cup Final. He left a congratulatory message on Lee's voice-mail. He wanted to know how Lee was, how Michelle was getting on. And though Lee often left these kind of messages on his mobile unanswered, something in his father's tone touched him. He possessed the awkwardness of the middle-aged person who was still uncomfortable with answer machines, for they would never consider purchasing one themselves. He didn't come to games any more, but he said that he'd watched the final. Was proud of his son. Frank Sweeney had signed off in the following fashion: 'Take care of yourself, son.' It made Lee want to see his father, remember the good things about him. It made him wonder if there was some way the family that had started to deteriorate when Colin went into the army could ever be resuscitated.

After the McKays had stormed away in a black cloud of recrimination and threats Lee returned to the dinner table and necked the beer he'd left on the table. It was the first of too many, a gargantuan all-night session that made up for his fortnight of abstention. He hadn't slept that night, and kept drinking into the afternoon when his Nokia had chirruped innocently. There was nothing for him to belong to any longer. It was all gone. His friends, the football club, Michelle . . . all of them were over, forgotten, distant. He had hoped that he and Colin might be able to rebuild what had been lost, but after the Jessica incident and what he'd told the Twomacs the previous night he knew it was just him now. Him and his dad who had been left when Lee's mother had died five years previously, just before Lee had gone to Italy. The life squeezed from her by bone cancer. It happened quickly, the disease was merciless. Hushed doctors would warn Lee and his father that the tumour was expanding through Mary's body with a relentless appetite. The time for 'medical intervention', as they put it, had passed. She left them one still August night after telling Lee that she was happy that she'd lived to see him married a couple of months before. He held her hand, but her body was so sapped and frail that the weight of it barely registered.

The loss of his wife had aged Frank Sweeney. He ate sparely now; painful gums meant that he could manage little more than tins of Heinz soup. His preference was for tomato, into which he would dip sliced white bread until it was steeped in the liquid. He liked other tins of liquid as well, although he had a strict rule about not drinking before five in the afternoon, which was generally the time he had finished when working. He drank four cans a night, every night. Hardly excessive, but enough, after a life on the roofs, to give him something of a pickled appearance. Whenever Lee went to see him, which was not regularly, he would be watching TV or doing a crossword. In the summer he might potter in the garden, but with no intent; there was just one purpose – to kill off a lingering afternoon.

So Lee knew his father would be indoors if he went over, which he duly did after listening to the message. There was something else his father had said: he left word that he'd been seeing a lot of Colin over the previous few weeks. Said that he visited most days. This was not like his brother, and his father admitted as much by the tone of his voice and the very fact that he'd thought it worth mentioning.

Lee stood in front of the porch surveying the street. It looked little different from when he was growing up. The place just seemed a little more glossy, like the colours had been turned up. Only the cars that, undoubtedly, were still washed by men in Umbro T-shirts on Sunday mornings, had changed: traded up from Sierras and Cavaliers to Mondeos and Vectras. PAS, ABS and aircon were standard these days.

Lee pressed the bell and waited. His dad had elected to stay in the house when Lee's mother had died. He said that it was like she was still there. Lee could understand that. His mother had always been so vital, bustling about the house keeping the three men in order, it hardly seemed possible all that energy had been hushed for ever. His father had never asked him for anything. Lee chose to transfer £2000 a month into his account, although it seemed unlikely that his father managed to spend it. Lee would have given him more if he'd needed it.

His dad eventually answered the door wearing an M & S V-neck against bare skin, Farrah slacks and a pair of tartan slippers which he replaced every six months ('whether I need to or not' he always joked). His hair was still thick but had turned white and he had started to comb it back away from his face which had begun to sag a little. His nose had small burst blood vessels flowering upon it. But this was up close. From a distance Frank Sweeney looked as good as anyone who was his kind of age, who had lived his kind of life, had any right to.

'Dad,' said Lee when the door opened.

Frank raised his eyebrows. 'Well, what a surprise,' he said, but not ungraciously. 'Come in, come in.'

Lee stepped into the hallway.

'Can I take your jacket, son?' asked Frank. Lee was about to offer it up when he remembered the half bottle of Teacher's secreted in the pocket to which he required easy access.

'I'm all right,' he said.

His father ushered him into the front room.

'So to what do we owe this unexpected pleasure?' he asked. 'Cuppa?'

'If you're making one for yourself,' said Lee. He glanced over at the television. Racing. The *Mirror* was folded open at the gee-gee pages. Lee sat down on the sofa he'd sat on as a kid and watched the television he'd watched as a kid. On top of the set there were two framed pictures. One a black-and-white studio shot of his mother which had been taken when she was in her late teens; the other, taken a few years later, was of his parents on their wedding day, fresh-faced and hopeful, impatient to taste the life ahead of them.

Lee took a swig of Scotch and placed the bottle back in his pocket. It was instinctive drinking. He didn't even notice it. He scanned the room. There were no pictures of him or Colin. His dad had taken down the watercolours his mother had painted from pictures of the Scottish Highlands.

Frank returned with two steaming white mugs of PG.

'Don't know about you, but I'm parched,' he said, offering Lee a Fig Newton, which he declined.

'You been keeping all right then?' asked Lee.

'Not bad for an old 'un.'

'You ain't old.'

'Sometimes I feel it,' said Frank laughing.

'Bet you thought I was Col,' said Lee fishing.

'No,' said his father settling back into the sofa, 'Col's got a key. Asked me for one. Sometimes he slips in and out without me hardly noticing. Just leaves a note. One time I found a cuppa warm in front of me. That's how I knew he'd been here. No one else could have done it, you see.'

'Yeah,' said Lee. Even with the damping effects of the whisky his mind was rushing.

'He sits with me for a bit, then he goes and sits in mum's room, the one we put her in when she got ill,' said Frank. He took a noisy slurp of tea. 'Must be difficult when you come out of the services. Don't know where you're going, what to make of life. Expect he's still upset about your mum.'

Frank looked up at the television. 'Here we go. Three thirty at Chepstow.' He diverted his attention back to the screen. Lee wanted more, but didn't want to force it.

'You got money on it?' asked Lee.

'In my head. That way I can only win, can't I?'

Lee furtively took another swig from the bottle. His father must have smelt the spirit but pretended otherwise. Best not to get into it.

With his horse trailing Frank lost interest in the race, although he didn't avert his eyes from the screen.

'He comes most days,' said Frank. 'Around this time usually. I expect that he'll be round soon.'

Lee raised himself from the sofa. 'Quick slash,' he said. His father sat mute. Lee trailed upstairs to the bathroom. It seemed strange to be taking the stairs one at a time: when he'd last lived in the house he'd always taken them in pairs when going up (good for the quads) or rushed halfway down before leaping into the hallway, which had always earned him a scolding from his mother. Pressing upon each step somehow didn't feel right, the pace was wrong.

The room – the smallest in the house – his mother had lain in for long, terrible months before being shunted into the hospice was at the front of the building next to the room she had shared with Frank. Colin had selected the room when the family first moved in. This, after all, was one of the inalienable rights of the older brother. Lee was pleased – he'd wanted the room at the back, next to the bathroom, anyway. It was bigger and looked out over the garden and the identical houses beyond. He liked seeing the houses at the back, the uncelebrated lives played out against a background of lawncare and barbecues. He pushed open the door and looked through the room to the houses beyond and yearned for the averageness of it. That, after all, was who he was.

The pile of the landing carpet had been flattened over the years. The trail from both Lee and his parents' rooms was smooth and well trodden. But outside what had been Colin's room the green textile was still elastic. He pressed his Swish! trainer against it and watched as it sprung back up, mosslike. That was Colin all over: present and absent at the same time; the heedless, truant son returning to bait wistful hearts.

Lee turned the handle and pushed the door open with his foot. Greying net curtains shaded the window, muffling the light, making the room feel cloudy. He remembered visiting her as she lay fighting for life, her eyes fading while she told him how she had kept a few of her sons' things in the drawers beneath the bed. Articles and trophies that Lee couldn't even remember possessing. Blankets, pictures, toys . . . He sat on the bed. The mattress was too soft. He tried hard to recall what the family had been like before she left them, before it all went bad. He remembered the soft beds, the blankets not duvets, a Viyella pillowcase with rabbits printed on it. The room was blank. Magnolia walls, a Chinese lantern over a bulb in the centre of the room. A chest of drawers – white, plastic veneer – offered no clues to history or identity.

Crouching on the floor Lee lifted the olive-green valance and pulled open a drawer. His memory stirred, although the recollection was ill-defined. He picked out a pillowcase, neatly folded since his mother had laid it there years before. He studied the image – a cartoon rabbit riding a bicycle, its long hind legs hanging over the pedals – which was repeated over a dozen times.

They'd bought it together, him and his mother, at Barnet market, where London melted into the greenbelt. It was worn thin from use, hundreds of nights of his shifting, restless head. There were tiny baubles of cotton all over its surface. He wondered what else was in the drawer. Directly beneath the pillowcase were sheets of various colours, like geological strata. He pulled the sheets up to see what was beneath. Packed at the bottom was a Tesco bag. He drew it out and looked inside.

Lee froze. In his hand he held a tightly wrapped package weighing perhaps a pound. His heart flipped an ugly somersault – stuffed inside the bag were four more packages identical to the one he was holding. He knew what it was, but he couldn't quite bring himself to take it in – cocaine. He'd never seen so much of it. Not at one time. Not in *his dad's* house.

He opened the other drawer. It was the same story, except, inside the Tesco bag there were bundles of used notes. Scores and bull's-eyes. He couldn't tell how much. Probably a couple of hundred thousand pounds. Maybe more. He pulled an Aertex blanket out of the draw and laid it on the floor next to the bed. Its smell stirred scattered moods and sensations archived in infancy. There was so much that had slipped away from him, so much beyond his recall.

Lee carefully pulled packages of cocaine and bundles of cash from beneath the drawers, jumbling it all into a pile on the blanket. He sat on the bed and examined the last bundle of gear, its pure, uniform whiteness beneath the plastic. It weighed more than powder had any right to. Packed neatly the small white brick was wrapped in prophylactic-tight plastic. It had been done with attention to detail, with some *care*. Colin. That's what the army had done to him. It had taught him to be conscientious, stripped away his lampoon sloppiness.

As he came down the stairs, the blanket slung over his shoulder, the booty cradled inside as if he were the sacker of some pebble-dashed semi with his reward safely stowed, Lee heard the ebb of his father's snoring beneath the trickle of the word game on the television. He passed through the hallway into the back of the house. Rummaging in the kitchen cupboard, among the cans of cleaning products and defunct insect sprays he ferreted out what he needed. There, as he knew it would be, was a canister of white spirit. Frank had always kept some in the house for DIY and domestic use. Swore by it for all kinds of purposes.

Lee picked it up along with a box of cook's matches. One hand for the white spirit, the other clutching the ends of the blanket, he passed through the back door into the garden. It was a fairly typical suburban plot, a hotchpotch of horticultural victories and botches. A grim patch of grass, a few borders of flowers – semi-loved roses, a scraggle of pansies and busy Lizzies, wooden fences that could have done with a splash of creosote – and, at the back, a shed with its own particular smell, the structure masking a feral area that was used for dumping and burning. Lee's father had always had a fondness for burning waste, something that had, on occasion, caused conflict with his neighbours and eventually the council.

Lee looked upwards. A single white boa of cloud floated in a careless expanse of anaemic blue. At last. It was summer; scant reward for the unremittingly dull spring, but summer nevertheless. Lee stopped his mind from wandering and concentrated on the matter in hand. He approached his dad's incinerator, a glorified rubbish bin with holes in the bottom and a funnel in the lid, and opened it. His father always left twigs and newspapers at the bottom so that he had no trouble lighting the thing.

He laid the blanket on the ground and unwrapped it. He reached for the whisky. His Adam's apple bobbed three times before his lips parted from the neck of the bottle. He lit a match and put it to a piece of newspaper at the base. Within moments the flames worked their way upwards to the twigs which started to crackle and spit. He pulled one of the bundles of cash from the pile and removed the rubber band that secured it. The wind rippled the end of the cash making it hum momentarily. Then he fanned it out and threw it into the incinerator. The money browned before bursting into flames. The smell was different from the smell of burning paper, it was a dirty, muddy smell, slightly metallic. It smelt like waste. Lee continued the process: removing the rubber bands before fanning out the cash and dropping it on to the rapidly growing fire. He went into the shed and grabbed sticks of wood from a neat pile which he slung on to build the flames.

Next came the coke. He cautiously unwrapped the packages before tipping the contents into the incinerator. The flames died momentarily. Lee poured white spirit on to the powder. The flames roared out of the contraption; Lee jumped back smelling the bitter odour of burning hair. He'd learnt his lesson; from then on he mixed the white spirit with the cocaine before he threw it into the fire. He stood, admiring his work, his face turning rosy as the heat escalated.

There was whisky fresh in his mouth when he heard the voice.

'Lee! What the fuck are you doing?'

He turned to see his brother striding towards him, his body tense, all business. Colin pushed past his brother and approached the incinerator, attempting to look in.

'You've really gone and done it now,' he said to Lee. His tone was somewhere between bitterness and disbelief. There was a rawness about it, a vulnerability that Lee recognised only from a day in October when his brother was sent away by a juvenile court.

'What have you done, Lee? What have you done?' Colin pressed his index fingers against his temples. 'You're mad, you know that? You're fucking insane.'

Colin paced quickly but aimlessly around the garden before approaching the shed and kicking it. The noise rolled over the manicured gardens of suburbia, but Lee did not react, just stood, taking the occasional nip from the whisky bottle, his stare buried in the flames.

'You've fucking done it this time, you've really fucking done it this time,' shouted Colin. 'I'm dead, Lee. I'm fucking dead. I'm extended as it is . . . The people I'm working with, they don't accept excuses . . . I'm fucking dead.' Smoke filled the sky so thickly that you could slice it. 'That was my last chance, Lee,' said Colin. 'My chance not to be a shoe man. You remember the shoe man?'

'I remember,' said Lee, still staring into the flames. The wind changed and both brothers raised their hands to shield their faces from the heat.

'You fucking prick, Lee,' shouted Colin. Spittle flew from his mouth, his eyes were reddening. The sweat of desperation soaked him. He came at Lee, tried to throw a punch, but it missed. Lee dropped the bottle of Scotch and pushed him away. He could feel that Colin had no strength to fight.

'I'm dead, Lee – and you killed me,' said Colin.

'No, I didn't,' said Lee. He took a deep breath of the smoke-filled air, searching for more words. None came.

There was no second attack from Colin.

'Looks like you're going to have to go away again,' said Lee.

Colin tilted his chin upwards, his eyes closed as if he were trying to imagine himself out of this situation, whisked from the burning wreckage.

Approaching his brother slowly Lee placed something in his hand: one of the bundles of notes. There was no hope for them now. He wished that he had never told the brothers about Colin; the guilt Lee felt weighed heavily upon him. He thought about his mother and what she had told him before she died.

'I love you differently to Colin,' she had said. 'I know you'll be all right, that's how you are. But I worry about your brother. When I go, and that might be soon, you've got to remember to take care of him. Promise me that, Lee.'

Lee had squeezed her hand, trying to will life back into her, and nodded.

His brother made no acknowledgement of the money, just held it loosely.

'You and me, Colin,' said Lee. 'We're over.'

'I'm gone,' Colin said. He took a few backwards steps towards the house before a hooked smile took shape across his face.

'You should know this,' he said. 'Because Michelle won't tell you. She's pregnant. The baby, it's mine.' He nodded at Lee meaningfully as he turned and walked quickly into the house and was gone.

Trying to catch his breath Lee stared bug-eyed after his brother. His nervous system spun wildly in improper directions. He squatted down on the grass and pulled the whisky bottle from the floor. He tipped it skywards to drain the final elusive drops.

He tried to think straight with fear and confusion tumbling through his head. This was something for which he had made no emotional contingency. It was too much to bear.

On all fours on his father's lawn he puked sour whisky and bile until the tremors ceased through his shocked, shot body. Hot bitter tears mixed with vomit in the dry grass beneath his face. He laid on the lawn until the sky stopped spinning. It was finished.

His dad was still snoring as he left the house.

Chapter Thirty-Four

He drove with just one eye open – his old trick to avoid double vision. There it was, spooled on to tapes, transcribed into notebooks. The whole deal, his whole history. It had taken him some time to work out where to buy a notebook and a decent pen. But then he remembered W. H. Smith – they did pens and paper. It had taken him the best part of the evening, but he was pleased with the results: line after line of scrupulously detailed, painstakingly recalled, dirty laundry. The story of his life; or part of it anyway. He would send it to Mike Stallone at the *Sun*. He'd think it was a phoney, a wind-up, but Lee could prove it all. He pulled from a bottle of Scotch that he was resting between his legs.

He thought: Colin was fucked. The McKays were fucked; although, stung, they would seek bitter revenge, of which he was fearful. What about him? What about Lee Sweeney? After all, as the song went, there's only one Lee Sweeney. What about him? He glanced around for old bill and took another lightning nip of liquor.

He was fucked as well.

He just wanted to see her face. He just wanted to see if everything could be all right between them. He was cold, freezing cold. All he had on was a Gucci shirt he'd half inched from a photo shoot. No jacket. He'd stuffed all the shit that he usually carried around with him in crevices in the motor; squirrelled away his change, sneaked away his keys and a wrap of gear.

He didn't even bother turning the engine off. Just left it

idling. The driver's door was wide open, like some snidey little car thief's wet dream.

Michelle's mum's house was plush: five bedrooms, two bathrooms (Jacuzzi, naturally), Magnet kitchen, top-of-the-range garden . . . Lee should know, he fucking paid for it. It was on an estate – a luxury one – just outside Harpenden in Hertfordshire, ideally located for access to the M1 up the road near Luton. Michelle and Brenda had originally gone to have a look at the development before it had been completed. None of the houses was ready, but that didn't matter to Chelle and Brenda: they bought the show home instead. The whole damn thing, fixtures and fittings, the lot. Brenda had liked it because it was plush without being flash. No point in ramming it down people's throats, was there?

He had to find out if Colin was telling the truth. He'd tried calling, but they didn't pick up. His only choice was to go face-to-face. Lee rang the bell. It chimed twice, echoing through the hallway. Impatient, he pressed the button again. He winced as a sharp pain shot through his index finger. He examined it under the light of the coach lamp. He'd chewed the nail right down. There was barely a sliver of nail left. Above the nail his finger was scarlet and swollen; it seemed that the skin was so thin that it could barely contain blood.

A window opened above him. A voice.

'Go away, Lee. We're asleep.'

It was Michelle. It was an order, not a request. He stepped backwards to try and see her, but she'd already moved out of sight.

He shouted her name. There was no answer. He rang the bell again. The window opened.

'Lee, get this into your thick skull . . .' His wife again. 'If you don't go away we're calling the police.'

We're. She was using the plural. Nice touch. Like she wasn't responsible for her own actions – everything was done collectively now.

'I just want to talk to you, Chelle,' he said. 'We *need* to talk.'

He clapped his arms around himself, trying to stay warm. He was trying to sound reasonable. Maybe he was even being reasonable. He wasn't trying to make a big hit, like some desperate heavyweight trying to connect with a haymaker before his weakening legs gave way.

He could feel the whisky inside him: a trickle of calmness that served to douse the heat of the moment. Within him, like a pearl hidden in an oyster lost somewhere in a heaving ocean, he harboured a hope that Michelle might just save him, might just reach into his contaminated, ruined soul and make him whole again. Addled, drunk, confused and exhausted as he was, Lee perceived something – hope? – that he'd not felt since before the drink, football and drugs had squeezed everything else out. All he needed was the truth. He could take it.

'Please, Michelle,' he shouted. 'It won't take long, I . . .'

'You're not listening, Lee, are you?' came the reply from above.

'This time we'll talk properly . . .'

'Open your ears, Lee . . .'

'I just need a few minutes . . .'

'Right, I'm counting to ten, and if you're still there I'm calling the police. One, two, three . . .'

A light went on in the next house. Some big-nosed busybody enjoying the action. Lee picked up a fistful of gravel and peppered the window with it. The light went off. Must have made their evening round there, him and Michelle going at it. Spiced up another night of *Lovejoy*, Horlicks and dewberry face masks.

The door opened. Michelle leant against the door frame in a thick, white towelling bathrobe. There was a crest and the words Four Seasons Resort, Santa Barbara on it. He didn't know she'd been to Santa Barbara. Didn't know where Santa Barbara was. Thought they did cartoons. It was just another void in a shared life, a gap never to be filled. It upset Lee, upset him more than he cared to consider. He supposed that relationships and marriage were all about time passed in each other's company, hours and minutes clocked up favourably, dogged time-serving in separate grooves until it was time to expire. It occurred to him that he and Michelle had gone the full twelve rounds and, exhausted, had fought to a kind of standstill, like two old sluggers too tired to throw the final knockout punch.

If he had one complaint, it would be this: that since the beginning of the relationship Michelle had never fully submerged herself in cementing the bond. The shop, her friends, her mother, her trips to Florida had taken precedence since the marriage went off target. To Lee, Michelle was like a bad swimmer: she had thrown herself on top of the water rather than actually into it.

And standing there that night, seeing her half asleep with no make-up, with her hair unkempt (how she would have hated anyone but Lee or her mother to see her like that) and with thick red lines marking her left cheek, like slashes from a cat's paw (Michelle always slept on her front), Lee had never felt further away from her. He knew then that his fantasy of salvation possessed as much substance as a drunken Hail Mary. Michelle and Lee were no more; moreover, Michelle and Lee had never been.

'Please go,' she said, tired.

'I won't be long,' he insisted.

A light came on above them. Her mother.

'I know it's late,' he said.

She gave in, waving him inside with a lazy sweep of her arm. It was clear that she was allowing him entrance to shut him up, to take the row out of the public realm as much as to appease him. Life in north Herts was like this.

He walked through into the kitchen. It was where they always ended up. The place was a mess. Dirty plates were stacked up on the draining board next to brimming ashtrays; empty tubes of Pringles next to menhirs of Diet

Coke. A pair of high heels rested next to the breakfast nook.

'Delores is away,' said Michelle. Delores was her cleaner. 'Gone back to Portugal – or wherever. Three weeks.' She yawned, suddenly losing her aggressive edge.

'You seen Colin recently?' he asked.

'What do you mean?' she said. It took her unawares. Her eyes widened and she became more alert. He knew then that Colin was telling the truth.

'What are you talking about, Lee?' She was feigning indignance and anger. She grabbed her lapels and pulled them closer together so that there was no brown sliver of chest to be seen. 'Lee, it's late . . .' She opted to return to tiredness and confusion instead.

'I saw him this afternoon, Michelle,' he said. He'd thought that his anger would make this easier. He didn't want to have to go any further. To have to spell it out.

'You all right, love?' It was Brenda. From her voice he could tell she'd sneaked halfway down the stairs to eavesdrop on the conversation.

'Fine, Mum, I'll be up in a minute. Lee's not staying.' Brenda didn't say anything else. Didn't offer Lee any kind of greeting. He heard her padding back up the stairs.

Michelle traipsed over to the breakfast nook, as if prompted by the state of the kitchen, and picked up her shoes. He could make out vague imprints where her toes had been, and the name of the maker in black.

'So hurry it up, Lee,' said Michelle. She'd hooked her index finger under the strap at the back of her shoes and waved them about impatiently.

'I've asked you a question,' he said.

'Can't this wait 'til tomorrow?' asked Michelle. 'It's not like we've got to get this sorted tonight.'

'Have you seen Colin recently?' he persisted.

''Course,' replied Michelle. 'He had that thing over at his place. He invited me and mum. Two weeks ago now. You weren't there. You were probably too pissed or something.'

'Oh, come on, Michelle,' he said. She had frayed his nerves with her games.

'You *were*, Lee, Colin said that he'd phoned you. You can't even remember, can you?'

'I wasn't drinking two weeks ago,' said Lee. 'Colin never rang.'

Michelle just laughed a jagged, hurtful laugh.

'You and Colin, Michelle,' said Lee persisting. He wanted the truth this time, he wanted it so badly that his body seemed to coil tight with pain and need. 'You know what I'm talking about.'

'It happened once and once only. A mistake. All over. End of story. Now, it's time to go, Lee.' She was insistent this time.

'Are you pregnant, Michelle?'

Michelle stopped swinging the shoes and stared directly at him. Some of her hair had swung down so far that it was touching the tip of her nose. She grabbed a shoe in each hand. Her knuckles white with pressure.

'Get out, Lee.'

'Give me an answer.' He stood his ground. 'Yes or no.'

'Get out now. I won't tell you again.'

'At least give me an answer. Don't I deserve a fucking answer? Don't I deserve that?' He was trying to sound reasonable, even when his insides were boiling.

'I don't know what you deserve, Lee, but I know that I deserve better than this, better than a drunk fuck, better than a druggie. That's all I know.' She was crying now, tears creeping down her scrubbed ready-for-bed face, dripping on to the towelling robe.

He knew that he only had to nudge her just a little more to get an answer. 'Tell me, Michelle.'

'Yes, yes, what do you want to know? Yes, I fucked Colin. Yes, yes, yes. What else? What else do you want to know? Where else do you want to drag yourself? You want the whole thing? Yes, I'm pregnant. Yes, you're a lousy husband. Yes, you're a fucking shit. Happy now? Sleep better tonight, will you?'

'The baby, Michelle, the baby . . .' He had to know, more than anything on earth he had to know. His body coursed with tension.

She laughed at him.

His impulse was to hit her. His anger was more powerful than anything he'd ever felt before. He turned around so that he couldn't see her laughing, so that he could control himself.

'Don't you turn your back on me!' Michelle screamed at him, enraged.

'Fuck you!' he shouted.

He felt her fists furiously upon him, beating his back. He turned, covering his head and face. She flailed at him, trying to hit him with her shoes and kick him. He grabbed one of her arms, which was extended upwards, and slid his hand along it. He grabbed the shoe from her grasp as she pulled his arm down and the shoe slammed into her skull.

Her limbs stopped moving. Her eyes no longer registered anything. He tried to pull the shoe towards him, but it was stuck, jammed in a place it was never meant to go. Michelle collapsed on the floor, the heel of the shoe lost inside her head, while the sole rested on her matted hair. She lay on the floor as still and silent as he had ever seen her, while a serpent of blood wound its way across the tiles. He looked at his wife's face and he no longer knew it. The pink marks from the sheets were fading. Fifteen minutes before she had been lost in sleep. He fell upon her not knowing what to do. Everything was stretched too thin.

He would never see her again.

Epilogue

No one was paying attention but Lee.

There she was, bombarding congregated millions with her technically, cosmetically applied amusement. There she was *giving it up*, giving it her all, right where she had always fancied she might belong.

Terrestrial.

It was not until she had introduced the latest all-girl pop sensation, Nice 'n' Nasty, with their requisite combat trousers, tattoos in cute places and hourly-upkeep hairdos, that the other prisoners took any notice. The girls mimicked their ditty and went through the motions of their ersatz homeboy strut.

The other prisoners argued about what they'd like to do, how often and to whom. According to tabloid enquiries two of the girls had been to stage school, one had been a stripper, and the other was a songwriter. Only three months before, during Lee's trial, they had been slaving their way up fame's broad but indifferent back. Now they had scrabbled their way to the summit: the thickset treasure of an appearance on the *National Lottery Draw*, with its host Jessica March.

A red-band got up and changed the channel. Lee raised himself from his plastic moulded seat.

'Ain't you staying for *Match of the Day*, Lee?' joked one of the cons. Lee didn't hear him, his mind elsewhere. There was something he had to do.

A glazed look would come over his face whenever he watched the *Lottery Draw*, which he did, religiously, every week, shutting out the slammer's biff-bang commotion.

It reminded him of the life he used to have, the one he wanted back. In his mind he had tried to reclaim it, but his memory was largely derelict now apart from a single image: despite all the years he had spent with Michelle, the picture of her lying on the kitchen floor with blood coiling upon the tiles beneath her head overrode all else. He could not see her in any other way. It was too much.

So, on Saturday evenings, he would try to obscure it with the studio lights, celebrity guests and the fallacious anticipation of the Lottery show, emblem of the forlorn and the counterfeit. He was pleased for Jessica. She, at least, had not succumbed. She had outstripped them all. She had written to him twice, sending her sincere condolences for what had occurred and promising to visit. She never came. Lee understood. She had her reasons. It's difficult to forge a career in light entertainment when you're a known associate of a notorious drunk convicted of manslaughter for laying low his wife.

Lou had written. He'd called. His messages were confused, distraught, earnest. He was trying to reach out, to be supportive, to make some sense of the upset. He told Lee to place him on his visitors list. Lee never bothered. He didn't want to see anyone anyway. Since he'd been banged up he'd missed the drink, desperately. But he'd stayed off the various distillations of Hooch and White Lightning that a known juice freak got offered. Other pleasures were easier to come by, lent themselves more readily to concealment. That was what his errand was about.

He was usually two-ed up in his cell, but the last one, some career crim, had been liquid coshed and ghosted out during the night after making some ill-advised all-sails-to-the-wind threats to a screw.

Lee got what he needed. The exchange had been swift and discreet. A job well done. He passed along a steel walkway back to his cell. Every time he walked in he felt ruined, thought back to seeing his name chalked on a cell door in the local nick with the word 'murder' next to it. He killed some time lurching in and out of sleep and staring at the peeling paint on the ceiling. It was no good. Michelle always came back to him. He knew that he couldn't live with that picture in his head.

The clatter of lock-up passed him by. A while later the screams of the wackos and saddos died down. A screw momentarily stared at him through a grille. Lee imagined the hardness of his eyes matched that of the coroner who had revealed the results of the autopsy at the trial: the baby had been Lee's.

There was no absolution. He was alone now. The screw wouldn't return for at least an hour. He had time. He emptied the contents of the packet on to the spoon that he had liberated from the canteen. They had told him to use about a quarter of the packet, plenty enough to get him high.

Lee didn't just want to get high.

He mixed in some water and cooked the mixture until it bubbled like caramel, sweet and delicious. He soaked it up with a cigarette filter and carefully drew it into his fresh works, courtesy of a star-struck trusty in the infirmary. Years of gym work ensured that he had little difficulty in finding a plump, juicy vein.

He punctured the thread of blood, waited for the bloom of scarlet and pressed the plunger down.

He was going. He was going . . . He was gone.

But it didn't matter. He'd been there before, and it felt just like home.

DIAMOND GEEZERS

Greg Williams

Polo geezers and page three princesses rub shoulders with gangsters and politicians in this brutally realistic and darkly funny
urban thriller set in the East End of London.

'A streetwise saga of London low-life with dialogue that
crackles and spits off the page like a pit bull with a hangover.'
DAILY TELEGRAPH

£6.99 1 85702 749 3

HOW TO ORDER

All Fourth Estate books are available from your local bookshop,
or can be ordered direct from:
Fourth Estate, Book Service By Post, PO Box 29, Douglas, I-O-M, IM99 1BQ

Credit cards accepted.   Tel: 01624 836000   Fax: 01624 670923
Internet: http://www.bookpost.co.uk   e-mail: bookshop@enterprise.net

All prices are correct at time of going to press, but may be subject to change.
*Please state when ordering if you do **not** wish to receive further information*
about Fourth Estate titles.